Super Nova

LEIA SKYY

Copyright © 2022 by Leia Skyy
www.LeiaSkyy.com

First Edition: October 2022
Second Edition: January 2024

ISBN 978-1-959039-51-8 (ebook)
ISBN 978-1-959039-52-5 (paperback)

Published by Books to Hook Publishing, LLC.
www.BooksToHook.com

Contents

Chapter One

Nova Scott was something of a shadow. Not many people knew who she was, but the ones that did, either loved her or hated her. She was used to it though, not that she would take abuse from anyone because that's the last thing she'd do. She hated injustice and she didn't tolerate it when she saw it. Her math teacher found out the hard way when she graded her friend unfairly.

"I'm sorry, this was supposed to be a good last week," Scarlett, Nova's best friend, and frankly the only person who could truly tolerate her ways, said. They were walking back home after a detention they didn't deserve.

"Don't worry about it. She had it coming. I would have been bothered by the eighty-nine percent if it wasn't the end of the year and I hadn't already been accepted to college."

"Ugh, right. College." Scarlett was a little touchy about that subject. She hadn't gotten any acceptance letters yet. As a last resort, she was planning on attending the local community college.

"Hey, don't worry about it. Your acceptance letter is probably sitting on your desk right now," Nova said.

"I don't care about that, you know that. I don't want to be

away from you is all. Did you have to be this freaking smart and get into colleges that the rest of us idiots can't get into?" Scarlett complained.

Nova chuckled. "Don't worry. Accounting isn't anything to write home about." Nova wasn't thrilled about her major but she didn't want to be homeless, and there were less interesting things out there that she could have been stuck with. Like archaeology. At least she wasn't majoring in that.

"If you hate it so much, why even do it? Stay here, start a YouTube channel and go viral. I told you I would help you edit the videos. I'd be half-decent, you know?" Scarlett said in a convincing tone. Nova was one of the best singers Scarlett had ever heard, but no matter how many times she tried to convince her friend that she was *amazing*, Nova denied it and pretended her friend was biased.

Nova looked at her friend fondly; she really did hope Scarlett had that acceptance letter on her desk today. "Easier said than done. My parents are too invested in my career for me to tell them I'm going to be a social media influencer who is secretly hoping to become a singer."

"You're no fun. Your parents know you can sing. They encourage it more than most parents would."

Nova stopped walking and looked at her friend. "They need a good retirement plan. That's me."

Scarlett bumped her shoulder to her best friend's. She didn't know how Nova did it most days. She was the perfect kid. Her parents hit the jackpot. Her younger sister, Skylar, too. It was like that little girl was the center of Nova's universe. "You're too good to be true. For now, though, let's hope I have an acceptance letter by the end of the day."

"You'll be fine, Scar." Nova hugged her best friend, before going their separate ways to their homes.

Scarlett lived in one of the suburban homes, where Nova once lived. But the mortgage became more than her parents could handle, so they had to give up her childhood house. Her current home wasn't too bad, though. She even liked how cozy it was. It was a two-bedroom apartment, just enough for the three people that would be left when she'd leave for college.

"I'm home!" she called out and went to the room she shared with Skylar to drop her bag off.

Skylar was lying in bed on her stomach, doing her homework.

"Hi, baby." She leaned down to kiss her sister's forehead. "What've you got there?" She sat down and watched as her sister continued writing.

"I have to write a short story based on writing prompts. This stuff is boring. I'd rather come up with my own story." Skylar let go of her pencil and collapsed on her back. "Is school always this boring or does it get better?"

"It'll be better." Nova wasn't a fan of lying to Skylar, she hadn't even maintained the illusion of Santa for her, but she was going to let this one slide.

"Good. What's for dinner tonight? Oh, and Dad's not going to come back home tonight."

Nova didn't like the sound of that. Their Dad, Derek, worked too hard. And he pulled double shifts whenever he could, but it affected his health more often than not. "What about hotdogs? I could make you some homemade fries to go with them?" She tried not to let the disappointment bleed into her voice.

"Yes, please. Can you also help me with math? I don't understand half of it."

Nova ruffled her hair and got out of bed. "Pack your things and come sit at the kitchen table with me."

⁂

Nova's mother walked into the living room just after she had managed to put Skylar to bed. Skylar didn't like going to bed without saying goodnight to her parents but there were nights she wasn't able to.

"Hey, sweetie." Mila smiled at her daughter softly, her exhaus-

3

tion evident in her eyes. "You're not supposed to be waiting up for me."

"I don't mind, Ma." When Mila dropped down next to her, propping her feet up on their small coffee table, Nova immediately snuggled into her. "Long day?"

Mila hummed and carded her fingers through Nova's brunette, purple-streaked locks. "Every day is a long day. How was school?"

"The usual. Ms. Jean gave Scarlett and me another detention."

"Again? Do you need me to talk to her? She's been a menace since your freshman year."

Nova laughed and shook her head. "There's no point anymore. School's out in a week. I have dinner on the counter for you."

Mila kissed Nova's forehead and rested her head on her daughter's shoulder. "You're the best, do you know that?"

"You're not the first person to tell me this today." Nova laughed.

"Good. You should be reminded. Did Skylar go down easily?"

Nova hummed. "She wanted to stay up for you, but I didn't know how long you would be. Dad's not coming anyway so she didn't argue about that."

"I'll see her in the morning before I have to leave." Mila stood up begrudgingly, groaning when her feet protested upon being used. "Oh, by the way, a letter came for you this morning after you left. It's under your dad's laptop."

Nova wasn't expecting a letter. What could it possibly be?

Nova got to her feet immediately and rummaged through the papers on the desk to get to the laptop. She picked it up and found a cream-colored letter. "What's this?" she whispered to no one in particular. She didn't usually get letters and all the colleges she'd applied to had already sent their replies.

"What does it say?" Her mother stood behind her, a plate of hot food in her hands.

She turned to her mother, and they both took a seat. "I haven't opened it yet."

"Well, what are you waiting for?"

Nova glanced at her mother before opening the envelope. The first thing she noticed was that the paper was a thick stock. Thicker than any letters she'd ever received, which meant it was really good quality paper. She felt a sort of impending doom as she unfolded the thing, her stomach half dropped. There was no need to feel like this, it wasn't like her college could take back her admission or her half-funded scholarship, but she couldn't help the feeling of dread.

Dear Miss Scott,

Congratulations! It is our pleasure to welcome you to Atherton University. We are delighted to inform you that we were absolutely mesmerized by your personal statement and entrance tape for the Musical Program. You happen to be one of the handfuls of students who get the opportunity to win a full scholarship to our esteemed University.
We have enclosed a welcome package to familiarize you with our campus and your curriculum. Feel free to reach out to us at any given point in time. We want to make your transition to Atherton University as easy as possible.
We look forward to having you at our university this upcoming academic year.

Sincerely,

Amanda Feri
Dean of Admissions

This felt like an elaborate prank. Nova didn't feel like she was in reality. This felt like a vivid dream. Nova was waiting to wake up.

"Sweetheart? What's going on?"

Nova turned to her mother sharply, realizing her mother was shaking her to get her attention, one strand of her streaked purple hair falling in her periphery. "I- uh." She didn't know how to explain it, so she handed the letter to her mother.

She watched her mother read the letter and realized there was another paper in the envelope, this one a normal letter paper. It had the curriculum details and her schedule. This had to be a joke. But the letter had the university's seal and address. It seemed to check out.

"Oh my God! Nova, this is *huge*. This is a full scholarship!" Mila turned to her daughter and immediately pulled her in for a hug. She squeezed her tight until she felt Nova squirm a little. Her heart was full, and her feet were off the ground. "Sweetheart, this is beyond amazing! I didn't even know you applied here."

Nova pulled back and took the letter from her mother's hand again. "I didn't think it would work," she whispered, her hands trembling a little. She had applied about six months ago and then forgot about it. She didn't even remember what song she sang for the audition.

It was something Scarlett had coerced her into doing. Everyone who ever had a creative dream knew Atherton was the place to be. There were actual Grammy award winners who went to Atherton University. It was the dream, but obviously, not one Nova could afford. She wouldn't even qualify for a student loan to attend there.

But this was a full scholarship. From the looks of it, housing included. She felt light-headed.

"Nova?! What's wrong, honey?" Her mother looked at her, eyebrows scrunched with concern.

"It's the musical program, Mom."

Mila's confusion wasn't going anywhere. "Isn't that a good thing, baby? I know you weren't the biggest fan of accounting."

Nova didn't like that. She never wanted her parents thinking she was making some colossal sacrifice. They did everything for her and her sister. It was only right to think about her parent's future the way they did for them. "That's not true. I don't hate it."

Mila wiped her hands and turned to her daughter, taking Nova's hands into her own. "This is a full scholarship, Nova. You won't have to get a student loan at all. This is good, right? Atherton is a good place?"

Nova swallowed the lump in her throat and slowly nodded. "The best."

"Then why aren't you jumping up and down like you have springs in your feet?!" Mila took her face in her hands and kissed her forehead. "We are so proud of you. Not just for this, but in general. You... are a good kid, honey. This is just another sign of that."

"But what about a job? You don't exactly make money if you aren't exceptionally lucky in this field."

"Oh, darling. Would you have gotten the scholarship if you weren't *exceptional*? You're not lucky, no. Just exceptionally talented."

Nova couldn't help the tears that sprang into her eyes. Her parents had always expressed their gratitude for her contribution to the family, but she didn't like hearing it. She felt it was her duty as their child. They took care of her, and one day, she wanted to be able to take care of them.

Her mother grabbed both of her hands and squeezed them gently. "Take the night and think about it. Weigh all the pros and the cons. If you decide you want nothing to do with it, no one has to know but us. It'll be our little secret." She wiped the two tears that had trailed down from the corner of Nova's eyes.

"Okay," Nova agreed. She put her head on her mother's chest and tried to curl up with her.

At some point, they both fell asleep with Nova having vivid dreams of big stadiums and seats full of a wild crowd. Was her future about to change?

Nova woke up with a crick in her neck. She opened her eyes to see Skylar staring at her from the chair across from her. She looked down and saw that her mother had put a blanket on top of her.

"Why did you sleep out here?" Skylar asked as she ate the scrambled eggs on her plate.

"I fell asleep on the couch with Mom. She must have gone into the room. When did you wake up?"

"An hour ago. I keep telling you I don't need such an early bedtime; I always wake up too early."

Nova gave her sister a look and shook her head fondly. "It's not a bad thing. Dad home yet?" She needed to talk to her dad about her decision. He was always good at helping Nova find the answers she needed.

"Yeah, he's taking a shower."

Nova hummed and got to her feet to stretch. She could deny it as much as she wanted but deep down, the answer was obvious. It wasn't even a competition, because Atherton would always win against any other university. It being completely free was just the cherry on top. Even if she had a full scholarship to Harvard, Atherton would still win out.

But it felt selfish. A degree in accounting would be... beneficial. A promised future, if not the most interesting one. Money won out against fun, right?

"Why are you making that face?" Skylar asked, bringing her out of her reverie.

"What face?"

"The one where you look like you're solving triometry."

Nova laughed. "Trigonometry. It's called trigonometry."

"Yeah, that. Why do you look like that?"

"Just doing some thinking. Go get dressed for school."

"You're so bossy." Skylar pouted but got up, nonetheless.

Nova stared at the letter on the coffee table. Why is this so hard?

"Nova?" Derek said and smiled at his daughter when she turned around.

"Morning." She hugged her father, melting against him. He smelled like fresh laundry.

"What's wrong?" He put a hand on her shoulder.

She didn't know how he did it, but he *always* knew when something was wrong with her. "Something came in the mail yesterday." She picked up the letter and handed it to him.

Her father took the letter and started reading it. His face went through the same emotions her mother's had.

"Nova!? This is huge, why didn't you call me last night?" Derek pulled her in for another hug. "Kiddo, this is amazing!"

"Did you read the whole thing?"

"Of course, I did! I've heard of this university. It's humongous."

"Dad, it's the musical program."

Derek raised his eyebrows at her. "And?"

"It's... it's risky, isn't it?"

"Elaborate, please." He folded his hands and watched as Nova struggled to find the words. His daughter was much like a thirty-year-old trapped in an eighteen-year-old's body, but sometimes the teenager won out.

"It's too ambitious. There's no future."

"What's wrong with a little ambition? It's not like you don't have the skills. They wouldn't give you a full scholarship if you didn't, would they?"

Nova didn't understand how her parents weren't scared. Nova was always... well, not scared, but worried. She was always worried.

"You don't have to feel responsible for everyone, Nova," Derek said with a heaviness in his voice. Their house went through foreclosure when Nova was just thirteen. It was hard on everyone, but it was her childhood home, and it left a big impression on her.

"But I *want* to be." Nova didn't like crying. But around her father, and sometimes around her mother, her emotional quotient decreased to that of a toddler.

"Maybe I need to be clearer. You are *not* responsible for everyone. We are your parents, and we are the ones responsible for this family until there comes a time when we can't be. Who says you won't be successful as a singer? You're amazing at it, just like you are at everything else. And yeah, you will be amazing at accounting too, but you love singing. You always have. Does a tallied balance sheet bring you the same joy?"

Nova rolled her eyes. "No."

"Then, that's your answer. Atherton is where you belong. Opportunity is knocking at your door; don't be stupid, sweetheart."

"So that's it? I go to Atherton and forget about accounting. That's what you're saying?"

Derek laughed. "Good things shouldn't be this hard to accept, Nova. Take it. Actually, I forbid you from doing accounting if that's what you're indirectly asking me to do."

Nova giggled. "It's... too easy. I'm used to fighting for things, you know?"

The familiar pain returned, the one that feels close to helplessness. "I know. Take it anyway. Maybe the course won't be as easy as you think."

Nova shrugged. "The university is far. Further away than the one I was going to."

"Aww, are you going to miss us?"

"Something like that." Nova ran a hand through her hair. "I had a plan. Things were supposed to fall in place in a week."

"Plans don't always work out." Derek led them to their kitchen, frowning at the sight of it. "Skylar needs better kitchen skills, look at this mess."

"I won't be able to come over on the weekends to help."

"Nova. We'll be fine. Scarlett will come over. She practically lives here anyway. Last week she texted me saying I need to buy her coco cereal because we ran out."

Nova banged her head against the kitchen counter. "Jeez." She had completely forgotten about Scarlett. How was she going to tell her?

"I will have to tell Scarlett."

Derek scoffed. "If I know anything about that girl, it's that she'd beat you up for not going there."

"She's the one that made me apply," Nova said thoughtfully. Maybe that wouldn't be the hard part of this ordeal. There wasn't a hard part yet. When would the other shoe drop?

"See? She'll be fine. And don't worry about Skylar. She's your mini-me. She'll be fine."

"I know. I... I'm going to miss her. Wherever I go."

"Atherton," her father said in a sing-song voice.

"So, you told him?"

Nova turned to her mother who looked like an older version of a sleepy Skylar. Her hair was a mess and the bags under her eyes were only a tiny bit better than last night.

"I did."

Mila came up behind her daughter and put her hands on Nova's shoulder. "And? What college is my pride and joy picking?"

Nova wasn't sure what she would do, so she evaded the question.

Nova wasn't sure what she would do, so she evaded the question.

"HEY, why haven't you replied to my texts?" Scarlett jogged up to her at their meet-up spot.

"It's been a crazy morning. I forgot to charge my phone last night." Her phone's battery was as old as time. It didn't work if she didn't charge it every two to three hours.

"Oh, is everything okay? It's not Skylar, is it?" Scarlett looked tense.

Nova couldn't help but love her best friend. Scarlett really did care about Nova's family. She *was* family. "No, everything's fine. Unsettlingly so."

Scarlett frowned. "What's that supposed to mean?"

"I got a letter last night. From a university."

Scarlett's mouth fell open. "Again? Dude, I haven't even gotten one acceptance letter. And now I won't. That's what I've been wanting to text you about. I received the rejection letter."

"Scar," Nova took a deep breath, "I'm so sorry to hear that. Are you okay?"

"I'm fine. I had already mentally settled on going to the local community college. But tell me your news."

"Do you remember the audition tape we made? The one you forced me to after we dyed our hair?" They had just gotten their streaks, Nova her purple ones and Scarlett her green ones. It was Scarlett's birthday gift to her best friend. She wanted it bad enough and Nova was never good at telling her no.

"Oh yeah! You sounded so good; I still listen to it sometimes. Why?"

"I got in. The letter was from Atherton University. A full-ride scholarship."

Her best friend's face lit up, her eyes going wide and her face curving into a big smile. "Oh my God!" She jumped on her, hugging Nova tight, and letting out a little scream. "You made it! I always knew you would!"

"Scarlett." Nova hugged her back; again her father was right. She didn't know why, but she kept looking for something to go wrong. Something out of place enough to make her want accounting. "It's so far away. I'll only come back for the holidays. And I'll be all alone," she admitted.

Nova was headstrong, she always had been, she had an answer for everything. But she'd never been alone. Scarlett, her parents, her sister. They'd always been around. But at Atherton, she was going to be all alone. Miles and miles away from home.

"It's Atherton, Nova. You love that university, it's your dream."

"Yeah, the dream that's supposed to make you feel better when you feel like crap. Not one that comes true."

Scarlett glared at her friend. Nova was a bit of a nut job sometimes for someone so smart. "You're weird, dude. Like a real weirdo. This isn't something to think twice about. You got in and now you're going to go there. Start packing your bags."

Nova tsked. "You seem awfully excited for me to leave. Yesterday you were praying for an acceptance letter."

"You know, it's almost a relief I didn't get one. I wasn't built for academics; you and I both know that. The best part is, I get to be here and take care of Skylar. She likes me better than you."

"Fine. I'll go and you won't see me for months and months. Then maybe you'll realize how much it's going to suck without me."

"Ugh, leave first. Come on, we have Ms. Jean's class right now."

Nova faked gagged. "Now that I'm not doing accounting anymore and you're not doing... well, university, we could... skip?" She looked up at her friend through her eyelashes. She'd never skipped a class in her life unless she was sick, or some other teacher required her elsewhere.

"Nova Scott." Scarlett gasped and eventually smirked. "Did you just ask me if we can skip a *math* class?"

Nova bit her lip and shrugged. "It's the last week, and it's not going to be the end of the world or our careers anymore, so?"

Scarlett put a hand on her mouth. "Where's my best friend, and what have you done with her?"

"Ugh, cut it out. Do you want to skip or not?"

"Of course, I want to skip!? I can't believe this is happening. Atherton has already made you a hundred times cooler than you ever were."

"Just shut up and let's go."

THE TWO OF them spent time together, sitting under the bleachers with junk food that cost Nova a month of her savings. It didn't matter though.

"You're going to call me all the time, aren't you?" Scarlett asked after they caught their breath laughing about the time she thought she would drown at the water park.

"Of course," Nova reassured. Scarlett looked genuinely concerned. "Stupid question."

"No, it's not. People change once they leave for college."

"Yeah, but it doesn't change for the people they care about."

Scarlett nodded. "I guess not. But... you were right. Atherton is far."

Nova looked at her friend; she put her hand out. When Scarlett put her hand into it, she squeezed it. "I wish you could come."

"I wish I could, too," Scarlett whispered. "At least I'll still have Skylar. She's a mini-you."

Nova couldn't stop the bark of laughter. "Oh God, you sure you're my best friend and not my dad's? He said the same thing. And he knew what your reaction would be even before I did. I'm pretty sure you two text more than he and I do."

Scarlett beamed. "Maybe your parents will like me better and officially adopt me."

Nova shook her head. "You don't need to be adopted."

Scarlett sighed. "I for one am the happiest person in the country today. Let me tell you, I was *terrified* at the thought of being an accountant's best friend." She fake gagged. "I'm so relieved."

Nova threw a piece of her gummy bear at her. "Now you can be best friends with a future broke person."

"Oh, shut your mouth," she said laughingly. "Does Skylar know?"

Skylar was a little more than unsettled by the thought of Nova not being around all the time. She had warmed up to the idea of Nova going away after she had explained to her how it was for the better, but Skylar was still under the illusion that Nova would visit on weekends.

"I mean we did a celebratory breakfast because I finally decided it's where I'll go but she doesn't know where Atherton is. Or how far it is."

Scarlett cringed. "Yeah, I wouldn't want to be you. I remember what she was like when you told her about the concept of college."

Yeah, that was something Nova wasn't looking forward to either. She went home to face the music with Skylar.

S kylar was not happy. She was excited her sister was going to the university which made her happy, but *she* was *not* happy. Derek was the one that explained where Nova was going, with a lot of interruption from Nova, but Skylar got the gist of it.

"What about my birthday?" Skylar glared at her sister. "What about *yours*?"

"I'll come for your birthday," Nova said; her sister's birthday fell in the summer anyway, so she should be able to uphold that promise.

Skylar folded her arms and looked away. Nova was packing her bags. Now that she wouldn't be coming home on the weekends, she didn't have the choice of slowly moving her things out. Scarlett was over to help, too.

"I don't get why you're so sad. I throw your birthday parties anyway." Scarlett pouted and folded Nova's jeans. "Your sister's the one who won't let you eat more than two pieces of your *own* cake."

Nova scoffed, and threw a pair of socks at her friend. "Yeah, you're not the one who has to deal with the sugar high."

"Are you guys getting any packing done or are you just throwing things at each other?" Derek came in looking every bit as exhausted as he felt. Still was smiling like a loon though. "Nova, I got you something."

Nova turned to her dad and raised her eyebrows. "What is it?"

"Want to step out for a second?" He offered his hand to her, pulling her up when she gave it to him.

Once they were in her parents' room, she sat down on the bed and watched her father pull out a box. "This is from Mom and me. It's not all you deserve... but it's a little something."

Nova's eyes watered even though she didn't know what was in the gift-wrapped box. "Dad, you shouldn't have."

"Yeah, well I wanted to. Open it."

She carefully opened the box, making sure not to rip the gift wrap. It was a new phone. "Dad? What...? This must have been expensive, why did you get it?"

"Don't worry about it. We've been saving up for it for a while."

"Daddy." She got up to her feet and hugged her father. "I don't..." She didn't think words could express how thankful she was. Yeah, it was just a phone, and it was common for parents to get one for their kids. But they must have been saving for *months*.

Derek kissed her forehead and smoothed his hand down her hair. "You need something to keep in touch with us. It wasn't a lot, I promise."

Nova knew exactly how much it cost. No wonder her parents were pulling shifts left, right, and center. "Thank you."

"You're welcome. Go set it up." Derek hugged her once again and watched her jog back to her room, her colored hair cascading down her back.

***

"It's going to be okay, sweetheart." Mila held her younger daughter and wiped her tears. It was a sad morning. Nova was leaving today, in five hours. Everything was packed and Derek had taken the day off to drop her to Atherton.

"I don't want her to go." Skylar sobbed. She was just like Nova, she didn't let her emotions out a lot, but she was a little more than emotional today. Mila had been, too, but she was doing a far better job hiding it.

"Me either, but she has to go. She's going to have so much fun there; you want your sister to be happy, don't you?" She pulled Skylar away from her chest and fixed her hair.

"Is she going to forget about us?" Skylar asked, looking the picture of innocence. Most days it was hard for them to remember she was only seven. She was way more mature than any seven-year-old they knew.

Mila smiled sadly into her hair. She tried reminding herself Nova was only going to college, but it felt like yesterday when she was dropping her daughter off at daycare and now, she was going away to college. "She couldn't forget about us if she tried. We'll call her every day on her new phone; it'll be fun. Plus, she won't be here to decide your bedtime for you."

Skylar nodded, but it didn't seem to make her feel any better.

In Skylar and Nova's room, Nova wasn't doing any better. Derek was ticking off their last-minute list of things to be packed. "You have your charger?"

"Dad, there's like four more hours. Are you really that excited for me to leave?" Nova joked, but it sounded completely serious.

"Sorry, I'm just…"

"Distracting yourself?" Scarlett finished for him. She knew how he felt. She had already given up on distracting herself with kitten videos on the internet.

"Yeah, that." Derek sat down on the bed and watched as Nova squirmed uncomfortably. "Have you gotten your dorm number and everything? The campus is huge." This past week, that's all they'd done. Looked at every bit of Atherton University on the internet.

"Yeah, I'm rooming with someone named Harper."

"Oh my God." Scarlett perked up. "You already know who you're rooming with?"

Nova nodded. "They emailed us a list of room numbers and people."

Scarlett gasped. "Please tell me you texted her."

Nova gave her friend a look. Who did she think she was? Of course she hadn't. "I haven't, besides I don't have any contact information. It was just the names."

"Ugh, you're honestly so clueless sometimes. We have the internet, and everyone has social media. What's her name? Let's look her up."

Nova didn't want to. "I... let's not, okay? If I don't like her, I'd rather just find out when I'm already there and can do nothing about it. I have enough things to dread."

Derek chuckled. "You're so negative."

"Thanks, Dad," Nova said sarcastically and hugged herself, her thumb trailing over the new tattoo on her left upper arm. Scarlett and she got tattoos as their last "activity" as best friends who live ten minutes away from each other. Nova wasn't all for it but like all things, Scarlett convinced her.

In hindsight, she didn't hate it. At all. It was a tattoo of a supernova, to reflect her dreams of becoming a massive star. It was pretty and looked nice against her tanned skin.

"Come on, enough sulking. Today's an exciting day, go shower and get ready," Derek urged.

Nova finished getting ready, and although she felt sad to be leaving her family, she began to feel the first flutters of excitement for the new stage of her life she was entering. It was a bit scary, the unknown, but it was also exciting. She decided that she would make the best of the opportunity that was presented to her. She was ready for her journey to face a new chapter in her life.

The car drive was long. Painfully long. Nova hadn't realized leaving would be this hard. Overall, she had tried to tone down her excitement about Atherton for the benefit of Skylar. She didn't want Skylar thinking she was happy to leave her; but now that she was on her way, she couldn't help but be both terrified and excited.

Goodbyes were always hard. This one wasn't any different. She could see it on her mother's face, the worry in her eyes. Mila had done a good job of not fretting over the fact that her daughter was going to be alone for the first time in her life. It's not like Nova wasn't independent, but she was still a mother. It was her job to worry.

If only Nova had taken Scarlett up on her offer to contact the people whose names were on the list, at least she'd be able to put a face to their name. But of course, she hadn't. No one had texted her either, so it wasn't like she was being cold to anyone.

"Sweetheart, you're going to get frown lines before you turn twenty at this rate," her dad said.

Nova sighed and shook her head. "Sorry. I have butterflies in my stomach."

"Being nervous is normal. I'm sure all the other kids are feeling the same."

Something told Nova that wasn't true. There were parts of her research that she hadn't shared with her parents. While Atherton was known for its prestige and extremely famous alumni, it was also known for rich brats that pretended like they owned the place.

Atherton's tuition was extremely high... Most people didn't even qualify for a student loan for that much. So, people who had excessive wealth were the only ones who could attend. Those kinds of students never lifted a finger in their lives and were born with a silver spoon, crusted with diamonds, in their mouths.

Nova didn't have anything against people with money, and she most definitely was not jealous but... the rich people she'd previously met had an air about them that didn't sit right with her. There were a couple of them in her high school, but they weren't Atherton rich. They were not kind people. So, one could only imagine what Atherton rich people would be like.

"Is it something other than the first day jitters?" her dad asked, knowing as usual that Nova was upset about something she hadn't admitted yet.

"I'm not... We aren't the same kind of people. The students that go here and me."

"Are they aliens? I didn't know Atherton took applications intergalactically."

Nova laughed, not able to stop herself. "Dad."

"Sweetie, they're all kids. Doesn't matter where they're from or what their major is."

Nova nodded, not really believing him. It wasn't as easy as he was making it seem. It was a whole lot harder when you were being made to feel less of a person because you weren't a trust fund baby. "I guess. I just need to get the first day over with."

"You'll be fine. In a week you'll be calling us asking if you can skip coming home for Christmas."

Nova turned to him. "You know I'd never do that, right? Not even if I have the best time ever."

Derek nodded, holding out his hand for Nova to take. "I know. You're too nice for your own good."

Nova scoffed. If only her father didn't have an angelic image of her, he'd know just how *nice* she can be. She wasn't rude per se, but she wasn't going to be nice to people who couldn't extend the same courtesy.

The rest of the drive went similarly, Nova feeling like she was going to throw up and Derek making her feel better.

The road turned into a greener path, buildings appearing less and less. The view was nice; it even helped Nova calm down. They made a couple of stops for gas and food, which Nova refused to eat, but Derek convinced her eventually.

Somehow, she managed to fall asleep. She had been trying for a long time, but her mind wouldn't shut down. She woke up when she felt the car slow down. They couldn't be stopping again; her father had told her they wouldn't.

"What's happening?" She straightened up groggily, rubbing the sleep out of her eyes.

"We're here." He smiled at her.

Nova opened her eyes to see huge gates. Huge was a bit of an understatement; they were unusually large.

"Woah." She let her mouth hang open. Seeing pictures online did not prepare her for what it was like in person. This was surreal. This place seemed almost magical.

"Take a picture, it'll last longer," Derek joked, but he seemed just as mesmerized. This place had an aura about it.

Nova felt small. She wasn't tall, she was an average height, but right now she felt small. After they checked in with security, the gates opened up to a road that had a mansion at its end. That was Atherton's main office.

"Kiddo, this place looks like it's right out of a movie."

Nova nodded, not really paying attention to anything but the campus around her. Taking walks here was going to be her new favorite thing. "It's so pretty." All the buildings were Victorian, made of red and maroon bricks with white lining. Only the main office was cream in color. It looked like someone washed down the building every day. It looked brand new. These buildings were built around the 1950s.

The roads were spotless, nothing was out of place. Nova had never seen greener grass in her life. It all looked so expensive. She understood why the tuition was the way it was. It couldn't be easy to maintain a campus this big.

The car halted in front of the main office. Another security guard stood there, donning the same black uniform as the one at the front gate.

Her dad held her hand and kept squeezing it until they entered the building. They got to the desk and Derek started talking to the receptionist. She was a kind old lady named Tara. She gave them a map of the campus and said that Nova had an induction event for freshmen in the evening.

"One of our staff will take your luggage to your dorm," Tara said in her melodic voice.

Nova was trying to play it cool, but her insides weren't getting the memo. They had staff to drop off their bags like they were in a hotel.

Nova turned to her father as her bags were loaded onto the trolley and taken toward her dorm. "So, this is goodbye?"

Derek nodded and opened his arms. "Yeah."

It didn't last long; it was better to get it over with quickly. "Call me when you reach home."

"I will."

With that, he got into his car and drove away.

Time to meet Harper Jones, her new roommate.

Chapter Four

Harper turned out to be the human equivalent of a golden retriever. She was *excitable*.

"Oh my God, you must be Nova?!" Harper jumped off the couch overflowing with clothes, sheets, and what looked like make-up products.

"Hey." Nova smiled and entered the room. Harper caught her in a tight hug. Her blonde hair tickled Nova's nose and smelled like lavender.

"It's so nice to meet you. I'm Harper."

"Nice to meet you, Harper." Nova pulled back and looked around. When she found out that she would be rooming with someone else, she thought it would be like sharing with Skylar, living in each other's pockets, but this place was almost as big as her house. "This place is huge."

Harper turned to look at the expanse of their "room"; it was bigger than most apartments that Nova had seen. "Yeah, but the kitchen is kinda small. I expected this place to be bigger. You should see the private suites, it's crazier."

"Oh." Nova had really underestimated this place. "What course are you in?"

"Dance." Harper beamed. "I've been a dancer for about

sixteen years. I started when I was two."

"You started dancing when you were *two*?" Nova looked at her incredulously. "That's impressive."

"I'm a quick learner. What about you?"

"Music. Singer."

"That's so cool. But we won't have any program classes together." She pouted. "What is your compulsory curricular?" With every course that was in the creative arts, the students were required to pick another course that was more academically inclined. But the main focus would be their field of choice.

"Business administration. You?"

Harper's mouth dropped open. "English lit. Also, you want to take *business* for your compulsory curricular?"

Nova shrugged. "It could be useful in the future. I was going to do accounting before I got the scholarship here."

Harper's mouth dropped once again but this time to the floor. "Shut. Up." She wacked Nova's right shoulder lightly. "You're a scholarship kid?"

All of a sudden, the things that were scaring Nova became extremely real to her. Was she about to be shamed for not being able to afford this... this stupidly expensive and extravagant place? "Uh, yeah. I got the letter last week."

"Dude, that's *so* cool. I had to beg my parents to let me go here. It's not exactly cheap but they're both neurosurgeons, so..."

Nova chuckled, hoping her relief wasn't evident. "Yeah, I guess. It was a surprise; I had forgotten I even applied."

"Do you know any other scholarship kids?"

Nova shook her head. "There was nothing on the university website. We have an induction thing in the evening though, so maybe I'll meet them then."

"Oh yeah, I forgot about that. Your bags were delivered; they're in your room."

Harper took her to her room. It wasn't humongous but it was more space than Nova ever had to herself.

"Cool tattoo, by the way," Harper said when Nova took her

jacket off, leaving her arms bare. She stroked it with her thumb. "What kind of star is it?"

"It's a supernova. Cliché, I know."

Harper shook her head. "No, it's not. It's pretty, I like it. Unique! I love your hair, too." She picked up one curl and twirled it with her finger. "I wanted to color my hair, but my mother wouldn't let me."

She looked down about it. It made Nova wonder if her parents were supportive. They were financing this crazy place, so, they couldn't be all that bad. "I like your hair. I can never get mine to stay that neat."

"Yeah, this is after a million salon appointments."

Nova nodded. "This room is really nice. I like the window." The setting sun was giving the room a soft orange glow. Mornings were going to be fun to watch.

"Oh, fair warning, we have to share a bathroom."

"That's okay. I'm used to sharing a bathroom. I have a little sister."

Harper jumped to her feet. "Really? That must be really nice. I have two older brothers." Her face twisted into a grimace. "They're all right but they're just so... they're boys. That's all I've got to say."

Nova laughed. "Have you seen the campus? The map says there's a café down the road. Do you want to check it out?"

"Sure, I can deal with this mess when we get back."

The two walked down to the café, Nova was enjoying the pleasant weather and so far, Harper seemed like good company.

When they entered the café, Nova immediately fell in love with the décor. It had two floors and the most comfortable-looking chairs. "Go sit, I'll get us something to eat," she offered.

Harper agreed and moved to go upstairs. Nova placed their orders and wondered if she could get a part-time job here. It would be better than any place she'd ever worked. She thanked the server and turned, bumping into a guy behind her.

The guy smelled slightly of cologne. Nova liked it. "Oh,

God. I'm sorry, I didn't see you there." She looked up at him and saw blue eyes staring back at her. He was pretty tall. As tall as her dad.

"It's all right, it's not every day a beautiful girl bumps into me."

Nova smiled. The boy had blonde hair that was slicked back with what looked like gel. It made him look sharper and older than he probably was. He had a nice smile. It was more so a smirk, but it was... hot. She had to admit, he was easy on the eyes. "I'm sorry, either way."

His smile widened and he put his hand out. "Andrew Rodgers." He was wearing an athletic jacket one size too big on him and his ripped jeans were a washed-out blue.

Nova shook his hand. "Nova Scott."

"Hmm," he hummed appreciatively, "You have a nice name."

Nova smiled. "Thank you, I, uh, I should get back."

"See you around?" He continued to smile at her, making direct eye contact.

Nova didn't think much of it and nodded. "Sure."

She jogged upstairs and dropped into the seat opposite Harper. "So, I met a boy."

Harper gasped and sat up straight. "Already? Girl, you move fast. You've been here for what? An hour?"

Nova laughed. "He said I have a nice name."

Harper squealed. "Great, now I'll be third-wheeling because no boy likes *my* name. It's boring."

They talked about everything, getting to know each other better. Nova decided she liked Harper; she was a lot like Scarlett. "My best friend, Scarlett, is a lot like you. You two would like each other," she said.

"Yeah? Atherton has lots of events that are open to the general public. She could come then."

Nova smiled. "Yeah, she'd like that."

"You'll probably be performing in some of them. I want to hear you sing."

"I've known you for all of two hours. I'm sure we'll get around to it by the end of the day."

Once they were done with their coffee, the two went on a walk around campus. Scarlett showed her the buildings that she would have classes in, maybe Nova would too, but she wasn't sure.

They made a turn and stopped at what looked like a jogging park.

"I think we should come here in the mornings. My dance studio building is just two minutes away," Harper suggested.

Nova cringed. "Sorry, I'm not a morning person."

Harper gasped. "Oh God. I can't sleep in after eight; my brain just wakes up."

"Lucky you. Don't get me wrong, I wake up early too, always have to, but I'm not... a nice person until after eleven."

Harper giggled. "We'll work it out. I won't bother you until after eleven."

"Sounds good."

Harper looked down at the watch on her wrist. "Come on, we need to get to the auditorium. The induction should be starting any minute."

They walked towards the auditorium; Nova didn't get to see much, but she still had two days before the semester started. "Do you know anyone that goes here besides me?"

Harper nodded. "I know a couple of people from my course. I met them last night. They're nice. Something tells me the parties here are going to be *wild*."

Nova smiled again; she was quite like Scarlett. Nova was glad for it too, sort of like a piece of home away from home. Oh, and was she ready for some partying. With this new chapter in her life, it was time to make some changes and let loose.

Just when they got to the auditorium, Nova saw Andrew. The boy was leaning against the entrance. "There you are." He smiled.

Harper leaned into her side. "Do you know him?" she whispered.

Nova nodded. "He's the guy I met at the café," she whispered back. "Hey," she said.

"I was waiting for you."

"You were?"

He nodded and stood up straight. "I was wondering if I could get your number?" he said, smirk still intact and Nova wondered if his face muscles ever hurt.

Harper got visibly uncomfortable. "Aren't you a bit forward? And they say chivalry isn't dead."

Andrew turned to her, and she leveled him with a glare. "Do you always gatekeep who your friends can talk to, or is Nova special?"

The way he said her name was as though he'd said it his whole life.

"She is special." Harper smiled at him. "Bye now." She pushed past him and moved to go get a seat.

Andrew continued to look at Nova and she was caught between a rock and a hard place. On one hand, she agreed with Harper, and on the other... she wanted to get to know Andrew. What harm could it do? "Give me your phone. Make it quick."

This time Andrew flashed her a genuine smile that made her feel better about doing this. Maybe Andrew wasn't that bad.

"I love your hair. Purple's my favorite color."

Nova smiled; it was a good thing he had a charming face. Some people might write him off as a creep otherwise. "*Purple's* your favorite color?"

Andrew tsked. "What? Whatever happened to colors being gender-neutral?"

Nova licked her lips and nodded. "Touché." She handed his phone back to him and walked away like her friend.

Harper had saved her a seat. "Please tell me you didn't give that jerk your number. He must be some entitled rich brat. I thought you would follow me after I left?!" Her view of Andrew had completely changed from the excited one she had at the café.

Nova wasn't too bothered though. If she was being

completely honest, Andrew was her type to the T. "You've known him for a whole minute. What harm could it do? If he's annoying, I'll just block him."

"Fine. But don't say I didn't warn you."

Soon enough the auditorium filled with people, everyone looking around curiously. Someone came on the stage and started testing the mic.

The lady was dressed in what looked like a designer red dress. She looked intimidating but her voice was nice. Almost calming.

"If everyone could settle down, we could get started here."

The whispers and murmurs of people shuffling around died down. It was eerily quiet before the lady in red smiled wide. The spotlight shined on her.

"Good morning, everyone, I am your Dean, Roma Devon. It's nice to see all these new faces. I'd like to welcome everyone that arrived today." She walked to the center of the stage and adjusted the mic on her lapel. "Atherton is delighted to have all of you. We hope that this semester proves to be everything you want it to be. The satisfaction of our students is our utmost priority."

"There are a few special people with us today. People who were handpicked to be here. Our scholarship students. If you could please stand up."

Nova knew this would happen, but she was really praying that it wouldn't. But of course, the university wanted to show that they were awfully nice and had accepted students who couldn't have afforded to go here otherwise.

Harper was smiling wide at her, patting her leg for her to get up. Unwillingly, she did. She looked around. The auditorium was huge, so it was possible she wouldn't be able to see everyone standing. There was another girl standing in the row above her. And when she turned to her right, just the row below hers, stood Andrew.

Andrew was a scholarship kid, too. Huh. Which meant Nova didn't make the worst decision by giving her number to him. She wondered what his scholarship was for.

"My God." Harper seemed to have caught on, too. "So, he's arrogant 'cause he's a scholarship student."

Nova shook her head in fond exasperation. "Shh."

Dean Devon started talking again, "These students who are standing, they have shown exceptional talent and proven themselves to be worthy of Atherton University. We have great expectations from you and hope to see you all live up to it. There will be a meeting for the eight of you in my office in the morning at ten o'clock sharp. See you there. You may take a seat now."

Nova scoffed. Talk about no pressure. She would have preferred if they just got an email saying there would be a separate meeting for them.

"What do you think the meeting is about?" Harper asked when the Dean continued to talk about how great Atherton was and how lucky they were to be here.

"I have no idea. Hey, can you do me a favor?"

"Course."

"Wake me up at nine? God knows I'm going to blow off my alarm."

Harper snorted. "Sure. But if you don't wake up, I'm throwing a bucket of water in your face."

DEVON TOLD them to head to the cafeteria for a special dinner. She also joked saying they shouldn't expect this kind of feast every day. Nova was sure her sarcasm detector was pretty good, but she would just have to find out if the food was always this good or not.

There was a whole spread of things. Things she hadn't even heard of. Who served scallops at a university?

Nova filled up her plate with food and she and Harper decided to go sit with the people that she knew from her dance course. The meal was pleasant, and the people were actually really nice. They all congratulated her on her scholarship but asked no other questions.

It was all going well until Andrew decided to crash their dinner.

"So, you're a scholarship kid, too," he said as he pulled out the chair next to hers and put his plate down.

He didn't even get invited but here he was making himself at home.

"She was in the middle of a conversation," Harper snapped.

It was funny to see Harper's peppy-girl persona leave the premises whenever Andrew came around.

"Sorry, darling. I thought I could join. I can leave if you want," Andrew said, words dripping in honey. Nova knew he had no intentions of leaving.

Harper continued to glare at him.

"You can stay," April, one of Harper's classmates, said. She smiled at Andrew, and Nova knew right away she had a crush.

Something about that... she didn't like. Andrew flashed her a grateful smile. "Thanks."

"You're a scholarship kid, too," Nova said, dragging Andrew's attention back to her. He did come here for her after all.

"I am." He leaned into her. "Athletics. You?"

"Singing."

Andrew nodded appreciatively. "I love music."

"I'm sure you do." Nova smiled. Now that she knew Andrew was a scholarship kid, the image that Harper tried to put in her mind about him being a rich snob didn't fit anymore. There was a shift in her mindset. Andrew wasn't that bad. Some people just suck at making first impressions.

"Maybe you can sing for me someday."

Nova nodded. "Maybe. Where were you before? Won't your friends be waiting for you?"

Andrew's jaw tightened, which would have looked weird, but it only pronounced the angles of his face. He really did look like an athlete. "Well, turns out being a scholarship kid means people look down on you here."

Nova felt a pang of sorrow for Andrew. She had gotten lucky with Harper, but what if Andrew hadn't?

"That bad, huh?"

Andrew rolled his eyes. "It's just boys and their egos. Everything is a competition. They're probably jealous that this is free for us while they're paying through their teeth."

"I haven't come across anyone like that yet." As an afterthought, she knocked on the wooden table.

Andrew laughed at her. "Superstitious?"

Nova shrugged. "Out of habit. I'll still go about my day if a black cat crosses my path. Are you?"

"No. You stop being superstitious when things go wrong despite you taking all the precautions," Andrew said. His eyes flitted away from Nova's.

Something about the way he said that made Nova want to hug him. She understood that on some level. Maybe it's why she even bothered with the small things. Just to make sure the things she had didn't disappear. "You can sit with us from tomorrow," she turned to the rest of the people, although they didn't seem likely to say no, "right guys?"

They all agreed politely, Harper staying silent next to her.

Nova elbowed her side gently. "Be nice," she whispered.

"Fine. You can sit with us," Harper said, looking down at her plate.

"Thank you, darling."

"Ugh, don't call me that."

Andrew continued to smirk. It seemed like he enjoyed making Harper mad. It would sure be interesting to watch the two of them when Andrew came over-

Wait, what? Since when was Andrew coming over, and since when did Nova think he was going to be interested enough to want to come over?

"I'm going to go hit the hay. I have an early morning."

Andrew got up and put his hand on Nova's shoulder. "I'll see you tomorrow in the Dean's office?"

Nova nodded and smiled. "Yeah."

"What's your house number?"

"Thirteen."

Andrew nodded. "Mine's fifteen. We can walk together. Be down at nine-thirty."

Nova could only nod. Somehow Andrew had ordered her to do something, and she was... going to do it. "I'll see you then."

Andrew nodded and left, leaving Nova feeling a little less than speechless. What was this feeling?

Nova hadn't indulged in boys back when she was in high school. Yeah, there had been crushes and she was with someone for a short month but that was it. Life got in the way, and there were bigger things to think about than boys.

The boys that went to her school didn't interest her. Maybe it was them, or maybe it was her. Either way, she didn't care at the time. But now, within a day, there was already a change in the way she felt. Scarlett was right. College changed people.

"Is there a reason for you smiling like that?" Harper asked. They were sitting on the couch, talking. Harper was telling her about her life back home.

Nova bit her bottom lip and cleared her throat. "Nothing."

"It's clearly something. Please don't tell me it's about that stupid boy."

Nova tried to hide the blush that was creeping up her face. "It's not."

Harper made a disgusted face, her hand coming up to cover her face. "Why can't you pick someone else? Literally, pick anyone else."

"What's your problem with him? Did something happen that I don't know about?"

Harper looked thoughtful for a second before she frowned. "No. I'm not really sure. He makes me... well, not uncomfortable in a way that I'd think I'm unsafe but, uncomfortable, nonetheless. He's creepy."

Nova didn't think so. Sure, Andrew was a little forward and bossy to some degree. At least from what she knew, considering it hadn't even been twenty-four hours, but he didn't make her uncomfortable. Her feelings were new, that was what was unusual. The weird feeling in her skin was just having a crush.

Her internal admission of her crush was a little too fast. But it was fine, right? It was only natural to see someone good-looking and to have feelings. Scarlett would be proud of her rationalization. "We'll get to know him, and if he's a weirdo, then we'll give him the boot."

Harper agreed but Nova could see how much she didn't like Andrew. She was sure Harper would come around though; Andrew had a charming personality.

That night as Nova lay on the unfamiliar mattress, she couldn't help but let her mind wander. What would it be like to be with Andrew? Would he smirk at everyone else but reserve his soft smiles for her? Would they go for walks together? Maybe they both picked business administration. Maybe he was thinking about her right now, too.

Chapter Five

Nova kicked at whatever was on her bed. Whatever time it was, she was not ready to be awake.

"Nova, you're going to be late. It's already nine. Andrew's going to be here in half an hour."

At the sound of his name, her brown eyes snapped open. "Oh, no. I forgot." She snapped up and ran her hands over her face. "I hate mornings."

"Hey, mornings are great. You're just a grump. Come on, you don't want to upset the Dean your first time meeting her."

"Right," Nova said under her breath and got out of bed, her legs wanting to wobble over and fall back into the soft mattress.

She took the quickest shower of her life and got dressed. She wore her jeans from last night and put on a sleeveless tunic blouse that flowed to the top of her thighs. It was comfortable and showed off her arms nicely. Now that she had her tattoo, it felt like a waste to wear long-sleeved shirts.

"You look cute," Harper said, sipping on a green smoothie.

"Thanks," Nova said as she wrinkled her nose at the smoothie. She never understood why people willingly subjected their taste-buds to that stuff. Sure, it helped but at what cost? She'd rather not have clear skin than drink *that* every morning.

"What? It's not that bad. I put mangoes in it."

"Where did you find mangoes here?"

"There's a store on campus and one like two miles away from here but I go to the one out. It has fresh produce."

She looked at the clock and realized she still had five minutes, so she had just enough time to make toast.

Atherton had a breakfast buffet, but it started at seven-thirty and ended at eight-thirty. There was no way Nova was waking up that early for just eggs. Maybe if she had a class around that time but otherwise it wasn't happening.

Her phone started ringing in the middle of her first bite. It was Andrew. She picked it up immediately. "I'll be right down, give me a second." She skipped the pleasantries and got to the point.

"Okay, beautiful. Good morning to you, too," Andrew replied and Nova just knew there was a smirk on his smug face.

She hung up without replying, her face still flushed despite her 'playing it cool' tone.

"God, you're embarrassing," Harper said in an exasperated voice.

Nova beamed at her exaggeratedly and put her shoes on. "I'll be back as soon as that thing finishes. Can we finish the tour from yesterday? Your friends should come, too."

Harper nodded. "I'll text them."

"Okay, bye!"

"Bye!"

She rushed down the stairs, tucking the hair falling in her face behind her ear. Andrew was wearing a pale green hoodie with a ketchup stain on the hem and gray sweatpants.

"You're going to wear sweatpants to see the Dean?" she asked.

"What's with you and the habit of not saying hi?"

Nova rolled her eyes, and they started walking toward the head office of Atherton. "What's with you and not answering my questions?"

"I just got back from a run. I'm here on an athletic scholarship; it's within my rights to be in sweats."

She smiled. "You went jogging this early?"

Andrew turned to her, and his mouth was slightly agape. "Nine in the morning is early? I usually wake up at four."

It was Nova's turn to be the one with her mouth agape. "That's... that's not possible. I don't know how you do it."

"Force of habit."

Nova nodded and they walked, talking about how surprised they were when they got their scholarship letters.

They were some of the first to arrive. Two girls were already out waiting. They said their hellos and introduced themselves. Jasmine had won a medical scholarship and Maria won one for culinary arts.

The rest of them arrived, everyone in different courses. It was really cool how many people excelled in different things.

"Great, everyone is here. I'm a fan of punctuality," Devon said and opened her door for everyone. She was dressed in a dark blue dress. "It's nice to see all of you personally. If we could go around and introduce ourselves, that would be great."

Everyone did as they were told, and Nova had been right; Roma Devon was an intimidating person because most of them fumbled with their words. She looked at all of them like she was doing a full-body scan and knew all their deepest darkest secrets.

"I'm sure everyone is wondering why you're here. Mostly because I wanted to meet the people our team chose. You all know that the submissions stopped six months ago, and we went through each of the candidates with a fine-toothed comb. You are all here because you're good at what you do and show potential." She paused for a second. "However, if we *think* that you're not doing your best every day or if you're slacking in your course, or in your compulsory curriculum, know that we do hold the power to take corrective measures."

In other words, if they thought we weren't being perfect little students, we'd be sent home.

"Our reputation precedes us, and we try very hard to maintain that. As students of Atherton, you represent us, so make sure to put your best foot forward every day. Am I making myself clear?" She ended with an uptick in her volume.

Everyone nodded, the tension had gotten thicker, and Nova looked at Andrew. He looked determined, like nothing in this world could take his scholarship away. Nova liked that.

"You can all leave, but please, if I ever have the pleasure of meeting any of you in person again, let it be for an achievement. I hate to be the crusher of dreams."

They all scurried out of the room like they couldn't get out fast enough and Nova related. Something about Roma Devon was so... powerful, you couldn't help but feel like you were two feet tall.

"That was exciting," Andrew said sarcastically. "Want to go to breakfast with me?"

Nova raised her eyebrows and tilted her head. "Are you asking me out, Rogers?"

"So, what if I am, Scott?" Andrew put his hands in his pockets.

Nova hummed like she was considering the offer. She was going to go but what would it hurt to make him suffer. "Do you put ketchup on your eggs?"

Andrew laughed and shook his head. "That would be a crime so, no, I don't."

"Good."

"Breakfast is on me." He took her hand and they walked to the café they first met in.

Nova didn't mind that he took her hand, in fact, she was all for it. Nova from a week ago would have been shocked.

Andrew was telling her about his achievements and all the medals he'd won. She understood how important this scholarship was to him. She had a feeling Andrew didn't take anything lightly.

They took a seat after they'd ordered. Nova shot a quick text to Harper, telling her she'd be late. Harper had texted back with a

. . .

NOVA SMILED and sent her a heart emoji, turning her attention back to Andrew.

"What's your compulsory curriculum? Mine is business administration." She had realized she'd never asked. Was it a sign that she had it bad because she was praying his was also business administration?

"Psychology."

"Wow. That sounds interesting."

Andrew nodded. "It does, but you know what doesn't? Business administration. I know you're way more interesting than that, so, why?"

Nova scrunched her eyebrows and leaned in closer to him. "How do you know I'm interesting? You've known me for a day. Less than, in fact."

Andrew smirked and leaned forward too; they were already head-to-head. "For starters, you have a cool tattoo, pretty hair, *and* you sing. That all sounds interesting to me."

Nova gave up and leaned back, giggling. "Fine. I picked business administration because it's a good backup plan. I like having a safety blanket to fall back on if singing doesn't work out."

"Yeah, I understand that. It's why I picked psychology, too. But something tells me we'll both work our way to the top."

Nova smirked. "I'm sure we will."

They talked more, and the more they spoke, Nova realized how mature Andrew was. He talked with confidence and wasn't afraid to let his personality shine. And because he was so open, she did the same. She told him about her high school life and how she got in trouble all the time for standing up for her friend.

"That sounds like something you'd do."

Nova shook her head. "You talk like you've known me forever."

Andrew looked at her, his blue eyes intensified. "It feels like we have, doesn't it? Known each other forever?"

Nova sipped on her coffee and nodded because it was true. She felt connected to him.

Andrew cleared his throat and intertwined his hands before placing them on the table. "Look, Nova, I'm not a casual guy. When I know I like something, or *someone* in this case, I go for it. Beating around the bush, waiting for the," he made inverted commas with his fingers, "*right time*. It's not my thing."

Nova licked her lips and waited for him to continue.

"What I'm saying is, I like you. And I think you like me. So, would you like to go out with me? Officially? I don't like the whole part where people don't label themselves, waiting for God knows what. If you agree, you'll be my girlfriend and I'll be your boyfriend."

Wow, talk about fast. Nova was expecting this though. Andrew wasn't lying, he was the type of guy who said whatever was on his mind. And Nova appreciated that.

All things considered, Andrew would make a good boyfriend. He was charming, determined, and *very* good-looking. If the thoughts she was having last night were anything to go by, she knew she liked him. So, why not?

"Yes," Nova said. She sighed once it was out, her skin littered with goosebumps. This was all so exciting. She now had a boyfriend and went to her dream school. "I would like that."

Andrew all but jumped out of his seat to get to her. They hugged, and Nova fit right into his arms.

"You smell so nice," she whispered and blushed when Andrew looked down at her.

"Come on, I'll walk you home," he said. He took her hand and walked out the door.

Nova was a little stunned and continued to look at him, not realizing her shoulder was about to hit someone.

Someone gave a high-pitched squeal and Nova broke out of her haze to look at the source of it. "I'm sorry!" she said and was about to walk away.

"Excuse me?" The girl stared at her like Nova had slapped her.

She and Andrew turned toward the girl, who was dressed up like she was going to a party. Who wears four-inch heels to a café?

"What's the problem? She only bumped into you and already apologized," Andrew spoke for Nova.

Nova dropped his hand and looked at the girl herself; she didn't want Andrew speaking on her behalf. "You didn't drop anything, did you?" She maintained a polite tone; she didn't want to pick fights before the semester even started.

The girl scoffed, "So, because I didn't drop anything you think you can just walk into people, rubbing your nasty self on them?"

Nova stepped a little closer to the girl. If this girl didn't have a problem being rude, then neither did she. "Did someone wake up on the wrong side of the bed, or are you always this unbearable?"

Andrew took her hand again and pulled her back. "Nova, don't. She's not worth it, okay?"

Nova looked at him over her shoulder and stepped back.

The girl had an angry glower on her face and muttered something under her breath that Nova didn't catch. Before she could say anything though, Andrew pulled her out of the café.

So much for thinking she wouldn't have to deal with this so early on.

Nova was seething. And not only because of that girl. But also because Andrew pulled her out of there like he had the right.

"Nova, you're practically blowing air out of your ears."

Nova stopped walking and turned to him. "Why didn't you let me talk to her? People like her are the reason people like *us* get bullied. That day in the cafeteria, you didn't have anyone to sit with because of people like her."

Andrew rolled his eyes at her. "We don't even know if she

knows if we're scholarship kids. She's probably like that with everyone; it's nothing to lose your cool over."

Nova shook her head and continued to walk away. "Next time, let me deal with it, okay?" She didn't want to pick a fight with him the first hour into their relationship.

"Fine, I'm sorry. I didn't like the way she was talking to you, and I didn't want things to escalate; that's it." Andrew put his arm around her shoulders and pulled her closer.

When they got to Nova's house, Andrew stood in front of her and looked down. "You're beautiful."

Nova bit the inside of her cheek so she wouldn't smile like a loon. "Thank you. You're not so bad yourself."

He tucked a piece of her hair behind her ear and cupped her cheek. "Do you want to go out with me tonight? Maybe we can go out on a walk or something?"

Nova nodded and hugged him. A walk sounded like a great idea. "Call me?"

Andrew pulled away and shoved his hands into his pockets. "I will. Maybe start with a 'hi' when I do."

Nova laughed and turned to run upstairs. She opened the door and rushed to get to Harper's room. "Oh my God." She landed on top of her roommate's bed. Harper was lounging there on her laptop.

"What?" Harper set aside her device and looked at her.

"I have a boyfriend," Nova announced.

Harper's hand flew to her face and covered her mouth. "No. No way, already? Nova. You've been here for a day, dude. How does that even work?"

The pure amazement on Harper's face made Nova laugh. She scratched her head and shrugged. "To be honest, it happened so quickly. Andrew's a go-getter."

"Yeah. Quickly is probably an understatement. He's your boyfriend, and you met like two seconds ago. Is he... I don't know because I'm not his biggest fan, but what do you like about him?"

Nova thought back to the first time she met Andrew. He was

so confident, and he didn't filter his words like others. He wasn't calculated. "He's just... he's so sure about himself, you know? Something about it is so appealing. I can't even explain it."

They spent the next half an hour talking about how Andrew asked her, and Harper went through a couple of emotions. In the end, though, she was happy for Nova.

"There's a party tonight. Jackson invited us. You'll come, right?"

Nova winced. She had already promised Andrew to go on a walk with him. "I sort of told Andrew we'd go on a walk together."

"So? It's a walk, and this is a party. Parties go on for the better part of the night. Come after you're done with your walk."

Nova hummed and took out her phone. "I'll invite Andrew, too."

Harper didn't say anything to that, only got out of bed and went straight into her closet. "We need to pick the perfect outfit."

Chapter Six

Nova was excited. She had picked out a pink top that she hadn't worn yet and a pair of jean shorts. This was her first party that wasn't a children's birthday party. Harper helped her put some makeup on, but she wiped a lot of it off; she preferred to go without any.

"You look cute either way," Harper complimented.

"Andrew's going to be here any minute. I'll wait for him downstairs." Nova wanted to avoid inviting him over. Harper needed more time adjusting to the whole idea of Andrew.

She didn't wait for too long because Andrew showed up in less than two minutes. "Hey, beautiful." He opened his arms for a hug, and Nova smiled wide before folding into his arms.

"Hi." She gave him a once over and grinned about how lucky she had gotten. Andrew somehow made sweats and a jersey look good enough for a party. "You look nice. Comfy."

"So do you. But, um, are you sure about the jean shorts?" He looked down at them but not in a way that made Nova feel good.

She was a little taken aback; she wasn't expecting to be critiqued. "Uh, yeah, we're going to a party after this, so...."

"You're going to get cold, is all, and there will be a ton of people there," he argued.

Nova sucked in a deep breath and nodded. "Yeah, I know. Let's go." She walked off in front of him; she didn't want to take the conversation any further. She definitely wasn't going to change just because he *said* so.

They walked in silence for a few minutes before Andrew grabbed Nova's hand and gave it a light squeeze. Nova felt herself relax again and stepped closer to him.

Nova's phone went off with a text ping, and she pulled it out to see Scarlett had texted her. It was a picture of Scarlett and Skylar making dinner together. "Aw," she cooed and sent heart emojis.

"That's Skylar?" Andrew asked and looked at the picture over Nova's shoulder.

"Yeah," she handed him the phone, "And that's Scarlett."

"Skylar looks just like you." Andrew grinned at her and handed the phone back.

Nova hummed. "You know all about my family; what about yours?"

Andrew stiffened a little and shrugged a shoulder. "I'm an only child."

"Oh," Nova nodded, "Must be nice, having all the attention for yourself."

Nova wasn't sure what was wrong with what she said, but Andrew didn't seem to appreciate it. He looked uncomfortable and had clenched his jaw. "Uh, sorry, I, uh, I didn't mean anything by it."

Andrew turned, looked down at her, and shook his head. "Don't be. It's a complicated situation, that's all."

"We don't have to talk about it." Nova hugged his arm. The cool air started blowing, and it got a bit chilly. "Maybe we should head to the party?"

Andrew stopped walking and turned to his girlfriend. "I'm not coming."

Nova didn't understand; he'd said that he would. "Why not?

It's the first party here; you can't miss it," Nova tried to convince Andrew.

"I have practice early in the morning, babe. And I'm not in the mood anyway."

Nova frowned and let go of his hand. "Why didn't you say so before?"

Andrew shrugged. "Parties aren't really my scene. And neither are the people." He shoved his hands in his pockets in a defensive stance.

Nova immediately felt bad. She knew some people were bothering Andrew. "You do know these people are just threatened by you? Come for an hour, and if you don't like it, we can leave together."

Andrew loosened up and stepped closer to her. "Yeah?"

Nova blushed and bit her bottom lip. "Yeah."

He tucked a piece of her hair behind her ear. "It's nice to know you care so much."

Nova scoffed, "Of course I do. Don't let others be the reason you miss out. They're mad they aren't as good as you, which sounds like a *them* problem."

Andrew nodded, his eyes going dark. "Nova, I'm going to kiss you now, okay?"

Words got tangled in her mind, so she only nodded.

When Andrew finally leaned in to capture her mouth, she sighed internally. It was amazing. The way he held her was gentle and caring; Nova felt safe in his arms. When they came apart, she didn't try to stop the grin that was making itself at home on her face.

"You'll come to the party, right? Come on, me being there should be incentive enough," she said because she wanted to spend more time with Andrew.

"Yes." He took her hand again, and they walked to the party. Nova was excited.

The party was already in full motion when the two of them got there. The apartment was huge, but the number of people was slightly overwhelming. People were dancing, and someone was hooting in the background. Overall, the place was packed with hyped people.

Nova could vaguely make out someone screaming out her name, and she looked around till her eyes landed on Harper. She looked tiny in the crowd.

She dragged Andrew to their friend group, and Harper hugged her. "Isn't this so much fun?" she shouted in Nova's ear.

Nova laughed and nodded. "I just got here, but yeah!"

The two of them started dancing together when her eyes fell on Andrew, who looked like a pillar between all the loose people dancing around him. She noticed he was looking at her, so she raised an eyebrow in question.

Andrew looked around and made a displeased face. Nova told Harper she was going to be right back. She put her arms around Andrew's neck and tried to sway with him, but he was as rigid as a tree. "What's wrong?" she said directly in his ear.

"Nothing." He didn't do anything to convey the fact that nothing was wrong. He had put his hands on her waist but made no effort to move with her.

"Let's go to the kitchen. I saw someone eating pizza." She dropped her hands and led their way to the kitchen, which was a little less crowded, making it easier to breathe. She saw the big box of pizza open on the counter and picked up a slice to give Andrew.

He shook his head and cleared the counter so he could climb and take a seat.

"You don't want pizza?" Nova asked, biting into the slice.

"I don't eat pizza."

Nova's jaw dropped. "Sorry, what?" She scoffed, "Please tell me you're joking."

Andrew chuckled but shook his head. "I'm an athlete. I don't put that stuff in my body."

She couldn't resist rolling her eyes. "You're more a sadist. How can you not eat pizza?"

Once again, Andrew chuckled but didn't explain himself further. He reached out and put a finger in one of the belt hoops of Nova's jeans and pulled her closer. He kissed her, and Nova smiled. "I guess it's not so bad when I can taste it on you."

"I promise it tastes so much better when you eat it yourself."

Andrew grinned. "I don't know; let me try again."

"If it isn't the cutest couple in town."

Nova turned to see the same girl from the café. Her fun-loving mood flew out of the building. The girl had two other girls in tow. "If it isn't the moodiest person in town," Nova retorted. Andrew jumped down from the counter behind her.

The girl scoffed. "There's a difference between being moody and being selective with the people I choose to associate with."

"Camille, why don't you leave us alone? We're just trying to have a good time," Andrew spoke.

"You know her?" Nova turned to her boyfriend and ignored the other three girls.

"Honey, everyone knows me." Camille moved closer to them. "And shouldn't you know whose house you're going to for a party? Or are you used to freeloading?"

Her words were said in such a saccharine-sweet voice that Nova wanted nothing more than to push her against the wall.

"That's right. I know who you are. Nova Scott, one of the scholarship kids. I didn't know who you were until I described...." She gave Nova a once over with a look of disgust, "*this* to some other people. And so is your boyfriend. Do you guys run in packs like wolves?"

Nova didn't know how she'd offended Camille enough to deserve this, but she knew no matter how nice she was to this girl, Camille would always be horrible. More people had gathered in the kitchen, watching as Camille belittled her.

"What are you so mad for, hmm? Is it because no one's given you any attention lately?" Nova said as she lifted her finger and twirled it towards all the people that had gathered, "Is this your thing? Is this how you feel better when you go to bed?"

"Excuse me, watch your mouth, loser," the girl next to Camille snarled.

The three of them were dressed alike, just in different colors. The two sidekicks, Nova thought of them as Skank One and Skank Two, were shorter than Camille. Her kitten heels added to her height, making her presence looming. Her face was covered with a thick layer of make-up, the professional kind that Scarlett tried but could never make look natural.

"Nova, let's go, okay?" Andrew took her hand. Nova snatched it away; he wasn't going to deal with this for her again.

"Yeah, listen to your boyfriend, *Nova.*" Camille smirked. "Or you know, you could stay and show us how you got that scholarship of yours." Her grin got wider.

Nova didn't understand what Camille meant at first, but Skank Two told her that Camille was basically demanding a performance.

"You've got to be kidding me," Andrew said under his breath, "Nova, please."

Nova didn't understand why Andrew was so adamant about getting out of here. "Can you stop?" she whispered harshly.

"What's wrong, Andrew?" Camille said in her sickeningly sweet voice. "If I didn't know any better, I would think you didn't have faith in your girlfriend's singing."

Nova saw Harper and her friends make their way into the kitchen. "What's going on?" Harper asked as she looked between Camille and Nova.

"Oh, more defenders. You have quite the fan club, Nova." Camille folded her arms.

"Okay, that's it," Andrew announced when it seemed like everyone in the other room was trying to see what was going on in the kitchen. "We're leaving. All of us."

Nova assumed by 'all of us' Andrew meant Nova, Harper, and Harper's friends. He didn't even wait for her to get a word out before he dragged her out by the wrist. She tried to fight it, but his athletic strength was shining through right now.

Harper followed them out with a bewildered look on her face, April and Dean following her. As soon as they were outside, Nova's struggling finally won out, and she freed herself from Andrew's grip.

"What is wrong with you?!" she yelled. "Why did you do that?"

"Let me drop you and your friends back to your room. You guys can party there."

Nova felt like screaming at the top of her lungs, but all she could do was stare at Andrew incredulously. "Are you kidding me? You dragged me out of there like a dog on a leash!? Who *died* and left you in charge of *me?*"

"Nova." Harper tried to calm her, but that only made it worse.

"Didn't I literally tell you *not* to do that this morning? I could have handled that on my own. I've dealt with a lot worse than Camille, okay?"

Andrew shook his head in exasperation. "Really, you want to do this right now?" He turned his back on her and started walking away towards her building.

"Why did you drag me out like that?!" she yelled as they all started walking. She was furious with him.

Andrew didn't look back once, and neither did he pay attention to Nova's rant. That made her even more upset. *How dare he treat me like this?* She fumed.

April, Dean, and Harper went up to the dorm room when they reached her building while throwing her furtive glances. Nova felt the boiling heat simmer down and settle into her. Andrew finally looked at her and opened his mouth to say something, but Nova cut him off.

"Don't even. Just go," she said, throwing her hand up in exasperation. He hadn't given her a chance to speak, so she wouldn't give him one either. She ran up the stairs and slammed the door shut behind her.

Her friends jumped in their seats, startled. She walked up to them and threw herself down next to Dean. She took a few deep breaths. "Sorry," she apologized.

"It's a good thing we left. People like Camille are only good for throwing extravagant parties," Harper said placatingly. "I was getting over it, too, so...."

"Stop it." Nova pulled her hair up and put it in a bun; she was getting annoyed with it falling in her face. "None of us should have been dragged out like that, I'm really sorry."

"Yeah, he did go all caveman on you; it was a bit weird," Harper admitted.

"What happened?" April asked.

"Camille and I had a little run-in at the café this morning, and she's still mad about it. I didn't know it was her place and party; Andrew and I were in the kitchen, and she walked in trying to start something."

Harper rolled her eyes. "And here I thought I wouldn't be part of any drama once I started university."

Nova scoffed, "Tell me about it." Then, when silence fell over the room, she sighed, "I'm sorry, this is bumming me out. I didn't mean to ruin anyone's night. I'm sorry I'm such a hothead."

"That wasn't your fault, though," Harper said.

"That's true," Dean said with a frown, "Andrew could have asked her to back off, and that would have been the end of it."

Nova didn't like the sound of that any better than what Andrew had already done. "Who is this Camille person anyway, and why does everyone know her?"

April gasped and turned to her. "You don't know Camille?"

Nova looked around the room to check if she was the only one confused, and she was. "Um, no? Am I supposed to?"

"She's only the biggest business tycoon's daughter. Anything you can think of, he probably has a company for it. And her mom," April became more excited as she went on, "I don't even know where to begin. She's this huge fashion designer and lives in Paris. Haven't you ever seen Camille in the magazines?"

"Um, I don't read magazines. And her parents are the famous ones, right? So, why is she all high and mighty?"

April hummed to that. "I mean, the girl has the world at her feet. It explains why she's so...."

"Entitled?" Nova filled in.

"Yeah..." Silence fell over the room, and Nova wanted to go to bed so this day would end.

"Why don't we watch a movie? Nova, do you want to set up the TV, and the rest of us will pick something?" Harper suggested.

Nova agreed, and they settled on some rom-com she'd never heard of. She wasn't paying attention, though. It felt like the right decision when she left Andrew without saying anything, but now her brain wouldn't stop rehearsing things she could have said to him *and* Camille.

She would have loved to prove to Camille that she was here for a reason and show her what she was capable of.

"Hey," Harper elbowed her arm gently, "You okay?"

Nova nodded, "I'm just still mad."

April patted her knee and offered her the candy she had found in Harper's room. The movie got harder and harder to pay attention to, and just when she was about to nod off on Harper's shoulder, her phone rang.

Andrew was calling.

Chapter Seven

"You don't have to answer that," Harper said, pointing at Nova's phone. Dean had paused the movie for her benefit.

Nova watched as the phone rang and then stopped. She thought he wouldn't try again, but she was wrong, he called twice more. "Ugh, fine, okay." She picked up the call and put it to her ear, not saying anything.

"Can you please come down?" Andrew said. He sounded calm.

Well, this would give her the opportunity to use all the comebacks she'd thought of after the fact. Once again, she hung up without saying anything and got to her feet. "I'll be right back."

"Do you want us to watch from the balcony?" Dean teased, but Nova slapped him lightly on the shoulder and walked out.

Andrew was waiting at the end of the staircase. "Oh, good, I was going to call again. Why can't you do pleasantries like normal people?"

"Yeah, clearly I'm not normal. At least Camille doesn't think so." She sat down on the last step, and Andrew followed suit. There was an obvious distance between the two.

"The last person to categorize you should be Camille. She's just a mean-"

Nova cut him off. "I don't care about her. I told you I've come across people like her before. Camille is the least of my problems for the night."

Andrew sighed, "You were getting mad. It was better if we left and you weren't going to make that decision in your emotional state, so I-"

"Emotional state?" Nova stared at him in disbelief. "Are you trying to make me angrier?"

"See," Andrew gestured at her, "this is what I'm talking about. You're not thinking. Do you not know who Camille is?"

Nova took a deep breath as she tried to keep her anger at bay, but she'd had about enough. "Please let that be the last time I hear that in my life." She looked at Andrew again. "I know who she is now, and frankly, I would have acted the exact same way if I knew before. So, whatever point you're trying to make is moot."

Andrew stood up and started pacing in front of her. "I don't know you all that well yet, which sucks by the way, but I do know how important this scholarship is to you. I know you love singing, and even though you've been here for like a second, you love this place."

"What are you trying to say?"

"All Camille would need to do is shed two tears to her daddy dearest, and before you know it, someone from the office is going to call you to say they regret to inform you that you won't be able to continue at Atherton." Andrew's face had gone completely red by the end of his speech.

Nova opened and closed her mouth, but nothing came out. Of course, she hadn't thought about that, but there would be no way Camille would ever be able to pull that off, right?

"Nova." Andrew sat back down. "I was looking out for you, that's all."

She didn't need looking out for, though. "I understand..." she said, calmer than before but still agitated, "I do, but Andrew, I *don't* like being spoken for. I'd rather do it myself, and now everyone at the party probably thinks I am some damsel in distress because of Camille. I don't know what I ever did to her, but I'll handle it. Whether that be with a fight or with civility."

Andrew didn't respond, only continued to look at her. "I've learned that being on the sidelines and not ruffling anyone's feathers works. But by all means, jeopardize the good thing you've got going on here for pride."

There was nothing kind in the way he said that. Before, she had detected a hint of concern, but now it was gone. "As I said, I can fight my own battles."

Andrew bit the inside of his cheek and nodded. "Okay, but don't say I didn't warn you," he said, walking off. Nova sat there for a moment, thinking about what just happened. They'd been dating a day. A *day* and there was already something wrong. To someone else, what Andrew had done may have been considered chivalrous, but to her, it made her feel weak.

She was still sitting there when she heard footsteps behind her. April and Dean were leaving.

"Hey, everything okay?" Dean asked.

Nova forced a smile for them and nodded. "I'll see you guys tomorrow?"

They nodded and said their goodbyes. Harper was waiting for her on the couch. "From your face, I'm guessing it didn't go well?"

Nova shook her head and sat next to her. "He's just so...."

"Annoying? Bossy? Cocky?"

Nova knew all those things to be true, but she did like him. However, it made her see that they really rushed into this. "I'm mad right now, so yeah. Don't use this against me tomorrow."

HARPER WOKE her up at eight in the morning for breakfast in the cafeteria, which, honestly, she was grateful for. She had a restless night filled with disjointed dreams, and she was glad to be awake starting a new day.

"Okay, our plans for the day include ignoring Andrew until the end of time," Harper joked, but there was a seriousness in her voice like she hoped Nova would take her up on her offer.

She was out of luck, though, because they ran into Andrew in the cafeteria. He was eating alone with a book open in front of him. Nova immediately felt bad for him. She was still mad about last night, but he was eating alone, and she hated that.

"I'm going to go say hi," she told Harper, who didn't even make a snide comment. It was a true testament to the sad picture he made. She walked over and sat down opposite him. His plate was almost finished. "Morning."

Andrew looked up and put his fork down. "Morning."

"Do you want to come and sit with us?"

Andrew shrugged. "I'm almost done."

Nova didn't do too well with unresolved fights; they usually led to more fighting. "Can we drop this? It's over now."

"Really? I came to apologize and explain myself last night, and it just got out of hand."

"It's fine. Going forward, though, let me deal with people who are coming for me."

Andrew nodded and swallowed the last of his breakfast. "Okay, my bad. I was trying to look out for you, that's it."

Nova nodded and tried to ignore the part where Andrew was trying to have the last word. "So will you come and sit with us?"

"For a couple of minutes. I need to get to the field soon." He got out of his seat and put a hand on Nova's lower waist. He leaned down to press a soft kiss on her head, and they called it a truce.

***

"What are we doing today then?" Nova asked once Andrew left for his practice.

"We were thinking of going to the theater. The drama students are holding an improv session. It'll be fun."

Nova agreed. She knew from her schedule that she had a class held there once a week. The route to the theater was pretty, too; there was a flower garden where some people took photos. So, Harper dragged them there to take a couple.

The theater was a lot like the auditorium but a little bigger. There was a balcony, and the seats were covered with red velvet. People were gathering and moving around. It reminded Nova of the time she had taken part in her school musical. That was the first time her parents had seen her perform.

"You'll be having your performance practices here, right?" April asked.

"Yeah."

"Omg!" Harper jumped in her seat. "See that kid in the green? He received an acting scholarship. He was an extra in a movie."

Nova looked at him and wondered what his experience was like at this school. It couldn't be as crazy as hers. One of the students went to the middle of the stage and announced that the show was starting. The theater seats were almost full.

The actors began to improv, coming up with a clever comedy. It was going well until there was a commotion that came from the theater entrance. Some of the performers were startled, but they didn't seem worried enough to stop. That was until they had something to worry about.

A group of people wearing masks burst through the theater doors. They were running and shouting while flailing their arms around. They were laughing loudly and charging towards the stage. It was clearly a bunch of boys.

Nova had no idea what was happening, but she knew this was *not* part of the improv. Those boys started running between the rows, scaring people out of their seats. They weren't doing anything but screaming and jumping uncontrollably like a pack of idiots. Was she back in high school again?

"What is going on?" Harper asked, her eyes following the boys who had spread out all over the theater, causing a ruckus. They were making so much noise that it was echoing throughout the theater.

"Oh, I think I know what this is! My roommate was talking about this!" Dean shouted over the noise, scrunching up his face.

"Well, are you going to tell us?!" April yelled.

"There is a group of guys that decided that they would go around crashing events, just for the fun of it."

"You've got to be kidding me. Are they insane?!" Nova said.

The actors from the stage had jumped down when a couple of masked boys climbed up and started chasing them around. Nova had never seen anything like this in her life; this was beyond immature for university students.

A tall guy with sharp, handsome features climbed up on the stage and stood in the center. He looked like he could be the leading man in a movie role. He just stood there and watched as people went crazy, including Nova and her friends, because two boys managed to terrorize her row. The guy on the stage looked on with amusement. He had a cold smirk on his face like this was entertaining to him.

He grabbed one of the discarded mics from the ground and tapped it twice to test it. "All right guys, that's enough."

As soon as the words were out of the guy's mouth, everything came to a halt. The masked boys stopped and turned to look at who Nova assumed was their "leader."

"People of Atherton, welcome." His voice boomed, and while his words were warm, his tone was mocking. "Since the semester starts tomorrow, we thought we'd let you people know how things *work* around here."

Nova looked around as all the boys shed their masks and shared his wolfish grin. She'd read about this stuff online, the ragging and bullying that happened in places like this because everything is about status at the end of the day. If there was a food chain, Nova was sure she was at the bottom of it.

"Okay, since a lot of you are here, let's make one thing clear.

There are people who lead, and there are people who follow. The majority of you...." he scanned the room with a look of disgust, "look like the latter."

Nova and her friends would have left, but those boys were stationed at the end of the rows, stopping anyone from trying to leave.

"The rules here are simple. Number one, don't get in our way. Number two, cover for us. At any given moment, you can become our alibi. If we say you were somewhere you were not, you will simply agree. Number three, and this one will be the hardest one for some of you, don't be annoying. Oh, and none of you want to find out what happens if you break the rules."

The hooligans, because that's how Nova thought of those other boys, made agreeing sounds.

Nova couldn't believe everyone was just standing here and listening to this nonsense. Why wasn't anyone speaking out or fighting back? Even Harper only displayed a slight grimace on her face like this was only a minor inconvenience. "Is no one going to say anything to him?" Nova asked her.

Harper snorted. "Yeah, sure, as if someone's going to say something to *him*."

Nova opened her mouth to reply, but *someone* didn't let her.

"Do we have a problem, ladies?" the guy on the stage said as he walked parallel to where she and Harper were standing.

Nova wondered if he was here for basketball; if not, that height was a waste. Harper had gone stiff next to her.

"Uh, n—no, we don—"

"Actually, I do," Nova cut Harper off. It must be a force of habit because she hadn't known herself that she would say that.

"Do you?" He jumped off the stage and walked over to them. Harper, April, and Dean leaned away as he came face to face with Nova. Except he looked down at her because she was considerably shorter than him. His eyes flickered between all her features, and his pupils dilated. "And what is it?" he asked softly.

Despite the scrutiny, Nova channeled her confidence. "Yeah, why do you think this is going to work for you? I'm sure I can round up some people who could confirm that you tried to pull this stunt, and I'm pretty sure you'd be suspended, if not expelled." She folded her arms. She was sure her argument was bulletproof, which was why she was confused when the guy's unwavering smug smile didn't go anywhere.

It got worse when he started laughing. The weird thing was that everyone else started laughing, too. Even the people Nova was trying to save from possibly becoming accomplices *or* culprits to crimes they didn't commit.

"*You're* going to get *me* expelled?" He put his hands in his pockets and leaned on his heel.

"Yes. It's not unheard of for Atherton to expel students for breaking the rules." Nova didn't actually know of anyone who had been expelled, but she was hoping it was a real thing.

The boy hummed in mock seriousness and nodded. "Sure, yeah. People *are* expelled, but not *me*. People like you."

"Like me?" Nova remembered Andrew telling her how these people could go crying to their parents, and all Nova would have left to show for her time in Atherton would be a traumatic experience.

"Yeah, like you. Scholarship kid, right?" His cattish smile got wider. "Yeah, I saw you at Camille's party," he said and looked around into the crowd, "Oh, you're alone. Where's your knight in shining armor? Is he off duty?"

The crowd laughed again, and Nova remembered something her mother once told her: when you were in the spotlight, things felt bigger than they were. So, she composed herself and cleared her throat. "I don't need him to fight my battles. I slay my own dragons. Unlike you needing your little hoard of pets." She smiled and waved a hand toward the boys that had come with him.

Her words definitely got to him because there was a twitch in his eyebrow. "Yeah, well, to save you the trouble and embarrassment, I can't be expelled. But *you* can. So, if I were you, I'd be very careful." He allowed his gaze to roam her face once again before stepping away from her. "Let her," he said louder, "be an example of exactly what *not* to do."

Nova wasn't threatened, and neither was she scared. Whoever this guy was, he couldn't be above the university's law.

"If any of you have any questions or concerns, get them cleared by someone else. I'm sure they'll help you. Or won't, I really don't care."

That seemed to be the end of his terrorizing as he took a final look at her and walked out with the others following him.

"Are you insane?" Harper pulled her back and stared at her like *she* was the one acting mad.

"What? He walked in here like he owned the place and told us that we have to take the fall for him whenever, wherever."

April and Dean shared a look. "Do you not know *anyone* here?" Dean asked.

Nova shrugged. "I don't. Isn't that the whole point of university? You come and meet new people."

Harper chuckled and squeezed her arm. "You're adorable, but so clueless, and that was stupid. Honestly, you're lucky he didn't do anything insane like have you thrown out. Or something worse. Based on his usual standards, he went lightly on you."

If Nova knew she needed a catalog of people and their backgrounds, she would have done her homework. "And is someone going to tell me who *he* is?"

"That was Dominic Lark," Harper said.

"Okay, and?"

April and Dean started laughing. "Girl, I'm going to make you a list. This is not normal." April put an arm around her, and they started walking.

"He's from the Lark family. One of the founders of Atherton."

Nova stopped walking, and the air got stuck in her throat. "So he *does* own the place?"

They all laughed at her, and she finally understood why they were all looking at her like she'd grown a second head.

"Harper was right, you know. You got lucky. I've known Dominic since we were in middle school, and he's not the most forgiving," Dean said with his lip curled in disgust.

Right, she forgot that the people she hung out with were filthy rich and ran in the same circles as those bullies; they were just nicer. This was certainly not the start she hoped to get when she came to the university, but here she was. "I would like that list, April. Please."

April smiled at her warmly and agreed.

The rest of the day was uneventful until Nova met up with Andrew. She attempted to tell him what happened at the theater, but he beat her to the punch.

"So, I heard something interesting from my roommate about the theater today." His voice was pinched, and he seemed irate. Nova was getting really tired of this back and forth with him. Their relationship had been four kisses and two days of fighting.

"Yeah, I didn't know he was from one of the founding families and quite frankly, I'm not sure if I would have responded any differently if I did. There is no part of me that is willing to allow someone to run over me."

Andrew softened a little. "I like how you defend yourself; I just wish you didn't self-sabotage in the process."

"I swear this stuff just happens to me."

Andrew laughed. "Okay, and I look forward to less of this happening to you. You've already crossed two extremely influential people."

Nova cringed. "I know. It's not looking good for me, is it?"

Andrew shook his head but smiled at her. "I hope you don't leave, Scott. I happen to like your company."

Even though Nova had her moments of thinking that Andrew was a bad decision, this wasn't so bad. "They'll have to do a lot worse than a little bullying to get me to leave. Are you excited about your classes tomorrow?"

Andrew shrugged a shoulder. "I think so. I have this compulsory math class; I don't know how I feel about that, considering math is not my strongest subject."

"Wait, math with Ms. Gina Hart?"

"Yeah. Wait, do you have that class, too?"

Nova smiled wide. "Yeah. Oh good, at least I'll have one class with someone I know. Harper and I aren't in any together."

"We should head back. I need to prep for my classes tomorrow," Andrew said suddenly.

"Right now? Can you stay for a little longer?" They were sitting on one of the many benches around the campus. She didn't want to go back yet, and she hadn't spent much time with Andrew when they weren't fighting.

Nova bit her lip. "Just a few minutes?" she said with an exaggerated cute pout to joke with him.

"I need to go, Nova." He stood up, but Nova caught his hand teasingly; he harshly shrugged it off. "Stop!"

She startled. That was unexpected. She was just teasing him. "Why are you getting mad?"

"I told you I need to go back, and you won't let me!" he yelled, his face distorting in barely contained rage.

Nova didn't know how to respond to his strange mood swing. Her cheeks pinkened in embarrassment and anger. "Uh, okay, go." She got up, too, and quickly walked towards her building. She didn't know what was wrong with Andrew, but he was giving off some seriously weird vibes.

Her dorm room was empty when she got back. *Why did Andrew blow up like that? He seemed totally unhinged.* She was really feeling like she made a bad decision rushing into this relationship with him. What should she do? She didn't want to think about it right now; today was just too much. She needed a distraction.

She lay on her bed and picked up the piece of paper she'd left there. It was the list of people she should know, made by all three of her friends. Hopefully, she wouldn't have to fight anyone else. But then again, tomorrow was only the first day of the semester. So, she scrolled on social media, getting to know who was who until she fell asleep.

Chapter Eight

"**D**ude, you better wake up before I throw a bucket of water on you," Harper said for the third time.

"I don't have a class until eleven!?" She groaned into her pillow. She didn't want to get out of bed, Andrew had ruined her mood completely, and it was more than a bit concerning how quickly his attitude changed. It was a testament to how little she knew about him.

"Still, we have breakfast."

Nova sat up and tried to keep her eyes open. "I hate today."

"It hasn't even begun yet. Come on; it's our first day, super exciting!" Harper hopped in bed, making Nova flail around.

"I hate you," Nova cried and got out of bed. She promised herself that even if Andrew was eating alone, she would not approach him. This time he needed to come to her. Because so far, he'd been messing up, and she'd been the one to make amends.

The cafeteria was emptier than it was yesterday, but there were still a lot of people, including Andrew, who was yet again alone, but Nova ignored him. It did tug at her heartstrings, but then she thought about yesterday and how he had pulled a *Dr. Jekyll and Mr. Hyde.*

"You're not going to him?" Harper asked as the two of them

sat. "Does he have to look like an injured puppy while eating?" Her words and her tone were a complete contrast. She seemed even more annoyed with him than usual.

"He's being a pain. He can have one meal on his own."

"You know I've heard you defend him like twice, yet complain about him ten times. Doesn't that say something?"

Nova was thinking the same thing. She pushed the food around on her plate, trying not to overthink Harper's words. She wondered if Andrew acted the way he did because he felt stressed. "We had a miscommunication. That's it," she defended.

"I might believe that if you didn't sound so unsure."

Nova had officially lost her appetite.

"Incoming." Harper coughed the words.

"Nova?" Andrew called out from behind her, and she sighed before turning to him.

"Hi."

"Can we talk?"

Nova looked at Harper and gave her a helpless look before getting out of her chair.

"About last night," Andrew started, he had his hands in his pockets, and his shoulders were stiff, "I think we were both a litt-"

"Both?" Nova folded her arms.

Andrew blew air out his nose forcefully and clenched his jaw. "Okay, I might have overreacted for a second." He took her hand and rubbed the back of it with his thumb. "I'm sorry."

"You can't keep doing things and apologizing, then think everything is going to be okay."

"I know. It's just... I was going through something, and I shouldn't have taken it out on you," Andrew said softly.

Nova loosened up a little; she didn't want to give in, but today was their first day, and it would be better to start it off on the right foot. "I just wanted to talk for a little longer."

"I know, but...." Andrew went a little red in the face, "I'm a little slow when it comes to actual studying." He chewed on his upper lip and looked away. "I have to read up on everything beforehand because… I'm not that good at academics, and I need to make sure I pass my classes in order to stay here. Failure is not an option."

Nova could see how hard this was for him to admit. She felt bad for him. "I had no idea. I get it, though." She hugged him. "I can help. Whatever you need." She got on her tippy toes to kiss his cheek.

There was a feminine gagging sound in the background, and Nova let her head fall on Andrew's chest in exasperation. She had a good idea who it was, and she was not in the mood to deal with her. Andrew held her when she turned to Skank One, who she now knew as Alexis, and Skank Two, known as Kat. And, of course, their queen bee, Camille, in the middle.

"Do you guys always walk around like *Mean Girls*, or is this a special occasion?" Nova tried to make it a light joke, but her tone betrayed her, and it came out prickly.

"Do you always walk around like you've just rolled out of bed?" Camille snapped, eyeing Nova's top with distaste.

Nova could feel Andrew's heavy breathing behind her. Not saying anything right now was probably killing him.

"Well, Camille, I hope you have a great day, too."

"I will. Not so sure about you, though." Camille walked past her, bumping Nova's shoulder in the process.

What a great start to the day, she thought. So much drama, and she hadn't even made it to her first class yet.

Nova decided she would try to keep a low profile in her classes; still, she noticed a definite chill in the air from her classmates. There was a lot of staring and whispering, with people going out of their way to avoid her. But at least she made one friend.

"I saw you in the theater with Dominic yesterday. That was so awesome. You've got guts considering you're here on a scholarship," her new friend, Riley, told her. So, she'd already made a name for herself. That explained the lack of people wanting to talk to her. Riley had to since they had been partnered for a duet performance. They harmonized well together.

Nova smiled awkwardly and distracted herself with the coursework. Her business classes weren't half bad. She sat in the front of her classes because everyone quickly filled the back seats. She didn't receive any welcoming looks from the students, so, sitting alone it was.

Halfway through economics, her mind flitted away from whatever was going on in class. Was she really going to spend her time at university as an outcast? Did Camille or Dominic add another "rule," stating not to go near Nova Scott?

"Miss Scott, is there a problem?" Mr. Noel snapped her out of her daydreaming.

"N-no, sir."

"Am I boring you?" He stood in front of her seat and folded his arms.

"No, sir. I was paying attention."

"Were you? Because it looked like you weren't."

Nova heard the whispers, and it made her want to run away. "Sorry," she said softly, just for the professor to hear. This was officially her least favorite class. The snickering in the background got louder, and she slid down in her seat a little.

"Don't let it happen again. Let it be your first and last warning."

What a jerk. She nodded, paid more attention, and answered as many questions as possible.

By the end of that class, Nova basically ran out of the building and waited outside the running track for Andrew. She needed to see a familiar face. When he came out, he was all sweaty and shiny. His blonde hair was slicked back and flatter than usual because of the sweat.

"Hey," she greeted.

"Hi." He leaned for a quick peck on the lips, which Nova would have liked to skip, considering the smell.

"I, uh, heard from someone that you got yelled at in your class. What happened?"

"*Yelled* at? It was more of a warning." How did he find out so quickly? As far as she knew, no one Andrew knew was in her class. "Wait, who told you?"

Andrew shrugged. "Someone said something in the locker room. I heard your name followed by a lot of other stuff, but I didn't think any of it was true. Unless you somehow managed to disrupt class with your *antics*."

"Oh God, what is going on? What *antics*?" She put a hand in her purple-streaked hair and ruffled it like it would make the stress go away. From Andrew's tone, she could tell he was leaving information out for her benefit. "This whole day went very differently than I thought it would."

"What happened?"

"Everyone's been talking behind my back and avoiding me like the plague. I'm just...."

Andrew didn't look surprised or sympathetic. "Why are you surprised?" he bit out.

"What?" Nova backed up and looked at him in shock.

"I warned you, but you didn't listen. Instead, you picked a fight with the worst people possible. You're lucky it's only social exclusion and a semi-bad rumor."

Nova scoffed. "This is unbelievable."

She struggled to keep her cool. "You're great at giving comfort, Andrew. I'll add that to the long list of things I've learned about you." She didn't wait for him to make the situation worse; she turned to leave.

"Nova!" he called after her, but it fell on deaf ears.

She must have blown past Harper because the girl was running after her. "Hey! Where's the fire?"

Nova stopped at their building and breathed harshly. She put her hands on her waist and looked around.

There were a couple of people walking, clearly staring at her, and she stared right back. "In me. I'm literally going to rip those two apart. And Andrew. Don't even get me started on him. I have never met someone so infuriating!"

Harper pursed her lips and guided Nova into the building. "Calm down, okay? You're fine."

"I know I am. And nothing anyone says matters because I don't let people bully me. That's not happening; I don't care who owns who or what, but nobody owns me." She would just have to deal with this like she dealt with everything else. Accept it and move on. She wasn't about to become Camille's Skank Three just so people would like her.

Harper nodded and fumbled with her keys. She let both of them in and sat Nova on the couch. "I literally have so much respect for you, I can't even begin to explain, but we need to correct this situation."

"There is no situation. I'm not some black cat that crosses your path and curses you. We don't need a correction; those two *idiots* need to take a good look in the mirror so they can see their ugly personalities."

"You're right. You are." Harper squeezed her hands. "But they are too influential for that. So why don't we settle for another way? An easier one that makes people love *you* and makes the hate go away."

Nova shook her head. "The hate doesn't bother me." It wasn't entirely the truth because some part of her wanted friends. But if she had to choose between standing up to bullies and being fake so others would like her, the answer was pretty clear.

"It might not bother you now, but trust me, it gets old. We can get this under control."

Nova didn't want to give in. She didn't need to pull strings or ask for favors to be liked. But she would like a fighting chance. And something told her that being liked by others would rub Camille and Dominic the wrong way. "Hypothetically speaking, what would we have to do?"

"It's simple. We throw a party, get lots of people to come over, and have a karaoke night."

Nova rolled her eyes. "What does this have to do with me?"

"Everything. You'll sing for everyone."

The more she thought about it, the more she warmed up to the plan. Singing was the one thing she knew she truly excelled in. "Would that really work?"

"Of course. Camille challenged your singing skills and what better way to prove her wrong?"

"But people don't want anything to do with me. Why would they come?"

Harper smirked and gave her a sly look. "Babe, all we need to say is that there's free food and drinks, and people will come like a moth to a flame. Just leave everything to me."

"Okay, then. Let's do it."

She didn't have to say it twice. Harper started making calls and texted about a hundred people. "You can call people, too, if you want."

Right, as though Nova had people to call. She did shoot a text to Riley and asked her to bring her friends if she was planning to come.

Harper placed a big order for pizza and wings. April and Maddie, another one of Harper's friends from dance, came over to help decorate the place. When Nova heard decorate, she thought with streamers and stuff, but they were basically trashing the place so that people would feel like the party's been going on for a while before they arrived.

When the first couple of people showed up, Nova started to get nervous. April tried to keep her busy with conversation, but it didn't help. People kept coming in, and eventually, the music got louder and louder.

April was dragged away by some of her friends, and Nova was left alone in the middle of the crowd. She could see Riley, but she was talking to other people. She didn't mind going up and starting conversations with people, but she knew what they thought of her, and she didn't need more crap.

"Hi."

Nova saw that it was Andrew. She didn't expect him to be here. "What are you doing here?"

"My roommate told me about your party. I waited for your text, but I guess you're still mad."

Nova nodded. "I really want to focus on what we're trying to do at this party tonight. I really don't want to discuss what happened earlier. I don't need any distractions." She kept her tone neutral.

"Okay. I'll be here if you need me," Andrew said, walking away.

The party became more crowded, and Harper found Nova in the kitchen. "Okay, I'm going to go set up the karaoke right now. You'll do great." She giggled and left.

Nova walked through the crowd. A lot of people stared at her once they realized who she was. She went to the middle of the room where Harper and Dean had the whole setup ready. Harper pulled her to the middle and tapped the now functioning mic.

"Hi guys, welcome. I know the first day of school can be hard on a lot of us, so my friend Nova and I decided to throw you guys a little party. Thank you for coming. Now, Nova here is going to sing a few songs for us, and then we'll go from there," she said, handing Nova the mic.

Harper looked around, expecting people to clap. When they didn't, she started the round of applause herself.

Nova held the mic and tried to regulate her breathing. "Hi, guys," she said into the mic. She hoped she wasn't visibly shaking. She whispered the song's name into Dean's ear, and he put it on for her. The music blared, and some people recognized the song and moved along to the beat.

The good thing about Nova was that she was not afraid to sing to a crowd. Whether that crowd was filled with fans or not. So, she sang. This was second nature to her. This was where she felt her most comfortable and her most confident. She was looking straight into the crowd but not really focusing on anyone. She just saw a blur of colors.

A part of the song contained a difficult to sing series of high notes. She pulled the mic away from her mouth to compensate for the lack of acoustics in the room, and she totally *killed* that song infusing it with all the emotions she had experienced since she arrived at the school. Once the music died down, Nova felt blood rush to her head, and she felt a little woozy.

Harper jumped to her side and cheered. When Nova finally focused her eyes on the crowd, people looked absolutely shocked—awed really, and for the most part, surprised. They probably realized that she didn't win her scholarship for no reason.

From what she could make out, people were whispering again, but the way they did about someone they admired.

"How have you *not* been singing to me since the second you got here. If I were you, I would never talk. Just sing. Like Disney princesses," Harper said in her ear.

Nova blushed and thanked her. "I can't believe this is working. They look like they don't hate me." She had remembered to turn her mic off, there was an incident back in high school with a mic, and she had no intention of repeating that.

"I told you it would work." Harper grinned and took the mic out of her hand. "Okay, was that something or what?" she said to the crowd.

People cheered and started chanting 'encore.' Nova smiled and felt relief rush through her body. Then, she picked another song and gave the crowd what they wanted.

Eventually, people wanted to sing karaoke themselves, so Nova gave over the mic to Dean to handle. She walked towards the kitchen to get a glass of water, and multiple people stopped her. They told her how great she sounded and invited her to their parties. Overall, this evening was turning out to be the perfect night.

"I'm so happy this is working!" April bounced by her side. "Also, I'm pretty sure you'll be all famous and completely out of my budget by then, but I'm booking you for my wedding."

Nova laughed. Being outside of April's budget was high praise indeed, because April was pretty rich. "I'll do it *pro bono*. Thanks for helping out." She hugged the girl. It was silly to think she had been slightly annoyed with her about her attraction to Andrew.

Right, Andrew. She still had to deal with him, but she'd like nothing more than to push it back until tomorrow. Tonight had come with its own challenges, and she had successfully overcome them all.

Riley came up to Nova to introduce her to her friends.

"You were *so* good." Andrew came up to her after Riley and her friends left. To his credit, he had left her alone for most of the party. Quite a few people had already left since they had classes tomorrow.

"Shouldn't you be in bed or something by now?" Nova had found that Andrew had a very strict schedule.

"I should be, but I didn't want to leave without talking to you." He pulled her closer by the waist. "Can we go to your room?"

Nova took him to her room. She really wanted to know what Andrew had to say this time.

"I'm sorry. I should have been more understanding of your situation."

Nova sat on the bed while Andrew stood. "You should have."

"I know, and I want to explain myself."

She'd had a wonderful night and hoped that Andrew wasn't about to ruin it. "Go on."

"Okay, the way you stood up for yourself, I can't even imagine doing that. All my life, I've been bullied for one thing or another. I was the skinny, lanky kid who didn't know what to do with his limbs, and then I was the guy with the drunk mom and no father in sight. Children are cruel from a very young age, and the best way to cope with it was to get on their good side. Giving in. So, I'm not used to doing what you did, and it set my teeth on edge. I was afraid of the outcome."

Nova felt a surge of pity for Andrew. "I didn't know you had gone through all of that. I'm sorry that happened to you."

Andrew nodded and hesitantly took a seat next to her. "You are such a good singer. You deserve to be here, and no one can take that away from you. Not Camille and not Dominic."

Andrew could be so sweet sometimes. The night just got better. "I'm glad we had this talk."

"Me, too." Andrew smirked and cupped Nova's face. "You're beautiful."

"You're beautiful, too."

Andrew leaned in for a kiss, but the door flew open. "I think you need to come out. Right now," April said.

Nova followed. Standing in the middle of their living room was none other than Camille.

"Oh, star of the show, there you are." She had a hand on her waist.

"Welcome, Camille." Nova looked towards the door as people were leaving. "I'm afraid you're late. The party's over."

Camille faked a smile, and Nova wondered what she would look like if she smiled for real. She had a beautiful... everything. Anyone with even half a functioning eye could see that. "I heard that you sang."

"Beautifully," Harper added.

Camille looked at Harper and gasped, which was fake, too. "Harper, I didn't know you had such a big heart. I heard about your mother's philanthropy. It looks like you've followed her footsteps and started your own charity."

Harper folded her arms. "I don't understand what you mean."

"Nova here. She's not your usual type to hang out with."

That made Nova's heartbeat speed up. She knew she probably wouldn't be this close to Harper had she not been her roommate; they really were different from each other. But then, Nova wasn't that similar to anyone here with her purple-streaked hair, tattoo, and fighting spirit.

"Nova is a good friend and a good person. That's more than I can say about my *other* acquaintances. Camille, I hate to do this, but it's getting late, and I have class in the morning. Can we continue this another time? I'm sure you're not one to overstay your welcome." As Harper spoke, she neared Camille to lead her to the door.

Camille got the message and turned to leave but not before she shot a look in Nova's direction. Nova wasn't scared of her, but she was pretty sure that she and Camille had a long way to go before things settled down.

While Nova and Harper were cleaning the house, Harper's phone started pinging from text notifications.

"What's going on?" she said under her breath and picked her phone up. "Oh my God. Nova. Look at this."

Nova took the phone to see what was going on. "Is that me?" Her jaw dropped when she saw all the comments and videos Harper was being tagged in. There was an insane amount of likes and comments. People probably couldn't find Nova's social media accounts because she had them set to private.

"I can't believe this worked *so* well! I'm a genius!" Harper did a little dance on her feet.

Nova gave her a side-eyed glance. "These people actually like me now."

"Harp," she gave the phone back to her friend and pulled her into a hug, "thank you so much. For this and for being my friend."

Harper tsked and pulled her back. "Is this about what Camille said?"

"I guess so. I'm sure she wasn't wrong."

Harper licked her lips and sat them both down. "I have had a lot of friends. And most of them look like real-life barbies. But I have *never* been friends with anyone as cool as you. You are a scholarship student whose earned her place here, and you sing like how I'd imagine angels sound. And you aren't scared of anything. Do you know how amazing that is? I'm constantly scared. Last night my own shadow from the fridge's light scared me."

Nova laughed but pulled her friend closer. "Thank you."

"You're welcome. And don't think this was for free. You owe me, Scott," she said jokingly.

"Anything, anytime."

The next day of school was better than she could have imagined. She had people to sit with, *and* her vocals teacher pulled her aside and told her he would keep her in mind for something exciting coming up. So, even the teachers had seen her in the videos. Things were looking up.

"Hey, do you want to come over to my dorm tonight?" Andrew asked her during lunch. "I have a couple of assignments I could use some help with."

Nova smiled and gave him a chaste kiss. "Of course. I would love to."

Andrew nodded. "I'll meet you outside your dorm at seven."

She chuckled. "You don't need to meet me; I'll walk on my own."

"Nope. I'll meet you."

"Okay." she blushed; she was glad to be getting some more time with him. Throughout their relationship, things have been hot and cold.

"I love it when you blush." He put a hand around her waist and pulled her closer. Unlike last time, there was no one to interrupt their moment.

"I'll see you tonight." She got out of her seat and happily skipped to her last class.

Chapter Ten

Harper was going out with some of her friends and had invited Nova, but Nova told her she was spending time with Andrew. "Babe, can I say something, and you promise not to get mad?"

Nova felt hesitation from Harper's side. "Of course."

"Don't you think it's a little weird that when things aren't great, Andrew's always on the other side of things? And when they are good, he comes back."

She couldn't really come to Andrew's defense, and Harper didn't even know the half of it. "I... I don't know." After hearing Andrew's side last night, she understood to some extent what he'd been through. But, explaining that to Harper would be unfair to him; it wasn't Nova's story to tell. "He's not a bad guy, Harp."

Her friend nodded. "Just be careful, that's all."

"I will. I'll see you later."

Andrew was waiting for her, and they walked to his place hand in hand. It turned out he needed help with research methods. He didn't have a desk in his room, so they set themselves up on his bed and got to work. It was nice helping Andrew; he listened carefully and didn't lose focus for a second. Nova smiled over his head while he figured out the notes she had written out for him.

"Wow, you really make things easy. You should write textbooks." He grabbed her face and pulled her in for a kiss. "Thank you for helping."

"You're welcome." She smiled.

They talked some more and ended up lying in bed. Andrew told her more about his mother. He had a neighbor helping out with her. "You're a good son, Andrew."

He smiled, but it didn't reach his eyes. "I try."

She threw an arm over his chest, hugging him.

"Nova, can I be honest?"

She nodded against his chest.

"I... I think I'm in love with you."

Nova shot up so fast that she could've gotten whiplash. *What in the world was Andrew saying? It hadn't even been a week! This couldn't be normal. What was wrong with him?*

"I..."

"Don't worry; you don't have to say it back." Andrew sat up, too.

"Andrew, I think..." She couldn't think of anything to say. How was she supposed to react to that?

"Nova, it's fine. It's my mistake. I shouldn't have said anything."

She shook her head, then nodded, but then shook it again. "I'm sorry, that was a lot."

"I know, I'm sorry." He took her hands in his own. "I mean it, though."

Nova's knee-jerk reaction was to pull her hands away and put some distance between them. "I think... I'm going to go. I'll see you tomorrow for breakfast, okay?"

Andrew didn't look too happy, but it wasn't like he could keep her there. Nova practically ran back to her place.

He said he was in *love* with her. She didn't think he even knew what that meant. It was nice to have him around sometimes, he was handsome and could be charming, but love? She wasn't in love with him. She was pretty sure she'd spent more time being annoyed with him than liking him.

It wasn't normal to fall for someone this quickly, especially with their track record. What did he expect from her? She pulled her hair up in a bun, so she didn't end up pulling it all out. She knew for a fact that even if she had fallen for him, which she had *not*, she wouldn't tell him so this early on.

She entertained the thought that maybe he was confusing love with growing affection. Love is a big commitment, not something to be taken lightly. She felt like she'd spent hours sitting and thinking about it before Harper came back.

"Hey, you. How was your night?"

Nova debated about telling Harper. On one hand, it would be nice to share this with someone, and on the other, Harper was clearly biased. She would probably ban Andrew from being around Nova if Nova told her. "Yeah, it was... it was fine." She scratched the back of her ear and chewed on her bottom lip.

Harper narrowed her eyes at Nova. "Why do you look nervous?"

"I-I'm not. I was just thinking about some homework."

"Okay... you'd tell me if something was up, right?"

Nova hummed and nodded. A little too quickly, maybe.

"Camille was at the party tonight."

Nova's ears perked up. Finally, something else to think about. "I didn't know it was a party."

"It wasn't until it became one. Anyway, she was trying *so* hard to bring you up. And she was all over Dominic."

"He was there?" Nova didn't like the thought of him any more than she did of Camille. He was all sorts of wrong. Anyone who abused their power like that couldn't be a nice person. She'd talked to a couple of people and found out that Dominic had a reputation for being nasty, like Dean had warned.

"Yeah. He was a lot less in-your-face than last time. He looked a little angry, actually. I heard that he had a big fight with his parents. They were threatening to cut him off or something."

If being in Atherton so far had taught her anything, it was that rumors were seldom true. "Glad I wasn't there then. I don't want any more trouble." Not that she preferred being where she was.

"Yeah, I'm sure Camille would have tried to start something again. She's probably just bored." Harper put her head on Nova's shoulder.

Nova agreed. She felt her phone vibrate in her pocket; it was Andrew.

ANDREW

Are you mad at me?

She sighed. This wasn't his first text since she left, and she wasn't mad. Just overwhelmed and confused. Well, there was also a hint of anger. It was unfair of Andrew to unload that on her.

"You look upset," Harper whispered.

Nova schooled her features into looking neutral again when she realized she was frowning.

"Did you fight with Andrew again? Nova, he's really not worth your time if he upsets you this often."

Nova turned to her. Huh, maybe Harper could give her some insight. "Why don't you like him? Tell me honestly."

Harper sat up. "I just think he's creepy. I've seen the way he looks at you, and it doesn't make me want to go *awwww*. He has this glint in his eye when he's watching you." She shuddered at the thought. "And like I said before, his behavior isn't supportive of you. I get the appeal, I do, but I think you could do a lot better."

Harper said that before, and Nova hadn't paid her any attention, but after tonight, she wasn't so sure if her friend was wrong. "Theoretically," she cleared her throat, "what would you think if someone confessed their love to you after knowing you for a very short time?"

Harper's eyes blew comically wide. "No. No, way. He told you he *loved* you?"

"No. No." Nova shook her head immediately. And it wasn't a complete lie. He said he *thought* he was falling in love with her. There was a difference. "I said theoretically."

"I would absolutely run in the opposite direction. What is *wrong* with him?!" She put a hand on her forehead. "Nova, please, you have to see how insane that is."

Nova chewed on her bottom lip. She did; she knew how crazy that was. "What am I supposed to do!?" She gave up all pretenses of this being 'theoretical.' She needed someone to talk to before she did something stupid.

"I think you know what to do, Nova. Saying he loves you at this stage in your relationship is... it's weird."

Nova stared at the four texts that Andrew had sent, but she hadn't replied yet. He meant well, didn't he? She would love to defend him, but she was a little creeped out. This seemed like an immediate deal-breaker. She couldn't continue to give in to him because she pitied him.

"Okay, okay." She took a deep breath and pulled up Andrew's text stream.

NOVA

We need to talk.

Chapter Eleven

Andrew stood in the middle of her living room in sweatpants and a tight t-shirt. Harper went to April's so Nova and Andrew could speak privately. Nova felt like a swarm of butterflies was about to take flight in her stomach.

"We need to talk? Really, Nova? You couldn't come up with anything better?"

"I'm sorry, but...." She took a deep breath. "Can we sit?"

Andrew nodded and sat. Nova felt really nervous about what she was about to say. She'd felt confident about speaking to him before Harper left, but now she didn't feel so brave. How would he take this? He was so unpredictable.

"Is this about me telling you I love you?" Andrew asked.

Nova nodded; there was no point in lying. "What you said was... it was a lot. I'm not saying your feelings aren't valid, but this is all really fast. I don't feel the same way. We spend more time fighting than getting along. This is too much for me, and I feel uncomfortable." She knew deep down it was best to be honest about her feelings, even if it was painful.

"Oh," Andrew exhaled and turned away from her to stare straight at the wall. "So, you're breaking up with me?"

Nova cleared her throat nervously. "I don't want to drag this out and end up hurting you more in the future."

"You don't feel anything for me?" Andrew spat out as he turned to glare at her.

Nova wasn't surprised at the angry tone. "I'm sorry."

Andrew stood up and began pacing. "You're unbelievable. I feel like this whole thing is a joke to you. You don't take anything seriously, not your scholarship, not this relationship!"

Nova stood up, too,and clenched her jaw. "I understand that you're upset, but you don't get to talk to me that way. I think you should go."

Andrew turned toward her furiously and approached her with his hands balled into fists at his side; she took a few steps back to maintain the distance. "You think it's okay to treat me like this?!" he yelled in her face, his neck strained in anger, his teeth clenched.

"Calm down, Andrew! This is exactly what I'm talking about! Why do you have to react this way? You just need to leave!" Nova shouted back at him. She didn't know how he would respond, and his posture seemed very aggressive.

He grabbed her upper arms and shook her slightly. "I love you! I told you that! You can't break up with me; I won't accept it! Just take it back, and we'll pretend none of this happened," he said trying to pull her into a tight hug and kiss her.

Nova snatched away from him and stumbled back. "Get your hands off me! What is wrong with you? Are you insane?! You need to get out of here now!" she said as she ran to the door and held it open for him.

Andrew didn't move. He stood there breathing heavily and just stared at her. The look in his eyes turned from fire to ice as his breathing calmed and his facial features relaxed. Nova felt a chill run down her spine at the look he gave her. He took a step in her direction. "Are you sure you want to do this?" he asked calmly.

"Yes," she said as she slightly trembled.

He took several more steps in her direction, and she began

to feel fear pool in the pit of her belly. She gasped as he came within inches of her, but he kept walking through the open door.

She quickly closed and locked the door behind him, then leaned her back against it. She felt shaken, out of breath, and incapable of standing. She slid her back down the door until she sat on the floor and rested her head on her knees. *What in the world just happened?*

It took her several hours to feel a semblance of normalcy. She'd explained to Harper what happened, and Harper hugged her and told her she had made the right decision.

"I told you! I can't believe he responded that way. Are you sure he didn't hurt you?"

"He didn't. At one point, I wondered if he would, but he left. Did I really hurt him that badly? It feels like I broke something inside of him. I feel bad for him, you know?"

"Don't. No one falls in love with someone in a handful of days. He sounds like a lunatic."

Nova nodded. "He *acted* like a lunatic. You'd think we were dating for years instead of days by the way he responded. The look in his eyes chilled me to the bone." She groaned with annoyance. "This is so much to deal with. I thought Camille would be the only bane of my existence."

"And Dom." Harper laughed, trying to lighten the mood.

Nova rolled her eyes. "So he's Dom now?"

Harper shrugged her shoulder. "He's not all that bad underneath the cocky exterior. He was playing around and flirting with girls when one of his brothers called. He walked right out and took the call like it would cost him his fortune if he didn't. It was sweet."

"It could be one of his tricks to get the girls to swoon. There's nothing sweet about Dominic Lark." She had searched his name on the internet, and it only confirmed what her friends told her. He was famous and rich. Filthy rich. He was the eldest of four, probably the heir to his family's dynasty. He had to be. There was no way anyone could be as arrogant as he was without that kind of security blanket.

"You've only had one interaction with him."

"Which was more than I wanted, thank you very much."

Harper laughed. "He has his good moments, although they are rare."

Nova scoffed. Harper was defending Dominic like she defended him after he tried to humiliate her and made a mockery of her relationship with Andrew. Although he did have a point regarding the latter. "I'll see him during my math class on Friday."

"All the best." Harper put a consoling hand on her shoulder and got up. "I'm going to bed; you should, too. Tomorrow just might be more interesting for you." She reached her bedroom and turned to face Nova as she leaned against the doorframe. "Life has been interesting with you, Nova Scott, and I'm *living* for it." She giggled and closed the door behind her.

Nova hoped her life would get a tad less interesting for others and more interesting for her.

As she lay in bed, her mind tried to remember what it was about Andrew that drew her to him in the first place. Good looks aside, it was the confidence. It turned out to be a façade to protect him from others. No one's life was easy, especially not Andrew's, but... he wasn't for her anymore. He never really was.

⁎

"You look awfully peppy for someone who just broke up last night," Harper commented as she passed Nova to get to the cereal box.

"I slept like a log."

"I'm aware. I woke up that log." Harper sat next to her. "You know this means we're both single. And this university is crawling with boys." She smirked at Nova and winked.

"I think I've had enough boys. My schedule is packed."

"Oh, come on, don't be a party pooper. I have the best idea, and you know for a fact that my ideas never fail."

Nova grimaced. "I don't want to throw another party and I want to avoid Camille until graduation." Her stomach churned uncomfortably at the thought of the girl.

"But it's going to be so much fun. You need this; plus I'm pretty sure people want to hear you sing again. So give the people what they want, Nova."

"And what would be the point of the party?"

"Getting over Andrew, of course."

"I already am."

Harper hummed. "So you're telling me that if you saw him in the cafeteria eating alone, you wouldn't feel bad?"

Nova bit her bottom lip; she didn't really know what she felt about Andrew, but she knew it wasn't anything good. She felt torn between anger at his response and guilt for hurting him. She also couldn't forget the look in his eyes the moment before he walked out. Maybe she did need to get over him a little. She had woken up this morning and checked to see if there were any texts from him. "Fine, but the party will have to be on Saturday. I need to have the rest of the week without seeing Camille and her minions."

"Deal! It's a party, and you're our lead performer!"

Chapter Twelve

Nova skipped two meals and decided to eat fruits and cereal because no amount of food was worth seeing Andrew.

"He looked like a train wreck." Dean told her, "You did a number for sure."

She hadn't told the others exactly what went down after the breakup. She just wanted to forget about it.

Harper swatted his arm. "Don't make her feel worse."

Nova didn't feel bad in the way her friends thought. She was avoiding him because she felt uncomfortable seeing him after his outburst. She felt bad that he might be sitting alone, but she could now see how that was probably his own doing. She didn't want to send him any mixed signals.

"I have a class with him tomorrow."

Harper grimaced. "Well, that might be awkward."

Nova nodded. She couldn't avoid him forever. Maybe things would feel better after she faced him once and for all. She'd told Scarlett about it. She, for one, had no advice for her other than to say how weird Andrew sounded and how unlikely it was for Nova to be in a relationship with him in the first place. Scarlett told her Andrew wasn't her "type," whatever that meant.

"Camille is in that class, too."

Nova spun to face April so quickly she had to balance herself against the counter. "No. Are you serious?"

April nodded. "She has Ms. Hart. At least you have that going for you."

"What?"

"Ms. Hart. She's very loved. People say she's very interesting."

Nova scoffed. "I'm going to have so much fun," she said sarcastically. Fridays used to be her favorite day, but it was becoming less favorable by the minute.

"Can we get back to party planning? Nova, these are the songs people requested last time; see if you like any." Harper brought them back to the task at hand.

✥

Nova sped down the path to her math class, berating herself along the way. Thanks to the overthinking she did in the bathroom, she was running late. She didn't know anyone in the class other than the people who hated her, so there was no one she could borrow notes from once she got there.

She had to get her head in the game and focus more on her studies. Contrary to what Andrew said, she took her scholarship very seriously, and her thoughts about her encounter with him were her only distraction. She hoped the teacher would let her slide this once.

It was her last class of the day, and she was carrying all her books by hand because she didn't have time to stuff them in her bag. She was doing a balancing act with her books, her music sheets, and her phone when she bumped into a wall.

A moving wall that wasn't really a wall. It was Dominic.

"Can you watch where you're going?" He looked down at her like she was a piece of chewed gum stuck under his shoe.

"If you saw me coming, why didn't you move out of the way?" Nova looked pointedly at the phone in his hand. She ended up dropping her phone. Dominic looked down at the device and picked it up, throwing it onto the pile of stuff in Nova's hands before jogging away. He looked as if picking up the phone was a big favor.

Nova stared at his back with her mouth agape. And Harper thought he had some redeeming qualities.

When she finally made it to class, it was completely filled with students. She knew this was a core requirement for a lot of majors, but she didn't expect there to be this many people in one class. She was standing at the door, looking for an empty seat, when the teacher noticed her.

"Nova Scott, is it?" She smiled at her. "I saw your video; you're a very talented girl."

Nova smiled. She understood why people liked Ms. Hart. She was a petite, slender woman with a kind face and shaggy long brown hair. She wore a tangled mess of colorful necklaces and looked like someone Nova wouldn't think twice before approaching. "Thank you."

"Come on in, take a seat." She pointed at the empty table almost at the front of the class. Nova passed Andrew's seat to get there, and she felt like she had a target on her back from his stare. When she finally sat and Ms. Hart was about to begin, the door flew open again.

Dominic stood at the door, panting and puffing. He was a little red in the face.

"Dominic Lark." Ms. Hart gave him the same smile she did Nova.

Nova couldn't help but think about her math teacher back home. If this were her, Dominic and Nova would have had to go to the principal's office and would have gotten detention.

"Take a seat next to Nova." She welcomed him in.

Dominic scanned the room to see if there were any other seats. Nova rolled her eyes, but she would have done the same. He sat next to her and dragged the chair away as far as possible without leaving the table. *How immature.*

"Okay, as I was saying. The class isn't hard if you pay attention. Other than that, my office hours are between two and five, so come see me whenever you need." She walked along the class. "I prefer having strong connections with my students, and there are quite a few of you here, so introductions first. I am Gina Hart; I've been teaching at Atherton for the last fifteen years. I love music, and I'm very excited to be teaching yet another group of extremely talented people."

Nova sat back and tried to relax. It was hard when Dominic's leg wouldn't stop moving. It was making the table vibrate. "Can you stop that?" she whispered.

Dominic threw her a blank look and increased the speed of bouncing his leg.

"Before I give out the first and most important assignment of this semester and year, I want you guys to know the person sitting next to you is going to be your project partner."

Chapter Thirteen

Nova sat up straighter, making her chair push back, causing a screeching sound. She whipped her head in Dominic's direction. He was staring back at her with the same look she was giving him—absolutely dead set against being partnered.

Dominic raised his hand. "Ms. Hart, I'd like to pick another partner."

Ms. Hart's eyebrows drew together in confusion. "Why is that? I'm sure you'll find Nova to be very useful for this assignment."

"I would prefer another partner, too," Nova said. So many things could make life at Atherton hard, and being stuck with Dominic would be at the top of the list.

"Oh."

"I'll partner with Dom," Camille offered.

Nova turned to look at Camille as she held her perfectly manicured hand up. Harper had said something about Camille wanting to be with Dominic, and what better way to do it than to be partnered until the end of the semester.

"Yeah, whatever. I don't care," Dominic said. He looked completely nonchalant about dropping Nova like a hot potato.

Camille looked absolutely delighted, her perfect face curved into a flattering smile.

"I'll be Nova's partner," Andrew said. He looked hopeful.

The blood rushed to Nova's ears, and she didn't even wait for her thoughts to catch up to her before she spoke, "I'll be okay with Dominic, actually."

Dominic turned to her sharply. "What?" he snapped through gritted teeth.

The silence in the room after Nova took back her words was palpable.

Nova looked down at her hands. She didn't owe Dominic an explanation, but if she really did end up as Andrew's partner, she'd have to find a way to drop this class. It would be impossible, but so was being around Andrew right now.

Ms. Hart cleared her throat. As awkward as it was, Camille still looked happy at the prospect of being paired up with Dominic, and Andrew looked pained. "I'm sorry, but I think you and Nova will work perfectly for the assignment, Dominic. So I won't allow it."

Nova sighed a breath of relief. She looked up and thanked her lucky stars. She shouldn't have because Dominic had pulled his chair a little closer to her so he could whisper harshly in her ear, "What is wrong with you? What do you want from me?"

Nova scoffed. She couldn't stand him. "It's sad that you think that. I don't want anything from you. Let's just do the assignment and get it over with."

Dominic's jaw popped. Nova was scared he'd break a tooth or two. "I can't believe you just did that. I'm not doing this with you; I'll speak to this hippie bimbo."

"You're so rude. She's probably the kindest teacher on campus." Nova took a deep breath and stopped when Ms. Hart started talking again. She liked Ms. Hart. Sure, she looked more like a preschool teacher than a college professor, but she wouldn't be teaching here if she wasn't beyond intelligent.

"Creativity is valued here at Atherton, and I can say with

confidence that each one of you here is creative. Some of you already know it, and some of you are going to find out soon enough and hopefully through this project."

Nova felt like she was attending a Ted talk, and it would've been nice if she wasn't fighting the urge to kick Dominic's bouncing leg.

"Math can be creative too, and I think we've all heard this, but there is math in everything. This is why most of you find yourself here despite your major. Math is all around you, even when you don't notice it. So the main assignment for this semester is about creativity and math." She giggled at the end. "For example," She looked at Nova and Dominic, "Nova's a singer, and I'm pretty sure Dominic can play the guitar, so your project could be math and music! An M&M project!" She beamed and clapped her hands together once. "There, I've already helped one pair. I know some of you may have trouble finding common ground with your partners, so come to me whenever you think you're at a hurdle, and I'll help you out."

Ms. Hart explained more of the curriculum.

"I can't believe you've done this." Dominic glared at her. "What happened? Did lover boy dump you already, and you're taking it out on me?"

Nova ignored him in favor of paying attention to their teacher.

However, Dominic didn't seem to get the message. "What happened? Were you as annoying as you look? The poor guy looks battered. Even I pity him."

"Will you stop it? I don't care what you think. We need to pass, and that's all I care about; shut up and pay attention," Nova snapped at him.

Dominic seethed and fisted his hands. "I really hate you, Nova Scott. I'm getting out of this assignment; I don't care how." He looked at her from the side of his eye.

Nova was stunned by his harsh words, but she wouldn't let him notice. She had done nothing to him to elicit such a strong response. She tucked a piece of her purple-streaked hair behind her ear. "The feeling is mutual."

Ms. Hart insisted everyone introduce themselves and state one thing they are passionate about. Nova imagined Dominic was passionate about ruining her life. He might be more against her than Camille. She hadn't even dared to turn in Camille's direction. Nova could feel the daggers directed at her; if looks could kill, Nova would probably be dead right now.

"Dominic, would you like to start?"

The boy sighed. "I'm Dominic Lark, and I'm passionate about nothing." He sounded bored out of his mind.

"Come on, don't be like that. Tell us." Her voice was patient and soft.

Nova was shocked that Dominic wasn't flaunting something incredibly pretentious like horseback riding.

"I play the guitar sometimes."

Their hay-haired teacher chuckled. "Okay, I can work with that. Try to be a little more enthusiastic next time. Next." She looked expectantly at Nova.

"I'm Nova Scott, and I'm passionate about singing."

Nova made the mistake of letting her eyes wander, and they landed on Andrew. His face was stoic and blank; he betrayed no emotion. It was like making eye contact with a stranger. She quickly looked away.

When it was Camille's turn, Nova expected her introduction to be artificial. "I'm Camille Rose, but everyone already knows that." She frowned, and for someone whose face was stuck like that all the time, it was surprising to see the lack of any frown lines. "And I'm passionate about animals. I love all animals and love taking care of them. My father owns several petting zoos as well." For a split second, her face went soft before she cleared her throat and went back to her default.

Nova tuned out the rest of the introductions in favor of over-thinking about her project. It would be too much to expect that she and Dominic could find a middle ground and agree to something. Dominic still looked like he was sitting on a porcupine at the end of the class.

Nova sprinted out of class as soon as it was over, noticing Dominic walk up to their teacher, making good on his promise. She hoped he could talk Ms. Hart out of them being partners by using some of that influence that he flaunts around. She was okay with anyone that wasn't him or Andrew.

"Nova!"

Nova stopped at the exit of the building at the sound of Andrew's voice. She turned slowly to see him walking towards her. She swallowed thickly and tried to act like she wasn't worried about him approaching her.

"Do you have a minute?"

"What's up?" Nova tried to sound casual. There was absolutely nothing casual about the two of them anymore. People were throwing glances at them as they walked by.

"I just wanted to say I'm sorry," Andrew confessed. He had his hands in his pockets. Nova took a small step back when he took one forward. "I... I know I said things that were uncalled for, but I didn't mean them. I was mad."

Nova nodded. "I understand that, but the way you reacted was not cool. The way you came at me and grabbed me... it was kind of scary, Andrew."

"I know. I'm sorry. I lost my cool, and I've reflected on that. I know I have to respect and accept your decision on us not being together, but I'd like to be friends at least. Can we do that?" Andrew asked as he gave her a small smile.

Nova shook her head slightly. She knew she had to be true to her feelings. "Andrew, based on what you said the other day, I'm not sure if that would be healthy for either of us. We've both made it clear what we felt for each other, and I don't want to lead you on in any way."

The smile slowly fell off his face. "Yes, it's been made clear, and I won't expect anything from you other than friendship. I promise," he said with a sad look on his face.

Nova felt conflicted on whether she should give him a chance. "Well, I guess we can give it a try."

Andrew nodded happily. "Great! Do you want to hang out? I'm free tonight." He leaned forward again, but Nova made sure to chuckle as she pulled back, so it didn't look awkward.

"I have a thing with Harper, so I'm not. Sorry."

Andrew tsked. "Maybe another time. Take care of yourself, Nova."

Nova stepped aside so Andrew could leave. She saw Dominic coming out of the class. He was stomping his way out, and his hands were balled into fists.

"Did it work?" She walked alongside him since he didn't stop to talk to her.

He ignored her. Nova didn't appreciate being treated like she was invisible.

She grabbed his arm to stop him from running off when he shrugged her off harshly. "Stop!"

The gasp was involuntary. "What the heck, dude? What could I have possibly done to upset you this much? I only asked you a question! Do I have 'Disrespect Nova' written across my forehead or something?" she yelled.

Dominic stared at her but made no effort to apologize. "Does it look like it worked?"

"You could have just said so."

He muttered something under his breath that sounded like a bunch of things Nova didn't think were true about Ms. Hart.

"It's just one assignment," she said, mostly comforting herself.

"I don't care. I'm not doing it with you. Figure it out on your own."

"What do you mean? I will *not* do the project for you if that's what you're thinking!"

Dominic turned to her. "I don't care what you do. Leave me alone before you end up in a situation you don't want to be in. What is it? Are you afraid you're too dumb to do it yourself, and you need me to hold your hand through it?" he said furiously.

"*I'm* the dumb one when *you're* the one running away from the project?"

Dominic scoffed. "Do you have any self-preservation instincts? It's like you're begging me to show you your place."

Nova laughed humorlessly. "Right, because I am so beneath you, and there's no one in the world like Mr. Dominic Lark. All hail Dominic Lark!" she said loudly enough to turn heads. She knew she was being immature at this point, but she didn't care. She pushed past him as she tried to hold in her tears.

Boys are idiots! she fumed. She was a good person; she knew she was. She didn't get in people's way and was hard working. So why did this boy think he was better than her? So much so that he wouldn't even do an assignment that was worth a large percentage of their grade? She couldn't be that bad. Of course, she knew she wasn't, but it didn't stop the tears that clouded her eyes. She wouldn't let them fall, though.

Chapter Fourteen

Nova was calmer by the time Harper got home. Harper had laughed when she heard about her being partnered with Dominic because she didn't know how terrible he had made Nova feel.

"I'm sorry." Harper wiped a fake tear from the corner of her eye. "I'm not laughing at you; it's Camille. She's probably clutching a framed picture of Dominic and crying right now."

"She looked at me like I kidnapped her favorite pet." Nova had never regretted being late to a class more than she did today. "I love Ms. Hart, but she isn't budging."

"It's fine. Dominic is prickly at best. But, uh, try not to rub him the wrong way, for your own good, babe."

Nova sighed. "I'm going to go call my mother and complain and then take a nap." She lugged herself into bed. Talking to her mother had been a good idea. She felt lighter. Her mother had an insane explanation for Dominic being a jerk, though.

"Maybe he likes you and doesn't know how to say it."

Nova gave a full belly laugh. "Thanks, Mom. I needed that."

"I wasn't joking, though. Boys are a little complicated like that."

If her mother was right and people were mean because they

secretly liked her, she had a whole community of people in love with her. "I think this might be the one time you're wrong."

Her mother hummed and continued to talk about things at home. After she hung up with her, Nova tried to nap, but all she did was toss and turn.

She put on a hoodie and packed her book bag so she could go to the library for a couple of hours before dinner.

"Did you see?" Harper stopped dead in her tracks. "I can't believe she's doing this."

"Who? What's going on?"

"Camille!? She's throwing a charity event tomorrow! She knows about our party, doesn't she?"

Harper had been planning all week.

"Oh wow, I'm sorry, Harp. I was the one who told you to push it to Saturday."

Harper looked extremely sullen. "I was looking forward to it."

"We can still have it."

Harper scoffed. "As if anyone's going to come here when they can go off campus."

"It's off-site?"

"Yeah. It's at a hotel not too far from here."

Nova bit her bottom lip. "What's the event for?"

"Animal welfare."

It was hard for Nova to imagine Camille being kind to anyone or anything. "Are you going to go?"

"Yeah. It would be stupid to miss it. It's usually really nice. I'm just mad about my ruined plans."

⁂

NOVA WAS LEAVING the library after completing a bunch of her coursework when she saw her math teacher. "Ms. Hart, do you have a minute?"

"Sure. Come to class with me."

Nova helped Ms. Hart carry some of her books. She was wearing a long skirt with flowers and a green turtleneck. The style didn't really make sense, but Ms. Hart made it look... comfortable.

"What can I help you with, Nova?"

Nova shifted her weight from one foot to the other. "I want to change my project partner."

"Oh." She folded her arms and jumped up on her desk. "Dominic asked for that this morning, too. Did he tell you?"

Nova nodded, but barely.

"Well, then you know my answer, don't you?"

When Nova didn't say anything, she tsked and smiled. "Okay, tell me one good reason you don't want to be his partner, and I'll consider it."

"We don't like each other," she answered honestly.

Ms. Hart laughed. "Okay, I like that you told me the truth, but that's not a valid reason."

Nova nodded. "I'm sorry to waste your time." She turned to leave.

"Wait!" The teacher jumped off the desk. "Listen, I've been here a long time, and I know quite a bit about Dominic Lark. He's an... acquired taste. And sometimes he's a downright jerk. But he's," she scratched her head and muttered something about 'being in too deep already,' "he's not the worst. A little troubled, okay? Give him time and if he's really being difficult, come talk to me again."

Nova appreciated the kindness, she did, but all she got from that conversation was that she was being knowingly paired with someone she didn't like. She didn't understand what troubled meant, but she didn't have it in her to care either. "Thank you, Ms. Hart."

"You can call me Gina when we're not in class."

Nova smiled and left. She was sure she could ask someone, and they'd tell her what 'troubled' meant as it relates to Dominic. April had the answers most of the time.

Nova invited her over after dinner. "What do you know about Dominic?"

"Why do you want to know about Dominic?" April asked with a smug smirk.

"He and I are paired for a math project, and Ms. Hart said something cryptic. I'm just trying to figure it out."

"Uh-huh," she said like she didn't believe a word Nova said, "I actually don't know much. He's very private."

"The guy who commands a whole team of minions on a theater stage is private?"

April nodded. "He's a mystery to most."

Nova blew air out of her mouth. "Great. Just great."

"What's the color of your dress for the charity event?"

Nova shrugged. "I don't know." She didn't have a dress to begin with, at least not a ball gown. And the entry ticket for the event was way more than her allowance. She couldn't possibly ask her parents to give her more. "I'm probably not going."

April gasped. "No! You have to. These events are fun."

"There will be others."

"Are you sure?"

Nova nodded. "I have to practice anyway; I'm auditioning on Monday." There was an upcoming play, and she thought she'd be able to get a good part.

"Good luck. Think about coming tomorrow, though, okay?" April hugged her and headed back to her room.

Nova hummed, but she already knew she wasn't going.

Chapter Fifteen

Nova made it to lunch really late, and there weren't many people left in the cafeteria. She saw her friends waiting for her.

"Hey, sorry I'm late."

Harper patted the seat next to hers. "Come sit. We were discussing how we're getting to the hotel tonight."

"Oh." Nova smiled awkwardly.

"Wait, I don't even know what you're wearing."

"I'm not going." She tugged a strand of her purple hair.

Harper seemed to notice that the topic made Nova uncomfortable. She turned back to making plans. She brought it up again when they got home.

"Why aren't you coming, Nova? The truth."

Nova swallowed thickly and licked her teeth. "I don't want to. It's Camille, and I have things to do. Plus, I thin-"

"That just sounds like a bunch of excuses to me." Harper folded her arms. "What is it? Did Camille say something? Because if she did, I can-"

"She didn't. I haven't even seen her since my math class."

Harper didn't say anything, only waited for an explanation.

"I... I, uh, can't afford the entry fee."

Harper deflated and gave her an exasperated look. "That's it? I'll cover for you, and you can give it back whenever. Or don't. I don't care; you know that."

Nova shook her head. "I can't let you do that."

"Please. I would literally *love* to pay for you to be there. Don't ditch me like that, come on. I want you there."

"Harper."

"What? Just come, please?"

She really didn't want to, but she considered it. "I don't even have a dress."

Harper shrugged. "I'm sure we'll find something in your closet. I'd offer, but you're taller than me. Come on, let's go pick."

She dragged Nova to her room. She hadn't even agreed to accept Harper's generous offer, but there was no convincing her otherwise.

This party better be worth it.

⁂

Nova's dress wasn't a ball gown, and neither was it as grand as what others were wearing, but she loved it.

It was a sleeveless, purple cocktail dress; the cloth was flowy and soft. Her supernova tattoo was on display just how she liked it. It reminded her that she was on the path to becoming a superstar shining brightly amongst the other stars.

"Woah, Nova." April ran to her, or at least as best she could in her dress. She looked like Belle in her yellow gown. "You look so nice. And way more comfortable than us." She made Nova do a twirl, her hair swishing as she did.

"Thank you. You look like you're about to start talking to the candles."

They laughed and got into the car Harper had booked. Dean helped the girls into the car, Nova getting in on her own, comfortably. The hotel was a twenty-minute drive away. As they began to pull into the parking area, Nova saw the grand lights and posters.

There was a navy-blue carpet in the entrance with photographers. So many photographers.

"Uh, what is this?" Nova asked when Harper got out of the car.

"Oh, it's a Rose event, so there's bound to be media. The charity is genuine, though, and it's all private on the inside, don't worry."

Nova turned to the people in the crowd, getting their photos taken. They were properly dressed for the event. "Harp, maybe I should go back."

Harper shook her head. "Nova, you look amazing. That dress is doing you so many favors."

"This wasn't the dress code." Nova rubbed her tattoo. "They won't let me in."

"They'll let you in as long as you have the ticket. And I have yours. You could be wearing pajamas, and they wouldn't care."

Nova knew Harper was saying that to make her feel better. She looked around for another entrance but couldn't see one. It got more uncomfortable when April and Harper pulled her between them and stood in the middle of the carpet. Both of them seemed to know exactly what they were doing. She stood out like a sore thumb.

"Just smile," April comforted, and Nova did her best to smile and breathe easy.

"See, that wasn't so bad." April took Dean's arm and walked in front of them.

Nova locked eyes with a couple of the guests. All of them looked at her face framed by her perfectly coifed, purple-streaked hair and then immediately down at her dress.

"Hey, look, it's Jamie!" Harper let go of her arm and walked towards a gorgeous man. He had shoulder-length blonde hair and had a muscular build framed by his suit.

Nova smiled at him. "Hey."

"Hi."

There was an accent that Nova didn't recognize. Harper told

her he was one of Camille's cousins from France. Jamie and Harper started catching up on things that happened since they saw each other last, Nova being side-lined.

"Want to dance?" Jamie offered his hand to Harper.

"Uh," Harper faltered and looked back at Nova.

She smiled and shook her head. "Go, have fun. I'll be fine."

Harper gave her a quick side hug and left. Nova stood awkwardly as people slowly made their way to the dance floor in their elegantly swirling gowns.

She found herself at the bar and asked for a glass of water.

"What are you doing here?"

Nova turned to see Dominic. He looked quite handsome in his perfectly tailored tuxedo. "It was an open invite."

"It is open to whoever is willing to pay, but I meant to ask how did you manage?"

Embarrassment crept down her neck. It wasn't like she could say that she managed just fine on her own. "Leave me alone, Dominic." She turned back to her glass and heard the boy laugh behind her.

"What are you wearing? Did no one tell you the dress code?"

Nova sighed and rubbed her temple with her fingers. "Don't you have anything better to do? Leave me alone." She got off her stool, but the heels she borrowed from Harper made her trip. She ended up using Dominic as support as she fell into his chest.

And to his credit, he caught her tightly at her waist before she fell on her face.

At that moment, while he helped steady her, he looked Nova directly in her eyes as they stood chest to chest, but she detected no... anger. None of the hoity-toity hatred he had for her. His pupils seemed to dilate. "Sorry," she mumbled. As if she wasn't embarrassed enough, life threw this her way too.

Dominic cleared his throat and let her go as she took a step back. "Is this your first time in a dress? You would have broken your nose if not for me."

Nova rolled her eyes. "Yes, Dominic, everyone in the room is helpless without yo-"

"Dom."

Dominic turned and stepped back from Nova when he saw Camille.

"Is she causing you trouble? Again."

Nova recognized the jab because of their math class.

"She almost fell on her face."

Camille laughed, a hand coming to cover her lips. She was wearing a beautiful pink gown with rose gold silk gloves. "You're funny, Dom."

There was absolutely no humor in what the boy had said, but it didn't stop Camille from putting one hand on his forearm as she laughed away.

"I didn't think you'd come, Nova. It wasn't exactly budget-friendly." She smirked. "Did you not know the dress code?"

"I don't have a gown in my dorm, Camille. People don't expect events like these when they go for higher education."

Camille chuckled again. "Will you look at that, Dom?" she said, looking up at Dominic before turning back to Nova. "Everyone else is following the dress code except you, so clearly, you're the only one. Don't be surprised if someone mistakes you for a waitress."

Nova looked away. She was wearing a nice dress, for goodness sake. Camille was making her feel like she had on a onesie.

"Do me a favor and stay away from the cameras. The last thing my family needs is a fashion scandal."

Dominic scoffed.

Camille turned her attention to Dominic. "Your mother asked me to find you. Dance with me?" Camille curled her hand around his bicep.

"No." Dominic turned back to Nova and gave her an appraising look. Then, he put out his hand to her. "Dance with me."

Chapter Sixteen

Nova stood there and stared at Dominic's hand. The boy who hated her had asked her to dance. In front of Camille, who already had enough reason to hate her.

"Excuse me?" Camille put a hand on her chest. "You want to dance with her?"

Dominic shrugged. "Yeah. Not like anyone else is going to offer."

Camille grabbed his arm, this time with force. "Dom, your parents are going to be livid."

The boy grinned. "Exactly."

Nova's mouth fell open. Of course, he only asked her because he benefitted from it. He wanted to make his parents mad, and Nova was the way to do it. "I'm not dancing with you."

"Yes, you are."

The absolute confidence in his voice was incredible. How could one possess such self-assurance? "No, I'm not. Now, if you'll excuse me." Nova picked up her dress to avoid getting it tangled again when he grabbed her wrist.

He yanked her toward him, and once again, they were chest to chest. He whispered in her ear, causing tingles to run down her spine, "Do you want me to cooperate on the math project or not? I can make your life a living hell, Nova."

Her breath got stuck in her throat. He could, he really could. She couldn't believe the level he was stooping to, but if her Fridays could get a little less stressful, she would take it. Camille being outraged by the suggestion was the cherry on top. "Fine. One dance."

Dominic clicked his tongue and nodded. He guided her to the center of the dance floor.

"I don't know how to dance," she whispered, not really knowing what to do with her feet.

"Figures. Just follow me; the song is slow." He put a hand on her waist and moved with practiced ease.

Couples slowed down around them, trying to stare, and Nova caught Harper's eye; she was dancing with Jamie.

"Why are you trying to upset your parents?" she asked, trying to avoid stepping on his foot.

"Because they upset me." He twirled her, her hair flying off her shoulders. He pulled her back to him, and Nova had to look away from his face.

"What did they do? Not buy you another sports car?"

Dominic's face stayed stoic. "Why are we talking again?"

"Because you want to upset your parents, and if you look like you're being tortured, that's kind of a point in their favor."

Dominic almost cracked a smile. "Whatever."

They swayed together for the duration of the song, and Nova caught Dominic looking at her intensely every now and then. Once the song ended, he let go of her.

He left without a goodbye. Nova didn't understand what had just passed between them, but it felt like a silent truce. Or at least an understanding.

"What was that?" April came to her, Dean trailing behind her.

Nova shrugged her shoulder. "I have no idea."

April smirked. "He likes you."

The laugh was too loud for the room they were in. "Yeah, sure. When pigs fly. He was... being weird."

"When is he not?" Dean commented. "Can we go eat, please? I'm starving."

Nova went along with them, relieved to finally be around people she knew. They sat at a table, and her dress bothered her less and less as the night went on. She had gotten up to get drinks for her friends when Camille walked up to her.

"Can I help you?" she asked as Camille blocked her way.

"What are you trying to do?"

"Excuse me?"

Camille folded her arms. "What do you want from Dominic? You do realize he'll never fall for the likes of you."

Nova sighed. "Listen, Camille, I don't really have the patience for this tonig—"

"I'm warning you, Nova. Stay away from him. Don't embarrass yourself. You reek of desperation. The Lark family would never approve of you, and the more you upset them, the more you upset Dominic. So pick someone from your own level."

"I'm not holding my breath for anyone's approval. I just want to get back to my table." She turned and walked away; she felt Camille's glare on her the entire way back.

This night might have been a complete disaster for various reasons but at least Nova knew what one of Dominic's issues might be. His parents.

"Can we go home?" Nova asked when she got back to her table.

"Sure. What was Camille saying?"

Nova snorted. "She was being possessive. Warned me to stay away from Dominic."

"She doesn't even like him."

Nova raised one eyebrow. "What do you mean? She's very... obsessed," she settled on. Camille had to be in love with Dominic. Why else would anyone want to constantly be around someone that insufferable?

Harper chuckled. "That she is. But she doesn't *like him*, like him. He's just the 'it' guy, so she wants in."

Out of all things Nova thought she would feel, pity wasn't one of them. But she did pity Camille. She also pitied Dominic for having to put up with it. "I can't imagine that."

They stuck around for another hour before Harper called for the car.

The cameras were gone by the time they left, which was a relief. "Please remind me to never come to events hosted by Camille."

"Oh, wow." Harper covered her mouth and laughed into her hand. "Nova!"

Nova's heart started beating really fast. This was the second time Harper had gotten excited and called out her name because of something she saw on her phone. "Just give it to me." She held out her hand for the device.

Harper's reaction made complete sense when her eyes fell on the screen. She heard April gasp and giggle too. Nova didn't find it funny, though; this meant trouble.

Someone had managed to get a picture of Dominic offering his hand to Nova while Camille stood next to him.

Camille's only saving grace was that her back was turned to the camera, so no one really knew the look on her face. The headline was pretty catty, too, Camille Rose being rejected by the infamous Dominic Lark: Read More to see who the Mystery Girl is.

"Camille is going to set my hair on fire, isn't she?" Nova chewed on her bottom lip. "This is not funny!" she yelled at Dean, who was snickering in the front seat.

"Oh, Nova. I'm sorry," Harper said before breaking out into laughter again, joined by April and Dean.

Nova gave Harper's phone back and checked her own for more pictures. There was one of her whispering into Dominic's ear, and the angle made it seem like they were enjoying themselves. If people only knew how awkward those few minutes were. There was another one in which Dominic was looking at her intently. She knew she wasn't imagining him staring at her.

"You look so good, though!" Harper comforted as she wiped her eye. "Dominic did this on purpose."

Nova shook her head. "I know that. Obviously, he didn't want to dance with me."

"Wait, why did you agree?" Dean asked.

"He promised me that he would cooperate for the math project. The last we talked about it, he had refused to do it with me."

She stared at the pictures until they were clear as day, even when she closed her eyes. When they got home, she couldn't get out of her dress fast enough. She scrolled through the comments on some of the posts on the university's page. People were wondering if they were dating.

"Are you still looking at comments?" Harper stood at her door.

Nova sat up and pulled a pillow to her chest. "Yeah. I have a weird feeling this won't end well at all."

⁂

Nova got dressed and went for her class as usual, and by now, she was almost used to people looking at her as she passed by. There were a handful of people she knew by name, and they always gave her a polite smile or nod. But there was a little extra something in their look today. Nova couldn't pinpoint it, but it felt wrong.

"Hey!" Riley smiled at her. "You looked lovely last night. I'm so glad Camille personally invited you to the event; that was really nice of her. I always thought of her as a cold person for some reason, but I guess you should never judge a book by its cover."

Nova opened her mouth to say something, but nothing came out. "Uh..."

"What's wrong?" Riley asked her and placed their lyric sheet on their table.

"I'm sorry, can you repeat that? I got lost in thought."

Riley smiled softly; she looked mildly concerned. "Camille. She invited you to the event, right? I know these events are super pricy, but it's for a good cause. I didn't think she was nice like that."

Nova nodded dumbly. "Where did you hear that?"

Riley's mouth curved into an 'o', as the realization had hit her that she was most likely misinformed. "People were saying that she invited you as a special guest because you couldn't afford the ticket. It's said that she arranged for Dominic to dance with you because you were standing alone at the bar..."

It took a minute for the information to settle in her brain. She knew it; she knew Camille wouldn't just let this go. "I-"

"I'm sorry, I had no idea it wasn't true."

"Why are you sorry? It's not like you started the rumor."

Riley put a hand on her neck awkwardly. Thankfully their teacher started the class. Nova was distracted the entire time, messing up some parts of her song. She earned a couple of warnings from her teacher, but that was the least of her concerns. Was that the look people were giving her? Pity? Oh, poor Nova couldn't afford the ticket and didn't have anyone to dance with.

"Nova, I'm really sorry about earlier." Riley shouldered her bag and walked out with her.

"Don't worry about it," Nova said, her tone neutral. She needed to find her friends, but she couldn't get to any of them until the end of her day.

***

HER PHONE RANG JUST as she reached her dorm about to call this day quits. "Hello?"

"Nova, it's Riley. Why aren't you at the theater? Auditions are about to start."

Right, Nova had completely forgotten about the play. "I forgot about that. Okay, I'll be right there." She turned and ran as fast as she could to the theater.

She was about to enter when she ran into Andrew.

"That's the second time." Andrew steadied her.

Nova tried to catch her breath; she could feel sweat soak into her t-shirt. "I'm sorry."

"You're here to audition, aren't you?" He brought his sling bag forward and pulled out a water bottle for her. "Here."

Nova accepted it. "Thank you." She took two sips and handed it back. "What are you doing here?" She had gone back to her normal breathing.

"Waiting for you, actually. I wanted to see you get the part."

Nova wondered how he knew she would be auditioning. It unsettled her; she didn't understand why he'd want to see it.

"You looked great yesterday, by the way. I saw pictures." His face went eerily expressionless when he said the words.

"T-thank you. You don't have to sit around for me; I'm sure it'll take some time."

"I want to."

She swallowed thickly and moved past him to enter the room. She internally winced when she felt him follow her in.

"Break a leg," he said, and Nova nodded at him.

From what she knew, she was pretty sure he had practice at this time of the day. Or another class, she wasn't too sure.

"Hey," Riley greeted when she got backstage.

Nova pulled out the tattered piece of paper that she had used for rehearsing her part.

"You're auditioning for the main, right?" Riley asked.

Nova was breaking into a nervous sweat. "No. Her sister."

Riley looked stunned. She put a hand on Nova's knee. "Are you sure? You're perfect for the main; you match the physical requirements, too."

Nova shrugged. "I didn't prepare for it. Plus, it's out of my vocal range."

"I've heard you sing. A little practice, and you'll be just fine."

Getting the lead part wouldn't be a bad thing. It would certainly help her image after what Camille had done to it. "Okay, I'll give it a try." Her nerves got worse, but the rush was nice. It was nice to be distracted from the rumor.

She stood on the stage when it was her turn.

"Nova Scott, correct?" one of the judges asked. Nova knew who he was, Mr. Bentley. He was the head director of the theater course.

"Yes, sir."

"You're auditioning for the sister, Kat?"

"Not anymore. I would like to audition for the main character, Venus."

He gave her the green signal, and Nova began. It was harder than she thought it would be, but Mr. Bentley looked convinced.

"That was good; could use some work."

Disappointment pooled in Nova's belly; she would have easily gotten the sister's part. She went backstage and got her bag.

Andrew met her at the door again. "That was phenomenal."

"He said I could use some work." Nova wanted him to leave her alone.

"Yeah, and he also said it was good. You should have heard the things he said to the others. He was *nice* to you."

She felt a sliver of hope. "Thanks. I'm going to head home."

"Uh, do you want to get coffee or something?"

Nova sighed and turned to him. "Andrew, why are you following me?"

"I'm not. I just wanted to see if you want to hang out."

"I have to get back home; I'll see you around," she said and left. He was clearly not over her. She felt bad for him. She wasn't heartless, but it wasn't okay for her to encourage such behavior.

Back in her room, Harper was stretching in her gym clothes.

"Have you heard?" Nova asked. She went to the kitchen to grab herself a glass of water.

Harper wiped a bead of sweat off her forehead. "I did. I tried telling others that wasn't what happened, but... it's spread far and wide. I'm sure it was her minions who spread the news."

"Everyone thinks Camille is the queen of the world."

"Don't worry about it, something else will come up, and everyone will forget about this."

"Yeah, well, I'm going to go talk to her." Someone had to remind Camille who Nova was, and she wasn't one to sit back and take it.

Nova walked up to Camille where she sat in the cafeteria. "Camille, can I speak with you?"

Camille turned to her and smiled. "Sure, Nova! Do you need something? I'm sure I can make arrangements," she said loud enough for others to hear. The people standing in the line for food turned to watch them.

"Why are you lying? I can just get Dominic to tell everyone that he didn't want to dance with you. I'm not going to let you spread some ugly rumor about me."

Camille smirked and folded her arms. "Why are you saying that, Nova?" Her volume increased, and so did people's interest. "Was the event not up to your expectations? I'm so sorry."

Her words were faker than her glued-on eyelashes, but she had somehow managed to make it sound genuine. People were staring at them, and it was evident whose side they were on.

"You should have been in the acting course, Camille," she said and turned away. In a way, she had made things worse for herself, but she wasn't going to go down without a fight. Hopefully, she had at least planted the seed of doubt in some people's minds.

There were a couple of girls who had fallen for Camille's sullen look; they probably offered her some words of sympathy too.

"I told you not to do that," Harper said when Nova got back to her seat.

"I... she can't get away with it."

April offered her the plate of food she had filled for her.

"Camille's known for being the ice queen. People comfort her and adore her because they're scared of her."

But Nova wasn't scared, and she would never stop standing up for herself. She ate and barely tasted anything.

Conversations were dull, and she saw Andrew from the corner of her eye. He wasn't sitting alone, thankfully. It seemed he had made some friends.

By Friday, Nova was exhausted. Her classes were never-ending, and she had really underestimated her coursework. She worked hard but was somehow still a little behind. She made it to her math class just in time.

Dominic was nowhere to be seen, but he had been late last class as well. When it was twenty minutes into class, and there was still no sign of the boy, Nova knew he wasn't coming. He might never attend another class. She felt stupid for believing him the other night. Of course, he'd used her and didn't keep his end of the bargain.

Camille was sitting right in front of her, a knowing smile on her face. She came up to her when the class was dismissed.

"Did you really think he would come?" she asked.

"I don't know what you're talking about."

"But you do. You don't know Dominic like I do."

"And I don't want to either." Nova placed her arms on the table and leaned forward. "What's it going to take for you to believe that I don't want him? Or anything that you have, for that matter. I'm not your enemy, Camille."

Camille rolled her eyes. "I know your type, Nova. The innocent nobody who wants to become a somebody. I know your tricks, and just know, no one's falling for them." She jutted her jaw to where Andrew was sitting. "Not even lover boy stuck around for more than a week."

"Okay, you can keep fighting a war that doesn't even exist. But don't think that I won't fight back."

Camille didn't reply to that; she threw her hair over her shoulder and walked away.

Ms. Hart was still at the front of the class, waiting for all the students to leave.

"Dominic didn't show." She hoped this would convince the teacher.

"It's one class, sweetheart. No one has perfect attendance. But I'm sure he'll reach out."

"And what if he doesn't? My grade is riding on his tardiness."

She considered her and folded her arms. "If he doesn't show up in the next class, I'll speak to him."

"And you still won't consider giving me another partner?"

"Patience is a very important skill. Maybe this is your chance to learn that."

Nova didn't even know how to reply to that. Why was everything at her expense?

She left class and stomped away. It just so happened that Dominic was in her way. "Dominic."

He looked at her, and it was like she wasn't even there. He looked right through her. She did read him wrong that night. There was no silent truce; he was only planning on ditching her. He turned back to the person he was talking to.

"Dominic."

He ground his teeth. "I'm in the middle of something."

"I don't care. Why weren't you in class? I was doing everything on my own."

"I'm not a tutor," he said, and the guy next to him laughed.

Nova wondered what it was like to have the world bow down to your every whim. "No, you're my assigned partner. I'm not going to get your grade for you."

He turned to her and took a step forward, looming over her. "And what's the alternative? You'll not do the project and fail too?"

Nova felt the vein in her head throb. Dominic had played her like a fiddle, and she'd had enough. "Fine. Don't do the project. I'm calling your parents, though."

Dominic stilled. He probably hadn't expected Nova to say that. "You're going to call my parents?"

Nova felt an unbridled amount of joy. It was a shot in the dark, but she had got it right. "Yeah. What would they think about their eldest, their pride and joy, slacking off in school? I'm sure they'll have a lot to say to you when they find out how irresponsible you're being with your education."

Dominic turned his head to look at the guy he had been talking to. He stared the guy down until he got the message and left. "Who told you?" He lowered his voice until it was husky.

"No one. Don't make me call your parents."

He pointed a finger in her face, and his tongue was poking at his cheek. "You don't scare me, Nova."

"No. But your parents do. I'll see you in class next week, Dominic." She walked two steps backward and turned to leave. She really would call his parents.

Harper found it extremely funny that she had threatened Dominic with his parents. "How'd you know it would work?"

Nova shrugged. "He wanted to upset them when we were at the party and then something Camille said. It was worth the risk, and it worked." She ended that with a smirk.

Dominic had better be in class next week because Nova already had the phone numbers she needed.

"I told you." Ms. Hart stopped her when she entered the class next week.

Nova made a questioning sound.

Nova followed her line of sight as the teacher looked at Dominic. The relief Nova felt was almost akin to the joy she had felt when her threat worked.

Unfortunately, Camille sat in her place before she made it to her table. Her week was going really well, a good amount of people somehow knew about the rumor being false, and she had been told that she was being seriously considered as the main character in the play. Overall, this had been the happiest she'd been since she got to Atherton.

She cleared her throat and stood next to her seat. "You're in my seat."

Camille looked up at her. "And I'm in the middle of a conversation." She gestured between her and Dominic. He looked bored like he always did.

"If everyone could get back to their seats, we can get this party started!" Ms. Hart said and clapped her hands once. Camille got up and shoved past Nova before going back to her seat.

Nova took notes, and Dominic just sat there. He didn't talk

to her; he didn't ask questions about anything he missed. Instead, he sat there like you would in a movie theater.

At the end of the class, she decided to talk to him about it. "This is the material we have to incorporate in the assignment. How will you understand any of this if you don't even take notes?"

"You're getting on my last nerve, Nova."

"And you on mine. Imagine the absolute nightmare it would be if your parents found out you're failing math."

Dominic cleared his throat and smirked.

Nova wasn't expecting that.

"You know, Nova, I did a little thinking after you ambushed me in the hallway."

She looked ahead at their teacher talking, but her ears were all Dominic's.

"I realized that if I fail, I might lose my credit card, my car, maybe summer vacation plans. But if you fail, you lose your scholarship. So, you tell me which one of us has more to lose?"

Nova's nostrils flared in frustration. "I'll still call your parents. I don't want to, but I will. I don't understand why you insist on being such a thorn in my side." She got up and shoved her things in her bag and regarded him once last time before leaving. "Have notes by next class, or I will call them."

When push came to shove, Nova was ready to call his parents, but he changed as the days went on. It wasn't all there, all at once, but he started taking notes. Nova had peeked at them and was shocked to see he was very organized. His notes were almost giving hers a run for her money. She hadn't thought it would work; she was close to going back to Ms. Hart and not taking no for an answer when she asked for a new partner.

Whatever had caused it, Nova was relieved to see him working.

Harper had gone back to making arrangements for her party, and Nova participated actively. In fact, she was excited about it.

"How are things with you and Dominic?" Harper asked.

She hadn't brought him up for a really long time. She had been complaining about Camille, though. She'd found interesting ways of annoying Nova. Most of them included speaking over Nova in class, making sure she was unheard, sometimes even stealing her answers. "Nothing. He's been... good." Nova thought the day would never come.

"I guess his threats were empty."

Nova nodded. "I guess. He's really good at school. I wasn't expecting that."

"Oh, babe, he was valedictorian back in high school."

Nova's eyebrows shot up to her hairline. She couldn't imagine Dominic with discipline. He did have a dominant personality, though. "Maybe he's especially a jerk for me."

"You know that's not true. But I might be a little obsessed with your pictures with him."

Nova chuckled. "So is Scarlett. She says it was the prom night I never had."

Harper placed a hand on her heart and made an aww sound. "I'm inviting him to the party."

Nova rolled her eyes.

THE NIGHT OF THE PARTY, Nova was excited as people entered and greeted her. When Dominic entered, everyone stopped whatever they were doing and looked at him. Nova understood how he would have made a good valedictorian. He certainly commanded the room with his presence.

He looked intimidating in his leather jacket and black slacks. His hair looked soft to the touch. It was short and cropped on the sides and a little longer on top. She looked away when his eyes met hers.

"What are you doing here?" Dominic sneered at her.

"This is my dorm room," she snapped back.

He looked around. "Must be Harper's doing."

Nova didn't know what that meant, but she didn't stick around to find out either. Instead, she hung out with a couple of people she'd met through the audition process that she was called back for. Her chances of getting the part had increased considerably. She thought being the understudy wouldn't be so bad either as a worst-case scenario.

"Nova, come on." Harper cut through the crowd and dragged her away from her friends. "You can sing if someone's playing the guitar, right?"

"As long as they're playing the right notes, I can sing to anything. Who's playing?"

Harper grinned. "Dominic."

Nova stopped walking, which caused Harper to stop too. "What?"

"What?"

Nova gave her a look. "You know what. Why do I have to sing with him?"

"You don't have to sing with him. He's going to play the guitar, and you're going to sing. It'll be fun. A bonding moment for you two!"

"Are you drunk? What's wrong with you?!"

Harper giggled and pulled her to their couch, where Dominic was sitting. He was tuning the guitar.

"Does he know he's playing for me?" Nova whispered in Harper's ear.

"Yeah." She shrugged. Nova tucked her hair behind her ear. If Dominic planned to embarrass her, she wanted no part in it.

"She's here!" Harper tugged her to stand in front of him.

"Finally." He huffed. "Hypocrite," he muttered.

Nova scoffed. "You're one to talk. So why are you doing this anyway?"

"Harper asked."

The statement made even less sense than him agreeing to play for her. "And aren't you the most agreeable person in the room."

He told her what song they were singing.

"Hi, guys!" Harper jumped with excitement. "It's our favorite duo performing for us today!" She gestured to the two of them.

Dominic's face soured when Harper called them the 'favorite duo.' People clapped, and Nova could already see cameras out and ready to record them.

Dominic played beautifully. Nova couldn't stop looking at the way his fingers glided against the strings. She had always been fascinated with instruments. Her parents had bought her a ukulele when she was young, but it broke before she knew what to do with it. After that, guitars were too expensive, and she could have never afforded the classes anyway.

Nova sang and put all the emotions she'd been feeling into the vocals. It was a song about feeling down and out, but working through the difficulties to become victorious in the end. She didn't know what made Dominic choose this song, but she was really feeling it.

As she sang, she closed her eyes on a particularly moving verse, and when she opened them, she saw Dominic staring at her with a look she hadn't seen on him before. It looked soft and gentle and caused her to flush from the top of her head all the way down to her toes. He didn't break the eye contact, so she was forced to look away.

When the song was over, Nova smiled at the clapping crowd. She looked around when her eyes landed on Camille.

She was standing with her posse behind her, glaring daggers at her. Nova shifted her eyes away. She thanked the people complimenting her and pretended to have never seen Camille.

"You're good at that." She shoved her hands in her pockets. She looked around awkwardly and smiled at whoever waved at her.

"Did you expect me to have no talent?" Dominic stood up. The look he had before was long gone and was replaced by his usual look of disdain. Nova felt even more nervous because of their height difference.

"I am trying to be nice; can't you accept the compliment?"

Dominic scoffed. "You have very judgmental eyes, Nova. People know when you're judging them, and I know you think I am good for nothing."

That was a first. Nova had never been told she had judgmental eyes. "You didn't treat me like I was a person when I first got here, so if anyone should be complaining, it should be me." Despite their words, their tones were light, not riddled with malintent.

Dominic smirked and walked away.

Chapter Eighteen

After her performance, Nova spent all of her time avoiding Camille. She knew the girl was not happy about her performance with Dominic.

She had seen the video posted of their performance, and it was getting a lot of traction.

"I'm going to get some food; I'm starving." Nova got up from the couch and walked to the kitchen. Luckily, the house was a lot cleaner than their previous party. She grabbed a sandwich and bit into it when a tell-tale head of blonde hair walked in with one of her minions.

Nova wiped the crumbs from the corner of her mouth and put the sandwich down. She cleared her throat. "Hey."

"Drop the act, Nova. I could see how smug you were from a mile away."

She loved being right, but there were times when it was better to be wrong, and this was one of them. "I didn't even know he was going to be here."

Camille nodded sarcastically.

"Camille, I don't have to justify myself to you. If you want to be with Dominic, be my guest, I don't care."

"It's funny how you say that and then do the exact opposite

of it. You're basically marking your territory whenever you're around him."

Nova couldn't stop the laugh. "I am not doing any such thing."

Camille's face morphed into a scary frown. "What will happen when you get him, Nova? His parents won't even let you in their house. Their help is better off than you. You're signing yourself up for a world of humiliation."

"Way better off," her minion supported her. She gave Nova a once over and stifled a laugh behind her hand.

"I'm leaving." Nova put the food back and walked to her room. She shut the door behind her and sat on her bed.

She texted her mother, but she was probably working. There was a knock on her door, and it was yet another person she didn't want to see.

"I don't want to talk, Dominic." Nova went to close the door again, but he stopped it with his hand.

"We need to talk about our project."

"Right now?!" Nova yelled. She put a hand on her mouth when she realized she was too loud. "Sorry, I'm sorry. Just meet me tomorrow or something, please."

"I want to talk right now." Dominic entered her room and shut the door.

Nova was sure he was annoying her on purpose. Camille had probably gone and gloated to him about how she made Nova feel like crap. About how weak she had been in front of her. "What do you want to do?"

"Not sure. I thought you'd know." He sat on the bed; his weight made the pillows jump.

"I was thinking we could use Ms. Hart's idea and relate it to music. I found a couple of articles that might be helpful," she said half-heartedly.

"No," Dominic said.

On any other day, Nova would have had the patience to put

up with his attitude, but today wasn't it. "Why not? You don't have an idea, and I do, so it doesn't matter what you want."

Dominic looked at her and leaned back on his palms. "I don't care. I'm not doing music."

Nova put a hand in her hair and tugged at it furiously. "Leave." She pointed to the door.

"No." Dominic smirked. Obviously, he loved getting a rise out of her.

"We'll figure it out in class; I really want you to leave." She used a tone that left no room for argument.

Dominic got up and opened the door to leave and Camille was standing on the other side with a hoard of people waiting for them.

"There! I told you guys, I told you!" Camille cried, her eyes red with unshed tears.

Nova walked to the doorway beside Dominic and looked out at the crowd while scanning the room. She didn't see Harper anywhere. Why was Camille in tears standing outside her door?

Camille's crying was making Nova nervous. Everything about the girl screamed, *Give me attention?!*

"What's going on?" Dominic asked. He looked the least bothered by the crying girl.

"I can't believe you'd do this to me." She sniffled and wiped a tear.

"Do *what*?"

Camille cried harder, and one of her minions, who was with her in the kitchen, decided to step in.

"Camille told you that she liked Dominic because she thought you were her *friend,* and now you're dragging him off to your room to be alone with him. Do you really have no value for friendship!? She's been nothing but kind to you."

Nova felt her eyes widen, and the urge to throttle rose higher and higher. "I didn't drag him in here. *He* was the one who wanted to discuss our math project!" After the words were out, Nova didn't understand why she defended the fact that she didn't drag Dominic in with her and not the part where Camille supposedly was kind to her. She looked at Dominic expectantly, but the boy stared back at her.

"I'm not involving myself in this." He raised his hands in surrender.

Nova blew air out of her nose. "I didn't drag him anywhere. And Camille and I have never had a *nice* conversation."

Camille let out a sob. "Wow. I really thought we were becoming friends. I came out tonight to see you sing even though I have an early start tomorrow."

People whispered, and Dominic stood next to Nova and watched everything unfold in front of him, not defending for a second. "I thought you were going to another party after this." Dominic pulled out his phone and opened an unread text from Camille. "You wanted me to go with you."

"Uh, y-yeah," Camille sputtered, "I wanted to spend time with you. That was before Nova made a move on you. You know what, Nova? Have him. I hope the two of you make each other happy." She wiped away a stray tear and left, her dress twirling with her.

Even though Camille had her dramatic exit, people were still murmuring amongst themselves, and Nova was so over tonight. "Party's over, guys," she announced. Harper was nowhere to be seen, so she would call the shots for the time being.

The crowd made its way out of their dorm when she saw Harper pushing through the crowd, her hands up, so people would actually notice and not crush her on the way out.

"Why is everyone leaving?" Harper distractedly said bye to anyone who said it to her first.

"Camille made a scene; I told them the party was over." Dominic was still standing next to Nova, though. She was still mad he had made no move to tell everyone the truth, but it was her fault for expecting Dominic to be fair to her.

"What did she say? God, I knew I should have asked her to leave."

Nova turned to Dominic. "Aren't you going to leave?"

"I don't want to." He smirked and sat down on the couch. "Come, Harper." He patted the seat next to him. "I'll tell you all about what Camille said. Nova, why don't you be a good host and get us something to eat?"

Harper smiled at Nova and shrugged a shoulder before taking a seat next to the boy. Dominic had taken his leather jacket off and talked to Harper like he did this every day. Nova placed a plate of chips and a sandwich on the table for Dominic, who didn't even have the courtesy to thank her.

"Nova, babe, I'm so sorry. I went down because my mother called. The last thing I need is for her to know I was hosting a party."

Nova nodded. "It's fine. But really, Camille should be in the acting class. That performance almost had *me* convinced that I was the bad guy."

"Who says you aren't?" Dominic smirked. He had his arm thrown over the back of the couch. She didn't really understand Dominic. One second, he wanted nothing to do with her, and the next, he was sitting in her living room willingly.

Nova chose to ignore his comment. At some point, Dominic started pointedly ignoring her and spoke over her. She took it as her cue to leave since there was no way she was picking a fight.

"Do you usually go to bed this early?" Dominic asked.

It wasn't early; it had just hit one a.m. "So what if I do?" She put a hand on her hip.

Harper giggled for whatever reason. "Let her go, Dom. Unless you want to be the one to wake her up tomorrow morning."

He laughed, and that was the first time Nova heard him laugh for real. It wasn't mocking; it didn't have any wrong intentions behind it. It wasn't a bad sound at all.

She left before saying something stupid, like 'you have a nice laugh.'

CAMILLE WAS STILL PLAYING the victim card come morning. It just so happened that Dominic was in front of Nova in the breakfast line. He wasn't even talking to her, she was sure he hadn't even noticed her, but that didn't stop Camille from glaring at her and looking downright morose when someone looked her way.

Nova didn't realize Dominic wasn't moving when she took a step forward and bumped into him. "I'm sorry," she muttered.

"Figures. Do you always look like this in the mornings?" Dominic placed his plate down and leaned on the platform like there wasn't a line behind them. Obviously, nobody said a word to him about it.

"You're doing this on purpose, aren't you?" Nova said and saw people whispering about them. "Why are you trying to get under Camille's skin?"

"Who says it's for Camille?"

Nova laughed humorlessly. "I hope you know it doesn't bother me. It's a wasted effort." She walked in front of him and began filling her tray.

"Meet me in the library at seven tonight," he said, leaning toward her to whisper in her ear, causing shivers to run down her spine.

Nova raised an eyebrow. "Why?" she asked, leaning back acting unaffected.

"I'm going to burn the place down and then blame it on you; I need you there to pin it on you."

"Uh…" Nova's mouth hung open.

Dominic rolled his eyes. "We need to figure out a topic. I have a couple of ideas since you're incapable of moving on from music."

Nova nodded and walked away. "He's a piece of work," she muttered when she sat next to Harper.

"Everyone thinks you're together," Harper whispered. "I've had ten different people ask me already."

"Thanks to Camille."

Harper winced. "That's there, but... Camille isn't the only one crushing on Dominic. There's going to be more like Camille who are going to show their true colors."

Nova put her head in her hands. "Ugh. This is just perfect. More enemies."

"Don't worry; no one can beat Camille." April smiled. "And you're handling her just fine."

THE LIBRARY WAS WAY TOO crowded for seven in the evening. The place was swarming with girls, but no Dominic in sight. She should have expected him to be late.

She sat in a corner and read articles that related music to math. Words started swimming around in her head, and she lost track of them. Dominic still hadn't shown. The crowd in the library had receded too.

She could see now that Dominic wasn't coming, and the anger simmering under her skin started to burn. She packed all her things and threw her bag over her shoulder. When her phone rang, she saw that it was Harper calling.

"Babe, are you still waiting for Dominic at the library?"

"He didn't show, so I'm leaving."

"Uh, yeah," she cleared her throat, "that's because he's here."

Nova fumed her way home. Dominic really knew how to waste someone's time and then infuriate them to the point of exhaustion.

She threw her door open and saw Dominic sitting there with his laptop on the couch, watching a TV show. *The audacity.* "Where's Harper, and why weren't you at the library?! I was waiting for an hour."

"Could have called," he replied, not even looking away from his screen.

Nova threw her bag next to him on the couch. She walked in front of him and shut the laptop. "What are you playing at?"

Dominic looked at her with annoyance. "Girls were following me. They would have crowded us at the library, so I came here."

"*No,*" Nova took a deep breath to try and calm herself, "So you let them follow you to *my* place? People already think we're dating because of Camille, and you're making it ten times worse!"

The boy had the nerve to laugh sarcastically. "Does it look like I care? And besides, wouldn't it be worse if they saw us together in the library?" He blew an exaggerated amount of air from his mouth. "And with the way that you look at me, it would only prove them right."

Nova scoffed. "Yeah, because *I* was the one who was asking me for a dance at the ball and *I* was the one who agreed to play the guitar for me," she said, waving toward the guitar lying on the floor against the couch.

"But we all know who's trying to steal me from Camille." He smirked.

Nova licked her lips and shook her head. "I'm not doing this cat and mouse chase with you. We're going to do our math, and you're going to leave me alone until our next class."

Dominic stared at her blankly, and she took that as an agreement. "Since you're dead-set against music, what have you come up with?"

"Why should I do all the work? You need to contribute, too," Dominic said in a mocking tone. He tried to replicate Nova's voice but failed epically.

"I sound nothing like that. And I've been finding articles and reading up on things all on my own. So where were you then, hmm?"

"It's not my fault you started on a topic your partner hadn't agreed to."

Nova sometimes thought that if she banged her head against a wall, it would feel exactly like trying to have a conversation with Dominic. "What do you want to do instead of music?" she said, cutting to the chase. They'd be here all night, and if Dominic didn't get to dinner on time, everyone would know where he was.

Come to think of it, the crowd in the library made more sense, too.

"I don't know yet. We still have one module to solve before we need to start."

"The faster we finish the project, the faster we can stop being partners."

"Then come up with something that's not music!" he snapped.

Nova gritted her teeth. "If you don't want music, then you come up with something."

They solved their homework together, Nova getting stuck every now and then because being in Dominic's vicinity was distracting.

"What's the third question's answer?" he looked up from his work and asked her. He twirled the pen around his fingers with skill.

She hadn't even reached the third question yet. "I don't know, I haven't gotten there."

Dominic scoffed. "What were you doing?"

"My brain's foggy," she admitted and bit the end of her pen.

The boy tsked and pulled her hand away from her mouth. "Don't do that."

Nova froze. She felt herself blush from the unexpected nature of his action.

"Take a break. You can't do your math when your brain's not working," he said and went back to his books.

She did take a break and went on her phone. There were a couple of texts from Harper. She was gushing about Dominic being at their place.

Her phone rang a couple of minutes into her break. "Sorry," she muttered and silenced the call.

"I don't care," he said under his breath.

Nova stared at Scarlett's name on the caller ID. "Hello?"

"Nova?!" Skylar's voice came through, and Nova felt a rush of anxiety.

"Sky? Are you okay? Are Mom and Dad okay?" She never called from Scarlett's phone. Instead, they usually talked when one of her parents called.

"We're okay. I used Scar's phone cause she's making me dinner. It's her birthday next week, and I want to get her a gift, but I don't know what."

Nova sighed in relief. "Okay, you could have called me from Mom's phone, though. I got scared."

"Sorry." Her sister giggled. She went on and on about her million ideas, asking questions and then answering them herself like she always did. Nova gave her a couple of ideas when she finally stopped talking, and they ended the call. She had gotten so lost in her words she didn't realize Dominic had shut his books.

"Sorry, I should have gone into my room."

Dominic shook his head. "Who was that?"

"Um, my sister."

He nodded. "I can't focus anymore either."

There was an awkward silence while Nova chewed on her lip.

"Is your sister younger than you?"

Nova nodded. "Yeah, Skylar."

"I have four younger brothers."

He sounded fond. Nova didn't question why he was being warm to her out of nowhere. She's learned that he had his fleeting moments, and she should appreciate them. "Can't imagine having that many Skylars," she joked.

Dominic nodded and cleared his throat. "We should go get dinner."

"You go first; I'll follow in a few."

He laughed, and this one Nova liked. It was funny to her that the same person could possess such different likable and unlikeable qualities. "Why, because you don't want to show up with me?" He scoffed. "God forbid someone might think we're together."

"I don't like complicating my life unnecessarily."

"You do realize, if we were dating, you'd be untouchable. You would get a social boost." He smirked, and Nova could see the pride shining in his eyes.

She chuckled. "I don't need a social boost, thanks. I don't want to fight Camille. Why won't you just tell her that you hate my guts, and then you two can bond over your mutual hatred for me?"

"I have no interest in bonding with Camille," he said, "What happened to you and lover boy?"

"Why do you call him that?" Nova asked. She remembered Camille calling him that too.

Dominic shrugged. "We all called him that. He's annoying."

Nova hummed. "I guess." A shiver ran down her spine at the thought of the night of their break up. "It just didn't work out."

"What did you do?" he teased.

"I didn't do anything. He and I are just not compatible."

He snickered. "You're one of those, huh?"

"One of what?"

"The ones who say things like 'not compatible' and 'it's not you, it's me.' Oh, and my personal favorite; 'it's the right person but the wrong time.'"

"I didn't know there were categories." She folded her arms and rubbed at them. Harper must have left a window open.

"Let's go. We'll be late for dinner."

Nova reluctantly agreed to go with him. He reminded her to take her jacket too. It was weird to hang out with him alone and not feel the urge to ram his head into a wall.

A couple of boys joined them on their way to the cafeteria.

"Where were you, dude? Camille was asking for you."

At the sound of the girl's name, Nova felt her breathing pick up.

"I was studying. Why was she at my place?"

The boy, Aaron, Nova thought was his name, said, "She wanted to talk to you about something."

Dominic rolled his eyes. "I'm not going to that stupid event with her. I'm not going, period."

"Your call, bro."

Nova eventually walked off to the side, leaving Dominic to his friends as it seemed he'd forgotten she was there. But it worked out for the best for her; she didn't have to enter with Dominic.

The hurt she felt about being sidelined and treated like she was invisible settled in her like a heavy rock at the bottom of a lake. Unmoving. Why did she feel this way when she knew not to expect any better from Dominic?

<h1>Chapter Nineteen</h1>

April was smiling at Nova coyly when she sat down next to her. "Word is getting around that Dominic was at your place."

Nova smiled a little; she knew April meant no harm. "You're having too much fun with this."

"I am." She giggled.

"It was... not the worst. I—I mean, it could have been worse."

Harper and April gasped. "You're so cute!" April gushed.

"Okay, calm down. I'm not waxing poetic about him. He still won't agree on our project topic, and we have about a week left before we *need* one." The stress she felt from before came back. "He needs to pick something before we have a real problem."

"Ask nicely, and maybe he'll do it," Harper said and then, "Actually, on second thought, don't ask nicely. He seems to be that into you."

"Stop. He's not into me. He likes messing with Camille. He told me." That wasn't said in so many words, but she got the gist of it.

The two girls made disagreeing noises and let the topic go. Camille showed up for dinner and pinned Nova with a look she prayed no one else would ever be a target of. The grapevine probably informed her about Dominic being in Nova's apartment.

Nova was called to the theater after lunch, and she was a big ball of jitters. Mr. Bentley was probably going to announce everyone's roles. Nova knew she thought she'd be okay with being the understudy, but the truth was that she wouldn't.

"Why do you look like a ghost?" Dominic said and broke Nova out of her reverie.

"What are you doing here?" Nova was sitting in an empty class not too far away from the theater. She decided against lunch because she couldn't imagine stomaching anything if she didn't get the role.

"Saw you enter. Got curious." He dropped his bag on the floor and sat one seat away from Nova.

"Creepy much?" Nova wiped her sweaty palms on her jeans.

"What are you doing here?" Dominic directed her own question at her.

"Waiting. I need to be in the theater in twenty minutes." She pointed at him. "Why did you follow me?"

He shrugged. "Wanted to see what you were up to."

"Right. What's the real reason?"

"Why do you need to go to the theater?" Dominic replied, ignoring Nova's side of the investigation.

"I'm not telling unless you tell me what you're doing here."

The boy sighed and laid back a little more in his seat. "My parents are here, probably looking for me. So, I'm trying to hide from them."

Nova nodded, not sure how to reply to that. She couldn't imagine hiding from her parents.

Dominic folded his arms. "Go on, make your jokes."

Nova raised her eyebrows. "I'm not going to make fun of you." She pulled out a chocolate bar, one she was saving for herself for after finding out whether she got the role or not. It wasn't for a reward, though; it was to make her feel better if she didn't get it. "Chocolate makes things better." She held the chocolate out to him.

The boy looked at her and then down at the chocolate. He finally gave in and took it from her. He unwrapped it and broke it into two. He handed one part back to Nova.

"Why are you going to the theater?"

"Mr. Bentley is holding a final performance before deciding who gets the available roles. I auditioned to be the main character, and I'm nervous."

"Why, do you think you won't get it? I'm sure Bentley knows about you."

Nova nodded. "He saw our performance,"

"Told you being with me would give you a social boost."

She laughed and looked at the time. She hated to admit it, but Dominic's arrival made the time move a little faster and distracted her from her nervousness. "I need to get going." She got up and threw her bag over her shoulder. "Thank you."

Dominic got up too. "For what? I'll come with you."

That was something Nova didn't want. She was nervous enough, and having Dominic there to watch her fail would be mortifying. "Oh, uh, I don't think it's open to an audience."

The boy gave her a 'duh' look and smirked. "It's me, Nova. I shouldn't have to explain this to you." He followed her out when she walked towards the theater.

"You really don't have to come."

"I have nowhere better to be. And my parents would never think to check in the theater."

Nova had more questions about that, but she needed to get into character right now.

"Uh, why's he here?" Dominic stopped her before she went backstage to gather with the rest.

Andrew was sitting in the first row when Nova turned to see who Dominic was talking about. "I...I don't know. I don't know how he knew this was happening today." He hadn't shown up to her practices for a while now, so Nova assumed he would leave her alone after she admitted how uncomfortable he had made her.

Dominic eyed Andrew like he did everyone he thought beneath him. Like he did to Nova sometimes. It was a quick reminder of who Dominic really was. Or at least one dominant version of him.

"I need to go."

He nodded at her and went to sit next to Andrew.

Mr. Bentley was rounding everyone up, and Nova stood next to her competition, Adrianna. She was a nice girl and really talented too. But she wasn't in the music course.

Dominic was sitting two seats away from Andrew. Andrew smiled at her, but she looked away. Her character was sad for the scene, so she channeled the emotions and closed her eyes until Mr. Bentley called 'action.'

Nova's name was last on the list. That was a good thing, but the wait was excruciating. It was a long time before her name was called out; she didn't think Dominic would still be there.

When it was her turn to perform, she channeled Venus until everything the character stood for swirled in her head. She was no longer Nova; she *was* Venus. She poured her heart and soul into the performance. She pushed herself until she felt herself heat up with effort. At the end of the emotional scene, she leaned over with the grief of Venus, putting her hands on her knees. By the time she finished, her breath was ragged, and sweat was beading her forehead.

Once she straightened up and returned to being Nova, her eyes zeroed in on Dominic. He was smiling. Not so much with his mouth, but she could see it in his eyes. Usually, she'd break the eye contact, but Dominic held her gaze.

"Okay, if everyone else could join Nova on stage for the results, please."

"Nova, you're going to be Venus," Mr. Bentley announced.

Nova felt her stomach drop; the anxiety bleeding out of her body in one fell swoop. "Thank you, sir."

"Don't thank me yet. You still have a lot of work to do. You'll need to build vocal strength, and you could do with more practice on the acting front."

She nodded and bit her lip to stop herself from letting her face split into a grin. "Yes, sir." Mr. Bentley was a known control freak and was strict.

After the man dismissed them, the other participants crowded Nova to congratulate her on getting the lead role, then she and Riley walked out together.

"Did you see Dominic?" Riley whispered.

Nova nodded. She understood what her friend was trying to ask her. "I did."

Said guy walked up to them. Nova looked around and saw Andrew waiting in the back. It was too much to expect him to be gone.

"Lover boy wants to talk to you," Dominic told her, his old jerk-self back in play.

"Okay."

Riley watched their exchange and then stayed back with Dominic to talk to him.

"Dominic said you wanted to talk."

Andrew smiled at her and nodded. "You were great. I was in awe."

Nova gave him a friendly smile but folded her arms. "Thank you. You really didn't have to be here."

Andrew bit his lip and nodded. "So you've said. I like watching you perform. I watched your video with Dominic." He shifted his weight and put a hand through his hair. "What's that about, hmm?"

"We've been spending more time together because of the… uh, assignment."

"Oh," Andrew swallowed thickly, "Must be exhausting."

Nova shrugged. "Not any more than I expected."

"Do you want to go for coffee?"

Nova was about to rack her brain for an excuse when Dominic interrupted the two of them. "Are we going or what?"

"Actually, we were just going to go for coffee," Andrew cut in.

Dominic looked at Nova with a raised eyebrow.

"I didn't say yes." She turned back to Andrew. "I need to go do my homework."

"Okay then, on your way, loser," Dominic told him.

Andrew narrowed his eyes at Nova and then looked back at Dominic. She felt like she was watching some weird masculine exchange where they were trying to see which was more dominant.

"Tomorrow, Nova?" Andrew asked the question to her but was still looking at Dominic.

"I'm going to be here all day after classes for rehearsals. Why don't you just text me? We really need to get going." She grabbed Dominic's wrist and dragged him out. "What was that?" she asked him when they walked in the opposite direction from their accommodation.

"What? He was being a creep. You didn't see the way he was staring at you when you were performing."

Nova looked at Dominic as they walked and saw the genuine horror on the boy's face. That was the same thing Harper had told her, and she wondered what they saw that she didn't. She really did get a creepy vibe from Andrew these days. "I don't know what you saw, but you don't have to be rude to people."

"You can't tell me he's not annoying. He should be glad that I haven't pounded his face into the ground yet."

"He's just..." Nova cleared her throat, "getting over our relationship."

Dominic shrugged. "It's not like I care, but if I were you, I wouldn't go near him. Ever," he said and then walked away.

Chapter Twenty

Nova was in the café working on her lines over a cup of coffee when Harper walked in with Dean.

"What's up?" Nova asked once the two sat down. They were looking back and forth between each other, making Nova nervous.

"Why is Dominic telling everyone that if anyone is seen with Andrew, he'll make their lives miserable?"

The pencil Nova was holding in her hand fell. "What?"

Harper nodded. "Did something happen?"

Nova shook her head and grabbed at her purple hair. "He's just being so weird! I'm going to go look for him, take my things back to our place, please." She walked out in a fit of rage. She wasn't even thinking.

In between her rage-paced walk, she realized she didn't even know where Dominic was. She walked towards the cafeteria. When there was no Dominic in sight, she gave up and started towards her room.

Dominic had his phone to his ear and was walking towards the cafeteria.

She stood in front of him with folded arms. "We need to talk."

"Jake, I'm going to call you back, okay?" he said and hung up on whoever he was speaking to. "What is wrong with you? That could have been my dad."

Nova rolled her eyes. If only he were scared of consequences like he was of his parents. "What have you told your minions about Andrew?"

"To stay away from him and beat him up if he looks suspicious. I thought you'd be thankful."

"*Thankful*? For what? You can't do that to him; he's a *person*."

Dominic scoffed. "I don't think you understand." He took a step closer to her and looked down with intense eyes. "I didn't do this because *you* have issues with him. I did it because *I* don't like him. You don't weigh in on my decisions, understood? Now move before I set up the same arrangement for you."

He walked away from Nova before she could say anything back to him. She balled and opened her fists a couple of times. She wondered why Dominic couldn't just be one person. She actually liked the guy she shared a chocolate bar with, the person who came to watch her get her role. It was a good day up until Dominic Lark decided it wasn't going to be.

"Nova!" Harper jogged up to her. "We were looking for you. I just saw you talking to Dom; what did he say?"

"He's not Dom!" She snapped at Harper. "He's Dominic, and he's the biggest jerk on the planet."

"I'm guessing it didn't go well."

"No. He's insufferable. He doesn't get to do these crazy things because of me and then gaslight me by saying they weren't for me!?"

"What's really bothering you? The fact that he did it for you or the possibility that he didn't?"

Nova wasn't sure what to do with that question. She was mad for multiple reasons. But she was mainly angry about being thrown from one emotion to another like a pendulum. "I-I, all of it!?" she admitted.

"Oh, Nova." Harper put a hand on her shoulder. "Come on; we'll eat ice cream after dinner."

"Fine." She felt dejected and confused.

"Besides, Andrew could use some of Dominic's *charm*."

"This isn't about what Andrew deserves or not. It's Dominic deciding for other people who they should talk to or not."

"I get it. Let's not worry about that right now, okay? We need to have dinner and make plans for this weekend. We need something fun to do."

HARPER'S WORDS had really gotten to Nova. She couldn't sleep because of them. Was she really bothered because there was a chance that Dominic didn't sideline Andrew for her? Did she want him to do it for her? *What am I thinking? I don't want him to do it at all!* She sighed and sat up. She checked her phone to see it was one A.M. already.

She couldn't look at her lines for the play anymore; she'd read them so much that they blurred before her eyes. So she texted Scarlett to see if she was awake. Her friend always had an answer, and she was a night owl.

"Nova? Are you okay?"

After explaining to Scarlett why she was still up, Nova hugged her pillow close to her stomach. "I wish I knew what to do about him."

Scarlett giggled. "I can't believe *you* want someone to like you. You're more of a take it or leave it kind of person."

"I don't want him to like me. I want him to treat me like a human being. He's a special brand of evil to me. He doesn't behave like that with Harper or April. He was decent to Riley, too!"

"Ask him."

"Huh?"

"Ask him. You'll never know if you don't ask him, and there's no one better to explain it than him."

Nova thought about it. It wasn't entirely a bad idea. Except, knowing Dominic, the answer could really crush her. "I don't think he'd have anything nice to say to me."

"You would find out, though. If he's really that much of a jerk, you know how to deal with those. You're getting confused because he's been nice on and off."

"You're right." Nova sighed; she felt a lot better than she had. "I'm going to try sleeping, okay? Goodnight."

She fell asleep, knowing she'd be asking Dominic questions tomorrow.

NOVA GOT to class a little earlier than everyone else.

"Nova." Ms. Hart stopped her. "How are things with Dominic?"

"Uh..." She wanted to be honest with Ms. Hart. She knew about Dominic's situation back home. "He's a tough nut to crack."

The teacher laughed and snorted in between. "That's one way to put it. But I'm glad you two are getting along; I knew you'd find a way."

"I didn't say we were," Nova said.

Ms. Hart smiled. "Oh, but you are. If you weren't, you would have come to ask me to change your partner again."

"That may happen any day. We still haven't decided on a topic yet."

"Take your time. I can give you an extension if required. I know you two will be fine, though."

Nova nodded and went to her seat. It was nice to know someone had faith in them because Nova lost hope every day. Dominic came right on time and dropped next to her.

"I want to talk after class," she told him.

"I still have no topic, so if it's about that, don't waste my time. Unless you came up with something non-music related."

The pencil in Nova's hand was about to crack because of the way she was gripping it. "It's not about that."

Dominic didn't reply and took out his books to take notes.

After class, Nova reminded Dominic to talk to her. Camille interrupted them once Dominic got to his feet.

"Dom, can you come with me to the café? I need help with some questions."

"Nova's taking me out. Get someone else," he told her and walked to the door.

Nova wanted to slap her hand to her forehead. Camille was glaring at her and gritting her teeth. Nova decided to make a swift exit before Camille started a fight with her and caused her to lose the opportunity to talk to Dominic.

"What do you want?" Dominic asked once she joined him on his way out.

"I wanted to ask what was going on with you."

He raised an eyebrow and looked down at her.

"One minute you act like we're normal partners working on a project together, and then the next I'm your arch-nemesis. So I want to know where I stand with you."

Dominic stopped walking and turned to her. "I don't like you. You're arrogant, and you judge people too quickly. And most of the time, your self-righteous act sets me off." He put his hands in his pocket.

"Really? *I'm* arrogant?"

"You're doing it again. You're not perfect, Nova."

"I never said I was. I just..." She sighed and felt really stupid about bringing this up with Dominic. He wouldn't let go of this chance to embarrass her. "I thought we were past this cat and mouse game."

"There is no game. Meet me at my place at six tonight. We need to solve the worksheet and decide on a topic."

"Nova? What are you doing here?"

Nova had feared this. It turned out that Dominic lived in the same building as Andrew but on the top floor. "I'm going to Dominic's."

Andrew clenched his jaw. "Did you lie to me?"

"Andrew, you know he and I are partners for math. And to be honest, I don't need to explain myself to you."

"Why won't you go for a cup of coffee with me?" He stepped closer to her.

Nova swallowed thickly and took two steps back. "I've been busy. And now I'm even busier because of the play."

"Those are excuses, and you know it."

"It's getting late. I'll see you around." She walked around him to the elevator.

"You know what he's done, don't you? My partner won't even discuss the project with me. He said he'd do it for us both. He's that scared of that monster you're going to spend the night with."

Nova turned to Andrew sharply. "I am *not* spending the night. And I didn't make him do that. In fact, I tried talking him out of it; you're welcome." All she wanted was for Andrew to go away. "And someone doing the whole thing for you doesn't sound like the worst thing to me." She stepped into the elevator and watched Andrew's red face as the doors closed.

She knocked and Dominic's door, realizing it was the only room on the floor.

He was shirtless when he opened the door, and Nova immediately looked away and tried her best not to blush.

"What?" he asked.

Nova sniffed and walked in, not looking at the boy. "Put on some clothes, for goodness sake."

"No one's here, Nova. They won't think you're dating me," he said and picked up the t-shirt lying on the arm of his couch.

His dorm was unreal. The floors were made of dark brown wood, and the walls were forest green. It was like an actual condo.

"Your comment this afternoon stirred up Camille enough."

Dominic had to nerve to smirk and wiggle his eyebrows. "I did that on purpose."

"I'm well aware." Nova sat down and took out her books. "Can we start?"

"Hmm." Dominic brought his things out from his room. "Before we do, I have a question."

Nova looked at him expectantly.

"What do you think of us dating?"

"Excuse me?!"

"Don't act so shocked. People have been talking, and I've been listening." He he draped his arm behind her on the back of the couch and smiled. "I'm a curious guy."

Nova glared at him. "What are you playing at?"

"Give me an answer."

She scoffed. "Who are you to demand answers from me?"

"Dominic Lark." The air of confidence didn't recede despite Nova's stubbornness.

"I'll answer it, on one condition."

Dominic considered it with his tongue poking out of his cheek. "What?"

"Look at my research about music and math. Just take a look; that's all I'm asking." She removed her folder with her articles and notes.

He took them from her and flipped through them quickly. He barely stopped at the paragraphs and threw the folder on the coffee table. "It's useless; I told you I don't want to do anything with music."

"Why not? It's not like you don't understand it. It might be good fun if you weren't being such a jerk!"

He gritted his teeth. "I don't have to explain myself to you."

"Then come up with a topic. I can't have you dragging us down."

"I'll do it when *I* want to."

Nova shrugged. "Okay then, I'll just ask Ms. Hart to change my partner, and when she says no, I'll ask her to speak to your parents."

Dominic stood up and pointed to her face. "Stop that."

"Then stop acting like a child. Either you give me a reason or a topic."

"Get out," he snapped. "Out." He pointed to the door.

Nova packed her bag and stood up to leave. "I guess I'll be talking to Ms. Hart then." She shut the door behind her and tried to regulate her breathing. This assignment must have been repentance for sins she didn't know about.

Chapter Twenty-One

ndrew was there when she got out of the elevator, most likely waiting for her. "Andrew, I'm really not in the mood, okay? I just want to go back to my room."

"That was quick."

She knew answering him would be feeding fuel to fire, so she walked ahead until Andrew pulled her back by her wrist.

"Go for coffee with me. I'll make you feel better."

"No, I'm good, thanks. I want to go back." She tried to free her hand from Andrew's grip. It was tight, and she was afraid it would bruise. She tried not to let fear take over. "Let go."

"Please," he begged.

"No, Andr—"

The sound of footsteps rushed from the stairs, and before Nova could realize what was happening, Dominic was shoving Andrew away from her.

"She said *no!*" he yelled at Andrew, slamming him back into the wall. Nova stood there in shock, and Dominic was in a rage.

"Dominic, don't." Nova pulled Dominic by his bicep when she saw him raise his fist. She didn't want this escalating to violence.

"What is wrong with you?" he yelled at Andrew. "Leave her

alone, do you understand? If you're seen within six feet of her, someone *will* show you your place." He clenched his jaw shrugged his arm from Nova's hand. "Come with me," he ordered, and Nova gave Andrew one last look before following the boy.

Dominic walked in front of her, not saying a word. Nova didn't understand why he came to defend her when he'd thrown her out of his room not even a few minutes ago. He was mad at her, and he still helped her. When she *really* needed it. She could act all tough and brave, but Andrew really scared her.

After walking for a while, Nova realized Dominic was walking towards her building. When they reached it, he turned to the door and held it open for her.

"Thank you." She looked down at her shoes. "You... you didn't have to help me, but you did. Thank you." She fiddled with the strap of her bag because Dominic was still silent. "How did you know I needed help?"

After what felt like an eternity, he said, "I was coming down to see if you were still there to tell you to come back up so we could get the project over with. Has that ever happened before?"

Nova shook her head and then nodded, not sure if she wanted Dominic to know or not. "It's complicated."

"Nova, this is serious." He stepped into the building and looked down, right into her eyes. "Has he hurt you before?"

"He— it was a rough night an—"

"*Has* he tried to hurt you!?" he cut her off. His voice was thunderous and sharp.

"He tried to force me into a kiss the night we broke up, but it didn't happen. He left after I asked him to and then apologized."

Dominic sighed. "Okay, I'm going to spread the word. He won't come near you anymore."

"Don't hurt him."

The boy's mouth hung open. "Why are you defending him?"

"I'm not. I just don't want anyone to get hurt because of me."

He dragged a hand across his face. "Go home."

Nova didn't say anything about the way he was ordering her

around. She went up to her dorm room and fell onto the couch. Nova didn't understand what she was feeling. She turned and curled into a ball. She could still feel Andrew's grip on her wrist, and she hated that. He was getting worse, and this had to stop. She was glad that Dominic had come when he did.

Maybe Harper was right, and Andrew deserved the social exclusion. But at the same time, Nova wasn't cruel enough to wish that upon him. And she didn't need Dominic protecting her by using his minions. If Andrew continued, she would be forced to report his actions to the administration. She really didn't want to do that because he'd more than likely get kicked out.

When Harper got back home from her class, she ran to Nova. "Are you okay, babe?" She hugged her.

"Yeah, why wouldn't I be?"

"I met Dominic on the way here. He told me what happened and to make sure you were okay. I mean, I would have done that anyway, but he *told* me to."

Nova shook her head. "I'm okay. Dominic was there at the right time."

"I'm glad. Thank goodness for Dom."

Nova couldn't stop the laugh. "I guess. I mean, I would have been inside his dorm room if he hadn't thrown me out."

Harper winced; she didn't even bother to ask any questions.

After her friend left her room, which she did after singing Dominic's praises, Nova read her lines and tried to get into character to practice for the play. Unfortunately, she couldn't focus because her mind kept replaying Dominic's face as he pushed Andrew away from her.

She really wanted to talk to him right now and didn't know why. She stalled for as long as she could before she picked up her phone. She was going to call him right now so that she could move on from these thoughts.

She dialed his number.

"Who's this?" Dominic picked up.

Nova couldn't help but roll her eyes. "I gave you my number

after you showed up at my place and conveniently left me waiting in the library."

"Of course, it's you. What is it?"

He threw her another curveball with the standoffish tone. "I... I think I want to talk."

"You think?"

Nova tsked and scratched her neck. "Forget it, my bad for calling you." She pulled the phone away from her ear and hung up, frustrated. *What am I doing?*

She took out her headphones and blasted music. She was never big on dancing; she wasn't that great at it. She started moving and closed her eyes. Her feelings were a mess, and the thrumming of music helped. Her hair was falling in her face as she moved.

She was lost in the beat, and the hand on her shoulder scared the soul out of her. She put a hand on her mouth to keep from screaming and removed the headphones.

"You really *can't* dance," Dominic said.

Relief swept her off her feet, and she plopped down on her bed, clutching her chest. "You scared me. Why didn't you knock!?"

"Yeah, cause if I did, you would have heard me." He dropped his bag on the bed and placed the box in his hand on the floor. It was a pizza box.

"What are you doing here?"

He shrugged a shoulder and opened up the box. "I felt like pizza, so I bought pizza."

Nova laughed despite there being nothing funny. After a moment of silence, she said, "I don't know why I called you."

"And I don't know why I'm here." He looked at her and then broke eye contact to pull over a chair to sit on. "Let's just eat." He tore apart a slice and handed it to her.

"Thank you."

The silence wasn't awkward. Nova didn't feel the need to fill it, and Dominic's gaze didn't feel like a burden.

When she laughed, surprising both herself and Dominic, the boy pushed away on the chair with his feet and put distance between them. "You're crazy."

Nova snorted without meaning to. "I am not." She covered her mouth with her hand and wiped the crumbs from the side. "I was thinking about something."

"Laughing in complete silence for no reason is more often than not a sign of crazy."

She sighed and dusted her hands off. "The first party at Camille's dorm? Andrew told me he doesn't eat pizza. That should have been my first and last red flag. Should have left him then and there."

Dominic made a disgusted face. "I really don't like him." He came closer again and took another slice. "Why did you actually break up? He didn't, um," Dominic sniffed, "he didn't try anything funny, did he?"

It took a minute for Nova to realize what he was saying. "Oh! No! He was just... a little too much."

The boy hummed. "You don't have to worry about him anymore; it's taken care of."

Nova bit her lip and nodded. "Thank you. I'm not really... I usually don't let other people handle situations for me."

"Everyone has a first." He smirked.

Nova groaned at the innuendo and threw her pillow at him. "You're impossible."

"Yeah, impossibly perfect." He smiled.

He had a beautiful smile. Nova liked the way his eyes almost disappeared when he did. "Impossibly full of yourself."

They finished the rest of the pizza without conversation. Dominic pointed to his face over his lip.

Nova smoothed a finger over hers, slightly mortified at the idea of sauce being on her face.

Dominic *tsked* and leaned forward. He wiped the one spot Nova had missed with his thumb.

"I don't like help," she reminded him, only half-serious. His touch felt too good for something so brief.

He rolled his eyes, licking the sauce off his thumb as her face burst into flames at the action. "Is that the musical's script?" he asked nonchalantly, as if he didn't just commit an act of intimacy.

Nova looked at her papers and nodded, trying to regulate her breathing by not making eye contact. "I was trying to practice my lines, but I couldn't concentrate."

"I can run them with you."

"You'll sing?" Nova jerked her eyes to his in surprise.

Dominic narrowed his eyes at her. "No, I won't, but I can speak and you can sing."

She handed him the papers.

"What? Are we seriously going to pass the sheet back and forth?"

"I don't have another copy."

The boy stared at her until she rolled her eyes and scooted to make a place for him on the bed. "Wipe your hands before touching my sheets."

They practiced for a long time, but it didn't feel like any time had passed. Dominic said the lines Nova allocated to him, and she sang her part. He provided criticism where he deemed fit and told her he was channeling his best Mr. Bentley.

They weren't ready to stop, but Dominic's phone rang.

"Jake," he said after picking up, "What's up?"

Nova watched him talk to whoever Jake was. Whoever it was, Dominic liked him.

"Okay, I love you. Call me tomorrow." He hung up.

The words 'I love you' were the softest words Nova had heard Dominic say. "Are you exclusively nice for *Jake*?" Nova asked and handed him her water bottle. They'd been going for nearly two hours.

"Jake and my other three brothers. He's the youngest in our family."

Nova smiled at him. "That's nice; who knew you could be a good brother."

"I have a mug that says 'the best brother.'"

They stared at each other until Dominic sighed. "Fine. I don't, but I've been told that multiple times."

"Without incentive?"

Dominic gave her the stink-eye.

"I'm only teasing." She giggled. She was giggling in Dominic Lark's presence. Life was full of surprises, it seemed.

"Not the kind of teasing I like."

Nova rubbed her hands together. "I'm not running any more lines. Venus has gone to bed for the night."

"Slacker," Dominic joked. "I'll get going then." He stood up and leaned over Nova to get his bag.

She froze when Dominic looked down at her as he threw his bag over his shoulder. His knee was placed firmly next to her thigh. Whatever was passing between them... it felt electric to Nova.

"Nova?!" The door flew open.

When Harper opened the door, she looked concerned. Her forehead was scrunched up with worry, and she was doing her little in-place jog, which only happened when she was nervous. "Camille's here. She's looking for Dom."

Dominic groaned and threw his head back. He got off the bed. "What does she want?"

"Um, she's sitting out in the living room, so you can just ask her yourself."

Nova wasn't scared of Camille, but she'd had enough drama for the night. "One night. I want *one* night of peace," she murmured and followed the other two out.

Camille was sitting on the corner of the couch with her legs crossed neatly. Her jeans fit her like a second skin, and her pink top, paired with her blonde hair, made her look like a barbie doll cosplay participant.

"Camille," Nova greeted her. "How can we help you?" She folded her arms.

"Where have you been? I was waiting for you at my place." Camille completely ignored her and didn't bother to answer her.

"I never said I was coming. Kyle told you I was because he's obsessed with you. Which you already knew because you use him to get to me all the time."

"Many people are obsessed with me, Dom. It's not my fault."

Nova couldn't hold in her snort. She slapped a hand to her mouth when Camille turned to her sharply, with disgust evident in her eyes.

"What are you doing *here* is my question, though."

"Nova called," Dominic said.

"Huh?" Nova turned to him. "You came here with pizza."

"*After* you called," he rebutted.

"I didn't ask—"

"Enough!" Camille stood up and took two steps closer to Nova. "I told you what would happen if you tried anything funny with him."

Dominic cleared his throat and smirked. "All right girls, as much as I love a good catfight, I need to go. Harper, be a doll and record this for me?" He gave her a side hug and left, not at all bothered by the way Camille was threatening Nova.

Camille glared at her after he left. "You've crossed the line."

"I don't know what line you're talking about. I didn't invite him."

"Sure, you didn't. You called him, though, didn't you? Dominic doesn't like desperate girls, Nova. They reek."

"Maybe that's why he preferred being here with me instead of with you, Camille. Your desperation is tangible," Nova said. She didn't know what came over her to make her say such a thing. Camille brought out the worst in her.

Camille's face turned beet red as she sputtered so angrily that she couldn't form words. Harper gently put a hand on her back and guided her to the door. "It's getting late. You should go."

When the tell-tale clicking of heels was out of earshot, Nova sagged and took a seat on her couch. "What am I going to do?"

"About what?" Harper closed the door and sat next to her friend.

She swallowed thickly before looking at Harper helplessly. "I think I like him," she admitted in a whisper.

"You what?!"

HARPER MADE THEM HOT CHOCOLATE, and Nova put an inordinate amount of whipped cream on top.

"I can't say I didn't see that one coming," Harper said.

"Of course, you didn't! We are supposed to hate each other. And, and he's insufferable and arrogant. He's not even a completely nice person!" She put her head between her hands. "I don't know why I'm feeling this way."

"You don't choose the people you like." Harper beamed.

"You didn't say that when I liked Andrew," Nova pointed out.

"That was different. Andrew gives off stalker vibes, but you and Dominic have natural chemistry."

Nova shook her head. "I am *not* doing this. I'm going to stop liking him, effective immediately."

Harper laughed. "Yeah, babe, if that worked, Romeo and Juliet wouldn't have had such a tragic ending."

"No. Dominic is all kinds of wrong for me."

"May I ask why?" Harper turned to her and looked at her with more calmness than she should, given the situation.

"Because we're so different. He's this rich guy, and the world is his oyster. And..." She fiddled with the handle of her cup. "I'm the scholarship student."

"So, what you're saying is, Camille is right and if you like Dominic, you should never do anything about it. Just back off, right?"

CHAPTER TWENTY-ONE

Nova hated that her friend was right.

"Do you think Dominic's worth the effort?"

Dominic may or may not be worth the effort; she couldn't be completely sure about that one, but she really liked their interactions when he wasn't being a jerk. "I don't know. I don't even understand where this is coming from."

Harper laughed. "Oh, to have a crush. Must be nice."

"Good to know someone's getting entertainment from my misery."

"What changed for you?"

Nova picked at the threads that were popping out of her t-shirt and shrugged. "I think... When he came to help me with Andrew. He'd just thrown me out of his place, and we were fighting, and he came down to get me—the look on his face when he protected me from Andrew. When I called him, not knowing what to say, he showed up with a box of pizza. He helped me practice for the play for *hours*, Harper. In those moments, it seemed that he might care about me. I mean, why would you do that if you were a bad person? So, then I started thinking maybe he wasn't the worst."

Harper's laughter was only a little annoying. Nova wanted someone who was just as horrified with the notion of her having a crush on Dominic as she was.

"I'm sorry." She put a hand on Nova's knee. "But if it's any comfort to you, I don't think Dominic feels any different. He came over with pizza for you. And you guys were in there for so long." Harper winked at her.

"I told you we were just running lines for the play." Nova really liked running lines with him. He was annoying with his snide comments, but there was something nice about that, too. "He might be warming up to me." Or she was delusional. None of her options were better than the other.

She'd forget all about him; he'd be out of sight and out of mind in no time because if that didn't happen, Nova was in big trouble. Bigger than any trouble she has been in so far.

Chapter Twenty-Two

Nova was miserable, all right. She couldn't seem to escape Dominic. Wherever she went, he was there. Standing in the hallway, sitting on the bench on her way around campus, everywhere.

"Is there a reason you see me and then look away like I'm Medusa and you'll turn into stone?" Dominic asked her.

He made her jump. She was on her way home from her rehearsal. "No. We don't stop for pleasantries. Not really *our* thing."

Dominic sucked his teeth and nodded. "Come over tonight."

Nova clenched her jaw and hoped that she wasn't blushing. He probably just wanted to argue some more about the assignment. "Will you throw me out again?"

"Maybe. But I'll walk you home, too." He smiled.

If the ground wanted to open up and swallow her whole, she wouldn't mind it. "I'll be there at six."

"Can it be later? I need to go to the gym."

Nova tried to get the image of Dominic working out to leave her head. "Sure. But we need to make it in time for dinner."

"No need, I'll order something."

"So, you're going to call all the shots?"

"No, never." He smirked. "You can decide if you want Chinese or Thai. I'm okay with both."

"Chinese."

"Smart girl." He put a hand on her back and patted it.

Nova felt a trail of goosebumps come alive on her skin. "Bye."

He waved at her and walked away in the opposite direction. *Dominic is not my type. I don't like being told what to do,* she tried to convince herself. She needed a long nap and a few moments of quiet before she went to his place.

SHE WAS GETTING ready to go to Dominic's house when she realized she probably needed to change. As she searched through her clothes, she realized what she was doing. She *didn't* need to look any better for Dominic. In fact, she was going to go as-is with her hair up in a messy bun and her shirt hanging off her shoulder. Whatever these new feelings were, they needed to leave.

On the walk there, Nova hoped she wouldn't run into Andrew. She knew he was smarter than to approach her, especially when he knew Dominic would sic the worst of his minions on him if he did.

The coast was clear, and Nova couldn't have felt more relieved. She knocked on Dominic's door, and he opened it. He was shirtless once again, but Nova found it a little harder to look away this time. Did she count an eight-pack?

"Come in." He made way for her and waved her to the couch. There were drinks on the coffee table, so he expected her to be on time. *Yet he couldn't find time to put on a shirt?*

He disappeared into his room and didn't come back out for a long time. Nova had taken her books out and started writing in her notebook. Dominic was still not willing to do music as their assignment, but Nova had enough material. And lately, her creative juices overflowed, leading her to start writing a song.

Dominic would nag her if he found out, probably would

demand she stop immediately, so she decided against telling him. "What are you doing?" he asked from over her shoulder. Thankfully, he was now wearing a shirt.

Nova shut her notebook as a reflex. "I was, uh, just working on something for my music class."

He nodded, but looked at her notebook intently. "Do you play any instrument?"

She shook her head. "I never got the chance."

"Want to try?" He picked up his guitar from next to the TV. He sat down next to her heavily and strummed aimlessly.

"Really?"

"I offered, didn't I?" He sounded a little annoyed, which was confusing since Nova thought they were past the point where her existence was a bane to his.

"Y-yes then. Show me how." She took the guitar from him and placed it on her lap. It was a big guitar, and it took almost all her space.

Dominic pulled it a little closer, making her move with the guitar. He asked Nova to place her fingers on the strings while he pressed on the notes. "Try strumming."

She did, and the music rang out flawlessly. She laughed. "I like that."

The boy looked at her and nodded. "Try again, but harder."

They went back and forth with the guitar, Nova strumming while Dominic pressed on different notes.

"Not bad," he said and put the guitar against the couch.

"My fingers hurt, though."

"It gets worse, which is why we have picks. I'll go get the food."

Nova bit her lip as she watched him leave. She thought she'd come here, he'd do his bit where he was mean to her, and just like that, Nova would stop feeling butterflies around him. But this was the exact opposite. She couldn't believe it, but she was hoping he'd be mean.

"What's taking you so long?" She'd gone to the kitchen to check on him when he didn't return.

"Plating the food." He was pouring out the orange chicken and noodles.

"We can eat out of the box; I don't mind."

He raised an eyebrow. "But I do. Were you raised in a barn?"

Nova fake laughed. "Aren't you funny?"

"It was a serious question. I don't know where you're from, so it's completely possible that you were actually raised in a barn."

"I'm not from a farm. City girl, believe it or not."

He looked at her from her feet to her head and then locked eyes with her. "I can see it." He put a plate in front of her on the counter. He'd equally divided all the dishes.

"Thank you."

He hummed and carried his plate to the couch while Nova followed. For the second day in a row, Nova found herself having dinner with Dominic. "Can you sing?" she asked. She knew he was musically inclined, but she'd never heard him sing. He had a deep voice, a good baritone, according to her. If he had training, he wouldn't be half bad.

"No," he replied curtly.

Nova didn't understand why he shied away from anything to do with music. "Sorry," she whispered and chewed on her food thoughtfully.

"I don't sing," he said after a beat, his voice a whole lot gentler. "I hadn't even touched my guitar until a few years ago."

"Why not?" Nova asked but realized that Dominic might not be in a sharing mood. "I'm sorry. You don't have to tell me."

Dominic chewed on his inner cheek. "My parents. They aren't very big on my love for music. They wanted me to take business administration so I can be like my father."

Nova knew what that was like. She was going to do finance until Atherton became an option for her. But she needed the money, and Dominic didn't. So he had no reason not to chase his dreams. "I'm sorry." She placed her plate on the coffee table. "I don't understand it; you probably wouldn't need to struggle as much. I'm sure your family has connections."

"They do. But I'm the eldest. It's my," he made air quotes with his fingers, "*destiny* to lead the business front after my dad. Can't really be a music artist and do that."

"I'm sorry."

"What for? It's not your fault." He picked up his and Nova's plate. Nova followed him to the kitchen and helped him clean up.

"Thanks for dinner." Nova leaned on the counter and stood with her arms folded. "Can we please talk about what we're going to do with our assignment?"

Dominic narrowed his eyes at Nova. "Have you noticed that every time you don't talk about the assignment, we don't fight?"

"It's not like I like fighting with you."

"With the number of times you bring it up, anyone would think otherwise. I told you, I'll come to you when I come up with something."

Nova comforted herself with the little music she had come up with on her own. If Dominic really had nothing, she'd submit the song for both of them. "The sooner, the better."

"Yeah, yeah, I get it."

They returned to the living room, but neither of them could concentrate on math.

"You don't have your lines, do you?" Dominic asked once they officially gave up.

Nova chuckled and nodded. She handed Dominic the sheet. She mostly had her lines memorized. "Why didn't you audition if you like the play so much? It was open to all majors."

"They'd find out and then guilt-trip me. I don't need that. Besides, I'd outshine everyone, and then people would complain about being in my shadow." He smiled wide. "It's not my fault I'm awesome. I'm sure I could get Mr. Bentley to like me, too." They both laughed.

Dominic offered to walk Nova home after they were done. "You don't have to walk me all the way. I'll be fine."

"I never said you wouldn't be. I want to walk anyway; we've been sitting around for too long."

Nova thanked him again once they reached her building. When she was inside her dorm, she closed the door and leaned her forehead against it. She'd expected to come back and feel some semblance of annoyance for the boy, but all she felt was bursting affection.

"Were you with Dominic?"

Nova jumped and turned immediately. "Andrew?! Why are you in my dorm?"

Chapter Twenty-Three

"How did you get in here?" Nova clutched the door handle, mentally prepared to make a run for it if needed.

"Harper let me in," Andrew said with his hands raised as if he meant no harm.

"That's right, she did." Camille walked out of the kitchen with a drink in her hand. "Sit." She nodded her head towards the couch.

Despite herself, Nova felt relief. She wasn't alone with Andrew. Harper stood behind them, looking guilt-ridden. Nova sat down and placed her bag next to her leg. "What's going on?"

"I was thinking about it," Camille said and sipped on her drink. "You told me once that we weren't enemies. Which is true, I don't think we are. Which is why I approached Andrew." She smiled at the boy, and Andrew stared back at her stonily.

He was hunched over himself and was blinking too rapidly.

"You should really consider yourself lucky, Nova. He really loves you." She kept smiling, and it was making Nova nauseous. Camille wasn't being nice. This was another one of her twisted schemes.

"Andrew, I told you. I don't want to hurt you. Why are you doing this?"

He looked up at her with red-rimmed eyes. "Because I love you, and you can't see it. There is nothing that Dominic can give you that I can't. I *respect* you."

"Scaring me in my own house and cornering me in your building isn't respect!" Nova stood up. "Camille, enough, okay? I don't want to do this. Dominic doesn't like you. He doesn't spare you a minute of his day, so why don't you both have some self-respect and leave us alone?"

"Self-respect?" Camille repeated, her eye twitching with anger.

"Yeah, do you know how pathetic it is to see you around Dominic when he doesn't even care whether you're in the room or not? You can have anyone you want, Camille; why are you embarrassing yourself like this?" She turned to face Andrew. "You knew I wouldn't change my mind, so why did you give in to her? It's time to move on."

Camille started clapping, and Nova rubbed her forehead with her fingers. "We're the pathetic ones when you're the one who keeps Dominic at the end of a leash?"

Nova couldn't stifle her laugh. "Dominic, on a leash? Do you hear yourself?"

Camille stood up; she slammed the glass in her hand on the coffee table, spilling its contents. "I tried, I really did, Nova." She came closer to her. "You know this what makes us?"

Nova glared back at her. She wished she could deny what Camille was saying like before by saying she didn't want anything to do with Dominic.

"*This* makes us enemies. And since you're so eager to find out what happens to my enemies, I'll give you a taste." She walked past her and slammed the door behind her.

"Andrew, I think y—" Harper started.

"Yeah, I know." He got up and left, too, not before standing by Nova for a minute. "I'll see you around," he said and left.

"I am *so* sorry." Harper ran to her and folded Nova into her arms. "I wanted to call you, but the two of them went on and on. Andrew always gave me the heebie-jeebies anyway."

Nova shook her head. "I should be the one apologizing. You're always getting stuck in these situations because of me. I'm really sorry."

"I can handle Camille, no problem. Andrew, on the other hand, is another matter. Anyway," she pulled away and smiled slyly, "how was your night with Dominic?"

Heat crept up Nova's face. "It was fine. He taught me how to play the guitar a little. And we didn't argue. Not once. Even after I brought up the assignment."

Harper squealed and bounced on her tippy-toes. "Oh my gosh, you two are so cute!"

Nova rolled her eyes but grinned along with her friend. But, boy, was she in trouble.

⁂

Nova stood in line for food when Camille cut in and stood in front of her. Nova didn't say anything. Camille swished her hair in Nova's face, and Nova still didn't say anything.

"It's a wonderful day, isn't it?" Camille asked the girl in front of her. Whoever she was, she was thrilled to be acknowledged by Camille.

"Y-yes, Camille. I love your shoes, by the way!"

"Thank you." She smiled at her and served herself the meatballs and spaghetti.

Nova put some on her own plate, not really paying attention since she was trying to figure out what Camille was up to.

Nova was going to exit the line when Camille smirked at her and put her leg forward.

Nova didn't have time to move out of the way; she'd already taken a step forward. Her foot got tangled with Camille's foot, and she tried to break her fall with her hands. The tray slipped out and dropped right under her.

While it did break her fall, Nova was covered in marinara sauce and meat. Whispers and giggles broke out in the cafeteria as everyone looked at her sorry state on the floor.

"Oh my goodness, Nova." Camille rushed to her, handing her tray over to the girl in front of her. She *tsked* and pulled out a handkerchief from her pocket. "You should watch where you're going. Don't want to fall into the wrong mess, do you?" She waved it over Nova's head.

"Thank you," Nova said sarcastically. She had chosen to wear her white pants today, and now they were a colossal mess. There was no saving them from marinara sauce. She collected all the stray noodles from her t-shirt and sat up.

"Dom." Camille's voice came from above her.

Nova was face to face with Dominic in the next second. He had crouched down to her level. "You okay?" He offered his hand to her.

"I'm sticky."

Dominic nodded. "Kyle, get her napkins. Now," he said to the boy standing behind him.

Kyle brought her the napkins, and Dominic helped her get rid of most of the sauce. Once she was on her feet, she thanked the green-eyed boy. He had beautiful eyes, Nova had noticed, but she found them prettier than ever. They had tiny gold flecks in them.

"I told her she shouldn't walk around with her head in the clouds." Camille put a hand on Dominic's bicep. "Move away, Dom. You'll get food on you."

Dominic shrugged her hand off. "Why don't you leave us alone, hmm?" He raised an eyebrow and turned back to Nova. "Can you walk?"

Nova nodded and looked between Camille and Dominic. "I'm okay. Just need to change out of this." She took off her flannel shirt, leaving her in her black tank top.

Camille eyed her, her nostrils flaring with resentment.

"I'll walk you to your place."

"She said she can walk fine on her own!" Camille yelled. She had her hands balled up in fists at her side, and her forehead was wrinkled because of the frown on her face.

"Did I ask you?" Dominic glared at her.

There was an audible, unanimous gasp in the cafeteria.

Camille sputtered in outrage as Dominic helped Nova up.

"Let's go." Dominic took the tray from Nova's dripping hands and set it aside.

"Dom!" Camille called after him, but Dominic didn't look back.

On their way to Nova's dorm, Nova couldn't help but stare at him. He was so... calm. "You shouldn't have done that. Camille—"

Dominic sighed. "You're covered in red sauce; you look like a murder crime scene, and what you care about is Camille's feelings being hurt?"

"I don't care about her hurt feelings. But people are going to make a big deal out of this."

"People make a big deal out of everything. I changed my cologne last week and that was the talk of the school."

Nova smiled despite herself. Dominic was being... caring. She wasn't sure if she wanted more or wanted him to stop. When they reached her room, Dominic offered to throw her clothes in the washer immediately while she showered.

Somehow Nova made it through the whole ordeal without blushing from head to toe. Her shower filled with fog, and she wondered what Dominic was doing outside. Could he have left? It wouldn't be like him, but he was too unpredictable for her to be sure.

He was in the kitchen when Nova came out.

"I thought we could eat sandwiches. I'd order a pizza, but it would take forever to get here." He cut the sandwich diagonally and placed it in front of Nova. "Your clothes are in the washer."

Nova chuckled. "There's no way those pants are ever going to be white again. I've made my peace with that."

"Couldn't you have been more careful?" he asked as he opened the fridge to pour orange juice for the both of them.

Nova blushed yet again. She didn't know why the universe was doing this to her, but she kind of preferred it when Dominic was being a jerk. At least she had comebacks to his taunts. She didn't know what to say to the person who was serving her lunch and looking like a Vogue model while doing it. "I didn't know she was going to trip me."

"It's Camille. You should assume she's going to do something crazy whether she will or not."

They both ate and sipped on their juice until Nova broke the silence. "Thank you. You could have just as easily joined them and laughed at me instead of helping me."

Dominic looked at her, and Nova felt herself wanting to shy away from his gaze. But she didn't. "I won't do that to you," he said after a beat.

Nova had to look away. He said that he wouldn't do that to her like she had actually made it to his list of exceptions. Not that she wanted to be on it or anything, but it made her giddy regardless.

"Do you want to practice your lines?" Dominic asked once they put away the dishes.

"Uh, can we not? I'm not really feeling like Venus right now."

"What then?"

"I was going to go to the library. I have a couple of assignments to catch up on."

Dominic bit his inner cheek and nodded. "Let's do them here. I don't like the library. No one leaves you alone in the *one* place they are supposed to."

"Okay, I'll clear the coffee table." Nova realized that she and Harper were a little more than messy, and it showed whenever they had company over unexpectantly. She'd been over to Dominic's twice, and the place had been spotless. Dominic did seem like the type of person who liked to keep everything clean.

Nova started with economics which was very much the bane

of her existence. She thought that math would be her most hated subject thanks to her partner, but ever since Dominic had lightened up, she'd started enjoying math.

Dominic must have noticed the way she was struggling with her work because of her constant sighing. "What are you working on?"

"Economics. I don't get how the graphs work."

Dominic put down his laptop and put his hand out for Nova's book. He read it for a minute before nodding. "This is the basic stuff; you'll get it. Come here." He looked at her expectantly, and Nova bit her lip.

She scooted closer to him and tried to keep their thighs from touching.

"I won't bite if that's what you're worried about."

Nova giggled, like honest to goodness giggling, and she felt a tinge of embarrassment. She was actually giggling over a boy. The same boy that she couldn't stand for longer than a minute just a week ago. "Sorry."

Dominic shook his head, and Nova thought she detected a hint of fondness in his gaze. She couldn't be sure because her head was all over the place. It turned out that Dominic was an excellent teacher.

"Do you need me to explain that again?" he asked her and put down the pencil.

Nova shook her head. She did lose focus because of the way her pencil looked in his hands. He had really nice hands. Nova didn't even think she had ever noticed or *liked* someone's hands. But luckily, she had listened enough to understand. "Thank you. I don't like economics."

"Me either."

"But you're good at it."

Dominic smirked. "I make it a point to be good at everything I do."

Nova smirked. "So, you don't sing because you're bad at it. Hmm, I wondered why that was."

"Okay, so I stop being a jerk and you start being one?"

She shrugged a shoulder and tried not to focus on his soft smile. "You rubbed off on me, I guess."

"I suppose I did." He closed his laptop. "Uh," he cleared his throat, "Andrew hasn't been bothering you again, has he?"

Nova couldn't stop the smile from splitting her face. "No. He's just sticking to intense glaring from afar."

"I can stop that, too."

"You're a very confusing guy, Dominic Lark," Nova whispered, not realizing she'd said it aloud.

"Excuse me?"

Nova blinked rapidly and shook her head. "Sorry, I didn't mean to say that."

"What did you mean by it?"

"N-nothing. It's just mumbling; ignore me."

Dominic threw the pillow from the couch at her. "Tell me. Right now."

She shook her head; she was not going to be discussing this with him. He could draw all the conclusions he wanted, but no matter how much she liked him, she wouldn't tell him.

"Tell me now, or I'm going to tell everyone we kissed."

"What!?" Nova sputtered. She looked at him and detected a hint of mischief in his eyes. Relief flooded through her veins. "Ugh, you're the worst." She threw the pillow back at him.

"It's not an empty threat."

Nova rolled her eyes. "I don't buy it. Can we not talk about this anymore?"

Dominic leaned closer with a sly smile.

"What are you doing?" Nova whispered.

Dominic didn't stop until they were sitting closer than when he was trying to teach her. Nova swallowed audibly and tried to look anywhere but his face.

He knows I like him, doesn't he? Nova thought frantically.

"Dominic?" Nova knew her face was red. Someone had gone

and told Dominic about her feelings, and now he was making fun of her.

"Tell me," he said softly while looking right into her eyes.

"I said you were confusing because you're nice one minute and a jerk the next." All words came out in a rush, and she was shocked by her compliance. It made her mad. She finally came to her senses and pushed him away, and thankfully, he went willingly.

Dominic still had a smug smile. "Works every time."

Nova gritted her teeth and shook her head. "I'm no longer confused. You're a jerk." She got up to leave in a fit when Dominic caught her wrist.

"Sorry, I'm sorry." He laughed and pulled her down.

She continued frowning despite the fact that Dominic seemed to be having the time of his life.

"What? I already apologized."

"I know. I want an explanation on your mood swings, though, since you forced that out of me."

Dominic took a deep breath and cracked his knuckles. Nova knew this was new for him, too.

"I now know that you're not as annoying as I thought you would be." Dominic bit the inside of his cheek. "I think you actually have talent, and Atherton was right to give you the scholarship."

Nova didn't know what to say. She expected him to tease her and maybe give her an unrealistic answer, but he seemed like he was being honest. The last thing she needed from him was transparency. It only meant falling harder for him. "T-thank you."

"You look surprised," he said. They were still in close proximity, and Nova accidentally knocked Dominic's foot with her own.

"I don't know. I guess I didn't expect for us to stop being... enemies?" She laughed. "Isn't that what we were?"

Dominic joined her in her laughter. "I think so. I have a lot of those. My parents are at the top of my list."

"I'm sorry about that, you know. I had no idea it was that hard."

He shrugged, and Nova was afraid she might have said the wrong thing. "You're doing great, though!" She knew some people didn't like displays of pity. "You're really good at... everything. And Harper told me you were valedictorian."

"I was." He smirked again. "You talk about me?"

Nova scoffed. "I whine about you more like."

"Whine about my perfect face and unbelievable physique?" He draped his arm over the back of the couch, causing his fingers to hang over Nova's shoulder.

"Your perfect capability to drive me up the wall," she said, slightly leaning forward.

Dominic rolled his eyes. "What are the chances that we've gone viral on campus?"

Nova had forgotten about the cafeteria scene. "Right. I would guess so. We have more pictures together than I have with Harper."

"They're good pictures."

"What?"

"The ball pictures. They're good pictures in spite of the circumstances."

"Even though I was in the wrong dress, you mean." Nova folded in on herself. She loved her dress, and given the chance, she'd do it all over again, but it would have been nice to hear that she looked good in it.

"No, I meant because I asked you to dance out of spite." Dominic looked at her with soft eyes.

Nova bit her lip and concentrated on her breathing.

"It was easier for you to dance in what you were wearing anyway. Most girls can't see their own feet and end up stepping on mine."

That made her laugh. She guessed that was the closest thing she would get to a compliment.

"You look funny on this one." He showed her a picture of herself covered in sauce and spaghetti.

"Can you send that to me? Sky's going to love it."

Dominic gave her a funny look and narrowed his eyes. "Your sister's going to like the fact that a mean girl tripped you?"

"She wouldn't know that. I'm a clumsy girl, so it wouldn't be farfetched for me to fall. Camille might have actually saved me the embarrassment of tripping over nothing."

"You don't look clumsy," he said, looking down into his phone.

Nova's phone pinged with the text notification from Dominic. "What do you mean?"

Dominic shrugged a shoulder. "You have a graceful walk; you glide across the stage. That isn't exactly a trait of a clumsy person."

Her face felt hot, and she did everything in her power to keep a straight face. "Uh, thank you?"

"You can't dance to save your life, though." Dominic shook his head. "Good thing there aren't any big dance routines in the musical, or you would be in serious trouble."

"You're allergic to being nice," Nova said teasingly.

"Only for you." He winked at her.

Nova *had* to figure out how to keep her face from stretching into a goofy grin every time Dominic pulled stunts like this. She didn't even recognize herself in these moments.

HARPER WAS NO HELP. She was a ball of giggles and smug smiles. "I can't believe this is real life. I *love* living with you!"

"I can't do this anymore," Nova whined. "He got annoyed before he left, and I wanted to kick myself for asking if he came up with a topic for math. I used to enjoy annoying him. What's happening to me?"

"I know!" she squealed, "I wish you two were dating already. It's so obvious he likes you."

"Right. Dominic Lark likes me. Pigs are flying somewhere, too."

"Oh, shut up. I've seen the way he looks at you. And he said that you looked beautiful at the ball."

Nova's mouth hung open. "He did not say that. He probably thought his face looked good when he complimented the pictures. He's full of himself." She folded her arms and wished she could mean the words like she used to.

"Maybe. *But* maybe not." She smirked. "I'm inviting him this weekend, too. He's going to play the guitar for you again."

She greeted that statement with silence. Dominic could play the guitar for her anytime he wanted.

"Have you told him about the song you're writing for math?"

Nova scratched her head. "Not yet. But I will." She would have told him already, but they had been doing so well and she didn't want to mess things up.

"I think you should do it soon."

"I will. Maybe once the song is done." She was still skeptical about it, considering how much Dominic was against singing. He wouldn't appreciate Nova doing the exact opposite of what he wanted.

Ms. Hart asked Nova to stay back after class.

"Do you need a new partner?" she asked her.

Nova's eyebrows rose to her hairline. "No, no. We're okay."

"Oh, good. So you two have decided on a topic, then?"

"Uh…" She looked away from her teacher. "Kind of. We have an unspoken agreement," she made up.

Ms. Hart smiled at her. "I see you've learned to be patient with him. That's good. Do you need any help?"

"I might?" She knew Ms. Hart was to be trusted. "Do you know why Dominic doesn't sing?"

"Ah." Her teacher folded her arms and leaned against the table. "Have you talked to him about it?"

"I've brought it up, but it didn't go down too well."

"I'm not sure why, but Dominic doesn't like... well, he likes to show off, but not things worth showing off."

Nova didn't know what to do with that information, but it was good to know he *could* sing. She knew it; he sounded good while talking, so it would only make sense for him to be good at singing too. That logic sounded good, anyway. She'd just have to convince him to sing the song with her once she was finished with it.

Chapter Twenty-Four

Nova and Dominic had started the habit of spending their time outside of classes together.

"I've been trying to reach you since morning," Dominic said as he placed his tray next to Nova's and sat down.

"Oh, uh, I was in the library. I have a test tomorrow," she lied. She needed time away from him to work on their song. Luckily, her afternoon was more productive than she had expected. She was almost done, and Ms. Hart had offered to look over it for her.

"For?"

"Uh, economics."

Dominic raised one eyebrow. "Right, I could have helped. I have a management class assignment I need to work on."

Harper elbowed her and smiled; Nova glared at her and mouthed a 'shut up.' "Sorry. I'm planning to head back there after my rehearsal. If you want, you can come."

"To your rehearsal?"

Nova turned to him. "Uh, no? I meant to the library after."

"I want to be at the rehearsal, though. I'll see you at the theater."

"Okay, your majesty." Nova rolled her eyes. "You're unbelievable."

"That's the public opinion, yes."

"Be ready to tell Mr. Bentley why you're there. He threw Andrew out."

Dominic turned to Nova sharply. "Andrew? He's been bothering you again? Why is this the first time I'm hearing this?"

"Woah, calm down. I didn't know it happened until Riley told me about it. I haven't seen him except in passing."

"Fine." Dominic flexed his jaw in annoyance. "I'll handle Bentley, don't worry about it."

"I'm not worried."

"You two really are something," April said from where she sat across from them. "If I didn't know any better, I'd say you two were together."

"Me with Nova?" Dominic scoffed. "Not when you're sitting right in front of me." He winked at April.

Nova's mood soured, and she tried not to let it show. She knew Dominic was only mindlessly flirting, but the way he disregarded the idea of them being together didn't sit right with her.

"Okay, Dominic, that's enough." Harper gave him a look, and Dominic smiled at her.

"I was kidding." He stood up. "See you later, Scott."

Nova nodded and watched him leave. "I hate him," she muttered, obviously not meaning a word of it.

"I think he likes spending time with you," April said, her eyes still stuck to Dominic's retreating figure.

"He likes having someone to make fun of."

"He has a lot of people to do that with," Harper said. "Just yesterday, he spent a long time bothering Kyle."

Nova raised an eyebrow. "How do you know? You two talk often?"

Harper chewed and nodded. "Sometimes. We have mutual... friends."

"Okay..." Nova had more questions, but she needed to get to rehearsal. There was a costume fitting today, too, so she was a little excited. Their costumes at Atherton were of the highest quality.

She'd probably have another dress to add to her small collection once the play was done. Scarlett would love it.

DOMINIC WAS ALREADY in the crowd when she arrived at the theater; he was talking to Mr. Bentley.

"You're late, Nova," the teacher said through gritted teeth.

"Sorry, sir." She wasn't late, she was right on time, but Mr. Bentley liked for them to arrive before time.

"We'll be starting from the third scene today."

Nova began to warm up and tried to remember her lines.

"Where is David?" Mr. Bentley asked.

"He can't come today. He has an exam tomorrow."

Mr. Bentley took a deep breath and balled his hands into fists. "Then why is Will not here? Isn't he the understudy? How are we supposed to work without the male lead?"

"Dominic can do it," Nova said. She immediately regretted it because of the way Dominic looked at her. "He's been practicing with me, so he knows the lines. Most of them anyway." She kept shooting herself in the foot.

Their teacher turned to Dominic. "Fine. Get on stage, Dominic."

"No. I don't want to be today's show pony. I'm fine where I am."

Nova shook her head to herself. She just wanted to know why Dominic was so against a little bit of singing. He clearly understood music.

"Either get on stage or get out of my theater." The man folded his arms and pinned Dominic with a glare.

"Yeah, I didn't want to be here anyway." Dominic picked up his bag and left, but not before sending a death glare Nova's way. Once again, Nova had created another problem for herself.

MR. BENTLEY WAS brutal after Dominic left. He had an issue with anything and everything. Nova felt bad for what was coming David's way at the next rehearsal.

Nova had texted Dominic three times, but there was no reply. She had just wanted him to participate and know what it was like to be part of the real thing. He obviously liked playing the part because he always volunteered to rehearse the lines with her.

"What's wrong? Why aren't you at the library with Dom?" Harper asked when Nova came home earlier than she'd said she would.

"I might have messed up a little."

She explained the situation to Harper and watched as she grimaced.

"He's being dramatic. He'll calm down, don't worry."

Nova put her head in her hands. "I don't know how to explain it to him." She just wanted him to enjoy the moment without having to commit the character.

"I'll find out where he is so you can go make up. Take some food with you; he's partial to pizza. Oooh, maybe get some from that place he loves." Harper picked up her phone and scrolled through her chats.

"Wait, Harp." In the midst of all of this, Nova really never understood how Harper knew *so* much. "How do you know all this? Like, you *always* know what Dominic is up to. And he sits here and talks to you like you guys are best friends. Are you?"

Harper sighed and bit her lip. "No, it's not like that. It's nothing really."

Nova tilted her head and looked at her friend. "You're not telling me something."

"No!" Harper shook her head. "I'm just really into the gossip, and Dom's, you know –"

"Harper." Nova folded her arms. "What's going on?"

Harper sighed and turned to Nova. "Okay, but promise me you won't get mad."

Nova nodded, hoping she was able to keep that promise.

CHAPTER TWENTY-FOUR

"We're cousins."

"What?!" Nova's eyes bugged out of their sockets.

"Hear me out." Harper raised her hands, asking her friend to calm down.

"No." Nova shook her head. "What does that even mean?!"

"We really are cousins."

Nova was profoundly surprised. When thinking back at all the signs, it all made sense. Dominic was comfortable around Harper, they seamlessly got along, and Harper always knew where or what Dominic was doing. Not just anyone could have gotten Dominic to play the guitar for her. "You're a Lark?! Harper, I thought you were a Jones?!" Nova started to pace because of the information overload.

"I am! I am Harper Jones. He's my maternal cousin. His mom and mine are sisters."

"Why the heck am I just finding this out?!"

"Because I never tell anyone." Harper blew air out of her mouth and tucked a stray hair behind her ears. "Will you please sit down? I'll explain everything, I promise."

Nova sat down but couldn't stop her leg from shaking.

"Okay, so now you know Dominic and I are cousins. And..." Harper groaned, "I've never really had to explain it to anyone before because practically no one knows. I never tell people that the Larks and I are related because it makes it harder to make friends. Back in middle school, people knew, and it was terrible. It was like they were scared of me or something. So then I stopped telling people after I changed schools for high school. Once no one had any idea we were related, I started making more friends, and people actually got to know *me* and like me."

"Harp, what happened?"

"Being related to the Larks isn't exactly easy. They have a reputation, and people clam up every time they find out that we're related. They think they need to behave a certain way and nit-pick their words, and it got really annoying. I like getting to know people without them knowing my connections."

Nova nodded. "I just can't believe you didn't tell me! I told you I liked him!"

Harper squeezed her eyes shut and covered her face. "I know. I really wanted to tell you. But I haven't told anyone since I started hiding it. I'm really sorry." She put a hand on Nova's. "I really am."

Everything Harper said made a lot of sense, but Nova still felt hurt. She had trusted Harper with her secret, but Harper didn't trust her with hers.

"You have to know I didn't mean to do this. I honestly never expected you two to get close."

"Neither did I! But I told you when we did, and you should have done the same."

Harper sighed. "I'm really sorry."

There was a heavy silence for the next couple of minutes, neither of them knowing what to say.

"Look at it this way. If you'd known Dominic was my cousin, would you have been my friend? Or would we only be room-mates? You would've never given me a chance!"

"That's not true."

"Yes, it is." Harper chewed on her bottom lip. "It's easy to say that right now because you *know* me, but you would have never been friends with me had you known. Especially after the stunt Dom pulled in the theater. Which I gave him an earful for, by the way."

Nova closed her eyes and laid her head back. "I understand what you're saying, but... you were my first friend, Harp. This is huge, and I don't know how to deal with it."

"For what it's worth, Nova, I love being your friend, and I know Dom really well, like *really* well. I know his deepest darkest secrets." She winked at Nova.

"I know that now."

"Hey, I owe you one for doing this, so let me help you make it up to him, okay?"

Nova folded her lips inward and nodded. She didn't want to

lose Harper's friendship and Harper did seem sincere. "Okay," Nova said as she ran her fingers through her hair, "Do you know why he doesn't sing?"

"Uh..." Harper nodded awkwardly. "I don't know how much I can tell you without being rude to Dom."

She was right, it wouldn't be fair, and it was wrong to use Harper like that. "I know, sorry."

"I can tell you that Dom's really a sweetheart underneath the jerk exterior. He's just a little hard to crack. But I love him, so he has to be awesome."

Nova cracked a small smile. "I'll take your word for it. People really don't know?"

Harper shook her head. "They just assume that I'm friendly with him because I'm friendly with everyone."

"I guess that makes sense. Okay, what do I need to do to get him to reply to my texts?"

"Food. I'll order his favorites, and you just show up with them. He'll calm down."

"Are you sure?"

Harper nodded. "If he doesn't, just text me; I'll straighten him out."

Nova laughed. "Okay, it's worth a try."

⁂

Harper had gone overboard ordering the food. There was way more food than for two people, but Harper assured Nova that Dominic would accept the peace offering.

Nova stood stiff and rigid outside Dominic's door with the food when he finally opened the door.

He looked at her, and Nova felt a pang of hurt when it seemed he was looking right through her.

"What do you want?"

"I got pizza and garlic bread." She swung the bag, drawing attention to it.

The branding on the bag must have done the trick because Dominic took the bag out of her hand and walked toward the living room. He had left the door open instead of throwing it shut in her face.

"What do you want?" Dominic repeated, too busy opening the pizza box to look at Nova.

"I'm sorry. About the rehearsal."

Dominic chomped on the slice, his eyes focused on her face. "Are you?"

"I just wanted you to enjoy the moment, that's all. I didn't mean to upset you," Nova said, and when Dominic didn't reply, she went to the kitchen and got him a drink.

Dominic watched her place the drink in front of him. "What are you doing?"

"Apologizing. You might not be familiar with the gesture." Nova smiled, trying Dominic's own technique with the ill-timed teasing.

He ate, and they sat in silence until he looked at her and back at the box, wordlessly asking her to eat, too.

Nova smiled and tore off a slice. Harper was right; he was melting. Slowly but surely.

"Don't do that again. I don't sing, period. I don't do it when it's just the two of us, so what makes you think I'd do it in front of people? And now, because of you, Mr. Bentley is mad at me."

"If it helps, he was a nightmare to me after you left. He even told me I walked funny when I was leaving the theater. I didn't know his criticism extended to my life, too."

That made Dominic laugh, and Nova felt herself relax.

"How did you know to buy this stuff?" Dominic asked.

"Uh, Harper told me." Nova wiped her fingers and sat more comfortably on the couch.

"She did?" Dominic raised an eyebrow.

Nova nodded. "I was wondering how she knows so much about you. I didn't think you two were friends."

"Harper is friends with everyone."

"Enough to know your pizza order and your favorite place too? Her brain must be filled with pizza places then if it extends to everyone."

"Um, yeah, I guess. She's really attentive and sh—"

Nova burst out laughing. "Sorry." She put a hand up to stop him while she covered her mouth with her other. "Sorry." She tried to control herself; Dominic was really trying to keep their secret. "I'm just joking with you. I know she's your cousin."

Dominic's response would've made someone think *he* was just finding out Harper was his cousin. His eyes went wide, and the pizza was close to falling from his hand. "H-how do you know?"

"She obviously told me."

"No." Dominic shook his head. "She *told* you?"

"Um, duh. How else would I know?"

"Wow." Dominic gave Nova a once over. "Unbelievable. Harper's never told anyone before."

"Yeah, I know. She explained that to me."

Dominic nodded. "She must really trust you. She's been hiding this since we were kids."

"I felt bad when she told me. No one should hide their cousins, especially not the ones they like."

"Perks of being a Lark," Dominic muttered. "I would hide it too if I could."

Nova saw his face morph into regret. "Don't say that. Family is important, even when you're not getting along."

Dominic rolled his eyes. "You don't understand what I have to deal with. My mother called today asking why I was in the theater."

"What?! How could she have possibly known?"

The boy shrugged. "Someone must have seen me there. She has her people all over campus. They aren't too nosy, so that's a relief. They give her some information here and there to keep her happy and leave me to it nine times out of ten."

"That's unfair." Nova said, "Sorry, but it is. You're a legal adult."

Dominic chuckled. "Yeah, I am. But there are some luxuries *you* can't afford and some that *I* can't."

Nova was shocked by the admission. "I guess that's true." She played with her fingers. "Is that... does your mother have something to do with you never singing?"

Dominic shook his head, his face neutral. Nova was expecting him to be annoyed with her prying. "She is and isn't. It's not all that simple."

"Are you done with your management assignment?" Nova asked.

"Uh, yes?" Dominic seemed surprised at the sudden change in subject.

"Oh, good then. We have time. Since your answer isn't all that simple."

Dominic smirked. "What makes you think I'll tell you?"

"We can either discuss that or our math assignment. You can take your pick."

"Right, so I was thinking carpentry. I think it's a perfect match. Measurements and volume, and of course the –" Dominic went on, and Nova felt sick.

Dominic had gone and chosen the worst possible topic, hadn't he? Maybe it wasn't too late to talk to Ms. Hart about a change of partners.

"You can't be serious!"

Dominic laughed. "I wish you could see your face."

Nova broke out of her horror. "I can't believe you're considering *carpentry*. Out of all things."

Dominic continued to laugh and wiped a fake tear from his eye. "Your face." He put a hand on her thigh mid-laughter, and Nova felt shivers run down her spine.

Even if carpentry wasn't something she'd *ever* want to do, Dominic's amusement made it worth the exploration. "You're going to find all the articles if we're doing carpentry."

"We are *not* doing carpentry. I enjoy messing with you but not at my own expense."

"Oh, thank God." She put a hand on her chest and tried her best to ignore the fact that Dominic's hand was still on her thigh. "What are we doing then?"

"My mother and father are both... strict. A little difficult," Dominic started.

Nova braced herself; Dominic was opening up to her. Harper was right, and she might as well forgive her if she could get to know the boy a little bit better.

"Ever since I was young, I had many tutors. *Many.* One for every subject. I haven't gotten anything below an A in my life, and I had very little to do with it. I did start to crave being the best after it was drilled in my head, but... it was always more out of obligation than my own will. And I never had a moment of peace. It was from one class to another. I almost drowned a couple of times during swimming because I was taking too long to catch on, so they thought survival would kick in if I was thrown into the deep end."

"Dom..."

Dominic shook his head. "Please don't say you're sorry. I don't need it."

"I wasn't going to say sorry."

The boy quirked an eyebrow and waited for Nova to continue.

"I was going to say that your parents don't know how to treat their children. No offense, but that's downright disgusting."

Dominic laughed. "I see why Harper likes you."

Nova's breath got caught in her throat. "Did you not have music classes growing up?"

The laughter disappeared from his face as soon as Nova mentioned music. "I did. For about a year. It was the only class I went to without a fuss."

"Good. At least you enjoyed something."

"I did. That is until they found out that I did. I don't remember exactly because it happened so long ago, but I think I threw a massive fit about something, and they stopped sending me. I thought they were bluffing, so I continued being stubborn. Guess they were not." Dominic swallowed heavily, and Nova wanted nothing more than to hug him. She wanted to offer comfort, but there were no words coming to mind.

"You don't have to look so sad about it. I never said I made life easy for them. Once they took away music from me, I had nothing more to lose. I find reasons to mess with them all the time. There is very little they have to hold over my head. Of course, I have help sometimes too." He winked, reminding Nova of the ball.

Nova smiled at that. "I'm happy to have contributed to that."

Dominic smirked. "They were a little mad about that, but only because Camille droned on about how I didn't dance with her."

"Are your families close? Yours and Camille's, I mean."

"It's business, nothing else. They benefit from each other, so they bear with each other's companies. The day there is no more profit, we'll be perfect strangers."

"Is that how it always works?"

Dominic nodded. "Yeah. My father always says to think with your head and not your heart."

Nova bit her lip and looked into her lap. Her father had the opposite advice.

"I'm making them seem like horrible parents." Dominic said, "They have their moments of kindness. My brothers are very happy. And I'm taken care of."

"Your mother has people stalking you, Dom. You don't have to defend them. Material things are just that, material."

"I'm not defending. My situation is very different from my brothers. I'm the eldest; it comes with responsibility. It could have easily been Jake, Landon, Matt, or Tristian. But it was me. My parents didn't choose for me to be the first. They want to ensure our family wealth doesn't fall into strangers' hands because I'm incapable of handling it."

Nova had to admit that Dominic was more mature than she

ever gave him credit for. He was making the best out of his situation. "That's very... unlike Dominic of you to say." She giggled.

"I know. I'm very unlike Dominic with you... it's starting to become a problem for me," he said in low tones.

Nova's hands started to tremble a little, and she had to squeeze them to stop.

"Can you sing, though?" Nova asked.

Dominic shook his head and chuckled. "You do not know when to give up, do you?"

"Don't you think that the best way to spite your parents is to enjoy your love for music? You don't have to become an international pop star, and you don't have to write albums. You can become a businessman *and* do what you love."

"Can I?"

Nova smiled softly and scooted a little closer. "You can do anything you want. You're Dominic Lark, remember?" The last bit came out in a whisper, unlike her intention.

Dominic looked at her, and for the first time Nova felt like he was *seeing* her. It shouldn't have made her as happy as it did.

Nova felt goosebumps litter her skin when she felt like Dominic was leaning toward her. She felt drunk on her roller-coaster of feelings, so she wasn't sure if she was imagining it. She held still, which took a lot more effort than it should. This was more unnerving than performing in front of a large crowd. She could almost feel his breath on her skin.

A knock sounded at the door and Dominic flinched away and was on his feet in a second. He opened the door, and Nova could see a head of perfect blonde hair through the space over Dominic's shoulder.

"Camille." Dominic said, "What are you doing here?"

"I didn't see you in the cafeteria for dinner, so I thought I'd check on you."

The calmness in Camille's voice indicated that she hadn't seen Nova yet.

"I'm fine, as you can see. You can go back now." Dominic was about to close the door, but Camille stepped in.

"I don't understand why you're still—" Camille's eyes finally landed on Nova. "Oh."

"Hey," Nova said, not sure what to do under Camille's scrutinizing gaze.

"What the heck is she doing here?" Camille turned to Dominic, her dress swishing along with her movements.

"That's none of your business. So now, if you could leave, that would be great," Dominic said from where he was still holding the door wide open.

"Dominic, do you have any idea what you're doing? Any idea of what would happen if people found out you were together? Your name would be drug through the mud."

"Enough! It's none of your business, and stop coming to my place unannounced. In fact, don't come anymore at all. You're not invited here, ever."

Camille started sobbing.

Nova watched it all unfold in front of her eyes, and she couldn't find it in herself to feel bad for the girl.

"I can't believe you're doing this to me. For *her*."

"She and I are not together, not that it's any of your business. Now, get out."

Camille wiped her tears, and Nova wondered how none of her makeup was running. It also stung a little to hear Dominic insist on the fact that they weren't together. Especially not when they were about to kiss, or at least Nova thought so.

"You'll regret this, Dom." She ran out of the apartment, leaving the door open after her.

Dominic shut the door and turned back to Nova.

"I think we're done here; I should be getting back." Nova picked up her things.

"Nova, I—"

"It's fine. I'll, uh, I'll see you around." She left, closing the door behind her softly. She wanted to slam it closed, but she didn't want to give Dominic the satisfaction of knowing he riled her up.

Harper was excited to know how well her plan went, so it meant Dominic hadn't told her anything about the end of their night.

"It was fine. He was in a much better mood after he saw the food."

Harper beamed. "Good. And? Did anything happen?"

"No, no. Why would it? I had just gone there to apologize."

"Nova, you were there for a while; obviously, it wasn't just pizza that occupied your time."

"We just talked a little about his childhood. He said he would hide the fact that he was a Lark, too, if he could."

"He's a good guy."

Nova nodded. "Yeah, I know. He is."

"Then why are you upset? Was it something he said? Nova, he says stupid things all the time; it's a twisted defensive mechanism."

"Harp, really, he didn't say anything. I'm tired, and I still need to finish our math assignment. It turns out I'm doing it all on my own, after all. He didn't call you or anything, right? I mean after I left?"

Harper shook her head. "I haven't spoken to him since you got there."

She either got the message or really believed what Nova was telling her because she left her alone.

Nova was lying in bed, wide awake. She had been trying to go to sleep for the past hour, but she couldn't. Her brain replayed her conversation with Dominic. The little time that he spent with her being real was amazing. But he shied away from the accusation of being with Nova like one would for a heinous crime.

She wasn't expecting her phone to light up with a text from Dominic. She sat up, her pillow falling off the bed because of the unexpected movement.

DOMINIC

Are you awake?

Nova had half a mind not to reply. She didn't need to do this with him right now, not when her emotions clouded her judgment.

Maybe it was the clouding of her judgment that made her reply.

NOVA

Yes.

The typing bubble came instantly, as though Dominic was waiting for Nova to reply.

DOMINIC

Why did you leave like that? I didn't like it.

His response confused Nova. What did he even mean?

NOVA

What do you mean? It had gotten late.

DOMINIC

You were perfectly fine before Camille got there. If it's something she said, you should know better than to take her words to heart.

Nova groaned; of course this oaf had no idea that it wasn't Camille that had upset her.

NOVA

I'm not mad at Camille.

Dominic didn't reply after that, and that made Nova madder. She wasn't going to think about it anymore. Which only made her think about it harder.

Chapter Twenty-Five

Nova woke up to a very heavy hand on her shoulder. Harper was never that rough.

"The heck?! Do you take sleeping pills?!"

Waking up to see Dominic's face was the last thing Nova expected. She had gotten about four hours of sleep, so she definitely wasn't hallucinating. "What?" She looked around for her phone when Dominic handed it to her.

"I got breakfast as a thank you for dinner. Harper's waiting in the kitchen." he said as he walked out of her room.

As she got dressed, Nova couldn't help thinking about how Dominic pretended like they hadn't texted last night.

Harper was already eating with Dominic when Nova came into the kitchen. They'd set a plate aside for her.

"Morning." Harper greeted, "Dominic got us your favorite."

"I wonder how he knew." Nova smirked and cut into her chocolate chip pancake.

Harper laughed. "You know, I love that I don't have to hide the fact that we're related from you. It's so much easier to be comfortable around him." She bumped shoulders with Dominic.

Nova hummed and refused to meet Dominic's eyes.

"I still can't believe you told her, though."

"It was only right."

Dominic looked up from his food. "Why?"

"Because she li—"

"Because I'm your math partner," Nova interrupted. Her blood ran cold thinking about what would have happened had Harper finished that sentence.

Harper realized her mistake and immediately nodded. "Yes, yeah. She, um, she's your partner, so she should know."

Dominic narrowed his eyes at his cousin. "You have friends that you've had for years and haven't told them, but she gets to know because we have math together?"

"I like Nova, okay? I trust her. Besides, now there will be two people laughing their butts off when someone asks why you won't ever hit on me," Harper said.

Dominic looked at her with more suspicion, but Harper didn't crack under pressure. "Fine. I'll find out one way or another." He went back to eating and looked at Nova.

Nova continued to ignore the fact that Dominic was in the room with her.

⁂

"Is there a reason for this?" Dominic asked once Harper left to get ready.

"For what?" Nova loaded the dishwasher and walked around Dominic, not paying attention to his staring.

"Listen, I have no idea what I did, so if you could just tell me, that would be great."

Nova sighed. "It doesn't matter, okay? I'm not even mad." She was about to walk away when Dominic caught her by the arm and pulled her closer and she stumbled against his chest.

"What happened?" he whispered.

Nova felt herself yielding under his gaze. She didn't like the way he was looking at her, or maybe she did. The butterflies in her stomach were more like elephants. This wasn't fair. "N-nothing."

He tilted his head and didn't let go of her arm. "I'm sorry, okay? I'm not sure what I did, but I'm sorry." His eyes fell to Nova's lips, his head leaning in to close the gap.

"Dom!?" Harper walked in with a phone in her hand. "Oh, shoot!"

Nova and Dominic immediately separated from each other.

"I'm *so* sorry!? I, um, Tris is calling you." She held out his phone.

Dominic took the phone and walked out of the kitchen.

Harper ran to Nova and took her hand. "I am the biggest idiot to exist. Ever. Nova, I'm *so* sorry."

Nova shook her head. "Why are you apologizing? Nothing happened."

"He was about to kiss you!"

"Uh, no he wasn't. We were just talking?"

Harper raised her eyebrows and folded her hands. "Right into each other's faces?"

Nova spluttered and struggled to get words out. "I, um, we—it was nothing. Really."

"Okay, sure." Harper nodded exaggeratedly.

"Cut it out, okay? I need to get to class." She gave Harper a quick hug before leaving.

"Where are you going?" Dominic asked.

"Class. It's held in the auditorium today."

"I'll walk with you." Dominic picked up his bag and walked out with Nova.

They walked in silence for a while. "I'm sorry too," Nova said; it wasn't fair to let Dominic feel bad about something that wasn't exactly his fault. He had done nothing but tell the truth.

"Are you finally going to tell me what it was?"

Nova chuckled. "Nope. Just take the apology, and let's move on. That okay with you?"

Dominic hummed. "No, but I'm not in the mood to argue. I'm going to head to the library; I don't have any classes until twelve. I usually sleep in, but I owed you two a breakfast."

"Thank you. I have only this class today and then I'm free. Do you mind if I join you?"

"Sure. I'll save us a table."

THE CLASS WAS interesting but exhausting. They were studying echoes, hence the use of the auditorium. Dominic wanted to know all about it, so Nova went on and on.

"Sorry, I didn't realize you were working."

Dominic shook his head. "Don't worry about it. I was getting bored anyway."

"It was just really cool. Oh, are you friends with Jacob Devone?"

"Maybe? I think I've heard of him; why?"

"His voice sounded like... like melted dark chocolate. It was the best thing ever. He was singing really low, and oh my gosh, I had goosebumps. I could listen to him forever."

"Oh, really?" Dominic asked, and Nova was shocked because of the clipped tone. "What was his name again?"

"Jacob Devone? What happened?"

Dominic bit his inner cheek and went back to typing on his laptop aggressively. "Nothing. Why?"

"Dominic. You're doing that thing where you become a jerk to me for no reason. What did I do?"

The boy sighed and fiddled with his wristwatch. "You sounded like you'd rather be here with Jacob than with me. That's all." And then back he went to the aggressive typing.

Was he jealous!? "I would have gone with them for coffee if I really wanted to be with Jacob and not you."

Dominic stopped typing and looked at her. "Why didn't you go?"

Nova shook her head. "I told you I'd be here, so... Plus, those pancakes really left no space for anything else. I might not even have lunch."

Their conversation lulled, and the two of them worked in silence. Every now and then, Dominic would ask Nova what she was working on and vice versa.

It was a surprise when her phone started going off. She thought it was Harper or Scarlett, but it was her social media. She was being tagged. She looked up to see Dominic looking at his phone as well.

"You, too?" he asked.

Nova nodded and opened her phone up. There were multiple pictures of her and Dominic. Ones from when they were together in math class and in the theater, one from their walk this morning, and even one of them working together in the library, which was *still* happening. Did they have a stalker?

Dominic muttered under his breath and balled his fists on the table.

"Who is doing this?" Nova asked. There were so many people commenting and saying all kinds of untrue things.

"This is not good. This is not good *at all*." Dominic stood up and started packing his things.

Nova watched in shock as Dominic got ready to leave without one word to her. And she had not missed the way he was disgusted by the photos. As if being seen with Nova was something to be ashamed of.

He left without so much as a goodbye. Nova's blood boiled, and one thing was sure in her mind. She was going to do her best to get over Dominic Lark.

Nova was going to pack her things and leave, too, but then she decided against it. Just because Dominic wanted to be a jerk and leave didn't mean that Nova had to stop working on her assignments.

Camille came into Nova's peripheral view. "You didn't expect him to stay with you, did you?"

"What do you want, Camille?"

"For you to understand that you and Dominic would never

work. He just left you here at the first sign of exposure. I actually think I did you a favor, saving you from heartbreak."

Nova took a deep breath before clearing her throat. "Did you take pictures of us? Camille, you have to know that's not normal. You clearly have a problem."

"It's not me who's going after a guy I can never have."

Nova scoffed. "I don't think you understand what you're saying. *You* are the one going after a guy you can't have. Dominic doesn't like you. I don't think he ever will."

"So you're an expert on all things Dominic now?"

"I think so." Nova got up and packed her things. She was about to leave when she turned back to Camille. She never was one to mince words. "Camille, can I ask you a question?"

Camille shrugged a shoulder.

"Do you even like Dominic? Like, do you actually care about him? Because to me it just seems like you want to be with him because he's just as... *known* and rich as you are. You two have nothing in common except maybe your net worth."

Camille laughed. "Oh, Nova. Your innocence is truly astounding sometimes. You don't understand how this world works. That's what happens when you try to make your way into places you don't belong."

Nova smiled. "I may not know much about social standing and public image, but I do know that you can't be in a relationship with someone you don't truly like. Dominic isn't a trophy. At least I know that much, and somehow," Nova shrugged, "that seems like enough to me."

⁕

NOVA WENT HOME and fell onto her bed. She didn't know why she was feeling many different feelings at the same time. Her sheets felt cool against her face, and her mind had enough going on that it was all barely comprehensible, so she fell asleep.

Her neck had the worst crick when she woke up to Harper

calling her name. That was much better than whatever Dominic was trying to do this morning. Right, Dominic. She specifically shouldn't be thinking about him.

"Are you okay? You aren't coming down with anything, are you?" Harper put a hand on Nova's forehead to check.

"I'm okay. I didn't get much sleep last night. What time is it?"

"Almost one."

Nova sighed. "I have rehearsal at three."

Harper nodded. "So, I'm guessing you saw the post."

Nova laughed humorlessly. "Oh, yeah. I did. And I know who posted it, too."

"What? Who?"

"Camille. She came up to me in the library after, um," Nova cleared her throat, "after Dominic left."

"Yeah, he called me after. He needed to find someone to get the post deleted."

"Oh." Nova drew her legs to her chest and sighed. "Did he manage?"

"Sure did. It took him a while, but he got it done."

"Great." Nova got out of bed. "I'm just going to shower before leaving."

"Babe, you sure you're okay? You seem a little upset."

Nova shook her head. "I'm fine. I'm glad you woke me up, though, thanks."

"Course."

Harper left her alone while she got ready to go to the theater when Dominic texted her.

DOMINIC

Where are you?

She was definitely not giving in and texting him back this time. What she hadn't expected was for her phone to start ringing. And when it kept ringing, it started to get on her nerves. Why was it that Dominic stayed with her or talked to her only when it was convenient for him?

Nova turned her phone on silent and spent the next hour rehearsing. It helped take her mind off what was happening in real life. Being in her character's headspace was a lot easier.

"Nova?" Simon, their sound guy, came looking for her, "Dominic's waiting for you at his place. He's asked you to go over."

Just when Nova thought Dominic couldn't make her angrier, he did just that. "Yeah, well, you can tell him that won't be happening."

Harper was sitting at the counter when Nova came home.

"Nova, I thin—"

"No. I don't want to. I've really just..." Nova sighed. "I don't want to do this. I get it, okay? It was stupid of me to think that Dominic was anything but the jerk I thought he was."

"I'm not going to defend him because I might be his cousin, but I'm your friend as well. Also, because I have no idea what he's done, he refuses to say anything, and you won't either. He says he wants to talk."

"If it's not about math, then I don't want to."

Harper nodded. "I'm going to stay out of it, but he asked me to tell you. So I am, that's all."

Nova hugged Harper. "Thank you. For not taking sides."

"You're welcome."

Once Nova was alone, she opened her phone to see the missed texts from Dominic. She didn't want to feel bad for him. But something about the incessant pleading to see her made her feel a little... better. She shook her head to get rid of the thought of forgiving him. She was better than that. She didn't need crumbs of someone's affection.

⁂

DOMINIC WAS NOT one to give up. He had done everything one could possibly think of. He sent more people Nova's way; he even tried to sign to Nova from across the cafeteria. Harper had come to her again, but she hadn't put a lot of effort into it. He had sent Riley, too. And that poor girl *did* put in an effort.

All the gestures were nice to a certain extent, but at the end of the day, *Dominic* never came up to her.

"You're really making him suffer, huh?" Harper asked when they were walking back home.

"This isn't really about that. I... I just don't think he'll ever get over social status."

"What about your math song?"

Nova hadn't had time to think about that. The music sheets had been lying in her bag for the past two days. She had completed it but still didn't have a way to let him know. They made their way up the stairs, and Harper opened the door.

"Dom?" Harper said as soon as she opened the door.

"Where's Nova?" he asked, and Nova entered the dorm.

"You've got to be kidding me," Nova muttered under her breath, "What part of I don't want to talk do you not understand?"

"Uh..." Harper took a couple of steps back. "I'm going to go to Dean's place. I'll be back in like an hour." She closed the door behind her.

"Are you always this stubborn? I've *never* had anyone take this long to respond to me."

"You broke into my house. I still haven't responded."

Dominic laughed. "You're impossible, Nova."

Nova folded her arms and stood in front of him; while she might be a little amused, Dominic did not know that.

"I'm sorry, okay? I didn't mean to leave like that. You have the right to be mad."

"I don't need you to tell me what my right is and isn't."

Dominic shook his head and put his hands in his pocket. "You have no idea, do you?"

"I know enough. I know that you'd rather be undercover than be seen with me. It's fine, really. I just got confused because... because we were spending time together."

"Are you done? Can I explain myself now that you've said your part?"

Nova shrugged.

"I didn't run away because I didn't want to be seen with you. I ran away because I needed to delete the pictures as soon as possible. My mind was running a hundred miles an hour, and I left abruptly. And before you say it, because I can *read* it on your face, no. I did not get it deleted for me; I got them deleted for *you*."

"For me?"

"Yes, you. What do you think Camille would do to you if she thought we were dating? She's already spread rumors about you."

"Camille is the one who posted them."

Dominic's mouth fell open. "I... I didn't stick around to find out. I just paid the guy, watched him erase it, and then tried to call you. But of course, you didn't pick up. I didn't know it was Camille."

Nova felt like the jerk in this situation. "I... I didn't like the way you left, and even when we were at your place and Camille said something about us being together you..." Nova stopped herself. "Never mind. I'm sorry, too, I guess."

Dominic nodded.

"For future reference," Nova smiled, "I don't care about what others think. And I don't care what Camille does or says about me."

"Noted. Next time you're drenched in marinara sauce, I'll let you swim in it."

Nova laughed. "Deal."

Dominic cleared his throat and opened his bag to remove a gift-wrapped box. "Olive branch." He gave it to her.

"What is it?" She took a seat next to Dominic and tried to shake it, but she couldn't tell what it was.

"Open it."

Nova took the gift wrap apart carefully. It was a box from a well-known jeans brand. "Dom..." She took the lid off to see the best pair of white jeans she'd ever seen in her life. They were so...

white. "I…" She set the box aside and put her arms around his neck for a hug.

Dominic's hand came around her awkwardly, but for the most part, he hugged her back.

"Thank you so much," she whispered and felt his hands tighten a little before he let go.

"You're welcome. You said you didn't have other white jeans, so I got them. I got your size from your play's fitting team, so I'm pretty sure they'll fit."

Nova patted the white cloth and felt her throat close up. "Dom, these are expensive… you shouldn't have."

"Okay, enough of that. I'm glad you like them. Am I forgiven?"

"Yes. For this time and the next time you upset me."

Dominic laughed. "Good, then I don't have to threaten Simon so he can deliver my messages to you. I should have known it was Camille. Wait, how did you know?"

"Because she told me. She was there at the library, too. She came up to me after she saw you leave."

"I feel like such an idiot."

Nova rubbed his shoulder. "It was a perfectly executed plan on her part."

"Yeah, but I've known her for long enough to have known. I should have *never* flirted with her."

"You flirted with her?"

"Unfortunately. But I was fifteen and didn't know any better."

Nova gasped. "This has been going on since you were fifteen?"

"Yup," he said, popping the 'P.'

"Wow."

"You know, Camille went through some embarrassing phases too. Want to hear about it?"

Nova had never agreed to anything quicker in her life.

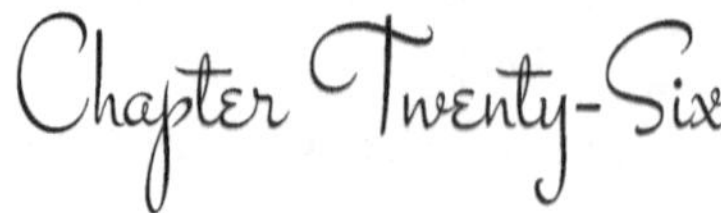

Chapter Twenty-Six

It had been about half an hour, and Nova hadn't stopped laughing. Her stomach hurt but in the best way possible.

"Did she really fall off a *pony*?" Nova tried to control her breathing, but it was a wasted effort.

"She did. Someone somewhere might have a video."

When both of them caught their breath, Nova sighed. She had to do this. Now or never, right?

"Dom, I... I have something to tell you."

"What?" Dominic was turned to her, giving her his undivided attention. She almost backed out because it was really nice to have things be smooth sailing for once.

"I wrote a song. For our math assignment."

Dominic didn't say anything. He backed away from her and turned to face the TV.

"You weren't coming up with any topics and we are getting dangerously close to the deadline. I couldn't just let it be."

Nova's heart sank when the boy got up.

"Dom, please."

"I told you. I explained to you why and you *still* wrote a song?"

"I had started before and you weren't coming up with a topic."

Dominic's mouth hung open. "So? What made you think I'd be okay with it just because I didn't have another topic?"

"Dom, we need to submit *something*. We both can't afford to fail. I could possibly lose my scholarship."

"So this was about your scholarship? Is that why we were spending time together, so you could *somehow* convince me to do your stupid song and you won't lose your scholarship?" Dominic asked; his eyes had gone a little glassy.

Nova shook her head fervently. "No! That's not what I meant. I was thinking about you too. I didn't want you to be in any trouble with your parents."

Dominic scoffed. "As if. You didn't even trust me enough to know that I would figure something out for us. That I wouldn't let you lose your scholarship."

The words hit Nova like a ton of bricks. "Dom, I'm so sorry, I di—"

"Honestly, Nova, don't," Dominic said and turned away from her to leave.

Once the door shut in her face, Nova fell on the couch feeling dejected. She shouldn't have told him. It could have waited forever. The assignment was already done, so she could have presented it alone and did both herself and Dominic a favor.

She'd had multiple people be mad at her; how is it that Dominic being upset hurt the worst?

⁂

"Harp, please." Nova was the one trying to get Dominic to talk to her this time. It was impossible to get a hold of him.

"I tried, babe. But he's stubborn." Harper hugged her as she sighed. It had been a whole day of trying to convince Dominic to speak to her for just a minute.

"I won't submit the music sheet. We'll fail; I don't even care right now." That wasn't true. Failing meant losing her scholarship. But losing her scholarship no longer meant just losing her dream. It was about losing everything she loved about her life right now; her friends, her dorm, her play, *Dominic*. "Maybe you can tell him you want to meet him, and then I'll show up."

"Nova, that wouldn't be fair. I didn't do that when you were mad at him."

"I don't know what to do anymore. The submission is four days away. We can still do something else that has nothing to do with music."

"I'll tell him, but he's being... Dominic."

Nova only wished she didn't know, but she knew what that meant all too well.

"He's not going to be mad at you forever. We're going out tomorrow; he'll be there."

"I think I'm going to pass."

"No, come on. It's not that big of a deal. You'll submit whatever you've done, and that'll be that. He'll forget about it."

Yes, he would forget about it because he'd forget about Nova. They would no longer have a reason to hang out anymore. Then that would be that.

⁂

HARPER WAS DOING her best to hype Nova up for the party, but Nova wasn't having it. Even her rehearsal had gone bad. Mr. Bentley had threatened to replace her.

"You look amazing. Can I please do your eyes?" Harper folded her hands and put them under her chin.

"Harper," Nova whined. She wasn't having the best time of her life, and sitting down to be Harper's guinea pig would probably be the last straw.

The place was already packed, and people were having fun. April and Harper tried to get Nova to have fun and sing songs, but all she could think about was where Dominic was.

When her eyes landed on Dominic, she felt a flicker of relief. He did not return the sentiment. The rest of the night was spent trying to see if he'd give Nova a minute. What was even worse was that she saw Camille sticking to him, and he *let* her. She'd never had a worse time at a party.

It kept happening over and over again like Nova was stuck in some hell loop. Every time Dominic ignored her, she felt a piece of her heart chip away. But she didn't let it deter her from trying to talk to him. She wasn't even doing it so he'd sing with her anymore. She just wanted to be forgiven.

None of it mattered, though. Dominic was stubborn, and Nova was tired. That is until *the* day arrived—the day of the presentation.

"Nova, calm down; he'll come." Harper tried making Nova feel better.

First, Nova's day got worse when she found out that the whole university was invited to watch them present. Meaning any random person could walk in and watch them give their presentation today. Ms. Hart wanted the rest of the kids to see what the others had come up with. Nova had never felt the urge to scream out loud in public more.

"He's not coming, and I'm going to have to explain to Ms. Hart what happened. I should go talk to her, right?"

Harper worried her bottom lip. "If you do that, I think she'll probably give you guys a lower grade or something for not doing it together. But you'll be fine because he'll come."

"He told you this?" Nova asked with bated breath. She hadn't had the chance to talk to Dominic still, mostly because the boy had an *excellent* escape plan set up for whenever he saw her.

"Not in so many words, but I just know."

Ms. Hart made it to the center of the class and started making announcements. She explained the assignment to the people that weren't in their math class. That's when Dominic walked through the door, and Nova thanked her lucky stars.

She swiftly made her way to where Dominic took a seat. "Dom, please, I ju—"

The boy got up and went to get another seat. He wouldn't even look at her. She didn't know what hurt more, being ignored or living with the fact that she had hurt the boy's feelings.

Once the performances started, Nova had resigned herself to thinking she would have to do it alone. She'd tell Ms. Hart that Dominic had written the song, and she'd perform it. Hopefully, that would be enough to get them a good grade.

When it was Andrew's turn, he was alone too. He had done his assignment on athletics and math. She remembered that Andrew's partner had refused to work with him. People actually booed at the boy, and Nova watched him speed through his presentation.

The closer it got to being Nova's turn, the more nauseous she felt. Her eyes met with Camille's by mistake when Camille went to present. She had the most self-satisfied smirk Nova had ever seen. She probably assumed Dominic was maintaining his distance because he didn't want to be seen with her.

Ms. Hart called out Nova's name, and she couldn't find it in herself to face the class alone.

"Is there a problem, Nova?" Ms. Hart asked.

Nova stared at her blankly, hoping she would understand that she didn't want to perform. At least not without her partner.

"Dominic dumped her," someone hooted from the back of the class, and the class broke out into laughter.

Nova got up slowly and walked to the front of the class, knowing that all eyes were on her.

"Ms. Hart, does she get a pity grade for a broken heart?" Camille raised her hand and asked. It made everyone giggle again.

"This is the *second* guy in *one* semester. Geez, Nova!" one of the boys from Andrew's acquaintances announced.

"That's enough, everyone!" Ms. Hart yelled. "Ready when you are, Nova."

Nova started the music that she had gotten her classmates to record for her. She completely messed up her timing, though, so she had to restart. The second time, her voice cracked in the first line, making everyone laugh.

Ms. Hart had to interfere with the crowd again, and she looked at Nova with pity in her eyes. Nova shook her head and cleared her throat. She was doing this with or without Dominic. She needed her scholarship; she could deal with her stupid heart, which had no business falling in love with Dominic in the first place, later. She turned to Ms. Hart and requested that she replay the music one last time.

"Hey, Nova, try finishing it this time. We don't have all day!"

By the time she turned back, Dominic was making his way down to where she was standing. He grabbed the paper out of her hand and looked it over. "You have your part memorized?" he asked.

Nova was too stunned to do anything but nod. "Do you need a minute?"

Dominic shook his head. "Let's do this."

"Can he even sing?" someone called out from the back of the class in a mocking voice. Obviously, they were doing everything to hide who they were. People started whispering, and cameras started to come out.

If happiness made you dizzy, Nova was very happy. Ms. Hart started the music right on time. Nova didn't even care if Dominic couldn't sing. He'd joined her to save her from the embarrassment of having to do this on her own. With just that much, Nova fell harder and harder until there was no more falling. She was already in too deep.

Nova sang the first verse and turned to Dominic when it was his turn. It was better than she could have imagined. His voice was *everything* she thought it would be. He belted the words out with no prior practice; in fact, he didn't even know how the music went except the notes that Nova had added in hopes that Dominic would agree to take a look. He didn't miss a beat.

He was perfect. Extraordinary, just like everyone said he was.

Nova fell in love with Dominic's voice, and she didn't know there was more to fall in love with. At the end of the song, there was a part where both of them had to sing at once. She closed her eyes as she always did when it came to high notes, so she wasn't expecting to be pulled toward Dominic.

When Nova opened her eyes, they were met with Dominic's perfect green ones. She could stare at them all day and still not tire. Nova didn't know if Dominic was feeling the same way as her, but the way the boy had his hand around her waist, she knew she wasn't alone. This was real.

The song ended, and their voices drained out. Nova *saw* the moment Dominic decided to make his move. He dropped the piece of paper in his hand and pulled Nova into his chest.

In a split second, Nova had her arms around Dominic's neck as the boy kissed her sweetly. He held her gently with one hand on the small of her back. Nova kissed him back with matched enthusiasm. Her feelings were completely different from what she was feeling only fifteen minutes ago.

Dominic pulled back and traced Nova's bottom lip with his thumb. "I've wanted to do that for so long."

"Then why did you stop?" she asked him as she leaned forward to kiss him again.

Harper later told Nova that the whole class had erupted into applause and cheers, and no one had stayed in their seats. Nova was none the wiser because she was too busy feeling like she was on cloud nine. Being kissed by Dominic was only a fraction better than seeing Camille's shocked face riddled with unabashed jealousy.

Chapter Twenty-Seven

Nova never truly understood what it was like to be smitten until she officially started dating Dominic. There were still things about him that annoyed her, but it wasn't a genuine annoyance; it always was accompanied by a tinge of fondness.

Dominic exceeded all of her expectations. Admittedly, she didn't have many to begin with, considering how everything came together; but he was perfect with her. He was sweet and loving but also teasing and competitive. It was everything she had ever wanted in a relationship, and they balanced each other out perfectly.

Harper was the one enjoying the situation more than anyone, though. "I'm sorry," she said as she entered Nova's room unannounced, interrupting Nova and Dominic.

"Harper, I swear, if you do that one more time," Dominic said through gritted teeth.

"I know, I know," she smirked, "but the play is tomorrow and the afterparty is less than twenty-four hours away. I need Nova."

"I need her more," Dominic said as he pulled Nova closer and nuzzled his face into her hair.

Harper put a hand on her waist and looked at Nova.

Nova sighed and squeezed Dominic's arm. "I'll be out in a minute."

"Thank you!" Harper said, shutting the door behind her.

Dominic looked at Nova with narrowed eyes. "Stop giving in to her. She's been stealing you away all week."

Nova laughed. It was the funniest thing seeing Dominic have no defense against Harper and her antics. "It's just another night, and then I'm all yours again. Don't you want to go see your friends?"

"I wanted to see you." He pouted cutely. "Scarlett's coming this weekend, so I won't get to see you then either."

"Says who? I will be the one who won't get to see *you*. Scarlett's been dying to meet you and Harp. That's going to trump her seeing me."

Dominic nodded and looked down at Nova's lips; his green eyes darkened as he rested his forehead against hers. "What if you came over to stay the night?"

"I don't think so." Nova smirked. "Okay, kiss me now so I can get this business with Harper over with."

Dominic obliged her, holding her face gently like he always did. When they came apart, he put his nose in her hair. "I'll see you tomorrow with breakfast. Don't go to the cafeteria; I'll bring you pancakes."

Nova blushed. She didn't know if she would ever get used to this kind of treatment.

⁂

AFTER NOT SEEING Scarlett for months, Nova excitedly ran up to her friend to hug her. There were so many people around her, but none of them registered when she saw her best friend. They squeezed each other as tightly as possible.

"You look great!" Scarlett said as she pulled away from the hug to look at Nova's dress. It was a lavender dress with embroidered flowers. It was gorgeous, and it was only the first costume.

"Thank you! So, do you!" she told her friend, hugging her again. "Harper saved you a front-row seat. You'll probably be sitting next to Dom. Be nice to him, okay?"

"I will. Break a leg!" Scarlett squeezed her one last time before Nova went backstage.

Mr. Bentley did the last round-up of the performers and was actually nice for a change. Well, nice according to his standard.

When Nova's eyes landed on Harper, Dominic, and Scarlett sitting in the front row, her nerves disappeared. She wished her parents could have attended, but they couldn't get a day off from work.

Performing with David was great. He was a great partner, and Nova had to admit they had good chemistry, but it was nothing like rehearsing with Dominic.

Rehearsing with Dominic was amazing even before they were together, but it got unimaginably better after the night Dominic asked if he could date her. Nova's whole world changed after that.

Dominic was not kidding about the social boost either. Everyone treated Nova like royalty now, and she wasn't particularly fond of that. Nova wasn't thrilled that people who once treated her like a peon now vied for her attention. But it was bearable because she loved being with Dominic. He was everything Nova had fantasized about in a boyfriend. He bought her roses for no reason, took her out on impromptu dates, respected her space, and left her alone when she needed a little 'me' time. Nova didn't know if she could be any happier.

Curtsying in front of the audience for the last time, Nova basked in the cheering of the crowd. Once she made her way backstage to change, she found a big bouquet of roses on her dressing table. There was a card on it.

She knew who it was from before she even opened it.

To the best singer in the world,
You were amazing, as usual.
Go on a date with me tomorrow? Be ready at 7.
Love, Dominic.

Nova blushed and put the card away before changing into her regular clothes. Scarlett, Harper, and Dominic were sitting around waiting for her when she came out.

Dominic stood up and pulled her by her waist for a kiss. It was chaste for all intents and purposes, but Nova still felt butterflies. He moved to back away, but she held him securely, pulling him back in for a second kiss.

"Thank you for the flowers," she whispered when she finally allowed Dominic to pull back.

"You're welcome," he said as he tucked a piece of her hair behind her ear. "So, go out with me tomorrow?"

Nova bit her lip and nodded.

"Oh, and I love Scarlett, by the way," he said directly into her ear while pressing a soft kiss to the side of her head.

"Ugh, are they always like this?" Scarlett fake gagged.

"Always. It was worse than this during their first week of dating."

Nova laughed. "Okay, I didn't bring Scarlett here so the two of you could gang up on us."

They made it out of the theater with Nova being stopped a couple of times by people wanting to congratulate her.

"Okay, can I have my best friend for the night? I'll give her back tomorrow," Scarlett said after they all had dinner at Dominic's place.

Dominic tightened his hold on Nova's hand before gently releasing it. "Of course," he said.

Nova leaned in to kiss his cheek. "I'll see you tomorrow at seven."

SCARLETT AND NOVA were lying on her bed facing each other after Scarlett had helped Nova touch up the roots of her hair to restore her purple-streaked glory.

"You've really made a life for yourself here, haven't you?" Scarlett asked with a soft smile on her face.

Thinking of her life at Atherton made Nova smile. She had never felt this content before. "I have. I... I don't know how to explain it, but everything is so... in place. I finally feel like I can call this place home."

"I'm so happy for you." Scarlett tangled her fingers with Nova's. "Dominic really loves you."

Nova chuckled, the mention of her boyfriend leaving her breathless despite it being three months since they started dating. "Yeah. I used to lie right here and complain about him all the time on the phone with you and Mom."

Scarlett gasped and whacked Nova's arm. "I had to pay your mom fifty bucks because she called this. I was convinced that you two were sworn enemies."

"Sorry." Nova chuckled. She remembered when her mother had suggested that Dominic might like her. At the time, it was the craziest thing Nova had ever heard. "Mom really did call it, though. I'm sure she was very smug about it, too."

They both talked more until they could barely keep their eyes open. It felt strange not to have any pressing issues in life.

WATCHING SCARLETT LEAVE WAS HARD, but Nova was excited about her date tonight. Leading up to the show, Mr. Bentley hadn't given them any free time between classes because they had to rehearse, so spending time with Dominic had gotten harder and harder. Because of this, they poured all their affection into the little time they had together, making each moment more precious.

But now, they could finally spend some uninterrupted time together. Nova put on a red summer dress and got ready for her date. At seven o'clock sharp, Dominic entered her room.

"How long did you hide out in Harper's room?" Nova asked with a smirk on her face. Dominic was a fan of showing up to places on time.

Dominic rolled his eyes. "Twelve minutes. Ready to go?"

"Yes. What have you ordered?"

"Oh, we're not staying in tonight. We're going out. Off-campus."

Nova raised her eyebrows in shock. Dominic usually hesitated to go off-campus because of his mother's spies. He wasn't ready for them to know about Nova yet, and she was okay with that. For the most part, at least. "Should I change then?"

Dominic stepped closer to her and cupped her face with one hand. "No. You look perfect, as usual."

"Watch Harper offer to do my eyes."

"No. Your eyes are perfect as is." He thumbed her cheek softly, and his eyes met hers.

Nova tried to fight the blush; she blinked away from the eye contact. "Okay, that's enough flattery. Take me to dinner now; I'm starving."

Chapter Twenty-Eight

The restaurant was very different from what Nova had imagined. It was a small establishment, but it still had private rooms for the customers.

"This place is charming," Nova said.

Dominic nodded. "Harper suggested it. It's her friend's place."

Nova had learned not to be phased by people's connections anymore. Everyone knew someone important. After all, she was dating the heir to the Lark empire.

The date was Nova's best one thus far, especially since they hadn't spent much alone time together.

"Are you okay?" Dominic asked once they placed their order.

Nova quirked an eyebrow. "Yeah, why?"

"Scarlett left. I know you wanted more time with her."

"I did." Nova hooked her ankle around Dominic's under the table. He was so observant of her feelings; it was the sweetest thing. "But I'll see her once the year ends and we go back home for the holidays. I was excited for our date anyway."

"You were amazing last night." He put a hand in his pocket and retrieved a rectangular brown jewelry box.

Nova's eyes narrowed and she sat up straighter. "Dom," she

said, her voice filled with exasperation. She loved the guy, she really did, but he could not take no for an answer when Nova said no more gifts. She had already accepted enough.

Dominic knew she was reluctant from the way she said his name. "Come on, it's for your brilliant performance. You deserve it. I can't *not* get you something."

Nova rolled her eyes. "The flowers were more than enough. I loved them, by the way." She still hadn't opened the jewelry box, intending not to take it.

"Please don't make me get Harper to force the gift on you. It took me hours to find this one. Please."

"I really dislike you," she said and pulled the box to her. Her eyes landed on the prettiest bracelet she'd ever seen when she opened it. It was comprised of thin strings of silver with tiny diamond-cut stars hanging off of them. "Dom. This is beautiful."

Dominic smirked and took Nova's hand in his. "Not as beautiful as you are. And there are stars because you're a star. You're my very own Super Nova." He winked, making her laugh.

"You're unbelievable. Let this be the last gift until Christmas, are we clear?"

"Yes, ma'am."

Dominic helped her put on the bracelet, and their food arrived. They talked about Nova's upcoming projects. One of her music classes had a solo performance coming up, and she thought about writing her own song. Writing the song for their math assignment gave her confidence about writing more. Thanks to Dominic, she was also able to play simple melodies on the guitar while she sang. She'd be even better if they'd had more time for lessons.

"You can help me, you know?"

Dominic shifted in his chair uncomfortably. He didn't lash out at Nova anymore when she brought up music, but it still didn't sit well with him. "I'll try, okay? I just…"

"I know, your classes are getting harder and you don't like them. I'm sorry."

"No," Dominic traced his thumb on the inside of her palm, "don't be. I like my classes just fine. They are not as bad as I thought they would be. I see why my father wants me to be good at business. I want to be, but…"

"But you want to do something that you want to do just for you?" Nova helped.

Dominic smiled. "Sort of. Music comes to me so naturally."

"Okay, so then just help me. And when you don't feel like it, you don't have to. Oh, and when I'm an international sensation, you can play the guitar for me when my crew needs a break," she joked.

"Done," Dominic promised.

They ate, talked more about music, and came up with silly future scenarios. Nova couldn't wait to live them out one day.

"Can we walk back?" Nova asked after Dominic paid. She knew she would have to return to her room after this was over, and she wasn't ready for it to end.

"It's a long walk, babe."

Nova shrugged. "I want to." She threaded her fingers through his.

The weather was chilly, but Nova didn't feel it since she was snug against Dominic. They were talking about vacation plans, which were still far away, but Dominic liked planning with Nova. They heard the sound of a car approaching and heard tires slowing down next to them.

A white SUV pulled up beside them. When the black tinted window rolled down, Camille's blonde head poked out. "Having car troubles, Dom?" she asked with her sickeningly sweet voice. She didn't even acknowledge Nova standing right beside him.

Nova sighed. She hadn't had to deal with Camille for a while now, ever since Dominic kissed her in their math class, but the blonde made her presence known every now and then.

"We're okay, thanks." Dominic kept it curt and took Nova's hand to start walking again. When Nova had told him about the things Camille had said to her, he offered to speak to Camille, but Nova didn't want him fighting her battles.

Camille's smile faded. "Where were you?"

"That's not your business," Nova interjected.

"Catty, are we? Just because you're dating Dom doesn't mean other girls aren't allowed to talk to him."

Dominic laughed. "How about I don't want to talk to you? Is that better?"

Nova licked her lips and faked a cough to hide her smile. She couldn't help but think about the time she thought Dominic and Camille would have been perfect for each other. Dominic had a heart, unlike a certain someone she knew.

Camille rolled up her window and drove away, leaving the couple in peace again.

Chapter Twenty-Nine

Before Nova, Camille couldn't remember a time in her life when she didn't get exactly what she wanted. There was nothing in this world that she couldn't have. And the same applied to Dominic. Dominic Lark was meant to be hers.

There was nothing anyone could do to keep him away from her. Her hands tightened on the steering wheel as she tried to control her breathing. She had been watching the two of them, hoping that Dominic would come to his senses and realize that a girl like Nova had no place in his life. But the girl had too strong of a hold on him.

Camille didn't want to resort to this. But, alas, she had no choice. At the end of the day, Dominic was for her and her only, by hook or by crook. It was time to find out more about how that Andrew guy felt about Nova.

Chapter Thirty

Nova was going to see Dominic at his apartment when she ran into Andrew.

"Hey." He stopped in front of her. He looked around to make sure no one was around.

"I'm in a hurry," Nova said and walked past him. She tried not to focus on her hammering heart; something about Andrew always set her on edge, and she never truly felt safe with him. She knew Dominic was a couple of floors away, and that kept her grounded.

"You lied to me."

Nova stopped in her tracks but didn't turn around to look at him.

"I don't understand; what happened? You hated him."

"I don't owe you an explanation."

"But you do. You told me you didn't break up with me because of anything other than me falling in love with you too early. But you did it because you fell in love with Dominic."

Nova turned and folded her arms. "Maybe I did. Maybe I didn't. It doesn't matter anymore, does it? I'm telling you this for the last time, Andrew. I tried to spare your feelings, but we were nothing. It would be better if you forgot it ever happened." She turned to leave, and this time, she actually did.

When Dominic opened the door, he immediately knew something was off. "What's with the frown?" He pulled her in for a hug.

"Nothing." Nova took her hair out of the bun it was in, and Dominic ran his fingers through the strands.

"Come on," Dominic pulled her closer on the couch until Nova's head was on his chest, "tell me."

Nova sighed; the sound of Dominic's heartbeat calmed her. "Promise me you won't do anything about it."

"It's about Andrew, isn't it?" His jaw clicked.

Nova nodded. "Leave it alone. I set him straight."

"He needs a good thrashing; that would set him straight."

"Do not do that, Dom. Promise me?"

Dominic shook his head. He looked away stubbornly, and Nova fought back a smile.

She stared up at him.

The boy tsked and stomped his foot like a petulant child. "Fine. I promise. But I still think we should nip it in the bud before he does something truly stupid. I don't want to take drastic measures, which you know I will."

Nova laughed and pulled Dominic's head closer to hers. "He's not planning anything. And you shouldn't be either."

"Okay, can we stop talking about him now? I wanted to plan something for the weekend."

Nova nodded and kissed Dominic softly. "Okay."

Chapter Thirty-One

S weat was dripping off Andrew's forehead as he took his fifteenth lap. Every time he saw Nova go up to Dominic's room, his blood ran cold. He wanted to break things into a million pieces. It didn't help that Nova wouldn't even look at him. Nothing he did got her attention.

He took a break and splashed water on his face with his bottle. "Andrew?"

He turned around to see someone he'd never seen here before. Four-inch high heels on gravel looked weird. "What do you want?"

Camille scoffed. "A little respect will go a long way with me."

Andrew gritted his teeth and turned to face her. "Camille, I don't have time for this. Unlike you, others actually have to earn their place here. So, if you'll excuse me." He picked up his bag and walked away.

"You still love Nova?" she called out.

When he turned, his bag almost fell off his shoulder. "Camille, I don't like playing games. If you're here because Dominic sent you, call your stupid guys and get this over with." He'd been through this enough times. He took it all for Nova, but the girl was the least bit bothered.

Camille sneered at him. "Dominic did not send me. I'm not one of his minions. Now answer the question. Do you or do you not want Nova?"

"Of course, I want her. She was mine first. Dominic doesn't have a freaking clue about a girl like Nova." Dominic didn't even know the kind of person it would take to be with Nova. She needed someone to tame her fire, and there was no one other than Andrew to do that.

"Right." Camille frowned. "I couldn't care less about that. But you want her, and I want Dominic. So clearly, we both have similar interests."

"Just spit it out already. The whole university knows you drool over Dominic; what's new?"

Camille folded her arms. "Help me break them up."

Andrew couldn't help but laugh. "Oh, yeah? Because that's so easy. What's your plan? You go up to Dominic and tell him how you can't live without him, and he'll drop everything? I would offer to do the same, but I would get beaten and expelled."

"You talk too much." Camille walked up to him. "I have a plan. And I need you to do your part. At the end of this, you'll get Nova and I'll get Dominic. It's that simple if you help me."

Andrew narrowed his eyes at the girl. "What's the plan?"

"Not here. Meet me at the restaurant off-campus. I'll text you the address," she said and turned to leave.

"Wait."

Camille turned to him with a hand on her waist.

"What happens if this doesn't work?"

Camille laughed. "You don't have to worry about that. This plan will work."

Andrew couldn't help but smile; had anyone else come up to him with a suggestion like this, he would have never even considered it. Camille was the one person he could trust not to mess this up. He knew for a fact that she wanted Dominic just as much as he wanted Nova. And now he was finally going to get Nova. No matter what it took, he would have her. She consumed his thoughts more than anything now, even his classes. He couldn't sleep thinking about her being with Dominic, and he became angrier and angrier each day. He spent all of his free time watching her secretly, and everything he saw only added to his determination. She would be his.

Chapter Thirty-Two

Camille knew Andrew was her best bet. If there was anyone she could rely on to get this whole thing to work, it would be him. She just hoped he wasn't dumb enough to screw it up. Not like she had much choice considering there weren't many people who would be willing to get on Dominic's bad side if this went south. Which it never would because Camille was just that good. Her plan was foolproof.

"How did you come up with this?" Andrew asked as he smirked and took a bite of his salad. "I mean, really? How do you sleep at night?"

Camille would feel offended if not for the smirk on Andrew's face; his words were basically a compliment. "Thanks. So, you're in?"

"Of course. I just need you to make sure Nova and I still graduate from Atherton."

"Yes, I already have that figured out. If Dominic insists on withdrawing the scholarship, I'll figure out a way to pay for it. And he'll be with me then, so I'll just... find a way to persuade him into keeping you two here." Camille's face morphed into one of someone daydreaming, with a small smile on her face at the vision of her future.

Andrew nodded and sipped on his drink. "So, when do we start this?"

"As soon as possible. The faster we get this done, the quicker we'll be able to get rid of our problem."

"Okay, give me the green signal, and I'll be ready to go."

It'll all be worth it in the end when she and Dominic rule Atherton together.

Chapter Thirty-Three

Harper and Nova were over at Dominic's for dinner. Nova had tried cooking for them, and if she was being honest, it turned out better than she'd expected.

"This looks great, babe." Dominic put his hands on her waist and turned her so he could kiss her.

Nova smiled into the kiss and grabbed the boy's hair. "Thank you. Did you finish your work?"

"I did. Harper's already whining, though, so let's get these plates out."

Nova felt true satisfaction when both of them enjoyed the food she'd made.

Harper closed her eyes and chewed while making appreciative sounds. "Wow, we've lived together for so long, and you never told me you could cook."

"I used to make stuff for Sky all the time. So I picked up a few things along the way."

After dinner, Harper left to see some of her friends while Dominic and Nova cleaned up.

"I'm going to the library tomorrow afternoon. I don't have any classes, but I want to get ahead in math. Join me?" Dominic asked as he passed the washed dishes to Nova so she could dry them.

"I probably have class at the time. Meet me in the lunch hall, and we can go wherever from there."

Dominic nodded and bent down to press a kiss to Nova's cheek. "Sounds good."

They smiled at each other while passing dishes. Nova didn't even know she'd craved these simple moments of domesticity, but now that she had them, she couldn't imagine living without them.

Chapter Thirty-Four

Camille had been following Dominic for a while now. She knew his entire schedule, what he liked to do during his free time and everything in between. Recently all his time was spent with Nova, and Camille had come very close to committing a crime on multiple occasions.

Luckily, Dominic was heading to the library according to plan. And Nova had a class. It was the only time Andrew could do his part of the job.

She shot him a text to make sure he was still stationed at the library.

Camille sat across Dominic's table. It was the perfect place to see him and Andrew who was sitting right behind Dominic. This was going to work flawlessly.

She gave Dominic some time to settle down and take out his things. She tried to dampen her excitement. She was one step closer to being Dominic's girlfriend with every passing second. She'd finally have a perfect life—a perfect college life experience with the perfect boyfriend. No one could possibly be better than Dominic.

After the most excruciating half an hour of her life, Camille finally put the plan into motion. She walked up to Dominic and tapped on his shoulder.

The boy looked at her and took off his headphones. He blew air out of his nose and looked at her expectantly.

"Dom, I need a book, but I can't reach it. Can you please help me get it?" she requested.

Dominic sighed. "I'm sure the librarian can help you."

"Oh, come on, Dom. It's just a book. Help a friend out? Or does Nova have the leash that tight that you can't even go with me for a second to get a book?"

"That's one way to ask for help. Upset the person you're expecting something from," the boy said with gritted teeth.

Camille shrugged. "It's all right, I understand. Nova would be mad. I'll find another book."

Dominic shook his head. "You're... impossible," he said and stood up, closing the book in front of him. "Where is it?"

"Right here." Camille beamed; she knew Dominic was too good not to help her. She led him away from his table where all his things were lying unattended. She cocked her head at the table to signal Andrew to get on with it.

She watched Andrew get up and make his way to Dominic's table. She had already told him Dominic's passwords. The boy was too simple; it was his youngest brother's birthday.

Dominic sighed and stared at her. "What book?"

"Oh, the one up there." She pointed at a random book on the uppermost shelf. Dominic lifted his arm to put his finger on one of the books, and Camille had to stop herself from shamelessly staring at the boy's perfectly sculptured bicep.

"Uh, no, the other one." She pointed to another book and looked past Dominic to see Andrew still doing his job.

They went back and forth with some books until Andrew left the library. It was dangerous for him even to be seen by Dominic. He'd know immediately that something was up.

"Thank you so much." Camille batted her eyelashes at

Dominic. "See, that wasn't so bad, was it? We should hang out more often."

"I think not. Now, if you'll excuse me." Dominic walked away from her in a huff.

Camille didn't think much of it. Soon enough, he'll be all hers, and she wouldn't need stupid excuses just to be able to talk to him. He'd be at her disposal whenever she desired.

Chapter Thirty-Five

Nova was just getting out of class when her phone pinged with a text from Dominic.

As soon as she realized what the text said, Nova's blood ran cold, and her skin lit up with goosebumps. There was something wrong with Dominic, and he needed her.

What in the world could have happened now!?

Nova ran there as fast as her legs could take her. Her mind had come up with the worst thoughts one could possibly have. She didn't even bother to collect her things from the class; she simply took off. Dominic could be badly hurt, or he was stranded and needed her. It could be *anything,* and the endless possibilities made Nova's legs tremble.

She wasn't even sure if she took the shortest route there, but the way there was a complete blur to her. When someone finally came into sight, Nova was too relieved that there was no blood in sight to realize it wasn't Dominic standing there.

Andrew. It was Andrew. She knew it from the back of his

head and her suspicions were confirmed when the blonde turned to her at the sound of her heavy breathing.

"What the h-heck is going on?!" she shouted and tried to get her breathing under control. "Where is Dominic?"

"He's not here. He'll be here in a minute, though."

"What?" Nova put a hand on her chest. Unfortunately, she wasn't the best runner. She doubted if she had ever run that fast in her life. "What are you talking about?!"

Andrew smiled at her and closed the distance between them. "Here." He took out his water bottle that he'd offered to her before. "Drink some water and calm down."

Nova looked at the bottle and wanted to deny it, but her throat was dry, and her chest was still burning. Water sounded really good at that moment. She took the bottle and took big gulps from it. The cold water felt good going down her throat. She handed the bottle back to Andrew. "Will you please tell me w-where Domin..."

Her sight blurred, her eyes got heavy, and the earth shifted beneath her feet. It was all blank from there.

NOVA OPENED HER EYES, and her head felt like it was about to split into two. She didn't remember going to sleep and she couldn't figure out why her bed felt like it was made out of rocks.

When she came to her senses, she remembered never going home. She was still at the hill where she was supposed to meet Dominic. It was all too confusing, and she was missing too many pieces of the puzzle to make sense of anything. She saw that her phone was lying next to her, so she picked it up as she got up.

She dusted herself off and slowly made it down the hill and back to campus, wondering what happened to her. Her head was still killing her, but she finally felt like her motor skills were back under her control. How did she pass out, and why did Dominic text her to come to the hill and never show up?

Being so caught up in her thoughts, she didn't realize that people were staring at her. She almost ran into a group of people looking at her strangely. No one had looked at her like that for a very, very long time. She was friends with most people now.

"Excuse me," she muttered an apology and walked towards her music class, where she'd left her bag. The walk to her class felt like the weirdest experience ever. It's like she had woken up in an alternate universe where all of a sudden, people hated her. What were they discussing? Did someone say something again? Nova got scared. She had an inkling it had something to do with Dominic; maybe that was why he asked to meet her.

There were people grouping up as soon as they saw her, then turning away from her so they wouldn't have to talk to her. They were even looking her up and down like there was something wrong with her. It made Nova feel more self-conscious than she had felt in a while. She smoothed her hair the best she could and checked to see if there was more dirt on her.

Once she got her bag, she sped through the murmuring crowd and walked toward her dorm. Maybe a cold shower and a change of clothes were all she needed. And a hug from Dominic. She was desperate for a good hug from her boyfriend. An explanation, too, but first came the cuddling.

Which was why she felt immense relief at the sight of him on the path she was on. She ran towards him and put her arms around his neck.

But no arms were holding her back. Confusion hit her like a ton of bricks when Dominic stood in her arms completely still. "Babe, what...?" She pulled back to see Dominic's eyes red and his face tear-stained. "Dom." She took his face in her hands and wiped the tears away. "What happened, babe? Are you okay?!" She ran a hand over his body to check for any injuries.

Dominic just stood there, silent tears flowing from his eyes. This was so out of character for him. Dominic never showed his emotions in public, so something horrible must have happened. Nova had never seen him like this before. She knew his parents were strict, but Dominic was so used to it that he'd never let them break him no matter what they did. But the boy standing in front of her looked broken. She didn't like the way he was looking at her like he was stricken. She needed him to communicate with her; she needed to hear his voice telling her what was wrong.

"Dom, please tell me what's wrong? What can I do? Just tell me, and I'll try to fix it, okay?" She felt her own eyes water at the sight of her distraught boyfriend. *Why won't he tell me!?*

"Tell me it's not true." Dominic finally spoke. His voice was as cold as the arctic winds.

"What, Dom? What's not true?" Nova was willing to admit to anything, as long as it would fix whatever it was that was breaking Dominic's heart.

Never in a million years would she have guessed that she was the reason for it.

Chapter Thirty-Six

Dominic's eyes were still filled with unshed tears when Nova felt an arm come around her shoulder. She knew it wasn't Dominic's because she was holding his hands. The strong waft of cologne filled Nova's nose, and she physically cringed.

"Hi, babe." Andrew's voice fell on her ears. He was standing so close to her, and that was not the only thing that sent her mind reeling. The other thing was that Dominic made no move whatsoever to push the boy away.

Nova didn't need Dominic to push Andrew away for her, as she was very capable of doing that on her own. But in the past few months, she'd let Dominic take care of her so she had come to expect him to continue to do that.

"So, it's true." Dominic snatched his hands away from hers.

"What is?" she asked as she shrugged Andrew's arm off her shoulder and pushed him away. She heard Andrew grumble, but she didn't care. Dominic looked more angry than hurt now.

"Woah, woah, babe." Andrew steadied himself and stood exactly where he was before. "We don't need to do this anymore."

Nova was going to pull her hair out. "No, I'm not doing this with you right now. Leave."

Dominic scoffed and wiped a tear from the corner of his eyes.

"Dom, let's just go to my room, and we'll figure this out, okay?"

Andrew laughed again. "Nova, babe, really. You don't have to pretend anymore. The cat's out of the bag. We don't need to hide anymore. You were dating him to get back at him for how he treated us in the beginning to teach him a lesson. Got him to open up to you and trust you and everything! You really got him good, babe!" Andrew said with glee hugging her against him.

"That's a lie!" Nova shouted. She put a hand on his chest and pushed him away again.

"It's okay, now, Nova. You can tell him that we're back together!" Andrew yelled with excitement dripping off of every word, despite being pushed away twice. "You've really gotten good at acting. But everyone already knows now, so you can stop."

Nova was so baffled at the words coming out of Andrew's mouth that her brain couldn't come up with understandable sentences.

"I-, uh, wh-" Nova was trying to come up with an explanation for the outrageous accusation thrown at her.

"I can't do this," Dominic muttered and turned and quickly walked off.

"No, Dom! He's lying!" Nova went to follow her boyfriend, but Andrew caught her by the wrist. "Let me go!" She fought against Andrew's relentless grip.

"Nova, baby, stop fighting this," Andrew told her softly and put one hand on her waist.

Nova had had enough of his crap. "Andrew!" She used her free hand to push him away with all her might while delivering a fierce slap to his face that he didn't even seem to feel in spite of his reddening cheek. "What are you doing?!" she yelled.

"He left you!" Andrew screamed back, his hold only getting tighter, and Nova's body couldn't fight against the force, so it got closer to his.

"Of course he did! You just lied to him by telling him I was pretending about our relationship and that you and I were back together! We are not back together. We will never be back together. And that stands whether I'm with Dominic or not."

Andrew stared at her, pinning her down with his uncomfortable gaze. "You don't see what's right in front of you? He just left you here with me, and you still want to be with him?"

"Yes!" Nova couldn't scream it out louder. Her feelings were all over the place. She was confused, angry, hurt, and sick, but all she knew for sure was that she loved Dominic. And she needed to go and make things clear. "Don't kid yourself, Andrew! We're never happening." She made sure to enunciate her words while still thrashing in his hold.

Andrew gritted his teeth and got closer to Nova. "When will you understand that you're mine, Nova? Not his!"

"Don't!" She tried to push him away when he leaned in for a forced kiss, but he was putting his all into his hold. "Andrew!" Nova screamed, hoping he would snap out of this. "Help!" Where was everyone? All of this was taking her back to the night she and Andrew broke up and how scared she was to be alone with him.

"Stop that!" Harper came from behind Andrew and started hitting his back. Being the small person that Harper was, Andrew was barely affected by her hitting. In the end, Harper used her legs to kick the boy until he buckled over and loosened his grip on Nova.

"Come on." Harper held out her hand for Nova, and they ran off towards their dorm together without looking back.

⁕

NOVA COULDN'T STOP the tears falling from her eyes. She felt sick to her stomach. She felt helpless because no matter how hard she was fighting out there, she was still scared of Andrew. She hated feeling that way.

"Nova..." Harper ran a hand up and down her back. "Calm down. You're okay. You're safe."

"I-I," she sniffled, "I'm sorry. I just…" Her voice broke because of a cough. "I just need to talk to Dominic. Please, I need to t-talk to him."

Harper sighed and hugged her. "Let's calm down first, okay?"

They sat like that until Nova got out all of her emotions. When her breathing returned to normal, Harper separated from her.

"Can we talk?"

Nova sat up straighter and nodded. She felt concerned by the tone of her friend's voice. "Yeah."

Harper licked her lips and nodded, her face stricken. "Why didn't you tell me about you and Andrew?"

"What?" Nova's mouth fell open. She couldn't understand why people thought there was something going on between her and Andrew. Especially Harper. "Harp, I don't understand. There's nothing between Andrew and me, I swear. Why do you think that?"

"Then how do you explain these?" Harper pulled out her phone and handed it to Nova.

Nova couldn't believe her eyes. "These aren't real." She scrolled through the pictures, seeing herself and Andrew hugging. There was one where her head was lying against his chest as he ran his fingers through her hair. And one where they were kissing. She felt violently ill, and a ball of fear tightened in her belly. None of that made sense.

"Harper." She looked up at her friend, her eyes desperate. "You have to believe me. I… I don't know what in the world is going on. These aren't real. I would never do that to Dominic. You know this. You know me."

Harper lowered her gaze and Nova saw how upset her friend was. "I'm sorry, Nova, but those are real. I was in the library and Dominic was waiting for you there. Then these pictures started being posted. You have on the same outfit you have on now and the timestamp is at the time Dom was in the library. They're actual pictures of you and Andrew. I… I don't understand why you'd go back to him. Why didn't you at least talk to me? Why did you do that to Dominic?"

Nova sobbed. "There was nothing to talk about, Harp! I don't know what's going on!"

Harper shook her head sadly.

How could those pictures possibly be real and she not know it? Nova thought hard about what happened when she saw Andrew on the hill, and she couldn't remember past that encounter. And then it hit her. The water bottle. That was the last thing she remembered about the interaction with Andrew. It all made sense. She had no memory of anything after she drank that water.

Was I drugged!?

The possibility settled in her stomach and made her want to hurl. Andrew had probably drugged her and then taken those pictures. But they were clearly taken by someone else, which meant he wasn't alone in this. If that was the case, she needed to report it. But that was a serious accusation, and Andrew would probably lose his scholarship when she came forward. Her heart clenched at the thought, but this was serious.

What else was he capable of if he could do that? One of those pictures showed them kissing and she didn't even remember it; she would have never consented to that. She shuddered. He was getting worse and worse. She had to make certain she was sure before she accused him; what she needed was proof.

She felt so overwhelmed with those thoughts that she pushed them to the side; she needed to talk to Dominic.

"Harper, please." Nova took her friend's hand in her own. "You have to get Dominic to talk to me. I can explain everything. I didn't do anything. I would never get back with Andrew."

Harper shook her head. "Dom doesn't want to talk to anyone right now. He was... he was feeling rough the last time I saw him."

Nova wiped her tears. "I'll fix this, I promise. Just get him to talk to me. Wait." She searched for her phone and opened up hers and Dominic's text messages.

When she opened the chat, the emergency text Dominic had sent her was gone. There was no message from him asking her to meet him on the hill. "What the heck?" she whispered and scrolled up and down the chat. There was no evidence. "Oh my goodness." Her eyes welled up yet again.

"What?" Harper asked.

"I... I had gotten a text from Dominic's phone asking me to meet him on the hill behind the science building. It said that it was an emergency, so I ran there. And when I got there, Andrew was there instead of Dominic. He told me Dominic would be there soon and gave me some water. And then... I just woke up in the middle of nowhere with no recollection of what happened. I was on my way here when I ran into Dom."

Harper swallowed thickly and looked like she was taking in all the information Nova was giving. "So, you're telling me that Dom texted you to meet him on a hill, and he wasn't there?" she asked skeptically. "Nova, that makes no sense. I told you that he was in the library waiting for you. I was there. He didn't text you."

Nova shook her head and hit her forehead out of frustration. "That's what I'm saying! None of this makes sense. I hate Andrew. You just saved me from him. What part of that says I'm with him and cheating on Dominic?!"

"But the pictures..."

"I know, I know. I can't even imagine what must be going through Dominic's head." Nova put her head in her hands and cried. She couldn't imagine how she would feel if she were to open social media and see her boyfriend hugging and kissing another girl. It would kill her. "Harp, I just want to talk to him."

"I don't know, Nova. Until you figure out a way to prove yourself... I think it's best if you give him some space. I've... I don't think I've ever seen him like this before. I know what I saw when I walked up on you and Andrew, but you two could've just been fighting about being exposed for all anyone knows."

Nova wanted the world to open up and swallow her. She unlocked her phone and dialed Dominic, but his phone went straight to voicemail. "I'm going to his place." She got up, adamant about putting this to rest. Dominic would believe her; he had to. He loved her.

"Nova, no." Harper stopped her. "Please, don't. Leave him be, just for today at least. He needs to calm down."

"He's hurting, Harper. And it's all because of Andrew!" Nova let her back fall onto the wall. "I can't let it continue."

"I know, but I don't think you being there will do any good. So for now... try to figure out what happened."

Nova slid down onto the floor and leaned her head against the wall. "I don't know how..." Her voice was barely a whisper. She had a massive headache.

"We'll figure it out. Let's get you into bed."

Nova let her friend help her to her room, remove her shoes, and help her get under the sheets.

"Harp..." Nova stopped her when the girl made a move to leave the room.

"Hmm?"

"Do you b-believe me?" Nova tried to keep her voice steady, but it cracked despite herself. She felt tears stream down her face, but after the day she's had, they felt natural against her skin.

Harper sighed. "I don't know, babe. I just think we need to figure out a way to prove your innocence. Until then... all I know is that my cousin is heartbroken."

With that, she switched off the light in Nova's room and shut the door behind her.

Chapter Thirty-Seven

Harper hadn't come to wake Nova up in the morning. The night before had been one of the most chaotic nights of Nova's life. She hadn't slept that restlessly before, and her headache was still persistent.

She checked her phone, and a part of her heart cracked when she didn't see a good morning text from Dominic. There were no pancakes for breakfast, no one to walk with to class. Even Harper had left without saying bye.

Somehow in the span of twenty-four hours, Nova's whole life had turned upside down. The last thing she should have done was open her social media. The comments on the pictures of her and Andrew were horrific. People could really be mean when they wanted to.

Not feeling like doing anything other than sitting and crying, Nova threw on whatever she grabbed first and walked out the door. She expected people to look down at her and whisper about her. But she did not expect the level of social exclusion she was met with.

She put her bag down on one of the tables in a secluded corner of the class when someone walking by pushed her bag off the table. She picked it back up and placed it next to her when a group of girls came and surrounded her.

"You can't sit here."

"I'm not in anyone's way," Nova said calmly.

One of the girls scoffed. "Move. Or we'll throw you out. We don't want any cheaters in our class."

Nova turned to look at her. "Class is about to start. You should sit down before you get in trouble."

"Like you did with Dominic?"

The girls laughed. "I get why Camille said the things she did about you. You really are worthless."

Nova shook her head. "I don't care what Camille says." She tried to stay as composed as possible. She needed to make it through her classes, and then she'd find Dominic and explain everything to him. He'd had plenty of time to calm down by now.

"Why is everyone gathered there?" the teacher called out to the group surrounding Nova. "Take your seats quickly; I don't have all day."

After her worst possible day at Atherton, Nova dragged her feet around campus, looking for Dominic. It didn't help that people were shoving past her, pushing her unnecessarily despite there being a lot of space to walk around her.

Apparently, Camille had spread lies about seeing her and Andrew in remote locations, making out, and that she had been trying to tell people for the past three months, but no one would listen to her. Camille said she was glad people finally saw Nova's true colors.

Every time she tried to call Dominic, the call wouldn't go through. He had probably blocked her. Just when she was going to give up and go home, she saw a similar build.

"Dom?!" She ran towards the boy.

Dominic turned to glance at her, but instead of waiting for her, he pointedly looked away and walked away.

Nova ran faster until she made it to the boy. "D-Dom." She slowed down and caught his arm. "Please. I just want to talk."

"And I don't. You've gotten what you wanted from me; now leave me alone." He picked her hand off of his and continued to walk away.

"Dom, please!" She was so tired. She just needed a chance, just one moment to explain herself to Dominic.

He didn't stop, and from the look of it, it seemed like he didn't care either. Nova didn't know what to do or how she would deal with this any further.

All she knew was that Dominic wouldn't listen to her, at least not without evidence.

Nova went back to her dorm and locked herself in her room. She had been on the internet for the past couple of hours, trying to find a solution. So far, she'd come up with nothing. She didn't even know how long she had been sitting there until there was a knock on the door.

"Hey." Harper popped her head through the door. "You didn't come out for lunch. Are you, um... are you okay?"

"Yeah, I guess. Don't worry about me." Nova shifted in her place. She knew Harper didn't believe her, and it made sense. Nova was an outsider and Dominic was her cousin. But... she thought that out of anyone at the school, Harper would believe her.

"Nova, your eyes." Harper's voice was dripping with worry. "What are you doing?"

Nova shrugged a shoulder. She blinked a couple of times to keep her eyes open, and a wet laugh escaped her throat. "I don't know. I literally don't know. I feel like I'm going crazy." Tears that she had been holding in came pouring out.

"Is this about what everyone is saying?"

Nova shook her head. "No. Dominic doesn't want to talk to me. And... I know he won't unless I prove to him that I'm not with Andrew and that Andrew was lying about me deceiving him. Those stupid pictures." Nova would have punched her laptop if it wouldn't cost her a fortune to get a new one.

Harper came and sat down next to her. "What happened today?"

"I got pushed and shoved in all my classes, and then Dominic said he didn't want to hear me out. I can't even read him anymore; he's back to being the Dominic he was when I first got here. Only this time, he *actually* hates me."

Harper tsked. "You need to eat, Nova. And get some sleep. Don't you have coursework to do?"

Nova continued to type away on her laptop.

"Okay, enough." Harper took the laptop from Nova and set it aside. "Get ready for dinner. You need fresh air."

"Why are you doing this?"

"Making sure you have enough food in you to keep you alive?"

"Being nice to me. You think I cheated on Dom."

Harper sighed and threw her hands in the air. "I don't know, Nova. I look at you, and I think there's no possible way it could be true. But then I see Dominic and how freaking pitiful he looks, and I can't help but blame you. You said you wanted to talk to Dominic. You said he'd believe you if you explained it to him. Clearly, he's not ready for that, so instead, talk to me. Go get some dinner while I go to the library, and then come home and tell me everything. Okay?"

Nova nodded and went to go get her dinner.

The cafeteria was buzzing, and just yesterday, Nova loved the fact that it was filled with laughter and life, but today she couldn't help but feel unsafe. She saw all the people that treated her like trash all day.

As she stood in the line to get her food, her eyes met Camille's. The girl had a sly smile, which annoyed Nova more than she would admit. She needed to get herself together. The last thing she should be doing in this situation is feel bad for herself. That stopped right now.

She held her head high and stood in line, not looking Camille's way again. Nova had no proof whatsoever, but she felt

CHAPTER THIRTY-SEVEN

Camille probably had something to do with this, and she was going to prove it.

Nova was about to step out of the line when someone put their foot out, and she didn't notice. Her tray went flying and she fell face-first on the floor. Some of the food had escaped and fallen right under Nova. She picked herself up and pressed a hand to her sore cheek, which was now hurting because of the fall.

Her eyes watered not because she was embarrassed but because Dominic was here to take care of her the last time this happened. And now he wasn't. She wiped the food off her t-shirt when she felt a cold splash of liquid on her head.

"What the heck?" she whispered as Camille poured her juice on her head.

"That's what we do to traitors around here," the girl announced.

The whole cafeteria broke into a cheer which scared Nova. It was like a battle cry, and before she knew it, people from every direction were throwing food at her. Something with curry got in her eyes and burned them. She needed to get out of there.

Nova got to her feet, almost slipping again because of all the food, but she steadied herself and ran out as fast as her feet allowed through the crowd. She didn't cry at all on the way back, and that was a feat in itself. It happened too quickly for Nova to realize she probably left a trail of food on her way back home.

She shut her door and sank to the floor. She wanted the whole world to stop for a minute. Just a minute. She couldn't afford a minute because the longer she sat on the floor, the dirtier it got. She needed to wipe everything down before Harper got back.

When Nova was all alone in the shower with just the sound of water falling around her, she let herself cry for what she promised would be the last time. The warm water helped soothe her sorrows for the moment.

She threw her clothes in the washer and wiped down the floor and door. She'd never felt this kind of exhaustion, but there was no time to rest because she had work to do. She needed to prove herself innocent. She also needed to find a way to get Dominic to talk to her now before she lost the last thread of her sanity and will to fight.

NOVA WAS BACK on her laptop when Harper came back.

"I heard what happened! Are you okay?" Harper asked.

Nova nodded. "I feel so bad for the staff that will have to clean up the cafeteria. I wish I could help."

Harper's mouth hung open slightly. "All of that, and you care about the cleaning staff?"

"They didn't even do anything. And now they'll have to stay back an extra hour or something cleaning up that mess."

"Nova," Harper said in the most exasperated tone.

"It's fine. I know they're hyper-focusing on me because there's nothing else of interest going on. Don't worry about me."

"Are you kidding me?" Harper shook her head frantically. "Okay, from what I've seen so far, you don't seem like you've been dating both Andrew and Dominic. You clearly want nothing more than to talk to Dominic; I can see that. But I still don't understand how those pictures exist."

Nova sighed. Nova had been studying those pictures extensively. "I know. I was just as confused as you. But I'm assuming Andrew deleted the text I got from Dominic calling me to the hill saying that there was an emergency. I drank some water Andrew gave me and then I woke up there alone. I...I think I was drugged, which was probably when he took those pictures of us. If you look at them, you'll see that my eyes aren't open in any of them."

"What?!" Harper screamed and got off the bed. "You think you got drugged, and you're only saying this now?"

Nova had thought about this for a long time. "I don't know how I can prove that. I don't know how to prove that the pictures are fake and that I wasn't cheating on Dom. I think I've been set up because the fact that the text was gone means that Andrew knew it was there. Does that mean that it wasn't really Dominic who sent the text?" Nova pondered. "There had to be a second person with Andrew taking those pictures, and my gut tells me it's Camille."

"Those are serious allegations, to be sure. Being drugged is not the same as social exclusion or having food thrown at you, Nova. That's a serious offense, and if that's true, something needs to be done about it."

Nova shook her head. "I'm still trying to figure out how to prove it happened. Right now, it'll be my word against theirs, and you already see the side everyone has chosen."

Harper sighed. "I'll go see what I can do."

"Thank you." Nova knew better than to hope. If she knew anything about Dominic, and she knew a lot, he was stubborn. More stubborn than anyone Nova knew. And she didn't blame him for it. It was hard for Dominic to open up to her in the first place, and now he was feeling betrayed.

***

"No luck?" Nova asked, a small smile gracing her face. It was almost masochistic of her to tolerate all of this. The Nova she was before she fell in love with Dominic would *never* let anyone treat her like that. But Dominic was worth letting her walls down for.

Harper shook her head. "He doesn't want to talk."

"It's fine, don't worry about it. I just need some time to clear my head and for everyone to move on from this."

"About that," Harper sat next to her, "I don't think that's happening anytime soon with the way that Camille's been talking about you."

Nova put her head on the pillow in front of her. "Does she ever stop? I've dealt with it before; I'll deal with it again. Not everyone is going to bother wasting their food every day to throw it at me."

"I'm sorry."

"Why are you sorry?"

"For not being there for you."

"You don't have to be." Nova said, "I still haven't proven to you that I didn't cheat on Dom. You're just choosing to believe me. Thanks for that, by the way. It's probably the only thing keeping me sane."

"I...I do believe you. I'm so sorry you got drugged."

Nova nodded. "Yeah, me too."

THE FOLLOWING days were hard on Nova. Everyone treated her worse than they had before she was with Dominic, and it hurt. But not as bad as when Dominic started looking right through her like he used to. It was like Dominic wasn't fazed by them not being together anymore. He walked around talking to people, laughing with them, being as Dominic as Dominic could be. But Nova couldn't be more different than who she was a few days ago.

She looked in the mirror and didn't recognize the girl staring back. She had become a shell of herself with no emotions on her face, bags under her eyes, and the spark that was once there was gone completely.

Nova had also become a sort of stalker. She followed Dominic everywhere he went in hopes that he'd finally take pity on her and let her speak. Today she followed him to the library as subtly as possible. "Dom." She found him in one of the corners of the library.

Dominic muttered something under his breath. "Please, Dom." Nova stopped him. "I just want a minute. Please."

"Aren't all the things happening to you enough to explain that I don't want you around me?"

Nova felt like she had been slapped. She was under the assumption that all the bullying was because of Camille. She didn't think that... never did the thought occur to her that it was

Dominic's doing. Dominic walked past her when she was trying to find her voice again.

Feeling the shame and hurt all at once made her bolt back towards her dorm. She didn't pay attention to her surroundings so she didn't realize when Andrew started following her. Once she was in her building, he called out her name.

"Andrew." Nova turned to him, pure fire in her blood. "I do not have time for this. Leave. Now."

"It hurts, doesn't it? When someone you love humiliates you in front of hundreds," Andrew asked.

Nova stood there with gritted teeth. "You said you loved me. Is this how you treat the people you love? I knew it from that night that you were trouble. You got what you wanted, Andrew; I'm miserable enough. Just leave me alone."

"I haven't gotten what I want yet. What I want is you. And to show you that Dominic never loved you. He's treating you like he treats me."

"That's because he thinks we're together. I don't blame him."

Andrew clenched his jaw and Nova saw the boy ball his hands into fists. She tried to keep the fear at bay and her face neutral, but she was scared. She had been in his position with Andrew too many times to know what was coming.

Nova took a few calculated steps back. "Go back to your dorm, Andrew. I don't want to talk to you anymore. And if you come any closer, I will report you for drugging me. I might not be able to prove anything, but Atherton loves its reputation; they will expel you. On mere accusation. Do not cross me, Andrew."

Andrew's eyebrows drew together, but Nova didn't give him the chance to say anything else. She left and locked the door behind her.

People say time heals all wounds, but she wasn't sure if she'd ever heal from being hurt by Dominic. How could he do this to her?

Chapter Thirty-Eight

When Harper got home, Nova was sitting in the kitchen, working on one of her assignments.

"No research tonight?" Harper asked.

"Did you know that all the bullying and food throwing was because of Dominic?" Nova questioned without looking away from her screen.

"No, it isn't. It's because of the rumors that Camille is spreading."

"He told me it was him." Nova kept the hurt out of her voice.

"You talked to him? What happened?"

"I didn't get to say anything. But he asked me if the bullying wasn't enough for me to stay away from him."

Harper shook her head. "That's not true. This is Camille and her minions. They've been saying a million different things."

"Then why did he say that to me?" Nova turned to Harper sharply. "Why can't he see that I'm dying over here?"

"Because he... he isn't used to this, Nova. He isn't used to people loving him for him. He's Dominic Lark, right? He gets what he wants when he wants it, and people think that he's their way of getting what they want too."

Nova gritted her teeth and stared ahead, and she remembered Dominic telling her about all his fake friends and girlfriends who were never really in it for him. Instead, it was for his riches and his cars. His contacts. But Nova thought he would know that she was better than that.

Dominic had opened up to her, told her things he hadn't told anyone else, but so had Nova. Nova had shared her deepest, darkest secrets with him. Her fears, everything. He should know better than to think she'd ever hurt him like this.

"Dominic may have told you a lot of things, but... I don't think he ever told you how afraid he was to lose you. He's being defensive. He's... he's doing what he does best. Being a Lark. They don't let others know that they are weak or have been weakened."

It explained why Dominic looked like nothing had happened after the first day.

"He hates to admit it, but he's like that. Too good to appear weak in front of anyone. He's not the one doing this, Nova. Camille is. And if you buy into this, she will succeed. She wants you and Dominic to be as far away from each other as possible."

Nova scoffed. "She doesn't need to do anything. Dominic's doing that all by himself without any help. I thought he loved me enough to at least hear me out. I'm not asking for him to give me the benefit of the doubt, but just to listen to me. He won't even give me a chance. This is all I'm worth to him."

"I know, and I'm trying to talk some sense into him but it's not working."

"So, what now? I have tried, Harp. I tried to find a way to get the text message back, but I couldn't. Do I just wait for him to wake up one day and realize that I love him? Why am I the only one fighting for us when I was wronged just as much as him?"

Harper hugged Nova and shushed her. Nova hadn't even realized that she had started crying. After days of the same thing over and over again, the hurt had washed away and all that was left was anger. Nova was angry that people that were once her friends now pushed her around like a ragdoll. People who once saved a seat for her now made sure that she couldn't even get to class on time.

"I'm going to ask him again. If not... we'll just have to trick him into seeing you."

"No," Nova said. "I don't need more trickery. That's what got me into this mess in the first place. He either wants me, or he doesn't."

"Okay." Harper nodded. "No tricks, it is."

THE NEXT COUPLE of days went by in a blur. Nova distracted herself with assignments and preparation for final exams coming up in a couple of weeks.

Dominic wasn't even talking to Harper now, but her friend assured her that it was only a temporary thing.

All things said and done, Nova's patience was running out. She knew Dominic was hurt, but it was about her, too. She showed up to talk to him every day; she went to class and the cafeteria every day despite knowing what she would be met with.

Camille had started a new rumor that Nova was now dating someone from outside Atherton because she didn't want Andrew anyway, that he was too poor for her. People were spreading all kinds of rumors about her, and they made their feelings about her very clear.

There were pieces of paper thrown at her with different threats and nasty things written on them. She paid them no heed, or at least she tried not to. But it kept getting worse.

It felt like the more days that passed, the less Dominic cared about her.

"I'm getting mad now," Harper said. "He's not even looking at my messages. I'm just going to go to his place. Do you want to come?"

Nova considered it, but she knew it would backfire. Plus, it was Andrew's building, too, and she'd rather not run into him, even by mistake.

"No, I'll be fine. Just mend your relationship first."

Despite all things getting worse each day, Nova was fighting not to give up because that would mean that Andrew would win. But fighting was becoming increasingly harder. She didn't know how much more she could take.

Chapter Thirty-Nine

"What are you doing, Dom?" Harper threw the question at him as soon as Dominic opened his door.

"I told you not to talk to me. Don't upset me, Harper. I'll tell everyone we're related, and then you're doomed."

Harper laughed. "That doesn't scare me. You can fool everyone and you can fool Nova, but you can't fool me. Why are you shutting me out?"

"Because you're here to defend her and speak for her. And I don't want anything to do with her." Dominic wasn't going to let anyone toy with his heart.

"Have you considered the fact that maybe I just want to check on you? And that I wouldn't defend Nova if she really was wrong?"

"Harper, I'm done, okay? I can't do this. If she wants to be with Andrew, so be it. I don't have it in me to care."

"You're worsening this for yourself. I don't think you understand the gravity of what's going on. Nova thinks you're the one who's behind all the bullying."

"Maybe I am." Dominic folded his arms. Of course, he wasn't. He wouldn't even know how to send out that order. Nova could get married to Andrew tomorrow, and he still wouldn't be able to do that to her.

"You and I both know that's not true. All I'm asking is for you to hear her out."

"And all I'm asking is for you to leave me alone. Nova Scott is no one to me anymore."

"You can lie to me all you want, Dom, but you can't lie to yourself."

She left after that, and Dominic was grateful for that. He needed one moment of his life where he didn't think of Nova. He didn't want to, but it was all he did. He was falling behind in his classes for the first time in his life and it was all because of Nova.

Nova had somehow crept into every tiny little crevice of his life. In the span of a small amount of time, Nova had become his be-all and end-all. He hated that almost as much as he hated what Nova had done to him.

Every time he heard Nova running up to him or trying to talk to him, he wanted to scream. He wanted to hold her and tell her that he didn't care that she cheated on him or deceived him. And that he didn't care about how hurt he was when he saw those pictures. But he couldn't do that.

This was not a forgivable sin in his book. He thought they were so happy. Nova seemed so happy. He thought she had let him in just as much as he had her. But it was all pretending. Dominic hated that he let his guard down enough to not even notice that the girl he loved was not faithful to him.

There wasn't anything Nova could say that would make what she did to him okay. He knew the majority of those thoughts were only him trying to convince himself not to take her back. But he really wanted to see her. He would allow himself at least that much.

DOMINIC KNEW if he went to the library at this time, he would run into Nova and she would try to talk to him. It was the little sliver of daily Nova he allowed himself as an indulgence. It was asking a lot of him to go from being with her every day to getting nothing of her at all. Besides, he wasn't going to change his routine for someone who cheated on him.

He sat by himself at one of his favorite tables while being completely aware of his surroundings. Recently, Nova had gotten good at sneaking up on him and taking him by surprise.

But Nova hadn't shown up yet, and he was a little... upset by it. Nova wasn't moving on already, was she? What was he expecting? For her to be here every day for the rest of their lives?

Instead of the person he wanted to see, Camille showed up with a cup of coffee. He was pretty sure he told her more than twenty times that he didn't drink coffee. "What do you want?"

"I was wondering if you wanted to go for lunch? I was going to pick out a dress for the gala tonight. I wanted to know what you were wearing so we could match."

Dominic sighed. "I'm probably not going, so we're not going to match. And even if I was going, why would I match with you?"

"Because I'll be your date, duh."

"You're *not* going to be my date."

Camille smiled. "Listen, Dom, I don't mind being your rebound. I'll do it."

"Camille, I'm not going to date you. I have no interest in you. I don't like you," Dominic said. He couldn't be clearer if he tried, and he succeeded in making the girl uncomfortable.

"You're just confused, sweetheart. Call me when you realize who's the right girl for you."

"Don't hold your breath for my call then; you'll pass out." Dominic put on his headphones and went back to work, leaving Camille to stare him down.

Nova didn't show up even though he stayed back for an extra hour. He packed up his things and got ready to leave. Once he went outside, the sun was already setting and it would be time for dinner soon. He hadn't been going to the cafeteria recently because girls kept coming up to him and he just couldn't take it. But he might go tonight so he could get to see Nova. Even if just for a minute. *I am pathetic*, he thought.

He shouldered his bag and walked toward his dorm, thinking of what his next step was going to be if Nova really had given up on trying to get him to talk to her. He had almost reached his dorm when he heard a familiar voice screaming.

"Dom!?"

Nova was late to the library today because a group from her vocals class thought that it would be fun to spray paint her. The paint was almost impossible to remove, and her skin felt raw against her clothes.

To her surprise, Dominic actually turned to look at her. He hadn't given her a second glance since this whole fiasco started, but he was looking at her now.

"Can we talk?" she asked as she got closer to the boy. She tried to dampen the flicker of excitement she felt about finally getting a reaction. Dominic must have missed her as much as she missed him; why else would he look at her?

She stood in front of him; the proximity almost felt like an embrace because of how long it had been since Dominic allowed this closeness.

"No. Actually, I'm putting an end to this. You disrupt my routine and I hate seeing your face. So, no more following, or you're going to be in more trouble than you already are. Leave me alone," Dominic said and walked away.

Nova stood there and let the words wash over her. She really thought for a moment that Dominic was ready to talk, ready to hear her side of this mess. But as he said, he hated her face. And he wanted nothing to do with her.

Hurt stopped converting to tears a while ago, and all that was left was her broken heart.

She walked home. She had been running around all week trying to catch Dominic whenever she could. Her classes and Dominic's ran at different times and on different parts of the campus, but somehow Nova made it work every day. Except there was no one to appreciate it, and Dominic was the last person who cared about her.

Nova had enough of this life of trailing behind her boyfriend, who she was pretty sure wasn't her boyfriend at all. With the way things were going, Nova was single again and all she had to show for the best three months of her life was a series of pictures of her and Dominic on her phone.

NOVA WAS LYING on her bed with her laptop in front of her as she watched a random video she found on the internet. She just needed some background noise to drown out her own thoughts. She didn't realize that she had zoned out for hours until Harper walked in and sat on her bed.

"I've been knocking for so long. Are you okay?" Harper asked.

Nova looked up at her friend but made no move to sit up. She was so tired; the bone-deep exhaustion she felt was beyond any she could describe. "Fine," she managed to whisper. She was never planning to leave her bed again.

"Nova, your eyes." Harper sighed and trailed a finger over the bags under Nova's eyes. She had noticed them in the morning, but she didn't have the time to do anything about it.

"What are these chafe marks?!" Harper immediately got off the bed and picked up the antibiotic ointment on Nova's table. "What happened?"

"Got spray painted," Nova said and coughed a little. She felt her stomach growling, but she didn't give it another thought.

Harper muttered something under her breath and sat back on the bed. She shut Nova's laptop, cutting out the sound of some late-night show host talking. "Sit up; you need this." She rubbed ointment onto Nova's lifeless limbs and looked at her.

"What?" Nova asked when Harper opened and closed her mouth a couple of times.

"What happened? With Dominic, I mean."

Nova cracked a small smile. Without even saying it, Harper knew that there wasn't anything that could put Nova in a slump like this except Dominic. Nova hated that. "He told me I was a disruption, and if I didn't want to get bullied more, I should stop bothering him."

Harper gritted her teeth and scoffed. "Well, I can't talk to him about this anymore. All he does is kick me out."

Nova nodded. There was a pause in the conversation, and Nova stared at her hands blankly. She took a deep breath and mustered her strength to say the next few words.

"I'm done."

Harper's hands stilled from where they were massaging Nova's elbow. "Done with what?" Her voice was low and hesitant like she was afraid to know what Nova was going to say next.

"Dominic. I can't run behind him anymore."

Neither of them said anything until Nova heard sniffling. She looked up from her hands to see Harper wipe her tears.

"I'm sorry, I'm sorry," Harper rushed to say. "I..." She shook her head. "I don't get to be the one crying."

"It's okay." Nova clutched Harper's fingers which were soft and cool because of the ointment. "I'm sorry, too. I couldn't get him to talk to me, but I... I just can't continue like this anymore. Everything about this situation is just... it's too much. Too much to think about and too much to feel."

Harper nodded. "I get it. I wish there was a way to help you."

Nova shrugged a shoulder. "There is."

"Hm?"

"Help me move on. From now on, you're just Harper Jones. No one's cousin. And I'm just Nova Scott, no one's girlfriend."

Chapter Forty-One

Moving on wasn't easy. Nova thought getting Dominic to talk to her would be hard, but she didn't even think about how hard it would be to forget him.

He was everywhere even when he wasn't. She was clearing her room and found the jewelry box that Dominic had given her. She opened it and took out the bracelet.

'You're my very own Super Nova.'

The words echoed through her mind, and she squeezed the bracelet in her hand until the points of the small stars started to hurt. She dropped the bracelet and closed her eyes. She needed to clear her room of all reminders of Dominic; it was the first step to moving on. Or so google said.

Last night after Harper left her room, Nova made a list of ways to get over Dominic. So far she was failing in all ways. As she looked around her mostly tidied-up room, she decided that it was okay to keep the bracelet on her bedside. Just for a week and then she'd get rid of it.

Her notes were a mess too with papers being all crinkled and strewn around. Most of them were not important so she made two stacks, one to keep and one to get rid of.

Nova didn't realize that sorting through papers would be her first step into relapsing. She found a couple of her math notes that had Dominic's handwriting on them. Just small little notes that he had written down on her paper because she'd missed them. Tears were quick to fall, and Nova looked for her phone to check the time. Dominic would be heading back to his dorm right now. If she ran fast enough, she would make it in time to see him.

It took every bit of the willpower and self-respect Nova had to keep from getting up and making a run for it. She had to stay strong. Dominic didn't want her around. He didn't love her enough to give them a fighting chance. She was done fighting alone. The math notes made it into the throwaway stack.

"ARE you sure you don't want to go? It's supposed to be fun. April's been asking about you," Harper said.

Atherton had organized a movie night in the auditorium for the students; the movie was made by the film and acting faculty and the big screening was today.

"I wouldn't be welcomed. I'd rather not deal with that right now."

"I'll be with you the entire time, I promise. You need to get out of the dorm, Nova."

Nova had limited going out for the time being. Harper thought it was because Nova didn't want to be bullied but it wasn't because of that. She didn't want to end up running into Dominic. She hadn't seen him in seven days. That was the longest she had gone since she got here. "I'm okay, really. You go have fun."

Harper sighed and left. Each day, Nova had found a way to dodge Harper's advances to get her to leave. She had started preparing food in her dorm instead of going to the cafeteria to avoid Dominic. She knew it was the coward's way out, but small steps were the way to go.

Once Harper left, Nova sat on the couch and stared at the

switched-off TV. The quiet was nice so she didn't want to disrupt it by turning it on. She ran a hand through her hair and put her head on the arm of the couch.

What am I doing? Nova often found herself wondering. Loneliness was new to Nova, despite her friend circle never being big. She'd always had Scarlett and her family with her, but now she was miles away from them and felt alone. Harper was there, but it wasn't the same anymore since Nova and Dominic stopped speaking.

Her phone pinged with a message, and she picked it up. Harper had sent her a picture of her and April with small frowns on their faces. Nova texted her back with smiley emojis. She didn't remember the last time she smiled genuinely.

Before she could even stop herself, she ended up opening the photos app on her phone. It was the only thing that brought her comfort now, and she wasn't going to deny herself. Maybe one day she wouldn't feel the urge to stare at the photos she took with Dominic but today wasn't it.

There were so many pictures. And in all of them, Dominic had wide smiles and soft eyes. He looked in love with Nova. Her favorite picture was the one that Harper took; Dominic and Nova were walking ahead, holding each other's hands as the sun was setting. It was the perfect picture to describe their relationship.

She stared at the picture until she tasted the saltiness of her tears. She wiped them away and switched her phone off.

ENOUGH!

But no matter how many times she told herself that it was enough, she always went back. Maybe she'd never stop going back. Maybe time would never heal her broken heart.

Chapter Forty-Two

Dominic hadn't seen Nova in a week, and what a long week it was. He couldn't ask Harper what was going on with Nova; she'd never let him live it down. He was worried about Nova, and he hated that every time he heard laughter coming from any corner, he'd try to find out if someone was bullying Nova again.

When he asked Nova to stop following him, he didn't think she'd listen. Nova never listened until she chose to listen. That meant that she didn't want to see him anymore. That she was moving on from him. He knew that she was already with Andrew, but she still always chased Dominic, trying to keep up the ruse. She didn't come to the cafeteria either, and Dominic knew from others that she had stopped going anywhere besides her classes.

Harper waved at him from where she was sitting with her friends in the auditorium. His own friends had dragged him to watch some movie made by Atherton students and Dominic gave in because he had nothing better to do. Watching a movie was a much better idea than lying in bed and looking at pictures of him and Nova. Anything was better than that.

"Hi," Harper said and sat down next to him.

His friends had gone to get some popcorn and drinks, so of

course, Harper thought this was the best time to corner him. "Hey." He continued to look ahead at the screen because he didn't need Harper scrutinizing his face.

"How are you?"

She sounded genuine, and Dominic knew his cousin had his best intentions at heart, but he couldn't help not wanting to talk to her. She still lived with Nova and was to some degree on her side. "Fine."

"Nova's sick."

Dominic didn't mean for his head to snap toward Harper as soon as the words were out of her mouth, but it did. And he could see Harper's eyes smiling. She might be very good at reading him, but he was pretty good at reading her, too. And right now, he had played right into her hands. "Why are you telling me this? I don't care. I don't go around giving you irrelevant information, so don't do it to me." He shifted uncomfortably in his seat. He should have known talking to his cousin would only cause him trouble. He clutched the armrests of his seat and blew air out of his nose.

Harper scoffed. "Then why do you look like you're dying to know more."

"I'm not. Like I said, I don't care. If anything, you should get away from me; I don't want to catch anything." Luckily, his friends returned and brought the noise with them. Harper took that as her cue to leave. Dominic should have felt relief but all he felt was sick himself. Nova was sick. It was probably why she hadn't come to the cafeteria and why she wasn't showing up to talk to him.

"Hey, man you okay?" his friend Kyle asked and handed him a soda can.

Dominic nodded. "Yeah."

"You sure? You look a little pale."

"I'm fine!" he snapped. He was tired of justifying himself. "Sorry," he muttered.

Kyle nodded but left him to his thoughts from there. If

Dominic had a dollar for every time he thought of Nova and worried about her, he would be able to build another Atherton university.

⁕

THE MOVIE WAS ONLY an hour and a half long, but it felt like an eternity to Dominic. He kept looking at his watch only to realize he'd only been there for forty-five minutes. If things weren't already excruciatingly annoying, Camille came and sat next to him. He ignored her until she tried to pick up his hand so she could thread her fingers through his.

"What do you think you're doing?" He snatched his hand back and narrowed his eyes at her.

Camille smiled at him, and it annoyed him to no end. Her perfume was unbearably sweet; it made him sick to his stomach. Her hair was disgustingly bright, nothing about her was... calming. Nothing about her was like... Nova. She was everything Dominic hated. She hadn't opened her mouth yet, but Dominic knew he couldn't bear to hear her sickeningly fake sweet voice.

He got up and left in an instant, quick on his feet so that Camille and her insanely high heels couldn't follow him.

Once he was outside and didn't hear anyone following him, he slowed down. He felt his heart beating furiously in his chest. He stopped walking and sat down on the bench nearest to him. His senses felt like they were all over the place and his head was pounding.

It was nearing the end of two weeks since he found out about Nova and Andrew. And despite it being so long ago, every time he thought about it, it was like it happened that very moment. The pain felt the same as it did when he was sitting in the library with Harper and his phone started going off because he was being tagged in the pictures. He wished he could go back in time and ignore it. He wished he never picked up his phone to look at that.

He wished he never fell in love with Nova Scott. He wished he wasn't dumb enough to get fooled the way he did. Everything he'd ever said and done with her, he wished he hadn't. He wished he could just... he wished he could just see her for a moment. Hold her like he used to. Smell the shampoo in her hair that had started smelling like home. Run his fingers through those locks one more time. Kiss her perfect face, look into her beautiful brown eyes.

He wished he could turn back time.

Chapter Forty-Three

Nova felt a crick in her neck when she woke up to the sound of her front door opening.

"Oh, sorry!" Harper whispered. "Are you feeling okay?"

Nova nodded mindlessly and moved her head around to get the blood flowing again. She hadn't realized she had fallen asleep. "How was it?"

"It was really good. You should have come."

Nova sighed and coughed into her hand. She had a small headache, but that was probably from being woken up.

"Are you feeling okay? You didn't look so good when I left either."

"I'm fine." She sat up and pulled the throw on the couch to cover herself. "Is one of the windows open?" she asked and rubbed her arms.

Harper looked around and shook her head. "I knew you were coming down with something. I keep telling you you're going to get sick. You can't run on peanut butter and jelly sandwiches forever, Nova."

"Well, I can't exactly go to the cafeteria. I can't do this right now," she said more harshly than she intended. She got to her feet but had to put a hand on the couch to steady herself. Maybe all she needed was a nap, and then everything would be better.

That's what she told herself all the time. Take a nap; it'll get better; shower, and maybe you'll feel better. None of it worked. But she was trying.

NOVA WASN'T FEELING any better the next day. She woke up with a scratchy throat, and her headache was still ever-present.

She had a morning class, so she had to get up and get dressed for the day. The weakness did not go away even after she ate breakfast, but she couldn't afford to fall behind in class. There wouldn't be anyone willing to help her catch up if she missed anything important.

"Nova." Harper stopped her for the fifth time this morning. "You shouldn't go to class. Look at you!"

"I'm okay," she said, and she'd argue more, but her throat hurt too much for it.

Walking to her class was another mammoth task, and by the time she reached it, she was sure she was going to pass out. She took the seat nearest to the entrance and pulled out her water bottle. She took long sips and pressed the cool bottle to her flushed cheeks. As she breathed out, she could feel how hot her breath was.

Their teacher walked in and looked at her curiously but did not comment, for which Nova was grateful. When her teacher switched off the classroom light so that she could use the projector, the sudden shift in light sent a painful zing to Nova's head and made her nauseous. She raised her hand and tried to ask for permission to leave, but she felt hot liquid climb up her throat, so she bolted out of her seat.

She put a hand on her mouth to keep it all in until she made it to the bathroom. The sound of the door banging on the wall behind her almost made her sigh in relief. She got on her knees and emptied her breakfast into the toilet.

Hot puffs of breath laced with the smell of vomit assaulted her senses and made her queasier. She wiped her mouth and did her best to clean the toilet seat before coming out of the stall. Her head felt lighter than before and her legs weak.

She didn't know that she had company until she heard a camera go off. She turned to see Camille and her two minions.

"Rough night, Nova?" Camille smirked.

Nova ignored her and splashed cold water on her face. She looked up at herself in the mirror and realized why Harper was so against her leaving that morning. The marble of the sink felt cool under her burning palms, giving her some relief. Her body was burning from the inside out, and she needed to make it back to class to get her things before she went home.

"What party did you go to, to end up like this?" Camille asked and got in her way when she grabbed the handle to the exit.

"Move." Nova put all her energy into that one word.

"Oh, come on, share with the masses. You look like you had lots of fun. Does Dominic know you party like this or was it another thing you hid from him?"

"Cam-" Nova didn't get to complete her sentence because she was once again emptying her stomach, but this time, down Camille's dress. It wasn't in any way on purpose, but Nova couldn't help but appreciate Karma's interference. She'd tried to warn the girl.

"What the heck!?" Camille shrieked. The blonde actually looked near tears and her friends recoiled away from her instead of helping her. Figures.

"I'm so sorry," Nova apologized despite not wanting to. She pulled out a tissue from the dispenser and tried to help Camille, but she pushed her away. So she just used it to wipe her own mouth and then threw it out.

"Get out of my sight. Right now! Do you have any idea how much this dress costs? More than your entire family's closet probably!" She continued to shout and Nova felt even more nauseated than before.

She decided to listen to Camille and left the bathroom. When she came out, Kyle, Dominic's friend was standing outside the ladies' room.

He was holding Nova's bag and notebook.

"Here." He handed both the things to Nova and left without any further conversation.

Nova watched his retreating back and wondered what had just happened. She looked down at the things in her hand and was so happy that she didn't have to walk back to class. She only had to power through and make it back to her bed.

NOVA HAD DROPPED her things on the floor and plopped on her bed. She shut her eyes closed and felt absolutely miserable. She hadn't been this sick in forever. Her mother would know what to do right now. She wouldn't be so alone if she was home. Skylar would run circles around her bed just to make sure she was fine.

Maybe it was the exhaustion or maybe the lack of nutrition, but her body was fighting something bigger than herself.

Quiet tears poured from the corner of her eyes, and she sniffled, turning her head into her pillow, wishing that it was Dominic's chest. He always smelled so good, like fresh laundry and sunny days. She missed him so much that it made her heartache. She missed her parents, Skylar, and Scarlett. She missed herself.

She had told her mother a little of what had happened, just enough to let her mother know she was having a hard time. She felt her hand gravitate towards her phone and dial her mother's number.

"Nova, sweetie, you okay?"

Nova sobbed, her mother's familiar voice being her last straw. "Mom, can I come back home?"

"Nova." Her mother's voice turned worried. "What's wrong?"

"Mom, I'm sick. And... and I can't be here anymore."

"Oh, honey, I'm so sorry to hear that you're sick. But is that the real reason you want to leave? Did you go to the medical facility on campus?"

"I hate this place, Mom."

"That's not true, Nova. You were saying how much you loved it there a couple of weeks ago. You're only saying this now because things have become difficult."

"I just want to be back home."

Nova heard her mother sigh and whisper something to someone; that's when she realized that she called her at work. She made it a point to never bother her mom at work. "Nova, come on. You're stronger than this. You're my brave girl."

Nova shook her head even though she knew her mother couldn't see her.

"Hey, you're Nova Scott. You don't let anyone push you around and you're smart, talented, and beautiful. Whatever it is that's bothering you, you need to push through it. Just like you always do. Your dad and I never taught you to run away from your problems."

Her mother's strong and steady voice soothed her. It reminded her of all the things Nova had been through to make it to where she was. Nova was a fighter, and she shouldn't give up her dreams because of a boy. She knew this. She just needed a reminder.

"You're going to make yourself some hot cocoa, take some medicine, and a nap. Then you're going to go right back to being Nova, am I clear? Don't forget who you are."

Nova chuckled, and dried her face. "Yes, ma'am."

"Good. Now go do as I said and call me before you go to bed, okay? I need to get back to work."

"Okay, I love you, thank you."

"I love you too, sweetheart."

Nova felt a lot better after that call. She wiped the remnants of her tears and made herself a cup of cocoa to drink, then took some medicine. She turned her phone on silent and put it under her pillow. She wasn't going to stare at pictures of Dominic anymore. Maybe one day she'd graduate to deleting the pictures.

⁂

"YOU LOOK BETTER!" Harper clapped and bounced a little on the couch.

Nova cracked a smile. "Why are you so happy?"

"Because I saw Camille walking covered in barf. It was amazing." She squealed, "She's cursing you out but everyone's secretly proud of you. This is basically your first step to making it back into the circle."

"I don't think that's ever happening, and I'm not sure I'd want to be back inside a circle that could turn on me so quickly. I was thinking about going for a walk; want to join me?"

Harper smiled wide. "Nova?!" The girl flung herself across the room to hug Nova. "You're feeling better." She pulled back and Nova saw her eyes water.

"Aw, Harp. I'm feeling better, I spoke to my mother, and she gave me a much-needed reality check."

"I love that! But I can't go on a walk with you because I need to practice for my dance routine tomorrow, but you go get some fresh air."

"Okay." Nova changed into a hoodie and some sweatpants and pulled her hair into a messy bun. She was ready to go clear her head.

As soon as the wind hit her face, she took a deep breath, and the air filled her lungs. She felt rejuvenated. Her throat was still a little scratchy, but other than that, she felt good.

She untangled her earphones and popped one in her ear. She kept one of the buds out for safety, but she let her favorite song wash over her. She walked around for a while, her thoughts quiet for the first time in a long time.

That was until her playlist played a song she hadn't thought about as "Her and Dominic's" song. She had never thought of it as their song until this very moment. She remembered it like it was yesterday; this was the song that Dominic tried to teach her on his guitar. According to Dominic, it was the first song that he had learned to fully play on the guitar too, so it was the easiest one to teach.

The lyrics played out and it made her breath hitch. It was a beautiful song and it sounded even better in Dominic's voice. She wanted to change the track, her fingers were itching to, but she couldn't bring herself to do it. The masochist side of her was taking control again. A three-minute song shouldn't go on forever.

She must have been going crazy because she could see Dominic right in front of her. It was like he was there in real life. Maybe her fever was coming back.

The boy was dressed like herself, in a hoodie and sweatpants. She knew exactly what that hoodie smelled like and what it felt like because she'd borrowed it more times than she had fingers and toes combined.

Nova stopped walking when the image of Dominic did too. She blinked a couple of times and realized he was real. That was Dominic, in the flesh.

She removed the one earbud from her ear and was standing three feet away from him. She knew that any sudden movement would send him running back to his dorm. She put her phone in her pocket and made the smallest move to take a seat on the bench next to her.

Once she was seated, she looked straight ahead. She could feel every breath she was inhaling and exhaling like never before. She didn't hear any footsteps, so she assumed Dominic hadn't left.

A strong gust of wind blew, and it made the hairs on Nova's neck stand up. She clasped her hands together tightly and tried to remember her mother's words. She was strong, and there was no reason to break down right now.

Then she heard the soft movement of shoes against gravel, and she dared to turn her head the slightest bit to see Dominic taking a seat on a bench a little further away from the one she was sitting on. He was far enough that he wouldn't be able to hear Nova if she just talked in her normal voice, but she could still see him because of the streetlamps.

She sighed and placed her hands next to her and held the wood underneath her hand. Dominic was sitting right there, not making a move to leave. Nova wanted nothing more than to go over and try one more time. One last time. But she knew Dominic. He wasn't going to give her a chance. And she knew for sure that she couldn't endure another round of being humiliated by the boy she loved.

"I didn't cheat on you," she said out loud. There was no way Dominic heard that, but Nova felt like a weight was lifted off her chest. "I would never do that." She allowed her tears to flow this time because, with every word, it felt like she was unlocking herself from being locked up under the burden of not being able to talk. "I love you so much, Dom." She sniffled and let the words sit on her tongue for what was probably the last time she'd say them out loud. With that, she got up and walked back to her dorm.

This time around, she was the one walking away from Dominic.

Chapter Forty-Four

Nova didn't look back at Dominic once, and she was very proud of herself. She unlocked her front door and sat down on the couch softly. She felt... empty. Blissfully empty. She said the main things she wanted to, and maybe they never reached Dominic's ears, but it wasn't for her lack of trying. He didn't want to hear her out and she couldn't keep going around in the same circles for a boy who did not respect her enough to give her a chance.

She let her head thud against the back of the couch, and she felt a smile hover on the sides of her mouth. That felt like the closest thing Nova would get to closure. She let out a breath and shook her head. She felt a sense of renewal.

"Hey there." Harper walked in from behind her, looking very sweaty and smelling it too.

"Hi."

"Fresh air did you good. You look better than you did when you left."

Nova nodded. "I puked out the demon living inside me, I think."

Harper chuckled and sat down next to her. "I'm glad. I'm even happier that the party rumors aren't getting to you."

"What party rumors?"

Harper's face fell and she hit her forehead with the palm of her hand. "What are the chances you forget I said that?"

"Zero, but I really doubt I'll be bothered by it. I'm feeling very different from the past couple of days."

"Okay then." Harper handed Nova her phone.

Nova had to laugh because for the first time she wasn't completely taken aback by something Harper was showing her on her phone. "I knew they took this. Moments before I emptied the second half of my breakfast on her very expensive dress, might I add." Nova gave Harper a little smirk. "She even asked where I was coming from."

Harper nodded and let out a breath. "Okay then I'm not ruining your good mood tonight."

There was silence in the room and Nova was enjoying it for the most part until she felt Harper shift a little next to her. She looked at her friend who was staring into her laptop and pulling at a loose thread in her pants. "What's wrong?"

Harper jumped a little, Nova pulling her out of her deep thoughts.

"What's wrong?"

"N-nothing, nothing."

Nova tilted her head and touched Harper's shoulder gently. "Clearly something is. What's going on?"

Harper sighed and turned to face Nova. "So it's really over, huh?"

Nova didn't know what to say. She hoped with every tiny cell in her body that it wasn't, there was nothing in this world that she wouldn't do for Dominic but... she wasn't going to lose herself in order to get him to believe her. "I... I think so?"

"Oh." Harper nodded minutely and nibbled on the skin of her thumb. "I guess," She started after a pause. "I guess I never really thought that this would happen. I figured the two of you would just... come to your senses."

"I know, I thought so too. I wish none of this would be

happening right now, but I guess we really can't always get what we want."

Harper didn't say anything just took Nova's hand and held it. They stayed there for a while and Nova tried to make do with the only part of Dominic she was left with at the end of this.

This had better be the end of this because she had about zero endurance left.

NOVA COULDN'T BELIEVE how the tables had turned. When she was trying her absolute best to see Dominic at any given point in time, he was never there.

Now that she didn't want to see him, because she had just started feeling more like herself, he seemed to be everywhere.

They ran into each other at the café, he ended up right in front of her in the food line, he was meeting up with a friend outside the theater when Nova was just leaving. She couldn't avoid him.

At night when she laid under her covers in the darkness, she had to admit it made her happy. At least she got to see him. Without the burning need to say something to him, Nova could just look at him.

Harper had shaken her out of her gazing one of the days and she had been a little embarrassed by it. She couldn't imagine how she looked to a third person. "S-sorry. I was just, um, thinking."

"Right." Harper smiled. She knew better than to tease Nova about this. "It's April's birthday on Friday, so we're having a little surprise party for her at Dean's house. You're in, right?"

Nova wanted to say no, she hadn't been to a social gathering in a long, long time and she wasn't sure she was ready for that yet.

"Don't worry, there won't be many people. We'll just do the whole surprise bit, eat some cake and head back home. You can sing happy birthday!"

Harper looked too excited and going to a party could be

Nova's first step back into reality. She couldn't possibly spend the next two years with Harper as her only friend.

"Okay. But cake cutting and back home."

Harper hugged her and nodded. "I promise! Come on, we need to go buy balloons and I have this really cool idea for the cake."

Nova let herself be dragged away, listening to Harper patter on about all things birthday-related.

Getting over Dominic might not be easy and there were still moments when her heart longed for him, but it was necessary. She liked being Nova—no, she loved being Nova, and that would always trump being in love with anyone else.

Dominic hadn't stopped following Nova since the night they both sat on the benches, not saying a word to each other. Nova had started to cry at some point because Dominic had seen her trembling shoulders. But then she left.

He really thought she'd at least come up to him, close enough so Dominic could reach out and hold her if he wanted. When Harper told him that Nova was sick, he wanted nothing more than to show up and be a good boyfriend. But he wasn't her boyfriend anymore, something he hadn't been able to come to terms with yet.

So, when Nova started to show signs of moving on, it angered Dominic. It made his blood run hot, and his veins light up with fire. He had no way of releasing his pent-up energy, so he did what Larks did best. Release it onto innocent people.

His friends had started to maintain a friendly distance, barring Kyle, who had been by his side to deal with his mood swings consistently, but Dominic was wearing him out pretty quickly too.

"Man, you need to calm down. Go to the gym or something."

"Do not tell me what to do! I didn't ask you to stay; you can leave when you want. The door's right there." Dominic opened and closed his fists many times to keep from punching the walls. His knuckles had just started healing from the grueling boxing session he'd had without gloves.

Kyle sighed and nodded. "Call me when you feel better. It's just a B, Dom. Not the end of the world and definitely not the end of your very promising career."

"Just get out," Dominic snapped and melted on his couch at the sound of the door closing shut behind his friend. When he saw the big, red, glaring B on his essay that was handed back to him this morning, everything had gone south from there. He hadn't ever gotten a B. Except for the times he deliberately underperformed to get back at his parents. And this wasn't one of those times.

Nova had managed to make things worse for him after she stopped showing up. Dominic couldn't concentrate on his work anymore because he wasn't sure if Nova would show up or not. If anyone even moved a muscle behind his back, he'd think it was Nova, and he'd lose track of what he was trying to study. His head would snap up to look around, only to feel crushing disappointment when there was no brunette with purple streaks in sight.

He thought that studying with friends would help keep him focused, but his friends were an even bigger distraction. And he couldn't study in his dorm for the life of him. He'd tried everything. And everything always led back to Nova.

She wouldn't even leave him alone in his dreams. There were mornings when he'd wake up, breaking a sweat and not knowing where he was. He was losing his mind, and it affected his overall mood more than anything else. And now his academics.

When there was a knock on the door, he thought it was Kyle again, trying to take him to the gym but it was Harper. Seeing her calmed Dominic a little because he never allowed himself to treat his cousin the way he did his friends. Harper wasn't his punching bag.

"I saw Kyle walk out."

"What do you want?" Dominic asked. He didn't move from

the door because he wasn't going to welcome Harper in. He wanted a moment alone.

Harper gritted her teeth. "I don't want to be here anymore than you want me to be. Tristian called me, he said you weren't picking up his calls."

"I told him I was busy. He'd send me an SOS if there was something actually wrong."

"He doesn't need an SOS to talk to his brother. Dom, you never let things affect you this deep."

Dominic punched the door with the side of his fist. "You don't think I know that!?"

Harper took a step back, frightened by the look on Dominic's face.

The green-eyed boy sighed and lowered his hand; he placed a hand on his eyes. "You should go," he hissed. This was why he couldn't take Tristian's calls. He wasn't able to control or even predict his own actions, and he didn't need more people dragged into this.

"Just call Tristian back. And... get a hold of yourself, Dominic."

Dominic shut the door after Harper got into the elevator and sat down on the floor. His hand hurt but not more than his heart. He needed to call his brother back, and his parents before they got wind of the B he scored on his assignment.

There was more damage control to take care of than Dominic was prepared for. He sat there in silence; he didn't know how long he sat there like that. He needed more of this. More of silence.

He needed anything and everything that made the thought of Nova go away. He needed the opposite of Nova.

Camille.

Chapter Forty-Six

Nova woke up from her nap in the evening when Harper came to wake her up for the surprise party. Nova couldn't say she was looking forward to it, but she tried her best to let Harper's excitement rub off on her.

"You really like birthdays, huh?" Nova said as she let Harper curl her hair. Her hair always fell into natural beach wave curls, and she liked them the way they were, but Harper said that she'd look better with some intervention.

Normally she'd argue her way out of it, but today Nova didn't feel like it. The internet said that sometimes a makeover is a good technique to start feeling better after a breakup. Unfortunately, the internet didn't have much advice for what to do when you're left heartbroken and basically ghosted. It was hard to put it into the search box in the first place.

"Oh my gosh, you're the prettiest girl I've ever known!" Harper got on her tippy-toes and did a little shimmy. "You look so good."

Nova got up and walked to her full-length mirror. She did look pretty. She was wearing her favorite purple dress with a black belt across her waist. Her neatly curled hair fell perfectly down her shoulders and the makeup made her face look... alive. Harper had really done a good job of making her look prettier than she thought she could be. Her under eyebags were gone and her face looked brighter. "I look good." She chuckled out.

"I know!" Harper jumped behind her. "This is what I'm always telling you. You look so good. Your eyes look gorgeous."

'Your eyes are perfect the way they are.'

Nova shook her head to get that voice out of her head. Her eyes looked good because Harper did her magic.

"You okay?"

Nova put on a smile and nodded. "Let's go; we need to be there to put up the balloons."

"Okay," Harper said and took her hand.

Dean's house was a little far away from theirs, so they got an early start. Nova wasn't very comfortable in the heels that Harper had given her, but the girl told her they were more like wedges than heels. It didn't make a difference to Nova, though, because they were hard to walk in either way.

"Ugh, these shoes are killing me. I wouldn't be able to run for my life if someone was trying to kill me," Nova joked.

"Come on. We're almost there. And I promise to throw you over my back and run if you were in danger of getting killed."

They laughed as they walked the last bit of the way. They decorated the dorm with pretty balloons and lots of candles. April would love it.

"Wait, come here, let's take pictures. We look super cute." Harper pulled Nova close to her and brought her phone out. She took as many pictures as Nova allowed until she had to pull away.

"Okay, enough, my cheekbones hurt."

"Ugh, we look so cute. I'm posting all of these."

Nova's hands slowed down from where they were setting up the table with the cake, "Um." She turned to Harper, who was still looking down into her phone. "Are you sure you want to do that?"

Harper looked up at her and smiled. "Of course. No matter what you think, I'm not ashamed of being your friend."

"Aw, Harp." Nova put her hands on her heart. "Stop it." She never understood how Harper said the mushiest things without a nerve moving on her face.

"I don't care, and you shouldn't either."

People started arriving and Nova placed herself in a far corner. Harper had said that there wouldn't be a lot of people, and to be fair to her, there weren't, but Nova was still more comfortable not being seen. She ended up heading to the kitchen and found odd things to do.

Harper came to get her when Nova was on the onset of panic. She had started to hear a lot more chatter and laughter coming from the living room. "Come on, April's going to be here in a sec; they're here."

"Uh, I think I'm okay here. I'll wish her a happy birthday and leave."

"No, come on, I promise you'll be fine. I'm going to sucker punch anyone if they say anything."

Nova reluctantly followed Harper, right on time because Dean and April walked in together at the same time.

Screaming of "Surprise!" ensued and Nova tried to keep a smile on her face, but she couldn't help but feel like there were so many eyes on her. She hugged April.

When everyone started crowding the birthday girl for the cake cutting, Nova blended out into the crowd and then eventually pulled back completely. She caught a couple of people looking her way and whispering to one another and Nova knew it was time to leave.

Nova once again took refuge in the kitchen to take some deep breaths. She placed her elbows on the counter and tried to relax and block all the noise from the living room. She turned her phone on and sent a text to Scarlett. She opened her social media app because she saw that she was tagged by Harper in pictures. She saw the post and liked it. Harper had made sure only select people could comment on it, for which she was very grateful.

She scrolled through other people's posts and came across one from Camille. Nova's back straightened and she had to hold onto her phone tighter so it wouldn't fall out of her hand. A picture of Camille with Dominic stared back at her.

Nova's vision blurred because of how long she stared at the picture without blinking. She almost thought that it was an edited image, that maybe, just maybe, someone was being cruel to her like they were to Dominic with pictures of her and Andrew.

"There you are; come on, I saved you a slice of cake!" Harper came from behind and put a hand around her waist.

When Nova made no movements, Harper's hold loosened, and she turned to her friend. "What? Is everything okay?"

Nova felt her lower lip tremble as she slid her phone towards Harper. "Tell me this isn't real."

Harper put a hand on her face. "This is some weird Déjà vu situation," she said after a beat. "That's what Dominic said after we saw your pictures."

"I want to go home," Nova said and wiped the tear forming in the corner of her eye. And to think that she was doing so well up until now.

"Nova, maybe this was just Camille cornering Dominic and forcing him into a picture. He doesn't even look like he wants to be next to her."

Nova wanted to laugh. "Did you defend me like this as well when you saw the pictures of me with Andrew?"

After a pregnant pause in the room, with no sound of anything but laughing and music from the living room, she said, "I didn't think so." Nova sniffled and cleared her throat. "I'll see you at home, Harp."

Nova walked through the crowd and shut the door behind her. To her ears, it sounded like thundering, but maybe that was just her heart in her chest.

Camille. Out of all the people in the world, with a population of seven billion, Dominic found Camille to go out with.

Everything they had been through in the past three weeks, and three months before that, did none of it matter to Dominic? He knew what Camille had done to her since the moment Nova arrived, and he knew how Nova felt about her. It was his perfect revenge.

She didn't think Dominic was petty enough for that. She didn't even realize she'd walked all the way back to her dorm when her phone rang. She picked it up without seeing who it was, and her tone was robotic when she replied, "Hello,"

She immediately heard laughter coming from the other end, a very familiar voice, sickeningly sweet. Camille. Nova pulled the phone away from her ear to see Dominic's name on her phone. Camille was calling from his phone.

"Dom, stop!" Camille laughed. "You're so sweet, gosh."

Nova knew it wasn't possibly a butt-dial. Dominic had blocked her the very same day everything went wrong. Camille had called her on purpose.

"Dom, we should go back to my place."

Nova disconnected the call and switched her phone off. Dominic really was with her. She didn't hear him in the background, but if his phone was there, so was he. It made her angry. It made her want to break things and scream. But mostly, it made her want to cry.

She decided that she'd had enough of this silent treatment from Dominic. She felt her resolve to be strong crack.

Nova balled her fist and wiped her tears with one hand. Dominic had come to her after the pictures of Andrew and her were released, so she was going to go to him. She was going to keep going to him until he explained to her why he didn't love her enough. Why did he pick Camille over her?

When Harper got home, only half an hour later than Nova, she found her friend in her room, makeup washed off her face, and back in clothes that looked more like Nova.

"Hey."

Nova nodded at the girl and sat on the corner of her bed to put on her shoes.

"Um, where are you going?"

"To find Dominic. Camille called from his phone, and they're headed to her place."

Harper nodded slowly. "Uh… so you're just going to Camille's dorm?"

Nova nodded and got up. She didn't know what she was going to achieve from doing this, but she was going anyway. She needed to see it with her own eyes that Dominic didn't love her enough that he'd end up with Camille.

"I'll go with you," Harper said.

"No." Nova walked out of the room.

"Come on; I'll just be your backup."

Nova sighed and turned to Harper. "Who are you going to protect me from?"

"Yourself," Harper said confidently. "Look, Nova. I know you're hurting, and so was Dominic. He was looking for Andrew to beat him up too. I'm not going to stop you because you two are more alike than any two people I've met, so I know it'll be useless, but at least let me come. Just in case anything goes south."

Nova swiped her tongue across her teeth. "Fine. Let's go."

⁂

THE LAST TIME Nova was at Camille's dorm was when she'd gone there for her first-ever party at Atherton. The building was quiet. Her head kept replaying the image of Dominic and Camille kissing behind those closed doors and it made her want to both run back home and break the door down; she wasn't sure which feeling was most dominant.

"I don't think there's a party going on in there," Harper whispered when they stood outside Camille's door and heard nothing but silence.

Nova looked at her friend and took a deep breath. She shook her hands to get rid of the nervous energy, then she knocked on the door and waited. She didn't know how she would react if Dominic was the one to open the door.

Lucky for her, he didn't. Camille stood in front of her, in a matching pajama set. "What the heck do you want?"

"Where is he?"

Camille laughed. "Dom? Oh, he dropped me back home and kissed me right where you're standing." Her voice softened at the end of her sentence and her eyes trailed away from Nova's face dreamily.

"Nova, let's go, she's lying. Dom isn't here."

Camille straightened up and glared at Harper. "Who died and made you an expert in all things Dominic? I'm sure Nova knows all about how Dominic likes to surprise people with kisses. He's finally coming to his senses."

Harper laughed. "You forced him into a picture. I would bet all my parents' fortune on it. Nova, either vomit on her again, or let's get out of here."

"You can't have him," Nova said, surprising herself.

"Excuse me?"

"You can't have Dominic," Nova said again, her voice not wavering once. "You can have anything in the world," she took a step forward so one foot was on the threshold and in Camille's private space, "but Dominic is mine." She backed up and turned her back. She was out of the building before she knew it and gasping for air.

"Woah, woah." Harper came and put a hand on Nova's back.

Nova was still gasping, and she tried to get as much air to her lungs as possible, but it just wasn't enough. She put her hands on her knees and bent over.

"Hey, you're okay, you're okay." Harper continued to rub her back. "What happened back there?"

What happened was that Nova pictured Dominic kissing Camille on her doorstep and it made Nova feel panicked. Every cell in her body hated the idea of that, hated the image that her head had created. She was not going to give up on Dominic because he was hers. He couldn't kiss anyone else because he was for her. "I need to talk to Dominic. I don't care how."

Harper nodded. "Okay." She waited for a moment before she started jumping. "Oh my gosh, you're going to get him back?!" She hugged Nova tight enough that she couldn't breathe anymore.

"Yeah. I'm going to get him back."

⚜

Nova's condition this time around was very different. This time she wasn't desperate, she was determined. Dominic was going to be leaving the library, and that was when Nova was going to stop him. She didn't care about the words that would come out of his mouth. He was going to hear her out and Nova wasn't going to rest until she had proven herself innocent.

"Okay, I'll make sure he leaves the library on time. You be ready, okay?" Harper said.

Nova nodded. "Thank you for doing this."

"No, thank you. Come on, let's get you a boyfriend."

"Yeah, no pressure." Nova reminded herself of what her mother told her. She was Nova Scott, and she was strong. She got what she wanted, and what she wanted was Dominic back. She wasn't going to let Camille fool her with her fake phone calls and lies about kisses.

The library was deserted since it was Saturday afternoon, and most people would be recovering from partying instead of being at the library. Nova was almost worried that Dominic himself wouldn't show up, but he had. She just had to wait for Harper's signal. Nova didn't have to worry about occupying her time because she was rehearsing her speech to Dominic in her head. Dominic was not going anywhere without hearing her out. "You got this," she told herself.

She was standing against a wall when she heard laughter coming from somewhere. She looked around but didn't see anyone. Nova heard multiple footsteps and her skin lit up with goosebumps. She couldn't help but feel that something was wrong.

"Hey, Nova!" a male voice called out to her from her right.

Nova turned sharply and stared at the boy in front of her. She didn't know him, but something about the look in his eyes scared her. "W-who are you?"

"Oh, you don't need to worry about that." He stepped closer to her, and Nova took a step back.

Her breath was quickening, and she knew she had to get out of there. Being around Andrew had made her quick on her feet and ready to get away from danger. She turned and was ready to bolt when she ran into someone.

"There's no point in running," another guy said. He was tall, almost as tall as Dominic. And he looked older than students attending Atherton.

"What do you guys want?"

The taller one shrugged a shoulder. "Nothing much from you, really. We just wanted to show you what happens when you cheat on someone."

Nova's chest started heaving and her sight was getting spotty. "Leave me alone."

The boys laughed and Nova felt her blood run cold when she heard more voices coming from behind her. There were two more men behind her, and Nova had never seen any of them here before.

One of the boys behind her tsked. "See, Nova, you wouldn't be in this situation if you just left our boy, Dominic, alone and didn't cheat on him. It isn't nice to break hearts." He pushed her with enough strength to knock her off her feet. She fell on her hands and knees.

"Dominic didn't send you," she said. She looked at her hand and saw scrapes on her palm. "He'd never do this. Who sent you?"

"He did." The tall guy smirked and kicked her left knee, making her fall flat on the ground.

"You're lying!" she screamed. Her hands and legs started

aching and the fear made her eyes water. "Who sent you?" She got up again and pushed a man who tried to get closer to her.

"Okay, enough talking already. Get her," the tall guy said and one of them grabbed her hair pulling her head back. It sent a wave of shock down her spine, and a groan escaped her lips. She whipped her elbow back to hit the man right in his face. He let go of her but not before he threw her forward.

This time Nova saw it coming so she steadied herself before she fell on her hands again. She turned to see the guy wipe a bit of blood from his torn lip.

He spat the blood out and gritted his teeth. "I did not get paid enough for this." He caught her hand again while the tall guy approached her.

Nova didn't know what else to do but scream. She shrieked, hoping someone would hear her. The library was soundproof though, to provide an "optimal learning environment'.

The men were immune to her screams and continued to hold her down. "Stop it!" She kicked and screamed.

"Now we're talking," the man said and they all laughed.

Nova cried harder and tried to take deep breaths. "S-stop it," she cried.

"Or what, huh?" He raised his hand to strike her, and Nova braced herself for impact.

But the hand never made contact.

Chapter Forty-Seven

Dominic was leaving the library to walk back to his dorm. He had ignored everyone and everything because he'd made a mistake going to that party with Camille. He felt... guilty. The guilt wouldn't let him live in peace. It was like he cheated on Nova, and he knew that she didn't care anymore, but it didn't make him feel any better.

Harper was in the library on a Saturday, so he was already suspicious of something going on, but he didn't have the will to ask her questions. He was looking forward to going home and maybe playing his guitar for a bit. His guitar had been his recent escape from reality. He strummed away until the music drowned out his loud and intrusive thoughts.

He was walking toward his dorm when he heard screaming. The screaming sounded terrified and frantic; it was clearly of someone in need of help. He ran toward the sound and as he turned the corner his vision went red at the sight.

Everything slowed down; the only thing Dominic could see clearly was Nova's face. She was crying and trying to free herself from the hold of the men who had surrounded her and held her down.

Dominic ran as fast as he could and caught the hand that was raised to hit his Nova. He punched the man in the nose and pushed him back. The guy staggered and fell over in surprise as the other guys drug Nova to her feet.

"What the heck?!" The guy screamed and got up and charged at Dominic, but all he was met with was Dominic's fist to his cheekbone. He fell to the ground with a satisfying thud and Dominic turned to Nova.

Her eyes were streaming with tears. "Dominic?" she whispered and looked at the ground. Her legs were trembling and the only reason she was still on her feet was because of the two men that held her. Dominic could see how hard their grip was; they were going to bruise her. He could see that her hands were bleeding.

Dominic roared and started swinging his arms to hit the first guy that came at him. He tried to focus on the swings the guy was taking, but he couldn't tear his eyes away from Nova's tear-streaked face. She looked so delicate that he wanted to tear apart every guy that laid a hand on her. Two of them decided to try and take him down and they almost had him. But Nova's sobbing got him up every time.

He ended up getting punched in his face because he didn't see the fist charging toward him. He took a deep breath and knocked the guy out with a headbutt. He turned to the only one left, who was still holding Nova's arm. "Let her go. Now. You have no idea what kind of hell I can raise in your life."

The guy looked like he was going to fight but all he did was throw Nova into Dominic as he ran away. Dominic wanted to go after him, but he knew he'd find out who these guys were soon enough.

For now, he held Nova in his arms. Nova, the same girl that had occupied his thoughts with every breath he took.

"Dom," she cried and held him by his collar to support her weight.

"I got you." He put a hand under her knees and picked her up bridal style. "Don't worry; I'm here."

"Dominic, I didn't cheat on you." She placed her head in the crook of his neck and cried. She mumbled more things, but Dominic couldn't focus on anything other than getting her to safety. He hated the way she trembled in his arms. He held her up higher.

"Hey, hey, look at me." He tried to place his forehead on hers. When she looked back at him with those perfect honey pots she had for eyes, he said, "Shhh, you're okay. We're going home, okay?"

Nova didn't say anything but continued to cry. She tightened her hold on his neck, and Dominic walked back to his dorm.

By the time he got to his front door, Nova had passed out in his arms. He couldn't open the front door without putting her down, so he shook her gently. "Baby," he whispered and pressed a kiss to her forehead. He pulled back to see a teardrop lying where he had placed a kiss.

He realized his face was wet. Nova's eyes fell open, and she looked confused.

"I need to open the door, babe. I'm going to put you down for a second, okay?" He put her down gently and continued to keep one hand on her waist as he dug out his keys from his pocket.

He opened the door and immediately picked her up again. He took her to his bedroom and placed her on the bed. He was so busy trying to see if she had any more injuries besides the scrapes on her palms that he didn't realize that she was shaking with silent sobs.

He sat down next to her and pulled her head to his chest. "It's okay; you're okay."

Nova shook her head. "I thought you'd never call me 'baby' again." She cried more and Dominic felt the tears soak his t-shirt.

Dominic sniffled and pulled her impossibly closer. "I never thought I'd get to call you that again, either."

"Wait." She pulled back but not really only enough to be able to see him. She put her forehead against his. "D-do you believe me?"

Chapter Forty-Eight

Nova tried to regulate her breathing, but everything was a mess. She was breathing the same oxygen as Dominic. She literally had his face in her hands.

Dominic's eyes told her everything she'd ever want to know. He loved her; he never stopped. He looked at her as he did when he first kissed her in their math class, in front of all those people who had made Nova's life a living hell in the past three weeks.

"Yes," Dominic whispered.

Nova didn't wait; she crushed her lips to his and sighed as soon as they made contact.

Dominic kissed back and eventually took control of the kiss when Nova couldn't do anything other than hold onto him. She never wanted to let him go. The feel of his soft laundry, the smell of his cologne, and his soft lips. She wanted to stay in this moment forever. A moment where only the two of them existed.

A moment where they didn't have to talk about the past three weeks, or Camille, or Andrew. All they had to do was stick close to each other until they somehow managed to become one.

Nova tasted her own tears and Dominic's in the kiss. She pressed one last kiss and came up for air. "I love you."

"I love you, too," Dominic said and held her face between his hands. "I'm going to kill them. Who were they?"

Nova put a hand on Dominic's and squeezed it. "They said that you sent them. For cheating on you."

Dominic's eyes widened. "I would never." He opened his mouth to explain more, but Nova kissed him.

"I believe you."

She hugged him again, happy to stay in his arms. "I'm so sorry. I promise I didn't cheat on you," she said again because Dominic was right there. She needed to tell him. She needed him to hear her out even if he said he believed her.

"I know. I... I just don't understand. I don't understand who is doing this to us." Dominic moved and positioned them so that they were both lying down in each other's arms.

"You're hurt." Nova traced a thumb on the boy's swollen lip. "I'm so sorry."

"It's not your fault. I'm going to find those men, and they're over. I don't care who they are; they are never getting away with this."

Nova rubbed her nose against Dominic's. "You smell really nice," she whispered and took a big whiff of Dominic's hair.

Dominic chuckled. "You smell pretty great too. I... I missed you."

Nova laughed, tears escaping the corners of her eyes. "Let's not talk about missing you. I... I never thought I could miss someone as much as I missed you. It was like..."

"Like missing a limb?"

Nova nodded and smiled; she put a hand on Dominic's face. "That's one way of putting it."

Dominic sat up and took a deep breath. "I'm sorry. I'm so sorry."

"Why?" Nova knew that between the two of them, they had about a million things to be sorry for, but she wanted to hear it.

"I'm sorry I went to that party with Camille. I didn't want to, I swear, I just... something came over me. I was so angry and... and

I just wanted to stop thinking about you. I promise nothing happened. I was barely there for an hour, and I left as soon as I could get her to stop clinging to me."

Nova clenched her jaw and nodded. She hated that. She hated that Dominic had willingly gone to Camille. "Why didn't you... why didn't you come to me? Why didn't you love me enough to listen to me?"

"Because I was mad, Nova. I do love you; I love you so much. Everything Andrew said that day kept echoing in my head."

"Andrew?!" Nova screamed. "Andrew said it. I didn't. You believed him over me!?"

"There are pictures. What was I supposed to do?"

"What I did. I saw a picture of you and Camille and knew you wouldn't do that to me. I knew that even if we weren't together or talking, you wouldn't do that to me. Even after she called me from your phone, I hoped that you loved me more than that. That what we had was real enough for you not to do that to me. That's what you should have done!"

Dominic scoffed. "Easier said than done. I saw the love of my life kissing another man. Don't you think that's the kind of thing that messes with someone's head? I didn't even know where you were, Nova. You wouldn't pick up your phone; Harper was with me, so she didn't know either. You were supposed to meet me at the library."

Nova didn't know what came over her, but she swung a pillow at Dominic and whacked him in the head. "Well, you would have known what happened if you had just talked to me! You would know that I was drugged and that Andrew staged those pictures after you left me alone with him!" She fell back on the bed and put her hands over her face. Her tears seeped into the cuts on her hands and made her skin burn. "You should have known that I was only ever yours, and I would never let anyone else lay a hand on me. Ever."

"He did what to you?"

Nova felt utterly defeated. She was finally having the conversation with Dominic that she was dying to have with him three weeks ago.

"Nova, he did what?" Dominic repeated himself.

"Now you care?" she whispered.

Dominic shook his head and paced the room. "Nova, you need to tell me now before I lose my mind."

"I was ready to tell you three weeks ago!" Nova screamed. It was a combination of all the anger she had suppressed caused by all the bullying, the ignorance, and the humiliation. "Why do you care now and not three weeks ago!?"

"I... I didn't know?!" Dominic sputtered. "Nova..." Dominic kneeled in front of the girl and took her bruised hands into his own. "I'm not good at this. I'm good at everything but not at this. I'm asking you to please tell me what happened. I swear I'll listen."

Nova could see the boy in front of her as he shook with desperation. She wanted to hold him longer, but she could feel a thrum of endless anger that ran through her body. Eventually, after she stared into Dominic's eyes longer, she had to give up. His eyes had watered, and she could feel from the grip he had on her hands how much he wanted Nova to talk.

"I got a text from you as I was leaving for the library. It looked like you were in some trouble, so I ran. I didn't care that it was somewhere we hadn't been before, all I cared about was you. I thought you were in trouble, so I ran. And when I got there..." Nova's words got caught in her throat. "A-Andrew was there. I don't know... it happened so fast, but I was there with him and he said you'd be there soon."

"You believed that?" Dominic said, exasperated.

Nova shrugged and tried to ignore Dominic's tone. "Look at what you believed! Can you judge? He gave me water because I was still dying from all the running, and that's... that's it. I can't remember anything after that. I woke up, and no one was there. I came down the hill and..." Nova laughed, but there was no humor behind it. "My whole life had changed."

Dominic clenched his jaw and shook his head. "I..." He opened and closed his mouth a couple of times. He threw his head back and groaned. "I can't believe this." He stood up and placed his hands on his waist.

"I kept trying to get you to listen to me..." Nova muttered. She looked at the boy in front of her, and everything about him screamed anger.

Dominic shifted on his feet and struggled to talk. Nova didn't sympathize with him.

"I don't have the text on my phone anymore; Andrew probably deleted it. I don't have any proof."

"Nova, you don't need any proof," Dominic said as he sat down next to her. He was bouncing his leg uncontrollably.

"Obviously, I do." Nova placed a hand on his leg and squeezed. "I... I need to talk about this more, but we have bigger issues at hand right now. Who sent those men? They said it was you, but it clearly wasn't."

"Well, it better not be Andrew, or he's taking his last breaths right now," Dominic said and pulled his phone out. Nova looked at him as he texted whomever he was texting, and she couldn't help but feel a wave of calm soothe her. She never knew how much she wanted someone to depend on. She had spent her entire life being independent. She was the perfect daughter, the big sister Skylar needed, and the rational best friend to Scarlett. Dominic had become her safety blanket, even without her ever realizing it.

"Okay, I have people on it. The other thing we need to do is to bring back that text. If it really did come from my phone, I can get it back."

"Really?" Nova turned to the boy. This is all she had wanted. She wanted to actually prove that she wasn't a cheater, regardless of whether Dominic believed her or not. She wanted some solid proof so she could finally rest.

Dominic smiled and put a hand around the back of her neck to pull her closer to him. They rested each other's foreheads against each other, and Nova looked into Dominic's emerald eyes. "I believe you, Nova. Even without getting the text back."

Nova let the words wrap her in the warmest hug. "I'm glad. But..." She leaned in for a hug. She didn't want Dominic to see her as the tears fell down her face. "I want proof, Dom. I've been looking everywhere, and I just didn't know what to do."

Dominic caressed the back of her head. "I'll do everything to get you that proof. I'm so sorry for not listening to you before. I'm so sorry for not believing you sooner. And," he pulled her back, "Andrew is over. And whoever is in on this. They're done, Nova, I swear it."

Nova didn't know what to say; she only wanted to kiss her boyfriend. Her boyfriend. "Wait," Nova said halfway to the kiss, "You're my boyfriend again, right?"

"Heck, yeah." Dominic pulled her in for that much-awaited kiss.

Nova broke away from the kiss when her phone started ringing. Dominic whined at the separation and pulled the brunette back in. Nova laughed and kissed him more until she couldn't ignore her phone any longer.

"Oh no!" She hit her forehead when she saw Harper was calling. "I totally forgot to update her."

Dominic hugged her side and placed his chin on her shoulder. "Can we get some more time together? Just the two of us?"

Nova turned to the boy, and she knew if Dominic looked at her like that, she'd do just about anything.

Except leave Harper in the dark. Harper was the one person who was there for her through this. "I'll just update her and come back." She stood up, but Dominic caught her wrist. She smiled at him. "Just in the living room, I promise."

Dominic nodded reluctantly and let her go. She walked out into the living room and picked up the call.

"Nova? Are you okay? Where are you?" Harper asked.

Nova immediately perked up at her friend's tone; she sounded scared. "I'm at Dominic's. What's wrong?"

"There is a guy here outside the library where you were supposed to wait for Dominic, and he's completely passed out. His nose is bleeding. I don't know what to do!"

Nova ran to get Dominic. "Harp, do not do anything. Just stay there; we're coming. I promise I'll explain everything."

Dominic and Nova ran back to the library to see Harper hovering over the passed-out man. Dominic pulled his cousin away from the guy and put her behind him.

He took his phone out and took pictures of the guy's face. Nova watched as her boyfriend crouched down and moved the limp body. Dominic tapped his face twice, but the guy didn't move an inch. Nova would think he was dead if it wasn't for his chest rising and falling.

"What do we do now?" Nova asked. She didn't want to be anywhere around the guy.

"Harp, get some water. I need to wake him up and ask some questions," Dominic said through gritted teeth.

Nova knew he'd rather be back in his dorm with her, but they had to figure out who sent them. Harper got Dominic a bottle of water, and he wasted no time pouring it onto the face of the passed-out guy.

As soon as the water went into the guy's nose, his body spasmed into a coughing fit, waking him up.

"W-what?" The guy sputtered and looked around, his wet shaggy hair falling onto his face as he sat up.

Dominic pulled the man closer by the lapel of his t-shirt. "Who are you?"

"M-mason," he stuttered.

Nova put a hand on Dominic's shoulder when he raised his fist to land another punch on Mason's face. "Calm down." She didn't let go of his shoulder. "Mason, who sent you?" she asked.

Mason tried to free himself of Dominic's grip, but he clearly didn't have a lot of energy. "I don't know."

Dominic looked up at Nova. "Get back."

CHAPTER FORTY-EIGHT

"Don't make him pass out again; we need answers," Nova reminded.

"Listen." Dominic tightened his hold on Mason's shirt. "I won't hesitate before doing something much worse than simply knocking you out. Tell us who sent you and you might get off easier than the rest of your friends."

Nova crouched down next to Dominic and locked eyes with Mason when he looked at her. "You all assaulted me, and I have bruises to prove it. You obviously don't go to school here and you're more than likely looking at jail time if this is reported. Tell us who sent you." She knew she had swayed him enough when the man's eyes widened.

"I'll tell you, but then you let me walk. No questions asked," Mason said. He was talking directly to Nova and ignoring Dominic.

"Fine. But if we find out you're lying, we'll find you."

He nodded. "Camille Rose."

Nova smiled and shook her head. *Of course, it was.* "Just go." She stood up and pulled Dominic up with her. Dominic was reluctant to let Mason go, but Nova held him back. Mason didn't waste a second, not giving Dominic a chance to stop him. He limped away as fast as he could, and when he was out of sight, Dominic faced Nova.

"I'm going to get her expelled."

Nova chewed on her bottom lip and tried to regulate her breathing.

"Dom, you know we can't do that," Harper said.

"Why the heck not?" Dominic turned to his cousin, and Harper rolled her eyes.

"She's Camille. Her parents and yours go way back, and they have just as much power as yours do. There is no way she's getting expelled. And—"

"Actually," Nova interrupted, "I don't want her expelled."

"What?" Dominic and Harper said at the same time.

Nova smiled; she was feeling like herself for the first time in three weeks. "I know what hell looks like, and it's not getting expelled. At least not for someone like Camille. She needs a taste of her own medicine."

Dominic and Harper looked at Nova with confusion etched on their faces.

"Uh, I'm not sure getting her beaten up is the answer here, babe," Harper said, her eyes moving between Dominic and Nova.

"Harp," Nova chuckled, "I don't want her beaten up. I hadn't even thought of that. I meant uploading pictures. Once we find out how that text was sent from Dominic's phone, we can compile proof and put it up online. I'm hoping people react the same way to her as they did to me."

Harper's face lit up, and Dominic nodded.

"I'm going to put this text thing to rest tonight. I want the person that's responsible gone, along with Andrew. We're going to the Dean right now."

"Dom, we need proof. He's a scholarship student; they won't suspend them without proof. He could probably sue them, and Atherton is not about to risk their reputation."

"Wow." Harper sighed, "You've given this some thought, huh?"

Nova shrugged a shoulder. "It's what all the research was for. I just couldn't get anywhere."

Dominic kicked the gravel and groaned. "I..." He curled his hands into fists.

"Hey," Nova took one of his hands in her own and untightened her boyfriend's fingers, "at least we know who was behind this. We'll figure it out. Why don't we go back to your dorm and get something to eat? I'm starving."

Dominic licked his lips and nodded curtly. "I'm going to have Jared, my tech guy, come over; he's going to figure out this text situation."

"What if he can't?" Nova whispered. She had prepared herself for never truly knowing what had happened, and Dominic needed to do the same. It was a bitter pill to swallow, but she had done it.

"He will. If he can't, I will find someone who can. I don't care how, but we're getting to the bottom of this."

Harper had left the two alone while they waited for Jared. Nova learned that Jared had always been Dominic's tech friend.

"I wish you would have introduced us before. I would have just gone to him, and all of this would have been fine."

Dominic dropped his spoon and sighed. "This isn't on you. None of this is. It's on me, and only me. I... I wish I wasn't so blind."

"I can't say I would have done anything differently if I were you," Nova admitted, "I have always been surrounded by people I can trust completely. I wouldn't even know what it's like to be in your shoes when everyone is just fake. I can't say I didn't blame you because I did. I was so mad at you but... I guess I made my peace with it."

Dominic swallowed thickly and looked away from Nova when she noticed his eyes had watered. "I always knew you were different, Nova. From the second you opened your mouth in the theater. I should have trusted my gut; I should have trusted you."

Nova smiled. She couldn't help but beam. "I can't even begin to explain how nice it is to hear that."

The green-eyed boy wiped a tear from the corner of his eye and shook his head. "You deserve so much better than me."

"I love you," Nova confessed. "I want to still be mad at you, but I'm not. I love you, and I will forever be grateful that you believe me and we're back together... I'm not letting you go."

Dominic leaned forward and captured Nova's lips. It was like all the stars had aligned, and Nova had everything she had ever wished for. Nova had tangled her fingers through Dominic's hair when there was a knock on the door.

"Ugh, Jared." Nova pulled away and licked her lips. She wiped Dominic's mouth and fixed his hair. She couldn't help but laugh; he looked adorable.

Dominic opened the door and let the boy in.

"Jared, this is Nova, my girlfriend."

Nova cleared her throat and smiled at Jared. She hoped her blush wasn't very obvious.

The two of them explained the situation to Jared and handed Dominic's phone to him.

"This will take about an hour or so."

Dominic nodded. "However long you need, just get me that text back."

"I'll try my best but... I can't get you something that was never there." He looked up at Nova and immediately shifted his gaze when Dominic straightened up.

"That text is there. And I'd watch my mouth if I were you."

Jared got to work, and Nova gave him space. She didn't blame him. The rumors that were spread about her would make anyone question. She needed to trust his skill, and it'd all prove itself.

"Hey, you okay?" Dominic came to sit next to her on his bed.

Nova looked at the clock and realized only fifteen minutes had passed. She knew that text was there. She saw it with her own two eyes, but... something about Jared's accusatory tone had got to her. She nodded regardless.

"Nova." Dominic pulled her to him and hugged her. "That text is going to be there. It is."

Nova buried her head in her boyfriend's broad chest. She had a small smile pulling at the corners of her mouth. Dominic was the one convincing her instead of the other way around. "I know. I just need him to get it as quickly as possible."

"I'll go talk to him." Dominic pulled away, but Nova held onto him.

"Don't. Let him take his time; you'll only make him panic."

Dominic tsked and settled with Nova in his arms. "Fine. But I think some motivation will go a long way."

Nova just hummed and hugged him as tightly as he allowed. She placed her head on his heart and let the steady sound of the beats lull her into sleep.

When Dominic woke her up, Nova startled herself into consciousness. "Did he get it, did you see?"

Dominic gave her a soft smile and shook his head. "He's still working on it. I got us food."

Nova tried to school her features and whispered a 'thank you.'

"He's not done yet, babe. He's just taking some time. He'll get it."

"Yeah. He will." Nova hoped her words weren't going to let her down.

She couldn't eat much, but she did for Dominic's sake so he wouldn't pester her.

"Guys." Jared walked into Dominic's room, and Nova dropped the piece of bread from her hand.

"What, what is it?"

"I guess Nova was telling the truth after all," Jared said sheepishly. He gave Dominic his phone, and lo and behold, the text was there.

Nova sighed audibly and fell against the headboard of the bed. She put a hand over her eyes and focused on her breathing.

"Thanks, Jared." Dominic led the boy out of the room and left Nova.

It took her a minute to get her breath back, and meanwhile, Dominic came and laid down next to her. "I told you he would do it."

Nova nodded. "I'm just so relieved; it's almost painful." She chuckled and curled in on herself. Dominic sat up and traced a finger on the side of her face.

"I know what we're doing next."

"Security cameras?" Nova smirked.

Dominic matched her expression and bent down to place a kiss on her forehead. "Security cameras."

Chapter Forty-Nine

Nova was a little jarred because of the amount of cash Dominic was holding in his hands. "Is this necessary? We can report Andrew and they'll dig up the evidence themselves."

Dominic tsked. "I know, but I can't have my parents finding out. At least not before I get straight As again."

"Huh?"

The boy's cheeks tinted pink. "I've been slipping lately... I had other things on my mind. It's fine, I'll just pay them off and they'll keep their mouths shut. We have the exact time we need footage of so it shouldn't be too hard."

Nova agreed and followed Dominic into the main building of Atherton. She'd only been here maybe two or three times. He was leading them into the basement.

"Lance." Dominic shook hands with a man who Nova assumed was the guard for this place. He nodded at Dominic and accepted the envelope of cash. "This never happened."

"No, it did not, Mr. Lark."

Lance took them to a computer, and Dominic gave him the date and time they needed footage.

"Here." Lance stood up and let Dominic take a seat. Nova stood behind him and put a hand on his shoulder. They were watching the footage beginning five minutes before the text was sent. Dominic was sitting at his usual table when Camille came up to him. He left with her, and Nova's grip on the boy's shoulder tightened.

Once Dominic had left, Andrew came into the picture. He was wearing a baseball cap and his Atherton tracksuit.

"That little-"

"I know." Nova cut him off and folded her arms. "Can we get this on a USB?" she asked Lance. The man nodded and Dominic gave him space to give them the clip.

"Camille's in on this too," Dominic said, his nostrils flaring.

"Yeah, but we can't really prove that with this clip. We need Andrew to admit to it." Nova knew Camille was in it all along.

"We already know she was the one who arranged the men who harassed you. I'm getting both of them expelled."

Nova decided not to reply to that. She knew Harper was right. Dominic wouldn't be able to have Camille expelled, at least not without his parents getting involved.

"Okay, one last task before bedtime," Nova said when they made it back to her dorm. Harper was waiting for them.

"I have everything compiled, I just need that last clip, and we're good to go." Harper had taken the deleted text from Dominic and made a statement of what had actually happened. She'd also gotten the picture Dominic took of one of the guys that harassed Nova, along with a picture of the scrapes on Nova's hands and knees.

"This is it." Nova sat between the two of them and held her phone in her hand. She just had to press 'post' and then wait for morning.

"Let's do it." Dominic squeezed her knee in support.

"Here goes nothing." Nova clicked on 'post.'

DOMINIC'S FACE stared back at her when Nova opened her eyes. "You're staring at me."

"I am," Dominic whispered. They locked eyes, and neither of them said anything.

"Have you checked your phone?" Nova asked once she remembered what they did last night. They wanted to see the full effect, so they set their phones on silent and put them away.

Dominic shook his head. "Not yet. I was waiting for you to wake up."

"What time is it?" Nova sat up. "Oh my gosh, Dom!? Why didn't you wake me up?" It was almost noon.

"You looked too peaceful. I didn't have the heart." Dominic placed his nose on her cheek and breathed her in.

Nova smiled and put a hand on his face. She hadn't slept like that in a long time. There wasn't a thought in her mind that troubled her last night. All that mattered was being in Dominic's arms and listening to his heartbeat in the darkness of her room. "I think we should check."

Dominic got their phones from the bedside table. He handed Nova's phone to her, and she unlocked it. Her notifications were in four-digit numbers. "Oh, jeez." She opened it up, and her heart skipped a beat.

There were apologies everywhere. All the people who were thirsty for Nova's blood were now begging her for forgiveness.

"Open Camille's page," Dominic said, looking at his phone. He had a big grin on his face.

Camille's comment section looked like hers did three weeks ago. People were threatening her the same way Nova was threatened. Of course, there was a smaller amount than what she had for herself, but that was only because the majority of the people were still scared of her.

"This is brutal," Nova said after she read a particularly gnarly comment.

"Nova, she sent men to beat you up."

"No, I know, it's just... people are horrible."

Dominic nodded and intertwined his fingers through Nova's. "They were horrible to you first. And I didn't do anything about it."

Nova swallowed thickly. "I know, but I'm Nova Scott. I can take care of myself just fine." Her mother's words hadn't left her since she had made the call.

"I don't doubt that. But you shouldn't have to."

Nova closed her phone and laid her head on Dominic's shoulder. "I'm okay. We're okay."

Dominic placed his head on top of hers. "We need to go see the Dean today. I want Andrew expelled and... I think you were right. Expulsion is going to do nothing for Camille. I'm going to keep her so that she can go through hell, right in front of our eyes."

Nova took a deep breath. "Yeah, let's go; we have people to expel and lunch to eat."

Dominic took her to the cafeteria, their hands intertwined. Everyone stared and whispered, but Nova felt fine. She felt safe.

Her heart lifted when people made way for her to get her food first instead of pushing her to the back of the line. No one tripped her, and no one made any snide comments.

Nova had officially shifted her universe right where it belonged. Even, still, she had learned how fickle these people were and how quickly they could turn based on a word, so she would guard herself against that in the future.

Chapter Fifty

"Ms. Scott, why did you not come to me immediately?" the Dean, Roma Devon, asked her. She looked through all the proof Dominic had laid in front of her. "This is a serious offense. Had you come to me in time, we'd have gotten you tested for a drug. This goes beyond breaking school rules; this is illegal."

Nova chewed on her bottom lip and stared down at her lap. She didn't know how to explain herself; she wasn't thinking clearly at the time and felt she had to gather proof.

"We want him gone. It's the only way Nova, or anyone else, in fact, can be safe," Dominic said.

"Of course. I need to speak to him, though. Have you decided whether you're reporting him to the police?" she asked Nova.

"I... I don't know. I can't do anything if he doesn't admit it. We were alone on that hill with no witnesses."

Dean Devon nodded. "I'm going to bring him in to break the news. It's completely understandable if you don't want to be here for it."

"I would like to be here."

Dominic cleared his throat. "Why aren't you saying anything about Camille? She's part of this; I can say that for sure."

"

Dean Devon nodded a couple of times and played with the papers on the table. "Mr. Lark..."

"Mrs. Devon, all due respect, I don't care what you're about to say. Camille needs consequences."

"I understand that, but some things are beyond my jurisdiction... if you understand what I'm saying."

"I do, and like I said, I don't care. I'll speak to whoever. Get them both in here and treat this like you would for any other student." Dominic folded his arms and looked at the Dean intently.

Nova could feel the Dean's discomfort. She knew she couldn't do anything about Dominic speaking to her that way.

The two of them waited for Dean Devon to get Andrew and Camille to come.

"Are you really okay to be here?" Dominic whispered in Nova's ear.

Nova nodded. "I am. I've met him a couple of times after the hill. Andrew is not the one I can't handle." She knew there was no way Camille was going to get the same consequences as Andrew. She deserved to be punished.

The door opened and Camille walked in, looking back as she talked to the Dean.

"Roma, honestly, I'm so happy you called. I have a list of people I need gone from here. The amount of crap I've been through this morning! Someone threw a tomato at me!? At—"

Camille's words died on her lips when she saw Dominic and Nova sitting in front of her.

"What the heck?" Camille turned to Dean Devon and raised her hand in a 'what is this' manner.

"Take a seat, Ms. Rose. Mr. Rodgers will be here in a minute."

Camille turned back and took a seat on the couch tentatively. "What am I here for, Roma?"

"As you already know, last night, there was a post made on the internet about something you did to Ms. Scott."

"I haven't done anything!" Camille screamed. "I don't know what this," she looked at Nova, "low life is saying."

"Ms. Rose." Dean Devon hardened her voice. "There is proof. There's nothing you can say that's going to erase that."

"Well, I di—"

The door swung open, and Andrew walked in. He had bruises on the side of his face. Nova immediately looked at Dominic.

Dominic shrugged a shoulder. "I didn't have anything to do with that," he whispered.

"Mr. Rodgers. You know why you're here, don't you?"

Andrew tightened his jaw. "Yes, ma'am."

"I have a couple of papers for you to sign, and then you will no longer be a student of Atherton."

"Huh?" Andrew's mouth fell open. "N-no, you can't do that. I got this scholarship fair and square!"

"You should have thought about that before you drugged Ms. Scott. We can't keep students like you around."

"Me?!" Andrew raised his voice and pointed at himself. "I wasn't even the one who came up with this plan. She was." He pointed at Camille. "Is she getting expelled, too?"

"That is none of your business, Mr. Rodgers. Now, whether Ms. Scott chooses to report you to the authorities is her decision. But your expulsion from Atherton is effective immediately."

Andrew shook his head. "You can't just expel me!"

Camille stood up. "I'm not staying. Both of these losers are accusing me of things I didn't do."

"Do you think I'm stupid?" Andrew turned to Camille. "I have screenshots of our chats. And I took pictures of you every time we met." He pulled out his phone and placed it on the Dean's table.

Dominic stood up and took the phone from in front of Dean Devon.

"I can't be expelled. My father will never let that happen,"

Camille said but her stance was wavering. Nova knew she didn't feel as confident as she was trying to come off.

"Yes, you can. I'll make sure of that," Dominic said. "Suspend her for now. I know we can do that much for sure," he told Dean Devon. "I want Rodgers out of here by tonight."

"I will sue," Andrew said from behind Dominic. The boy took one step back when Dominic turned and walked toward him.

"Then I will end you in court. Go on, try me," he said, his eyes never leaving Andrew's.

"Enough," Nova said. "Andrew, just leave. I won't press charges; just go. And never come back. You might also want to consider getting some therapy." Nova stood up and pulled Dominic back to her. She held his hand tightly. "Just go. Leave us." Andrew glared at their linked hands with a grimace.

Dean Devon tapped her fingers on the table. "Mr. Rodgers, please don't force my hand. There are other ways of going about this. But, I assure you, you won't like them."

Dominic moved out of Andrew's way and the boy sat down on the chair where Nova had been sitting. "There must be a way. Please."

Nova heard the waver in Andrew's voice and she almost folded. Almost. She couldn't possibly forget all the horrible things he'd done, all while trying to make her believe he loved her. Andrew needed professional help more than this scholarship. He was a danger to everyone around him.

"I'm sorry, Mr. Rodgers. It is what it is."

Andrew sniffled and signed the paper.

"Ms. Rose, you are suspended until further notice," Dean Devon said. She sat down at her desk and typed something on her computer. "I will be speaking with your parents, but until then, please refrain from showing up to classes and remove yourself from campus."

Camille was breathing heavily and staring right at Nova.

"This isn't over. The Larks will never accept you," she said and walked out of the office, her shoulder colliding against Nova's.

"I hope you will move out by tonight, Mr. Rodgers. I'll have someone sent to get your things. Please don't make a scene."

"Don't worry, Mrs. Devon; I'll see to it myself that he leaves tonight," Dominic said.

Andrew looked at Nova, his eyes were red, and his jaw was clenched. Nova saw betrayal in his eyes, like she was in the wrong.

Nova turned away from him to go and sit back in her seat. "Thank you, Dean." She heard the door open and close. She breathed out shakily and put her face in her hands.

"You're safe, Nova. I would have liked it if you came to me earlier with this."

"I know. I'm sorry."

"No need. Andrew will no longer be a threat. And as for Ms. Rose... I'm going to do my best."

Nova nodded. "Thank you so much."

Nova was going to get her life back. She was going to strive to accomplish her goals of graduating with the best grades and having a bright future. It was hers for the taking, and she wasn't going to let anyone get in her way.

<h1 style="text-align:center">Chapter Fifty-One</h1>

Nova never thought life could be this good. Dominic still felt fairly guilty about the way he treated Nova, and he spent every moment trying to make it up to her. He had also managed to get his head back in the game with his classes and had his As back.

"I'll see you in the evening, okay?" Dominic pressed a quick kiss to Nova's forehead and headed toward the gym.

Nova was walking back to her dorm, and there was a guard standing in front of her building. "Uh, is everything okay?" she asked him. He didn't look familiar; she'd never seen him around campus.

"Ms. Scott, you've been asked to the Dean's office."

"Oh, is everything okay?" Nova immediately knew something was wrong. Her stomach didn't feel right, and it wasn't because of something she ate.

"You're called right away, Ms. Scott."

"Uh, okay." Nova walked towards the main building of Atherton, but she felt a rising panic as she went on. She pulled out her phone and texted Dominic. The guard was walking behind her at a safe distance.

When Nova stood outside the Dean's office, she felt a sense of dread. Her only thought was, *did I lose my scholarship?*

"Ms. Scott?" The guard nudged her. "Are you all right?"

Nova nodded; her head felt like it was moving, but she wasn't too sure. Is this what Camille meant by this wasn't over? She took one last deep breath and put an end to those thoughts. She wasn't going to be expelled. It just couldn't happen.

She opened the door the stepped in. The first thing she noticed was that Roma Devon wasn't in the room. A pristinely dressed man and woman were sitting on the couch looking picture perfect. Nova recognized them immediately. Johnathan and Katherine Lark.

The knowledge didn't ease Nova's apprehension in the slightest. Her heartbeat shot up and pounded in her ears. "Mr. and Mrs. Lark," she greeted. Her voice was steady, but it took every bit of her will.

"Oh, so you know us," Katherine spoke. She put one leg over the other and sat sideways. "Take a seat, Ms. Scott."

Nova eyed the chair in front of the couch. She tentatively walked over and sat down, not making any sudden moves. "How can I help you, Mrs. Lark?"

Katherine's face was set in stone. It was as though it would kill the woman to smile. "Clearly you're aware of who we are, Ms. Scott, so I'm going to assume you also know the kind of background the Larks come from. Correct?"

"Of course."

Katherine nodded. "Ms. Scott, my family and I are very particular about the people who we choose to associate ourselves with. All of them being of high stature."

Nova controlled her features and tried to keep her nose from flaring. She had an idea how the Larks found out about Dominic and her. With the way the conversation had gone so far, she knew what was coming next.

"I don't particularly think you fit that category, Ms. Scott. Dominic has always been rebellious, and I'm sorry to inform you this is just one of those times for him. He doesn't really understand these things well."

"If you don't mind, Mrs. Lark. I think you underestimate your son's capabilities in evaluating the kind of company he keeps. Dominic is very well capable of making those decisions himself," Nova said with strength.

Katherine's eyes expanded a little, but only for a second. She wasn't giving Nova any other reads. The only thing she knew for sure was that Katherine wasn't impressed.

"Ms. Scott, my husband and I don't have a lot of time to waste. You and Dominic have no future together. Sometimes these things just don't work out. You're young, you both have ways to go, and it'll be best for you if you leave Dominic now. The Lark life isn't for everyone."

Nova ground her teeth and kept her mouth shut.

"I know your family... isn't well to do. I think we can help with that." Katherine turned to her husband.

Johnathan produced a rectangular piece of paper from the inside of his vest pocket. The man hadn't said a word yet.

Katherine took it and placed it in front of Nova. "A check for five million dollars. Sounds fair enough doesn't it, Ms. Scott?"

Nova couldn't help herself. A guffaw of laughter escaped her lips. "Sorry, Mrs. Lark, but are you trying to pay me off to leave Dominic?"

"Five million is a life-changing amount of money, Ms. Scott. This is a once-in-a-lifetime offer for you."

This time Nova had to cover her mouth to keep from laughing.

"What about this is so amusing, Ms. Scott?"

Nova shrugged a shoulder. "Simply the fact that you thought this would work, Mrs. Lark. With all due respect this isn't a K-Drama and my love isn't up for sale. Five million dollars *is* a lot of money, but if you really tried to put a number on how much I love Dominic, you couldn't afford it."

Katherine gritted her teeth and shook her head. "I really wish that it wouldn't have to come down to this. I hope you understand, we can make life for you and your loved ones very difficult, Ms. Scott. I think you should pick wisely; I would hate to implement those things."

Just when Nova was going to continue, Dominic burst into the room, his chest heaving, and beads of sweat layered his forehead.

"What's going on?" Dominic huffed. He walked in front of Nova and looked down at the table. "What the heck is this?"

Nova stood up and put a hand on Dominic's arm. "Babe, I've got this." She pulled him back behind her and stood in front of him facing his parents.

"Mrs. Lark, I appreciate your concern about me not fitting into your world, but it's not really up to you to decide that for me. As for this check, it holds no value to me. I don't want your money, and if you really thought it would be that easy to sway me, you were clearly wrong. This isn't just about me. You were planning to ruin your son's happiness, too. You can do as you please; I cannot stop you, but please don't think that money and power is the only driving force in the world. You aren't any better than the people who work themselves to the bone every day to make ends meet. I love Dominic. No amount of money could compensate me if I ever lost him. If you really think it necessary to hurt the people I love, then let that be on your conscious, but I will not let you bully me into leaving your son."

Dominic's father chortled, which made all of them turn their attention to him.

"I give you my blessing, Ms. Scott. I like this one, Dominic," he told them.

Nova's eyebrows rose in shock and she couldn't believe what she was hearing. She looked at Dominic and saw the same shocked expression on his face.

"Johnny, what are you saying?" Katherine whispered loudly. "You don't even *know* her. Imagine if everyone found out that Dominic was with a *nobody*!"

"That's enough, Kathy. Nova, you're a commendable young woman, and I shouldn't have expected any less; you were chosen by our experts here. I like your fighting spirit, Nova. A lot of people would have hesitated where you gave it to us straight."

"Johnny, wha—"

"It's decided," he said firmly, his voice never rising but it had the same effect. "You and Nova have my blessing." He stood up and put a hand on Dominic's shoulder. "Your mother and I will no longer interfere. Take care of each other."

"Johnathan?! I don't th—"

"I said, enough." Johnathan turned to look at Katherine, his eyes communicating what words weren't. "Like you said, we have matters to attend to. We'll be on our way now. Dom, call your parents once in a while, will you?"

With that, Johnathan escorted his wife away and left Dominic and Nova alone.

"Oh my goodness." Dominic shook his head and looked at the closed door. His mouth was agape. "Nova." He turned to her and pulled her closer. "Do you know what this means? Babe?! We just got over the biggest obstacle!" Dominic's face split into the biggest smile.

Nova smiled, too, her boyfriend's face being too contagious.

"This means we can finally be happy! Nothing and no one's in our way!" Dominic pulled her in for a hug and fit his head in the crook of her neck.

The happiness was practically radiating off him. She hadn't ever seen him this happy about anything.

Dominic pulled back and leaned in for a kiss. His lips were soft and sweet. Nova was glad she fought for her happy place.

"I guess the next order of business is our happily ever after."

Dominic laughed and wound his arms around her waist. He lifted her off her feet and kissed her again. "Happily ever after, it is."

Epilogue

4 YEARS LATER

Nova was backstage getting ready for her show. The past week had been really busy for her, and she hadn't had time for anything. Good thing she loved her job as much as she did.

She did a quick change of outfits and sat down for a vocal warm-up.

There was a knock on the door, and Nova expected her assistant to walk in. But instead, it was Skylar.

"Sky?!" Nova got to her feet and wrapped her hands around her sister. She wasn't so small anymore; in fact, she was now taller than Nova. "What are you doing here?"

"Surprise!" She pulled back. "There's more, but I couldn't wait."

Nova laughed and squeezed her hands. "What do you mean?"

"Just wait," Skylar said and pulled Nova to the couch. She started telling Nova about school and her friends when the door opened again. Nova's eyes grew wide, and a loud gasp came from her mouth.

"Mom, Dad, Scarlett!?" She ran to her parents and best friend and hugged them all. She lifted her head from their shoulders and saw Dominic standing at the door.

"Dom!" She ran to hug her boyfriend. It had been a while

334

since she saw him last. Dominic had been just as busy as her, if not more. "I thought you were flying out today."

Dominic kissed the side of her head. "I wanted to surprise you. I finally cleared my schedule, not for long but for now, I'm yours."

Nova smiled and caressed his face. "I'm so happy. Thank you for bringing them."

"Of course. Sky's been nagging me since forever now."

Fran, Nova's assistant, knocked on the door. "Nova, you're on in twenty."

Nova nodded. "Fran, please seat my family in the pit and make sure they have snacks."

"Of course." Fran closed the door behind her.

Dominic put a hand around Nova's waist and pulled her closer. "Can we perform together tonight? I want to perform our duet. It's been a while."

Nova beamed and kissed Dominic chastely. "I would love that."

"I know. My schedule's been crazier than usual, but it'll settle down soon, I hope. I'll get mic'ed up."

"Okay, I'll see you in a bit." Nova sent her family with Fran so she could prepare. She did her usual routine of getting ready for a show and felt excitement bubbling in her stomach. Dominic and she were going to perform after a really long time. Her fans loved when the two of them took to the stage together.

Dominic came to stand next to her before the platform raised her up on stage. He kissed her and whispered sweet nothings in her ear until she got the countdown for the performance.

Once Nova was on stage, everything made sense to her. Even on her hardest, most tiring days, the crowd never disappointed her. She felt the best kind of energy, and she hoped she was able to reflect that back. She had become an international popstar about a year ago, but she would never get used to this. She didn't want to. She wanted every day to feel like it was her first time performing.

She could see her parents and sister from the stage, and she waved to them, which made Skylar and Scarlett break into a funny dance.

Skylar didn't have to worry about college anymore. None of them had to worry about anything. Out of all things that Nova achieved after she got signed right out of college, her proudest moment was getting her parents their dream home. In many ways, Nova had made it.

"All right, guys." Nova stopped after her last song. "I have a surprise for you guys." She laughed into the mic when the crowd went wild. She had already seen some people with banners of her and Dominic.

"Please welcome on stage my boyfriend and surprise guest star, Dominic Lark!"

Dominic rose from the same place Nova had, and the lights changed colors as her drummer played a beat for his entrance.

The cameras had panned towards the green-eyed boy, and the whole arena could see what Nova saw. The most handsome boy in the arena. She put her hand out for Dominic to take and accepted the kiss he leaned in for.

"We're going to be singing the song I wrote for us back when we were in college. This song is the reason we're together today, so enjoy." She fixed up her mic, and someone brought Dominic his guitar. Nova toured with his guitar now so that they could perform like this together whenever they wanted.

The crowd took out their flashlights and started swaying with the music. There were some roses being thrown on stage. Nova didn't pay attention to anything, though. With Dominic in front of her, the whole arena could multiply by a hundred, but he would be the only person she could see.

By the end of the song, Nova's heart was pounding in her chest, and her eyes were clouded with tears. She had really missed Dominic. They both had incredibly demanding jobs, but Dominic always made the effort to come to see her. No matter where she was in the world.

Once the song was over, Nova hugged Dominic and buried her head in his chest. "I love you," she whispered in his ear and kissed it softly.

"I love you too."

Usually, once they were done, they'd call it a night and head for a quiet dinner together. Nova was about to grab the mic so she could thank her fans and her band when Dominic beat her to it. She raised an eyebrow at him and looked curiously as he untangled the mic from the wire laid around the stage.

"Before we say goodnight, I have an announcement."

The crowd started screaming again, and Nova had no idea what Dominic was referring to.

"Nova," Dominic turned to her and took her hand in his own, "In my day-to-day life, I meet hundreds of new people. I see what they're like, but I have yet to find anyone like you. You are in every shape and form the most unique person I know."

Nova squeezed Dominic's hand and put a hand on her fast-beating heart.

"Every person who has a business should be grateful every day that you are a singer and not a businesswoman because you would be the most ferocious competition they would have to face."

The crowd laughed and so did Nova. She had a couple of her own dealings with her brand, but Dominic wasn't very wrong. She would have made a killer businesswoman.

"I am the luckiest man in the world because I get to be yours. I get to wake up to your texts every morning; I get to call you mine. You have made me a better businessman, a better son, a better brother, and the luckiest boyfriend in the world."

When Dominic took a step back and took his guitar off, Nova knew what was coming. It made her skin light up with goosebumps and her head felt extremely light. "Oh, gosh," she whispered to herself and wiped the sweat from her upper lip.

"I have the honor of being all those things, but I'm missing out on something I've been waiting for since the day I fell in love with you. Nova Scott." Dominic put his hand in his back pocket and got down on one knee.

Nova felt all the blood rush to her ears, and her step almost faltered. Dominic was on his knee. Proposing. People were jumping up and down, screaming. Nova felt like doing a bit of her own jumping.

"Will you marry me?" Dominic opened the small box, and Nova's eyes fell on the prettiest ring she'd ever seen. Dominic had designed the most perfect ring with a diamond in the shape of a shooting star.

Nova's chest heaved with small sobs, and she could see Dominic was getting more and more desperate as she stood without answering. "Yes! I'd love to be your wife." She bent down and tackled him into a hug.

Dominic laughed in her ear and held her tight.

The crowd had basically gone feral, and Nova listened to it all unfold. Her parents, Skylar, and Scarlett looked happier than she had ever seen them.

Dominic took her hand and slipped the ring on her finger. It felt right; it felt like it belonged.

Nova felt like she belonged. Belonging to the love of her life. Now and forever.

Bonus Chapter

I am deeply honored that you took the time to read Super Nova!

If you want more of Nova and Dominic, make sure you download the free bonus chapter where you can read about Dominic's first impression of Nova!

Bonus Chapter (https://swiy.co/SuperNovaBonus)

If you enjoyed this book, please consider leaving it a review so that others may find it as well.

Check out my other teen/young adult romance novels by visiting LeiaSkyy.com.